Unbridled Dreams

Books by
Stephanie Grace Whitson

A Garden in Paris
A Hilltop in Tuscany
Jacob's List

PINE RIDGE PORTRAITS
Secrets on the Wind
Watchers on the Hill
Footprints on the Horizon

PRAIRIE WINDS
Walks the Fire
Soaring Eagle
Red Bird

KEEPSAKE LEGACIES
Sarah's Patchwork
Karyn's Memory Box
Nora's Ribbon of Memories

DAKOTA MOONS
Valley of the Shadow
Edge of the Wilderness
Heart of the Sandhills

NONFICTION
How to Help a Grieving Friend

UNBRIDLED DREAMS

STEPHANIE GRACE
WHITSON

BETHANY HOUSE PUBLISHERS
Minneapolis, Minnesota

Published by Bethany House Publishers
11400 Hampshire Avenue South
Bloomington, Minnesota 55438

Bethany House Publishers is a division of
Baker Publishing Group, Grand Rapids, Michigan.

Printed in the United States of America

Library of Congress Cataloging-in-Publication Data

Whitson, Stephanie Grace.
    Unbridled dreams / Stephanie Grace Whitson.
        p.   cm.
    ISBN 978-0-7642-0327-5 (pbk.)
    1. Women rodeo performers—Fiction. 2. Buffalo Bill's Wild West Show—Fiction.
I. Title.

    PS3573.H555U53   2008
    813'.54—dc22

                                                            2008014286

DEDICATED TO THE MEMORY OF
GOD'S EXTRAORDINARY WOMEN
IN EVERY PLACE
IN EVERY TIME

THANKS TO . . .

. . . MY EDITOR ANN PARRISH,
for working the magic that makes the stories better.

. . . COPY EDITOR KAREN SCHURRER,
and her amazing "eagle eye" for the details.

. . . BETHANY HOUSE PUBLISHERS,
for the great privilege of working for them.

. . . LINDA HEIN OF THE NEBRASKA STATE HISTORICAL SOCIETY,
for introducing me to the real woman
who inspired Liberty Belle.

. . . MARY ROBINSON, Librarian, McCracken Research
Library, Buffalo Bill Historical Center; and Lynn Houze,
Curatorial Assistant, Buffalo Bill Museum,
for sharing their knowledge of the Wild West.

. . . DR. LINDA ERMISCH,
for sharing her expertise in the field of horse behavior.

. . . MY WRITING FRIENDS,
for challenging me to be faithful to the call.

. . . MY DANIEL,
for being willing to make the sacrifices that unbridle my
dreams.

AND AS ALWAYS, THANK YOU, DEAR READER,
for honoring me by giving of your time
to go back in time with me. It is my prayer that God
will use the story of Liberty Belle to bless you.

ABOUT THE AUTHOR

A native of southern Illinois, Stephanie Grace Whitson has resided in Nebraska since 1975. She began what she calls "playing with imaginary friends" (writing fiction) when, as a result of teaching her four homeschooled children Nebraska history, she was personally encouraged and challenged by the lives of pioneer women in the West. Since her first book, *Walks the Fire*, was published in 1995, Stephanie's fiction titles have appeared on the ECPA bestseller list and have been finalists for the Christy Award and the Inspirational Reader's Choice Award. Her first nonfiction work, *How to Help a Grieving Friend*, was released in 2005. In addition to serving her local church and keeping up with two married children and three college students, Stephanie enjoys volunteering for the International Quilt Study Center and riding motorcycles with her blended family and church friends. Widowed in 2001, Stephanie remarried in 2003 and now pursues full-time writing and a speaking ministry from her studio in Lincoln, Nebraska. Learn more at *www.stephaniewhitson.com* or write stephanie@ stephaniewhitson.com. U.S. mail can be directed to Stephanie Grace Whitson at 3800 Old Cheney Road, #101–178, Lincoln, Nebraska 68516.

Charm is deceitful and beauty is vain,
But a woman who fears the Lord,
she shall be praised.

PROVERBS 31:30 NASB

CHAPTER 1

YOU are in SO MUCH TROUBLE.

Seventeen-year-old Irma Friedrich sighed. If only Momma hadn't shrieked a moment ago, Diamond wouldn't have startled. And if Diamond hadn't startled, Irma would have landed the dismount that involved a handspring off the dapple-gray gelding's withers and a high arc through the air. She would have been standing in the middle of the arena—uh, corral—taking her bow as Liberty Belle, the star of Buffalo Bill's Wild West. She would have been waving to the imaginary crowd of thousands and then going over to pat Diamond on the neck and reward him with a few cubes of sugar. But Momma *had* shrieked—at the worst possible moment, when Irma had just put the reins in her teeth and started her handstand on Diamond's back—and Diamond *had* broken his stride, and so here Irma was, sitting in the dirt trying to catch her breath and wondering why in the world Momma and Daddy had come out to the ranch at this time of day. They weren't supposed to drive out from town until suppertime, and it was barely past dinner.

As Irma got up and dusted herself off, Daddy stepped down off the back porch and hurried toward the corral. "Are you all right?" he hollered. When Irma nodded and bent down to pick up the hat she'd borrowed from her cousin Monte's room, Daddy stopped in midstride, put his hands on his hips, and sputtered, "Then get yourself up on the porch and apologize to your mother. You've frightened her half to death." Spinning around, Daddy stomped back across the patch of dirt that served for a backyard and up the unpainted stairs onto the porch of Aunt Laura and Uncle Charlie Mason's two-story ranch house.

Diamond ambled over and snuffled her pocket. Irma glanced toward the ranch house, where Momma was sprawled on the porch swing, Aunt Laura standing over her, fanning to beat the band. Irma could just imagine her cousins—Minnie and Mollie, Mamie and Maggie—all gathered at the kitchen window watching the drama unfold. The girls could be counted on to stay out of sight now, but they could also be counted on to take advantage of every future opportunity to tease Irma about everything from the missed dismount to their Aunt Willa's dramatic collapse.

With another sigh, Irma looked down at Monte's hat. The smooth felt yielded as she tried—and failed—to reshape the crown. Monte was usually understanding about Irma's borrowing his old clothes and hats, but he was going to be mad about his mangled hat. She hadn't exactly asked his permission to borrow his recent purchase, and she knew he'd had it all shaped and ready for tonight's barn dance over at the Double Bar J. She should have left it in his room, but it had looked so *right* when she tried it on and peered at herself in that little mirror Monte had on the back of his bedroom door.

By the time Irma caught her breath enough to duck between the corral poles and head for the house, Aunt Laura had stopped fanning and gone back inside. Movement at the kitchen window indicated her cousins had gone back to their chores—probably at their mother's insistence. Daddy was sitting beside Momma now, patting her arm and murmuring something that must have been reassuring because Momma was nodding. Irma very much doubted Momma had really fainted. How many women could faint in such a way as to land per-

fectly draped on a porch swing? Momma could rival any actress ever
to appear on the stage at Lloyd's Opera House in town.

Halfway to the house, Irma felt a twinge in her left ankle. Now
that she thought about it, her shoulders hurt, too. And her backside
would probably bruise where she'd landed. The closer she got to
the porch, the more she hurt. Everywhere. But Momma was crying
again, and Daddy was obviously in no mood to be wound around
his only daughter's little finger. Ignoring her aches and pains, Irma
swiped a strand of red hair away from her face. Tucked it behind
her ear. Lifted her chin and took a deep breath. *YOU*, she thought
again, *are in SO MUCH TROUBLE*.

"Sit," Daddy said, and indicated one of the two battered chairs
opposite the porch swing.

The chair creaked when Irma obeyed. She folded her hands in
her lap, newly aware of how dirty Monte's jeans were, how her hair
was falling out of the scarf she'd used to tie it back, and worst of all,
how she must look to Momma, a woman who believed in multiple
petticoats, corseted waists, and bustles almost as sincerely as she
believed in Jesus. And that was saying something about a woman
who never missed church, ran the Ladies Aid Society with an iron
hand, and could quote scripture as well as Reverend Coe.

"Apologize to your mother," Daddy said.

For what felt like the millionth time in her life, Irma read bewil-
derment and an expression she had come to label *What hath God
wrought?* in her mother's hazel eyes. It was no secret that, if Momma
had any say about it at all, Irma would never have been allowed
to spend summers on her aunt and uncle's ranch, reveling in what
Momma considered "unladylike pursuits." But Momma knew better
than to try and come between Daddy and Aunt Laura Mason—his
baby sister and only living relative. No one had expected the only
boy among her five Mason cousins to end up being Irma's favorite
and best friend. And no one would have predicted that Irma would

end up spending more time tagging along with Monte riding and roping than she did gardening and cooking with the Mason women. But no one minded. No one, that is, but Momma.

When, only three years earlier, Uncle Charlie and Aunt Laura invited Irma to go with the Masons on a holiday to Omaha, Momma waxed poetic about all the wondrous things Irma would experience in the city. She even helped Irma pack. Unfortunately—for Momma—Irma cared nothing for the bustling streets and well-stocked shops of Omaha. What impressed Irma was seeing the first performance of the Honorable W. F. Cody and Dr. W. F. Carver's Wild West, Rocky Mountain, and Prairie Exhibition.

From the moment of the Grand Introductory March to the firing of the last rifle during the closing act, fourteen-year-old Irma had been entranced. She returned home from that trip knowing what she wanted to be, and to Momma's horror, it had nothing to do with domesticity and everything to do with the Wild West.

In the ensuing years Irma fell off more horses than she could honestly count. She hid bruises and denied sore muscles and did everything in her power to make sure Momma never guessed that summers on the ranch were now about a lot more than playing cowgirl. Oh, no. Irma wasn't playing. Not one bit. She was working toward the dream of becoming Liberty Belle, headliner for the Wild West Show. Something Momma would never understand and never approve. Something that had been kept secret. Until just a few minutes ago, on this Friday in April of 1886.

Daddy knew about his daughter's dream, of course. He even encouraged it a little when Momma wasn't around. Oh, he didn't really believe Irma was going to leave home and be a Wild West star. Irma knew that. But he didn't seem outraged or, what would be even worse, laugh at her the way Momma had the one and only time Irma mentioned Buffalo Bill's adding cowgirls to his troupe. But the daddy who was proud of his daughter's riding and roping skills was nowhere in sight today. Right now, Daddy was holding Momma's hand as if it might shatter into a thousand pieces, and as he stared at Irma, his gray eyes showed no willingness to smooth things over for her.

Irma glanced down at her gloved hands. Momma would hate the old pair of stained leather gauntlets, but she would hate seeing the grime beneath Irma's fingernails even more. Momma already said Irma's hands were "masculine" and battled that perception by providing a silver-handled manicure set and an ever-expanding array of dress gloves, neither of which Irma appreciated. She sighed. Curling her fingers against her palms, she decided to leave the work gloves on.

"We're waiting," Daddy said.

Irma cleared her throat. "You drove out early. You weren't supposed to get to the ranch until suppertime, and I didn't think—"

Daddy interrupted. " 'You drove out early' and 'I didn't think' do not qualify as an apology, Irmagard."

Irma bit her lip. *Irmagard.* It was a bad sign when Daddy called her that. She looked at him and stifled a little shiver. Did he want her to lie so Momma would feel better? She *wasn't* sorry she'd saddled Diamond and practiced her trick riding. It had taken some serious finagling to arrange the last few days of practice sessions. First she'd had to convince Daddy and Momma to let her help Uncle Charlie drive a string of horses over to Buffalo Bill's ranch, Scout's Rest, in preparation for the daylong "doings," when most of Lincoln County would be in attendance to watch cowboys from all over audition for the Wild West. Then, once at Uncle Charlie's ranch, she'd had to convince Uncle Charlie to do without her so she could perfect the act she was determined to show Buffalo Bill. And she nearly *had* perfected it. Until Momma screamed and ruined everything.

Why couldn't Daddy admit to being proud of what he'd just seen? And if Momma couldn't be proud, why couldn't she at least acknowledge that her daughter had accomplished something that had taken a lot of hard work and perseverance? But all Momma could see was the borrowed outfit and the fall, and all Daddy seemed to care about right now was Momma's reaction. It made Irma want to cry.

"Are you going to answer me, Irmagard?"

What had Momma been saying? *Oh, brother.* Nothing upset Momma more than when Irma daydreamed instead of paying attention. She looked up. "I'm sorry, Momma. What did you say?"

Momma sat up straighter. "*You* said that we weren't supposed to get here until suppertime and that you thought— But then you didn't finish what you thought. So, I'm asking . . . what exactly *were* you thinking when you expressly disobeyed my wishes and returned to your cowgirl fantasy? What exactly were you thinking when you stole your cousin's clothing? What exactly were you thinking when you saddled poor old Diamond and ran him ragged? And, pray tell, what exactly were you thinking when you were sailing through the air risking life and limb for some ridiculous *stunt?*"

As Momma talked the words came more quickly, and her usually mellow speaking voice got positively squeaky. When Momma was like this it was better to just let her make the speech. Sometimes, by the time she was finished, she'd worn out the worst of her temper.

"Did you give one tiny little thought"—Momma held her hand up and indicated an imaginary inch between her thumb and forefinger to illustrate—"to how we would all feel if we came outside and found you . . . there"—she waved her lace-edged hankie toward the corral—"crumpled . . . *dead* . . . gone from us forever." She hiccupped, lifted her hankie to her mouth, and closing her eyes, began to cry. Again.

"Now, Momma," Daddy said, and patted the hand he still clutched in his.

Momma wrested her hand free. She glared at Daddy, and the two pink spots on her cheeks grew bright red. "Don't you 'now Momma' me, Otto Friedrich," she said. "This is your fault. *You're* the one who's let this . . . this"—she gestured toward the corral—"ridiculous . . . phase go on and on." She looked away. "If I had known this was going to happen, I never would have let her come out here. And I certainly would not have agreed to attend that . . . that hullabaloo at Bill Cody's ranch tomorrow." Her voice wobbled. She cleared her throat and said to Daddy, "The child has done nothing but try my patience ever since your family took her to Omaha. *Wild West* indeed!"

"Now, Momma," Daddy said "Half the county will be there tomorrow. You *love* socializing with the ladies. And you know we couldn't refuse an invitation from Bill Cody. He's been good to the bank. Good *for* the bank. And to have declined—"

"Tut-tut," Momma said, and waved her hankie again. She sniffed. Her voice dropped a notch. "I suppose, if I'm honest, I have to take my share of the responsibility." She gestured toward the corral again. "This started long before Charlie and Laura took her to Omaha." She paused. "I'm the one who arranged for her to go on that camping trip with the Codys." She sighed. "But I sincerely thought a friendship with Arta Cody would *help* matters." She shook her head. "If only I'd known back then that it would fuel this . . . this . . . *horse* nonsense."

It isn't nonsense, Irma thought. *Why can't you see that?* Being invited on the Dismal River camping trip with the Codys when she was eleven years old was a highlight of her life, second only to seeing the Wild West in Omaha. It was on that trip that Irma's love for the wide open spaces had been *praised* by Buffalo Bill himself. The other girls had shrieked and held up their skirts when they had to ford the river. Not Irma. Irma had urged her pony down the bank and across the water and let everything get wet and she hadn't minded a bit. The other girls had been so tired that on the way back, they put their saddles in the supply wagon and road in the buggy with Mrs. Cody. But not Irma. The other girls had been afraid when someone stampeded the ponies one night and Monte said it was probably Indians. But not Irma. After all, she reasoned, they were with the great Indian scout Buffalo Bill, who knew half the Indians in the West.

And she would never forget how, when they got back to North Platte, Buffalo Bill patted her on the head and told his friend Otto Friedrich that he had a "tough little cowgirl" on his hands and he should be proud of her. Most of the time it seemed that Daddy *was* proud. Monte and Uncle Charlie said she had a natural talent. Over the years even some of the wranglers working on the Mason ranch had given her grudging praise. But not Momma. Momma always acted as if the things Irma loved most were a disease to be cured.

". . . and you haven't been much help," Momma was saying to Daddy, "setting up an arena in my own backyard every time I'm gone for an evening!" She whipped her head around and glared at him. "Don't think I haven't known what's been going on behind my back!"

"Now, Momma," Daddy said. "I thought her enthusiasm would run its course. I was only trying—"

"Whatever you were trying," Momma snapped, "what *happened* is that now Irmagard actually *believes* we're going to allow this—" With a sigh, she gazed at Irma. "I don't suppose it really matters what you were thinking today. It's irrelevant anyway in light of—" She glanced at Daddy. "Tell her, Otto."

The look on Daddy's face was undecipherable. But definitely not good. Irma spoke up. "I'm not hurt, Momma. I fell off, but Diamond would never step on me. Not on purpose." She paused. "I-I'm sorry I frightened you. But as I said, you weren't supposed to . . . I mean, Aunt Laura said you were coming for supper. I didn't think there was any harm in—"

"It doesn't matter," Momma repeated. "It's all going to be part of the past soon enough. It took a great deal of talking on your father's part." She smiled at Daddy. "But reason has prevailed. In fact, part of the reason we drove out early was to give you the news. You've been admitted to Brownell Hall for the fall term."

"But . . . but . . . that school is for . . . for . . ." She held out her arms to implore Momma. "I'm nearly eighteen. I'm way too old for Brownell. Arta was only sixteen when she attended."

"Yes," Momma agreed. "And look what they did for her. There isn't a finer young lady anywhere. She has a leading role in North

Platte's social life and admirers wherever she goes. She can hold her own in any society, and that includes the finest circles in the *East.*"

Irma had overheard enough of Momma's conversations with friends over the years to know that, for Momma, the East was the shrine of all things desirable. Momma spoke of her arrival in what would become North Platte, Nebraska, back in '69 as if she'd entered purgatory. There were no trees, no lawns, and no flowers back in those days, and if it hadn't been for Daddy's building Momma a nice two-story house with a picket fence, Irma suspected Momma would be back in the hallowed East sipping tea right now. But with the house and the growth of North Platte, and with Daddy's hard work, the name *Friedrich* had come to "mean something." At least that's what Momma said. So Momma stayed to reign. Until, of course, the day Mrs. William F. Cody arrived. No one in the area would have been able to challenge the great Buffalo Bill's wife when it came to social rank. So Momma did the next best thing. She endeared herself to the Codys by being slavishly devoted to anything Louisa Cody cared about. And when Arta Cody went away to Brownell Hall, where all wealthy young ladies from Nebraska were educated, Momma had begun a campaign to see that Irma followed suit.

Just look at her, Irma thought, observing Momma's expression as she prattled on about the future. *She's so pleased with herself. I should have known she hadn't given up on Brownell.* And Daddy was siding with her. How could he? Didn't he know—didn't he care—that being forced to attend a place like that would *kill* her?

"No," Irma said aloud, and shook her head back and forth.

"I beg your pardon?" Momma said with a little frown.

Irma met her mother's gaze straight on, even arching her own eyebrow as she repeated a little more loudly, "No. I won't go. You can't make me."

Daddy opened his mouth to say something, but Momma held up one finger and he was silenced. "It isn't a decision that is yours to make, Irmagard," she said. "It may not feel like it right now, but we are doing this because we love you and we want what's best for you."

Irma snorted. "Right."

"Young lady," Daddy said. "Watch your tone."

She swallowed. Maybe begging would work. "Please, Momma. Daddy. You can't mean it. You can't."

"Your father and I," Momma replied, "have discussed this, and we agree. You need a chance to be around a more refined circle of—"

"I *don't*," Irma interrupted. She gripped the arms of her chair with her gloved hands.

"Do not interrupt me," Momma snapped. "You are not yet an adult, Irmagard, and as such you do not really know what is best for you. Certainly you have an unusual amount of energy and spirit. And a strong will, which—" she forced a laugh—"undoubtedly came from me. These are fine qualities and will stand you in good stead once you accept the path intended for young ladies to walk."

Irma groaned. "I'm not *made* for the path you're talking about, Momma. I'm sorry, but I'm just *not*."

"Every woman is made for the same great purpose. To resist our highest calling is to resist God."

"I'm not resisting God," Irma insisted. "I just don't want to get married and have babies right now. Maybe not ever. Is that so bad? Isn't God the one who gave me the ability to balance on a cantering horse's back? Isn't God the one who helps me run fast—faster than even Monte? If it isn't God, then who? Tell me, Momma, please, because I want to know." She put her hand on her pounding heart, leaned forward, and let the tears come. "I love God, Momma. Really, I do. When I'm riding out on the prairie and there's nothing but sky for as far as I can see, that's when I know God is there. He's around me and I can feel Him and, honestly, Momma, I feel closer to Him there than I ever have sitting in a pew listening to Reverend Coe drone on and on about the Israelites making bricks for Pharaoh."

"Irmagard!" Daddy scolded.

"No, Daddy, no. You have to listen." She looked at her mother and pleaded, "You have to listen, too, Momma. I know I'm a disappointment to you. I know you want a daughter who's a fine lady like Arta. You want me to like tea parties and fancy dresses, but I *don't*, Momma. Sometimes I feel like I'm going to *suffocate*." She stood up, sobbing, shaking her head. "I can't *be* who you want me to be," she finally said. "And if that's who God wants me to be, then I guess I can't be His, either."

Ignoring her father calling her name, Irma ran to the corral where Diamond stood half asleep. Jerking the gate open and grabbing the horse's reins, she leaped into the saddle, pulled his head up, and kicked his flanks. Crying harder than she had in a long, long time, Irma clung to the saddle as Diamond charged through the corral gate, past the barn, out onto the open prairie, and toward the horizon.

CHAPTER 2

❖⇒◎ ◎⇐❖

THE MIND OF MAN PLANS HIS WAY,
BUT THE LORD DIRECTS HIS STEPS.
Proverbs 16:9 NASB

After all the years of soggy bedrolls and cold winds, of howling wolves and stampeding longhorns, a feller would expect a real bed and a feather pillow to induce a near coma. But here he was, counting how many times that clock on the stairway landing gonged and thumping his pillow in a vain attempt to get comfortable. Again. Finally Shep sat up and slung his legs over the side of the bed. The last thing he wanted to do was hurt anyone's feelings—after all, Buffalo Bill himself had invited Shep to stay at the house—but he just couldn't sleep in this fancy bed. He got up and crossed the room to the window that looked out on the site of what was shaping up to be a magnificent ranch worthy of its renowned owner.

What in the— Shep ducked behind the full-length drape and peeked out the window, concentrating on what he'd thought was movement. *There.* There it was. He was right. A horse and rider just on the opposite side of the corral near the water trough. A little guy who shoulda known better than to linger out there in the broad moonlight if he didn't want to be seen, and by the way he was slipping down off the horse and almost tiptoeing around, it sure seemed like he didn't want to be seen.

Or maybe you've heard too many of Doc Middleton's stories these last few days. As far as Shep knew, horse thieves were generally a thing of the past around North Platte, Nebraska. Certainly no self-respecting horse thief would come near *this* ranch. At least not when half the cowboys in the territory were camped around the bunkhouse hoping to get hired on with Buffalo Bill's Wild West.

Moving slowly away from the window so no movement would be detected by the unannounced visitor—or visitors—should they look toward the house, Shep pulled on a shirt, slid into his jeans, and descended the ranch house stairs in his stocking feet. He exited the front door and pulled his boots on. Buttoning his shirt as he went, he slipped around the side of the house and, keeping low, headed for the row of scrub trees that bordered the cook's kitchen garden. Using the hedge for cover, Shep crouched down and watched for more movement by the barn.

Whoever it was had ridden in alone, and as he watched from his vantage point, Shep decided the visitor had no evil intent. He'd walked his horse away from the water tank and hitched him to a corral post in plain sight. He was probably just trying to keep from waking anyone up. Probably another cowboy hoping to try out. More likely a cowboy clown from the size of him. *Bet they call him Shorty.* Whether anyone else called the new guy Shorty or not, Shep would. Of course being six feet four inches tall, Shep could call just about anybody Shorty and get away with it.

As Shep watched, Shorty unsaddled his horse and turned him into the empty corral. Whoever the guy was, he took good care of his mount. Even now, in the wee hours, he was running his hand along the horse's back, checking for burrs where the saddle had been and lifting each of the animal's hooves to check his feet before ducking between the corral poles. Heading for the well pump Shorty took off his hat and . . . *Whoa*. Waist-length hair tumbled out of the hat while Shorty pumped water. Shep lost his balance and sat back with a jolt. Shorty was a *girl*.

"Come to bed, sweetheart. Irma could find her way back here in a snowstorm. And even if by some chance she couldn't, Diamond could. All Irma has to do is give him his head and he'll bring her right home."

Willa didn't move from her place by the narrow bedroom window. She shivered and rubbed her arms. "There's no use in coming to bed. I won't sleep, and I'll just keep you awake with my tossing and turning." When the bedsprings creaked she glanced over her shoulder. "Don't get up. I'll tiptoe downstairs and make myself some tea. Just because I can't sleep doesn't mean you should have to be dead on your feet tomorrow." She didn't let up, even when Otto pulled his dressing gown off the hook by the door and pulled it on. "Once Irmagard is back and I know she's safe I'll take a nap. It doesn't really matter if I go to the Codys' anyway." But Otto was already behind her, encircling her in his arms. She leaned back against him with a sigh. "What about wolves? What if she's hurt? What if she fell off—or got thrown?"

"Diamond is as gentle as a cow pony ever gets," Otto said. "You saw that for yourself. He let the girl climb on and around him like a monkey, and he didn't even break stride—"

"Until I yelped," Willa said. "*Coyotes* yelp."

"Irma's more likely to slip and fall down the stairs at home than she is to fall off that horse on a moonlit spring night."

Willa turned around and stared up into his face. "Indians," she said. "What about Indians?"

"I don't *know* about Indians, sweetheart. Just like I don't know what it is that makes you unable to put our daughter in God's hands and come to bed with me." He hugged her harder. "Isn't this one of those times when the faithful are supposed to watch and pray instead of tossing and turning?"

Willa fought back tears. Did he really think she needed to be reminded of how weak her faith could be when it came to Irmagard? She closed her eyes and leaned into him. "I'm sorry. I just—" Her voice broke. "I don't understand why she *hates* me so."

"The two of you don't mesh," Otto said. "But Irma does *not* hate you."

Willa looked back out the window and murmured, "She's so lovely. And graceful. She moves like a willow waving in the breeze. Doesn't she realize she could have her choice of any number of eligible bachelors in North Platte? Orrin Knox would—"

Otto interrupted her. "Which is why Irma isn't interested in him. She's too strong-willed to want a man who waits for her to beckon him into her life."

"Well, the Randall boy, then," Willa said. "Or perhaps she simply hasn't met the right one yet. Which is another reason Brownell makes so much sense. She'll have a chance to meet a different class of young men in Omaha. Louisa said the school plans lovely socials with all the best families."

"Irma's made it very clear more than once that she doesn't want to get married. At least not now. And frankly, even if she did, she'd be more likely to notice someone like Ned Bishop than Orrin Knox."

"Ned Bishop!" Willa shuddered. "He's an uneducated *wrangler*."

"He may be uneducated in the way you mean, but he has a sizeable savings account at the bank and a solid plan that will likely land him his own spread inside of ten years." He smiled. "Charlie says Bishop reminds him a lot of me back in the day." He touched her cheek. "I was somewhat of an uneducated wrangler when you met me." He nuzzled her neck. "And we've done all right."

"You," Willa said dutifully, even as she caught his hand in hers and stood back, "were an exceptional man with a great many gifts—including, even if I do say so myself, a wife who did her part to help you succeed."

Otto agreed. "And I can see Irma following your example in finding the right man. She's actually mentioned ranching to me for that far distant time when she's no longer performing."

Performing. The topic simply would not die. "She's living in a fantasy," Willa insisted. "She doesn't have any idea what it's like to travel with *show* people. Her reputation would be ruined forever. And as far as ranching goes, why doesn't she see the realities of that life? It isn't romantic. It's drudgery. Surely you cannot want that for our Irmagard." She let go of his hand and peered back out the window.

"What I want," Otto said, "is for her to be happy. And if she can make a life for herself that brings her half the joy that Laura has found with Charlie Mason, then—"

Willa cringed inwardly. She didn't dare bring it up, but surely Otto wasn't oblivious to what life as a rancher's wife had done to his sister. Countless hours standing over a wood-burning stove had transformed Laura Friedrich Mason's once porcelain skin into little more than a piece of tanned leather. And her hands. The poor woman had the hands of an overworked washerwoman. Happy or not, the once lovely Laura Friedrich become Mrs. Charles Mason would not be recognized by her girlhood friends these days. And Willa would not stand by and let that happen to Irmagard. God couldn't want that. He had to have a better plan. "I've prayed about it, Otto," Willa murmured. "Truly I have. And I just can't believe—"

"So that's it," Otto said. "You and God have it all mapped out, eh?"

His tone of voice said that, whatever her intention, Willa had managed to sound self-righteous. Again. Why did it always turn out that way? Why did Otto always resent it when she spoke of praying and getting answers? Sometimes she wondered if talk of God made him feel like he had to compete with the Almighty for her affection and loyalty. The truth was that were it not for her faith in God,

Wilhelmina Friedrich would have taken Irmagard and returned to the East long, long ago. But Otto didn't know about that. He did not share her faith and understood neither how much it meant to her nor how much it had benefited him. And so, once again, Willa cast a quick prayer to heaven and decided that the best thing to say right now was *nothing more.*

"Let's have that tea," she murmured, and turning from the window, she led the way down the stairs and into the kitchen. While Otto added wood to the hot embers in Laura's massive cookstove, Willa retrieved two cups and saucers, sugar, and cream. A few minutes later they took their tea out onto the back porch and settled on the swing. "Your sister is a fine woman," Willa said. "I mean that with all my heart." And she did. "In fact, it's because of Laura's hard work that Irmagard's summers sliding down haystacks with the girls and chasing after Monte and Charlie on horseback have been so wonderful."

"It hasn't been all fun," Otto said. "Irma's done real work out here. Charlie's told me so—and admitted that it surprised him. He didn't believe her when she first said she wanted to earn her keep. But she won him over. She has worked right alongside the men and then used every spare minute to practice her riding." Willa could hear him smiling when he said, "She's determined. Like someone else I know."

"I *am* determined," Willa agreed. "And all I'm asking is that she give one year to considering another way. *One year.*" She sighed. "She acts like attending a fine school is akin to banishment."

"Maybe for her it is."

"I thought you supported me in this."

"I did. But after today—" Otto shook his head. "I just don't know anymore. She seemed so desperately *unhappy.* She's wanted to be a trick rider with the Wild West ever since she learned Bill was going to add women to the program. And that dream has not abated with maturity. If anything, it's gotten stronger. Do you have any idea how long it's taken for her to learn to do what you saw this afternoon?"

"She is out of her mind if she thinks I am going to sit back and let her fritter away an opportunity to attend one of the best schools in the region so she can become a *circus performer.* I've seen what that life does to people. To women."

Otto squeezed her hand. "I've heard that Bill's troupe takes good care of one another—almost as if they were a family. The ladies are escorted wherever they go and their privacy is sacrosanct. Bill has taken every reasonable precaution to protect them."

Willa sat quietly for a moment, trying to calm her pounding heart. She shook her head. "I simply won't have it, Otto. The risk is too great. She must give Brownell a chance."

With a sigh, Otto nodded. "All right. Let us assume Irmagard capitulates and goes to Brownell. She learns everything they have to teach her. And yet it turns out that all that has been accomplished is a forestalling of the inevitable. She still wants a life that's . . . unusual. So Bill gives her a chance and she amazes him with her audition—which just might happen. Monte and Charlie both say she has real talent."

"Monte and Charlie are biased beyond belief when it comes to that girl," Willa said. "It won't happen."

"But what if it does? What then? Do you tie her to the bedpost and order up a wedding?"

The man could be so annoying. Like a dog after a bone he would not let a thing go. "Once she spends some time with refined young ladies and sees what the world has to offer she will realize how silly— how immature—this Wild West phase has been." In the moonlight Willa could see Otto's reaction. He might not be picking a fight, but neither was he convinced.

"Darling," Otto set his cup and saucer on the small table to his left and took her hand. "You say you have prayed, and I believe you. But I still don't understand how you can be so certain that God's will for Irma is the very thing she least wants."

How did the man do it? He didn't claim a faith beyond a generic belief in God. Willa, on the other hand, pored over the Bible by the hour. It had been her lifeline to survival more than once, and yet Otto was bringing up one of the great theological questions of all time—how to know God's will. Irmagard had brought up some of the same issues earlier when she asked if it wasn't God who had given her the balance and the skill to perform. Maybe they both had a point. Maybe God didn't *always* require what one wanted least. What if she was wrong? What if— NO. *Children, obey your parents.* That was in the Bible, and its meaning was as clear as it could be. No amount of theological quibbling could reinterpret *that* principle, and if Otto didn't have the backbone to make Irmagard obey, Willa did. And would.

Somewhere in the distance a lone coyote yipped and was answered by an entire chorus of yowls. Willa shivered and was once more in the moment, worrying over her only child alone in the wilderness.

Otto kissed her hand. "She'll be fine," he said. "Which is more than I can say for you if you don't get some rest." He nodded toward the east where the faintest paling of the indigo sky spoke of dawn. Standing up he took her cup and saucer, set it beside his own, and pulled her into his arms.

When he moved to lead her back inside, Willa protested about the teacups.

"Let Viola mind the teacups." He nuzzled her neck.

As Willa followed her husband up the stairs to the second floor, weariness descended like a shroud. It was always like this for her. Stress wore her out even as it robbed her of sleep. She sat on the edge of the bed while Otto removed his dressing gown. "I can't sleep," she murmured even as she rubbed her neck. "You know how I am."

"I do," Otto said as he got into bed and pulled her close. "But I have a remedy in mind." He kissed her.

"Mornin', ma'am."

A rumbling voice yanked Irma off the horse in her dreams. She opened her eyes to the feeble light of a dawn about to break. A tall stranger stood at the door to the empty stall where she'd slept in a pile of fresh hay. Moving to smooth her skirt, Irma remembered she was dressed in Monte's clothes. One of the snaps on his red flannel shirt was undone. Not that it mattered with her lack of endowments in that area, but Irma still felt herself blushing as she snapped it. She got up and looked around her, hoping to hide her embarrassment even as she picked hay out of her hair. And all the while the stranger was leaning on the stall door, watching with an amused twinkle in his eyes that made Irma self-conscious and irritated all at once.

"Who are you?" she blurted out. She reached for Monte's hat and pulled it on, realizing as she did so that Monte was going to be past annoyance and right into mad when she next saw him. He'd had to go to the dance without his new hat.

"I believe that's my line, ma'am, what with you sneaking onto the property and stowing away in my friend's barn." He reached over and pulled a long piece of hay out of her tangled hair.

"I didn't *sneak*," Irma said, "and I wasn't *stowed away*. And for your information Buffalo Bill is a friend of my father's. And mine. So I repeat—who are *you*, and what are you doing spying on me?"

"Wasn't spying," the stranger said easily. "Couldn't sleep. Saw you out by the corral in the middle of the night. Watched long enough to know you weren't bent on horse thievin' and figured I'd let you get some shut-eye before seeing what brings you onto the place." He touched the brim of his cowboy hat. "Shep Sterling, ma'am."

Shep Sterling? Irma peered up at him. She'd seen Sterling's likeness on a Wild West broadside. Shep Sterling had a drooping mustache and wavy, shoulder-length dark hair. This fella had a well-trimmed beard and short hair. He smelled of bay rum cologne and was dressed like he'd just walked out of a mercantile with an armful of new "cowboy duds." His boots were shiny. And that belt buckle was . . . ridiculous. No self-respecting cowboy would be caught dead wearing something like that. Irma smirked. "The last I heard Shep Sterling was billed as the King of the Cowboys with the Wild West. He has long hair and a droopy mustache, and—"

"And what?"

"Real cowboys just don't get all duded up in polished boots and belt buckles like that," Irma said. "At least not the ones I've worked with. Not on a day when they're going to be roping and riding broncs." She grinned. "And they *never* smell like a spice rack."

"Let me get this straight," the man said. "I can't be Shep Sterling because I don't have a mustache. My hair isn't long. My boots are shiny, my belt buckle is too fancy, and . . . I smell good."

Irma shrugged. "It's a nice outfit. For a drugstore cowboy."

"Drugstore cowboy?"

"Someone who has the outfit . . . but who wouldn't know a latigo from a lariat." Irma looked down at his boots. "And whose boots haven't ever set foot in a corral on branding day."

The "cowboy" grinned and shoved his hat back on his head. "Well, ma'am, the fact is, I do know a latigo from a lariat—"he looked down at his boots—"but the boots and the buckle *are* new. And if what you say is true about *real* cowboys, then I guess I ain't a real cowboy."

"*There's* a surprise," Irma laughed as she brushed past him and headed for the corner of the barn where feed was stored. Grabbing a bucket, she dipped into a bin of oats and walked out to the corral. Diamond came trotting over. Irma scratched behind his ears. "Ready to go home, boy?" she said. Diamond thrust his muzzle into the bucket and grunted with pleasure.

"You in the habit of borrowing grain from Buffalo Bill?" the man asked.

Irma shook her head. "Not in the habit. But he won't mind." She glanced sideways at him. "And you'd know *that* if you were a real cowboy, too. Ranchers always have the latchstring out for one another." Diamond finished the last of his grain, and Irma returned the bucket to the barn. When she got back, the stranger had stepped into the corral and was saddling the gentle gelding. "I'll get that," Irma said. The stranger stepped away and watched her work. She slipped the bridle over Diamond's ears and pulled his forelock from beneath the browband. When the stranger moved to grab Diamond's reins she shook her head. "You don't have to do that. He's ground broke."

"*What* broke?"

"As long as the reins are dangling like that, Diamond considers himself hitched to a post. It's actually called 'ground tying' a horse. Which is what you can do if they're 'ground broke'."

"No kidding." The man put his hands on his hips and shook his head. "That's amazing." He looked at Irma. "And you'd trust him not to run off? Even if he was out of the corral?"

Irma nodded as she hooked a stirrup over the saddle horn and checked the girth strap.

"No offense," the stranger said, "but I thought girls always rode on one of them, uh, them . . ."

"Sidesaddles," Irma said as she reached for the reins and mounted up. "Some do. I don't."

"Well, don't that beat all," the stranger said. "Now that's something to write home about. Meeting a pretty girl who sits a horse like a man."

Irma peered from beneath Monte's hat, suddenly suspicious of the stranger's supposed ignorance. She nodded at the corral gate. "If you'll open the gate for me, I'll be on my way."

When he obliged, Irma rode through. "You never did tell me your real name," she said, as the stranger closed the corral gate.

"Henry Mortimer," he said, then shrugged. "Not a very good name for a cowboy, is it?"

Irma laughed. "You could try Hank."

He smiled up at her. "You think that fits?"

Irma nodded.

"Well then, I guess that's it. I'll be Hank to you, Miss . . . ?"

Irma smiled. "When I get my spot with the Wild West I'll be Liberty Belle."

Hank whistled low. "What's your act?"

"Trick riding."

"I'd like to see that."

"Keep an eye out later today," Irma said. She hadn't quite figured out how she was going to manage an audition with Momma in attendance, but she was determined it would happen. Nudging Diamond forward, she headed for the ranch, wondering about Hank Mortimer and what kind of connection earned him a room in Buffalo Bill's ranch house. He seemed nice enough. Maybe she'd seek him out and explain things to him so he could appreciate what he was watching when the auditions started. Folks couldn't really understand how much skill it took to ride a cutting horse until they understood how hard a calf would try to stay with its momma. The partnership between a good cowboy and a good horse was a sight to behold—once a person realized how long it took for that partnership to solidify. It had taken her nearly two years to teach Diamond how to partner with Liberty Belle. There was a lot to learn in order to really appreciate the West. It would be fun to enlighten a greenhorn. And besides, Henry had nice eyes. Broad shoulders. *You sap. You're blushing.*

As the sun rose above the horizon, reality crashed through Irma's daydreams about the day ahead. She had run off and stayed away *all night.* Momma would be beside herself. What if, when she got back to the ranch, Daddy punished her by making her stay at the ranch while everyone else headed for Scout's Rest? She hadn't thought of that. She might not even be allowed to *go* today.

You are in so much trouble. Again.

Urging Diamond into an easy lope, Irma argued herself around to accepting the only sure way for her to deflect her parents' combined wrath. Reluctantly she realized that she'd best forego the idea of auditioning today. Maybe she could talk to Bill Cody and arrange for something on another day. It would be over a week before the Wild West train pulled out of the station. Maybe it would work out to her advantage *not* to audition when half the world was at Scout's Rest. And now that she thought about it, having plenty of time to explain ranch life to a certain handsome drugstore cowboy wasn't exactly a bad thing. Her stomach growled. As she urged Diamond into a gallop Irma decided it was a good thing she was hungry. She had eaten some crow in her life, but to get her parents' permission to go to Scout's Rest, she was going to have to wolf down the whole bird.

CHAPTER 3

BE KIND TO ONE ANOTHER, TENDER-HEARTED,
FORGIVING EACH OTHER, JUST AS GOD IN CHRIST
ALSO HAS FORGIVEN YOU.

Ephesians 4:32 NASB

"I'm *sorry*, all right?" Irma said as she dismounted and handed Monte his misshapen hat.

"Do you have any idea how long it took me to steam this over Ma's tea kettle? To get it just right?" Monte struggled in vain to shape the crown with his hands. "I can't believe you'd just steal a man's hat, Irma. That's so wrong."

"I'll find a way to make it up to you. But first— you've gotta help me." With a glance toward the house, Irma led Diamond into the barn. "Can you take care of Diamond while I get changed?" When Monte didn't move, Irma said, "Come on, Monte. Alice Carter thinks you hung the moon. She wouldn't care if you came to a dance in a pink dress, let alone a new hat. The way she stares into your eyes every time she sees you, she probably wouldn't have even *noticed* the hat." Irma touched the brim. "And besides, it isn't ruined. I'll take it to town with me when we go home and have Mr. Hamilton fix it up like new. Daddy says he's the best haberdasher in town."

"He's the *only* haberdasher in town, *Irmagard*," Monte said, still refusing to show any signs of forgiving or helping her.

Irma batted her eyelashes at him and shimmied her shoulders in a pantomime of the way she'd seen Alice Carter flirt. "So . . . am I right? Did she save you the first dance?"

Monte shrugged. "All of 'em," he finally said, and there was the grin. Monte could never stay mad at her for long.

"I told you so." Irma led Diamond into a stall, grateful when Monte followed her.

"Are you all right?" he asked. "I heard you took a bad fall before you ran off."

"I'm sore, but it wasn't that bad a spill." She put her hand on Monte's arm. "I *did* it, Monte. The whole routine. I just slipped at the end. But I *did* it. And yes, I'm all right. I ran off because I just—" She nodded toward the house. "I just couldn't listen to her anymore."

"Well, they're *both* really upset. You should have been at supper. Everyone around the table was trying not to talk about the only thing we could think about." One corner of his mouth curled up. "You really did that dismount?"

When she nodded he whistled softly in appreciation. "Wish I woulda seen it." Picking up a stirrup, he slung it over the saddle horn and undid the girth strap. As he pulled saddle and blanket off Diamond, he shook his head and murmured, "You are in *so much trouble.*"

Irma slipped Diamond's bridle off and, pushing the stall door closed with her foot, followed Monte into the tack room. "Is anyone else up?"

Hoisting the saddle onto an empty rack, Monte took the bridle from Irma and hung it up. "Pa's over at the old barn harnessing up the team. The girls are awake, although I don't think they're downstairs yet."

"My parents?"

Monte shook his head. "Didn't hear anything when I walked by their room. But there were two cups and saucers on the back porch. Like someone had a midnight meeting. Unless Miss Viola had a visit from a secret admirer." He laughed at the joke about Miss Viola, who seemed delighted with the fact that she was approaching her sixtieth birthday having never been "hog-tied-by-any-two-legged-varmint-lookin'-for-a-servant-he-don't-have-to-pay."

"Finish up with Diamond for me, and I'll do all your chores tonight," Irma promised. "And I *will* make it up to you about the hat."

"I don't think you can fix it this time, Irm, and I'm not talking about the hat. Aunt Willa's gonna want to hustle you straight home. Even if I wanted to make a deal about hats and chores and stuff, the fact is I don't think you're gonna *be* here for chores tonight."

"I'll handle Momma," Irma said. "Just, please . . . for now. . . ?"

"Oh, all right," Monte said. They walked back toward Diamond's stall. "Ned and me are trying out for the Wild West today. Having someone else to do chores here at home would be fine with me. That way we can stay later if we want."

"*You're* trying out?" Irma glanced toward the house again, where a light was now glowing in the kitchen. She wasn't surprised about Ned thinking of signing on. He had an ambitious streak as wide as the Platte River and no local family ties, but Monte never spoke of anything but the riches to be made in the sandhills, which he called the "best cattle country in the world"—as if he'd actually seen the world.

"I didn't think you ever wanted to see the other side of the South Platte, let alone the other side of the state line," Irma said.

Monte shrugged as he opened the stall door and began to go over Diamond's dapple-gray coat with a curry comb. "Pa could do a lot with forty dollars a month. Might even be sixty if I can impress Bill and get into more than one act."

"But Uncle Charlie would have to hire someone to replace you."

Monte shook his head. "Nope. We talked about it already. Not much of a herd left to run since the blizzard. Fact is, Pa's thinkin' he might have to let some of the hands go. Ned volunteered to try and find something else. Then we decided why not Wild West together."

Irma knew untold numbers of cattle had died last month when a blizzard dumped eight inches of snow and left drifts five and six feet deep all across Lincoln County. But Daddy's talking about the damage from his perspective as a banker was different from hearing Monte talk about how the blizzard had hurt Uncle Charlie and Aunt Laura—and how he was trying to help.

"If *you're* trying out today," she murmured, "I just have to be there."

"You aren't still thinking of trying to sneak in your own audition are you? Your momma would—"

Irma shook her head. "No. That was probably a bad idea all along. I'd need Diamond there, anyway, and—" She put her hand on Monte's arm. "But I can't miss seeing you and Ned ride. Please, Monte—help me out."

"Isn't that what I'm doin'?" Monte waved the curry comb at her. "But you gotta wash my britches and—" he thought for a moment— "polish my boots before the next dance."

"Agreed."

"And iron my shirts. And . . . I need a button sewed on my—"

"Don't press your luck, Monte Mason," Irma protested. "You may be my favorite cousin, but a girl's gotta draw the line somewhere. I'd have to love you a lot more than I do before I'd be your seamstress. Besides, you have a sister who's almost as talented as the seamstress in town. And Minnie actually *likes* to sew."

Monte shook his head. "How you gonna' find a husband with an attitude like that?"

"What makes you think I want to find a husband?" Irma sassed back. "Part of me thinks Miss Viola has it right about men."

"Well, that's good, because you're practically an old maid already,"

Monte teased. "Minnie seems to think eighteen is the last gasp age for getting a man."

"The only thing *I'm* feeling desperate about this morning is how to smooth Momma's ruffled feathers. As you said, I'm in trouble. And believe me, I know it."

"Go on in there, then, and fancy yourself up while I tend Diamond," Monte said, nodding toward the house. "And do a good job of it, too. I want you there when I make a darned fool of myself trying to impress Mr. Cody. Swipe on some of that lemon verbena stuff. Maybe Aunt Willa will see there's hope if you're all gussied up like a real girl when you come down for breakfast. Shoot, maybe she won't even know you've been gone all night." Monte paused. "Which reminds me, where were you, anyway? Diamond doesn't look all that wore out."

"If I tell you," Irma said, "you have to swear never to let anyone know."

Monte raised his right hand. "Swear."

"I got lost." The dimple returned to Monte's cheek. Irma tapped it as she said, "You promised not to tell. And now you'd better promise not to laugh." She sighed. "I fell asleep in the saddle. When I woke up, Diamond had gone home. Only to his *old* home."

Monte stroked Diamond's neck. "You old devil, you," he said. He chuckled and looked at Irma. "So you spent the night at Scout's Rest?"

Irma nodded. "Slept in the barn—and don't you forget that you promised to keep that secret. I can't have Momma thinking I got *lost*. I need her to believe I can take care of myself." With a sigh, Irma turned toward the house. "Now, if I can just get upstairs without anyone hearing me."

"I left my window open," Monte said.

Irma went back to hug him. "And that," she said, "is why you will always be my favorite cousin."

Monte waved the compliment away. "The rooster's gonna be crowing any second. You'd best be climbing that trellis."

Irma kissed his cheek. "Thank you. And I'll help you with chores for a week if this all works out." She trotted quickly across the open space between the barn and the ranch house and ducked around the corner of the house. With a last wave in Monte's direction she grasped the trellis Uncle Charlie had built only last year and climbed up to the second story, where, as promised, Monte had left his bedroom window open, just in case his runaway cousin needed to sneak home in the middle of the night. The rooster crowed just as she pulled herself through the window.

———

Suffering from a stiff neck and a headache, Willa had just given Laura's coffee grinder a crank when the answer to her midnight prayers walked into the kitchen dressed in the double pink housedress Willa had had made by North Platte's best dressmaker. Irmagard's red hair shone from a good brushing and was piled atop her head in the most becoming style. And—what went past the realm of answered prayer and ventured close to the miraculous in Willa's mind—the girl had donned an apron as if she intended to help in the kitchen. Willa's spirits soared momentarily but plummeted back to earth as she wondered if, instead of sincere repentance, this might be yet another performance by the actress known as Irmagard Determined to Get Her Way.

Clearly caught off guard by the sight of her rumpled mother cranking the coffee grinder, Irma offered a muffled greeting before hurrying out on the porch. She came back inside bearing the cups and saucers Willa and Otto had left behind last night, then collapsed into a kitchen chair and, with her most repentant expression on her fresh-washed face, moaned, "Oh, Momma. Will you ever forgive me?"

Willa didn't answer. Instead, she fumbled her way through mak-

ing coffee. When she reached for the dirty cups and saucers, Irmagard hopped up.

"I'll do it," she said.

Barely managing to refrain from another emotional outburst—
this one fueled by anger, Willa waved Irmagard away while she went
to the dry sink, pumped water enough to rinse the dishes, dried
them, and put them back on the wooden shelf hanging above Laura's
gateleg worktable. She began to set the table for breakfast. When
Irmagard moved to help, Willa acquiesced. Plates clunked against
the table. Silverware rattled. Coffee cups and glasses landed in place
with a thud, all of it unnaturally loud as the two women worked in
emotionally supercharged silence.

The three younger Mason girls—fifteen-year-old Mollie,
thirteen-year-old Mamie, and eight-year-old Maggie—came downstairs and, with nervous glances from Willa to Irmagard and mechanical
"good mornings," hurried outside to do the milking and egg-gathering.
Minnie, Laura, and Miss Viola all came in at once, and tried to act as if
nothing was wrong as they moved through their morning routine.

Willa poured herself a cup of coffee and excused herself, heading onto the back porch where she settled on the porch swing and
thanked God for helping her not create another scene just then. In
a family of high-strung women, Wilhelmina Ludvik had once been
the one most given to fits and fainting. The Ludvik family history
included words like *asylum* and *suicide*—words that not only embarrassed Willa, but also, on occasions like yesterday when she gave in
to her emotions, terrified her. Convinced that without her faith her
own life might have had a tragic end, Willa prayed. *Only you know
how frightened I've been, Lord. Help me. Please help me know what to
do now. I don't want to be an emotional shrew.*

When Irmagard finally came out onto the porch and settled
uncertainly next to her, Willa waited to speak until she thought she
could trust her voice not to wobble. Finally, with a last unspoken
plea for help from above, she said, "It would seem that we are at

an impasse, you and I. You insist that you cannot be the daughter I want you to be, and I cannot seem to be the mother you want me to be." She reached for Irmagard's hand and squeezed it. "It's not always easy for a mother to stand her ground. But in this, I feel I must." She was tempted to once and for all spread the ugly cloth of her family's past before Irmagard, so the child would understand her feelings about the Wild West. But then, with a little shudder and a faint heaving of her chest, Irmagard leaned over and rested her head on Willa's shoulder.

"I'm sorry, Momma," she muttered. "I'll try. I really will. I-I don't want to go to Brownell. I think—no, I *know* I'll hate it." With a deep sigh, she sat up. "But it's only one year." She looked away. "It was wrong of me to run off like I did and even more wrong for me to stay away for most of the night." She gave a little shrug. "I wasn't going to tell you this, but the truth is I-I got lost. And I couldn't find my way back in the dark."

"Your father said that Diamond would find his way home even if you couldn't." Willa pressed her lips together and tried to rein in her temper. She was trying to be calm, but it wasn't easy in the face of a willful child's prevarication. "How can you expect us to trust you and to respect your choices in life when you lie to avoid punishment?"

"I'm not lying. Diamond *did* find his way home. Just not to *this* home." With studied sincerity, Irmagard explained. "Uncle Charlie got Diamond from Scout's Rest. So when I lost my way in the dark and gave him his head, the stubborn old goat took me there." She sighed. "I fell asleep in the saddle, and when I woke up Diamond was standing by the corral over there. It was late and we were both tired. So I put him in the corral, and I slept in a pile of straw in the barn. I woke up a couple of hours ago and headed back." Her blue-gray eyes pleaded. "I'm so sorry, Momma. I can't imagine how you must have worried. Or maybe you weren't so much worried as wishing you get hold of me and give me a good thrashing. I certainly deserve one."

"If your father hadn't been here I don't know what I would have done." Forcing herself to sound calm, Willa returned to the topic she had raised with her first sentence. "The truth is, Irmagard, most of the time I feel quite ill-equipped for the task of parenting you."

Irmagard blinked away tears. "You'd be so much happier with a daughter like Arta Cody."

"Shush," Willa said, and patted her daughter's arm. "You mustn't talk that way."

"Why not? It's the truth. All my life you've tried to make me into a lady, and all my life I've resisted." Irmagard fiddled with the tatted fringe on her apron pocket for a moment, and then, taking a deep breath, she said, "Words aren't enough to make up for what I've put you through this time. And I meant it when I said I'd do what you want. And . . . and . . . I'll try to make you proud of me at Brownell." She sniffed and put her hand on Willa's forearm. "Please say you'll forgive me for yesterday. For scaring you with that stunt in the corral and not seeming to care. And for running off and scaring you even more." Swallowing, she said, "After the way I've behaved I don't even deserve to go to Scout's Rest today." She paused. "But I hope you'll say I can, because Monte and Ned Bishop are trying out, and with all my heart I want to be there."

Willa patted her daughter's hand. The phrase *seventy times seven* came to mind. In spite of her suspicion that she was being manipulated, she could not bring herself to impose a punishment that would deny Irmagard the delights of a day at Scout's Rest. Taking a deep breath, she said, "Whatever you may think, I do appreciate how difficult it was just now for you to agree to give Brownell a chance." She cleared her throat. "It would be rude to snub Mr. Cody's invitation. And even if our absence went unnoticed by Mr. Cody, the entire family would be disappointed if you didn't go."

Irma kissed her on the cheek. "Thank you, Momma. Thank you so much."

CHAPTER 4

YOU HAVE MADE MY HEART BEAT FASTER
WITH A SINGLE GLANCE OF YOUR EYES.
Song of Songs 4:9 NASB

"Stoooopppppppp," Irma gasped. She put her hands to her waist and stared into the dressing mirror at Minnie, whose dark brown eyes were just visible behind her.

Minnie stopped tugging and tied off the corset. "There you are. A perfectly breath-defying twenty-one inches. Congratulations. You're assured the tiniest waist at the hoedown."

"And likely assured a need for smelling salts before the day is out."

"Perhaps, but you're going to look like a fashion page straight out of *Peterson's Magazine*." Minnie fingered the teal plaid walking skirt lying on her bed. "You know, if you weren't so nice to me, I'd have to hate you." She smiled as she handed over one of three petticoats. "Put these on, and I'll help you button your new shoes."

"I can get the shoes," Irma said from beneath the first petticoat. She pulled it on before asking, "Don't you have your own dressing to do before we leave?"

"Of course, but it'll take me all of three minutes to pull on the same old blue calico I wore to church all winter." Minnie shrugged. "Not that it matters. It's not like anyone's going to take a second look at me anyway, with the town girls strutting around like peacocks." With a look of remorse she added quickly, "Present company excepted, of course. You don't strut unless you're out in the corral pretending to acknowledge the adoration of thousands."

Irma reached for a piece of lace lying on the bed. "How about a new collar for your dress?"

"Oh, no you don't," Minnie said and backed away. "You're not blaming me when Aunt Willa throws a fit about you giving away the trim she paid so much for."

"She won't throw a fit." Irma said. "I wasn't going to wear it anyway. And with the dark blue from your dress showing up the pattern in the lace, it'll look really nice." Inspiration struck. She opened the small velvet box sitting in the tray of her traveling trunk and held up a pair of earrings. "Put these on. The dangles don't do a thing for my scrawny neck. In fact," she said, tucking her hands into her armpits and bobbing her head back and forth, "they make me look like a chicken." She squawked and strutted her way across the room as Minnie held the earrings up to her ears and then joined in the clucking and strutting. Finally, the girls collapsed on the bed in a fit of laughter.

"Now *you* stop," Minnie gasped, trying to regain her composure. She handed the earrings back, "They're lovely but I can't. I don't want the responsibility. If one fell out at Scout's Rest we'd never find it, and Aunt Willa *would* throw a fit about that. So would Ma, for that matter."

"All right," Irma said and, returning the earrings to her jewelry box. She held up a length of ivory-colored ribbon. "Then we'll braid this into your hair. Between that and the lace frill, no one will even notice the dress isn't new."

"Thanks." Minnie accepted the ribbon.

"I'll do a French braid. Orrin Knox won't be able to take his eyes off you. Of course I expect to get some credit when that happens."

"Should that miracle occur," Minnie countered, "there is not a *chance* that I am going to put *your* name in Mr. Knox's head by telling him you had anything to do with my ensemble."

"Why not?"

"You know exactly why. Your mother has her own plans for Mr. Knox. It's going to take more than a bit of lace on last year's dress to get him to notice *me*."

Irma reached for her cousin's hand. "You listen to me, Minnie Mason, and believe what I am about to say—I have *no interest* in Orrin Knox."

Minnie shrugged. "I do believe you. But Aunt Willa has her ways . . . and any man would be an idiot to choose me over—"

"You stop right there," Irma said. She glowered at Minnie. "You have everything any man in his right mind would desire in a woman. You're lovely. You can cook and sew with the best of women. I, on the other hand, hate to cook and sew, and the last thing on earth I want is to settle down and raise a family. A man would have to be crazy to be interested in me right now, and if Orrin Knox doesn't have enough sense to see that, then I'll just have to corner him and tell him!"

Minnie's hand went to her mouth. "You wouldn't!"

"I won't have to," Irma said as she shimmied her way into another one of the petticoats. "Orrin doesn't care for me a bit." When Minnie looked doubtful, Irma insisted. "He doesn't. Momma is always talking about how my dreams are ridiculous. Well, trust me. When it comes to 'ridiculous,' Momma's notions about my future win the prize. I am *not* going to stand for being courted by the likes of Orrin Knox, and that's that." She reached into Minnie's wardrobe and pulled out the blue dress. "Now get thyself primped and proper, Miss Mason. The buggy departs directly."

Minnie changed while Irma grunted through the process of

buttoning her shoes and grimaced as she donned the ridiculous bustle that made her backside wiggle when she walked. Glancing at herself in the mirror, she wondered at the dichotomy between what Momma called a "virtuous reticence of manner" and the reality that dressed in this getup she would be shaking her tail feathers at every man on the ranch today.

With a sigh of resignation, Irma pulled the teal plaid walking skirt over her head, tucked in the ivory waist, then added the plaid jacket cut to suggest a plunging neckline that emphasized the veritable waterfall of ivory lace spilling down her front. The idea that *this* was somehow more demure than a simple denim split skirt was ridiculous. But Minnie was right about one thing. The dressmaker had done a good job of replicating the walking suit Momma had declared "perfect for next spring" when it appeared in last fall's issue of *Peterson's Magazine*.

"Do you want the hat before or after you braid my hair?" Minnie asked.

Looking in the mirror and checking the security of her upswept hairdo, Irma made a face, then motioned for Minnie to hand her the hatbox. "Let's get it over with." Minnie removed the lid, and Irma reached in and withdrew the hat for which Momma had paid a breathtaking price. It was a complicated arrangement of lace and feathers accented by the latest thing—a dead bird.

"It's stunning," Minnie said.

"It's ridiculous," Irma countered. "Just look at this." She turned toward the mirror and held the hat in place. "Once this thing is perched on my head, I'll hardly dare move." She jabbed one of the long hatpins into place. "Which is, I suppose, exactly the point. And also the reason Momma loved it so much. It's the perfect hat for someone whose primary activities of the day will include climbing down from our buggy—with male assistance, of course— sitting at a table having tea, and strolling about the grounds on an escort's arm." Irma wondered if what Minnie had said was true.

Did Momma have plans to find a son-in-law? Thinking about that possibility made Irma feel as if she were dressed in little more than a plaid cage.

She stared at herself in the mirror. "Can you see me elbowing my way up to the corral or cheering on a bulldogger dressed in this getup? And target shooting is going to be out of the question." She raised her skirts to inspect her thin dress boots. "They already pinch. Walking out to the shooting range will be agony." She dropped her skirt. "If only I hadn't turned my ankle yesterday."

"I thought you said you weren't hurt."

"I'm not. Really. Just a sore ankle." She shrugged her shoulders. "And my back hurts a little." She looked over her shoulder at the way the dark teal trim accented her waistline. "My backside is probably going to bruise, but—"

Minnie started to laugh. "Well, I'm glad you weren't hurt."

"Sorry," Irma apologized. "I'm whining when I ought to be grateful. Especially that Momma is letting me go. I really was disrespectful." She took up another hatpin and anchored the hat more securely before waving Minnie into a chair and beginning to braid her hair. "I acted like a spoiled brat."

"You *are* a spoiled brat sometimes," Minnie said. "I love you, but if the shoe fits—"

Irma yanked playfully on a lock of Minnie's curly dark hair. "You want a braid or a rat's nest?"

"Braid, please," Minnie said. "But face facts while you're braiding. Running off like that was hardly the best way to convince your mother that the Wild West isn't just one more childish dream. If anything, it's going to make her even more determined to get you settled down."

Irma looked up. "Explain, please."

"Well . . ." Minnie pondered. "You have that luncheon coming up. It could be the first of a long line of luncheons designed to parade potential husbands through the house. And all that partying would definitely interfere with a summer out here on the ranch."

Irma paused in midbraid. She looked up and met Minnie's gaze in the mirror. Her cousin was serious. In fact, Irma realized, she might also be right. Momma might not interfere with a day at Scout's Rest, but she could most certainly raise all kinds of objections about a last summer on the ranch. What was it Momma always said? That words alone didn't really mean much in the way of an apology. It was actions that counted. Irma realized that, while it was a good thing she had already abandoned the idea of auditioning today, she dared not stop there. Not after what Minnie had just said might happen.

"You're right," Irma finally said as she handed Minnie a small mirror to check out the braid. "I have to be a perfect lady today." She reached for the parasol Momma had purchased as "the perfect accent" for the new walking suit.

"Stunning," Minnie said.

"Thanks." Irma touched the fringe of curls framing her cousin's face. "You know, I'd kill for your hair. It takes about a thousand hairpins to get my mop into anything approaching a nice hairdo. And it's *red*, for heaven's sake. No one wants red hair. You, on the other hand—"

"I wasn't talking about the braid," Minnie said as she laid the hand mirror down. "I was talking about you. *You're* stunning. I'm just fair to middling plump and pretty." She motioned for Irma to follow her. "And we both need to get downstairs."

With a last regretful glance toward the mirror, Irma headed after Minnie, who really did look lovely with her hair braided that way and the lace frill at her collar. Inspiration struck. If the day was to be a complete loss for her personally, the least Irma could do was find a way to make Mr. Orrin Knox notice the abundant charms of one Miss Minnie Mason.

Minnie and Irma were two steps from the kitchen when Momma appeared in the doorway and crowed approval. Just behind her, Monte crossed his eyes and pretended to gag. As Irma walked into the kitchen, thirteen-year-old Mamie looked her up and down with undisguised envy and a self-conscious smoothing of her own drab brown dress.

"Why can't I wear my Sunday dress?" she begged her mother, who was just taking a pan of biscuits out of the oven. "You're letting Minnie and Mollie wear theirs."

Aunt Laura set the biscuit pan on the stove top and untied her apron strings as she said, "Because Minnie and Mollie are almost grown up. But you aren't and it isn't Sunday."

"Doesn't Minnie's hair look lovely?" Irma said, and looped her arm through her cousin's.

"It does," Momma agreed. "Now hurry and eat something, girls." She glanced at Irma. "Daddy's already gone to fetch the buggy."

Irma pressed the flat of her hand to her corseted waist. "I can't possibly eat," she said. "I'd throw it up all over the buggy halfway to the ranch."

"Irmagard!" Momma scolded. "There's no need to be coarse."

"I'll pack you a little something just in case you change your mind," Aunt Laura offered.

Irma followed her mother outside just as Daddy drove up in the buggy. "Aren't you coming with us?" she asked when neither Aunt Laura nor the girls moved to join them.

"I've a few things to do here," Aunt Laura said from the back door. "Charlie and I and the girls will be along soon enough." She smiled and pointed at Irma's parasol. "Just send up the parasol, dear. It'll shine like a beacon guiding us right to you."

"Well, at least let Minnie come now," Irma said, motioning for Minnie to climb aboard.

When Minnie held back, Irma spoke louder. "Come *on* Minnie. Times a-wastin'."

Momma said nothing.

Minnie looked over her shoulder toward the house. "Ma still has some things to do before she can leave. I should help her." She smiled at Irma. "I'll see you there." And before Irma could say a word, Minnie had rushed past Aunt Laura and back inside.

Are you really going to let this happen? Irma tried to telegraph the message to Daddy, but he was talking to Uncle Charlie, who was standing on the opposite side of the buggy. *Just like Daddy. Conveniently unaware of the way Momma treats people sometimes.*

" 'Bye now," Aunt Laura called.

Daddy took it as a signal, and with a glance behind him to make sure Momma and Irma were seated, he bid Uncle Charlie good-bye and headed the team up the trail leading to Scout's Rest.

"You may not realize it, dear," Momma said as they bumped along, "but sometimes Minnie is made to feel positively frumpy in your shadow. I thought it best for her to have an opportunity to arrive *without* you in tow."

"Minnie's lovely," Irma said. She glowered at Momma.

"Of course she is," Momma agreed. "Lovely in every way. You did a beautiful job with her hair. And the lace collar was an inspiration. It makes her Sunday dress look almost new."

Well, what did a girl say to that? Especially a girl who was trying to be careful not to pick a fight. *Nothing. It's best if you say nothing at all right now.* And so that's what Irma did. She settled back and closed her eyes and pretended to take a nap even as she imagined ways to bring Minnie out of her shadow—if what Momma said was true—and into the light of Mr. Orrin Knox's world.

———

"I know this isn't your cup of tea," Daddy said to Momma as the buggy rumbled over the prairie. "But I think you'll be glad you've seen it for yourself. When this next round of building is completed,

Scout's Rest is going to be the talk of the county for some time to come."

Irma spoke up. "Arta says her father is building the biggest barn ever seen in this part of the country. He's going to have *Scout's Rest* painted in four-foot-high white letters across the roof so people can see it from the train."

"From the train?" Momma echoed. "Is that even possible? Aren't the tracks over a mile away?"

Daddy nodded. "They are. But isn't it just like Bill Cody to want people to know whose place they're admiring?" He laughed and shook his head. "Ever the showman." He teased Momma. "And after you see the house that's going up, our place is going to feel like a hovel."

"Don't be silly," Momma said quickly. "We have a beautiful home." She sighed. "It really is a shame the Codys aren't on better terms. Mr. Cody's sister selected the house plans—and all she did was tell the builder to copy Judge Peniston's home in town. I don't think Louisa plans to ever live there. Such a pity. They are a handsome couple. If only they could find a way to settle their differences."

Irma had nothing to say to that. Momma's commenting on someone else's marriage rankled and set Irma to remembering her first encounter with Buffalo Bill. She was six years old and North Platte's most famous citizen had invited Daddy and Uncle Charlie to drive supply wagons on a hunting trip. But it wasn't just any hunting trip, and when Momma objected to Daddy's being gone, the two of them fought. Irma could still remember lying in bed crying while she listened to her parents arguing.

Daddy yelled something about a Grand Duke and that he wasn't about to miss out on a historic event. Irma remembered hearing the front door slam and then, after what seemed like a long time, hearing Momma crying. The next day, when all of North Platte went to greet the Grand Duke's train, Momma and Irma stayed home. And when the long procession of cavalry and infantry filed right by their house, Irma was alone at the front window waving at Uncle Charlie and Daddy. Too bad Momma hadn't practiced what she preached about married couples settling their differences.

Momma was out of sorts the entire week the hunting party was gone. Irma got what she considered more than her fair share of spankings and was sent to her room so many times she eventually set up a play area there just to stay out of Momma's way. Even that didn't seem to please Momma. One day it was barely past suppertime when she ordered Irma to bed. Irma went, but she could not sleep. Thinking Daddy had come home when she heard voices downstairs, Irma had just reached the carved cherry railing when she realized the man in the foyer was not her father. A *stranger* was hugging Momma. What was even worse, Momma was hugging him back. She even kissed him on the cheek. And she was crying as she said something about wanting to go.

"Then do it," the man said. "Get Irmagard and come with me."

Confused and afraid, Irma crept back to her room. Closing the door, she curled up on the bare wood floor just inside her room so she could listen through the crack between the floor and the bottom of the heavy door. After what seemed like hours, she heard Momma's footsteps on the stairs. The minute Momma's bedroom door closed, Irma slipped down the back stairs. The house was empty. Creeping back up the front stairs, Irma pressed her forehead against the leaded-glass window that graced the landing. The stranger was riding away. Irma paused outside Momma's door only long enough to hear Momma crying before returning to her own room, her own bed, and her own tears.

Daddy came home the next day. Standing in nearly the same place as she had with the stranger, Momma kissed Daddy on the lips, then whispered something in his ear. She even cried a little. Daddy wrapped her in his arms and hugged her tight. With a little laugh he lifted her off the floor and spun her around, then bent to do the same with Irma. Things went back to normal. And Momma, who had never been a religious woman before that, started going to church every Sunday.

Irma never saw the stranger again, but the memory would not die. It planted Irma firmly on her doting father's side of any issue, and tore at the fabric of the mother-daughter relationship in a thousand tiny ways. As Irma grew, so did her differences with Momma. When Momma pointed out some mention of Arta Cody in the newspaper, Irma nodded, thinking as she did so that she wouldn't mind being mentioned in the newspaper—as long as it was for something besides hosting a tea party or attending the new play at the opera house. When Momma praised Irma for a bit of needlework or for learning to play a new hymn on the piano, Irma wished for more time to practice roping or riding. By the time she was in her teens, trying to be different from Momma had become second nature.

And so it was that, as the buggy drew near Scout's Rest and Irma's attentions returned to the present, her earlier resolve to be Momma's "dutiful daughter" for the day waned. She began to hope Daddy would chaperone her around the grounds. She would, of course, have to pay her respects to Momma's friends at first, but she began to hope she and Daddy would find the Masons and, together with them, join the rest of the crowd who'd come to admire horses and watch cowboys demonstrate their skills. The entire Mason family would undoubtedly watch Monte and Ned Bishop try out, and while no one expected Momma to participate, it only seemed right for Daddy and Irma to be there.

Watching Monte's audition wasn't the only thing luring Irma away from playing dutiful daughter today. Last fall Bill Cody had asked Uncle Charlie and Monte to keep an eye on the local horse crop for promising mounts to replenish the Wild West stock. Cody had offered Uncle Charlie two dollars a head as a finder's fee for anything worth looking at and a percentage of the purchase price for anything he bought. Monte's favorite was a chestnut mare with a black mane and tail, four white socks, and a crooked white blaze. Irma just had to get a look at her. And then there was a certain handsome greenhorn. With Momma happily gossiping with friends, Irma might have a chance to explain the finer points of bronc riding and bulldogging to Hank Mortimer.

"Good heavens!" Momma's exclamation startled Irma right out of her daydream about horses and Hank. "Someone must have walked a thousand miles these past few weeks just planting trees. Look at them all, Otto. It's hard to understand how we can't seem to manage a few trees on our property in town. I'd like the promise of some shade."

"All right, Momma," Daddy said. "I'll talk to Al about trees before we leave today. Maybe he can hook us up with a supplier who'll send out something bigger than a seedling. Something hardy in the west."

"Ask about a rosebush or two while you're at it," Momma said. "Something impervious to wind and drought. And maybe a climbing rosebush for that trellis Charlie built Laura."

Daddy chuckled, "You don't want much, do you, Mrs. Friedrich?"

"Just a little civilization, Mr. Friedrich."

While Momma groused and Daddy teased, Irma took in the recent changes at Scout's Rest—none of which had been visible last night in the dark and none of which had caught her eye when she made her hasty exit earlier that morning. Half-listening to Arta talking about her father's plans was entirely different from seeing the progress for herself. For the first time, Irma could actually see a huge house and barns, a lake large enough for canoeing, and entire groves of tall trees. Tempted to be envious, she wondered if she might be able to afford a nice ranch of her own someday—once she'd toured with the Wild West as a headliner for a few years. Headliners made good money. At least that's what Monte said.

Daddy parked the buggy. As he prepared to help Momma and Irma down, Irma glanced toward the far corral where a crowd was already gathering to watch a couple of wranglers saddle a dancing pinto. Daddy glanced that way and said, "That must be the horse Charlie thinks will be the new star bronco. They've named him Outlaw."

Irma glanced toward the house, where someone had built a shelter of upright poles supporting a frame topped with brush. There, Irma knew, the "real ladies" would hold court in the shade, sharing news about this family or that and talking over the upcoming social season and the new opera house in town. There, Momma would revel in announcing that her daughter had been accepted at Brownell, and Irma would be expected to sit primly and pretend to be pleased. She was formulating a way to escape when Momma spoke up.

"I can see the wheels spinning, Irmagard," she said. "Pay your respects to the ladies, and then I won't keep you tied down."

Daddy winked at Irma as he offered an arm to each woman. They crossed to the shelter. As always, Irma was proud to be on the arm of Otto Friedrich, Buffalo Bill's friend, founder of the First Bank in North Platte, leading citizen, and all around likeable gentleman. Daddy had accomplished a lot since the days when North Platte was little more than the end of the line for the Union Pacific track being laid west. He had, in fact, built himself, if not an empire like Buffalo Bill's, at least a respectable part of one. Daddy worked hard to provide Momma with the kind of life she expected.

"Irmagard?" Daddy patted her hand.

What had she missed this time?

"You'll have to excuse our daughter. She's preoccupied with the opportunity to meet so many famous people today." Daddy smiled at her. "I was trying to remember the name of the sharpshooter who's scheduled to appear at the opera house this week."

"Lillian Smith," Irma reminded him.

"Ah, yes. The California Girl," one of the mavens said with obvious distaste.

"Bill said she makes him look like a novice when it comes to target shooting," Daddy said.

"I wouldn't know about that. But I hear . . ." The old woman went on to express her personal opinion about the kind of woman who engaged in "that sort of thing."

"Well, well," Daddy said. "You'll excuse me if I respectfully disagree with judging a young lady based on gossip." He bowed, then kissed Momma on the cheek and excused Irma and himself.

"Daddy," Irma huffed, trotting alongside, "I'm going to need those infernal smelling salts if you don't . . . slow . . . down."

Daddy stopped midstep and apologized, then shook his head. "I can't abide those old hens and their peck-peck-peck at anything or anyone who doesn't toe the line they've drawn about what's proper and what's not. How can they possibly know anything about any of the women Bill's adding to his Wild West when they haven't so much as—" he broke off, chuckling. "My, my, who do I sound like now?"

"Me," Irma laughed. "And I'm glad to see at least one of my parents isn't horrified by what they witnessed in Uncle Charlie's corral yesterday." She hurried on before Daddy could backpedal. "I know, I know. It was foolish of me not to consider that you and Momma might arrive earlier than planned. And it was downright wrong of me to refuse to apologize when I'd frightened her. And running off like that and not coming back for most of the night—"

"Yes. I've been meaning to discuss that with you. Your mother said you got lost?"

Irma sighed. "Embarrassing as that is to admit, it's the truth." She looked past Daddy and scanned the group of cowboys watching as a potential rider approached the pinto bronc christened Outlaw. "I didn't tell Momma, but I met someone here this morning—a greenhorn, in fact—and I promised to help him understand what would be going on today." She tugged her father's arm. "I'll tell you all about it later." She pointed to the cowboy in the corral. "Isn't that Monte? Let's hurry!"

"Here you go," Uncle Charlie said and waved Irma to a spot in front of him even as he said to Daddy, "Wait 'til you see this. I was right about that pinto. It's taken them half an hour to get a saddle on him. Cody's going to want him for sure, and I bet he pays me top dollar."

"Where *is* Bill?" Daddy said, craning his neck.

"Socializing. Monte said Cody gave Shep Sterling the go-ahead to check out the broncs and riders this morning."

Irma didn't have time to find Sterling in the crowd, because at that moment Monte finally got one toe in a stirrup and the wranglers who'd been holding Outlaw's head let go and dove for the fence, scrambling under the lowest rail as the pinto exploded into a frenzy of bucking. The bronc was good, all right, but Monte wasn't giving up easily. Even when the horse sunfished, sending a cloud of dust toward the side of the corral where Irma and the rest of the Mason family stood, even when he left the ground with all fours and landed with a jarring thud that made Irma wince, even then, Monte stuck in the saddle.

Finally, a nasty spin sent Monte's hat flying in one direction and Monte in the other. When he didn't move for a moment, Irma's hand went to her mouth and her heartbeat quickened. After what seemed at least part of an eternity Monte opened his eyes and scrambled to his feet. Irma joined the crowd in applauding with relief.

A few feet away, a tall cowboy ducked between the corral poles and retrieved Monte's hat, then walked toward him. Clapping his hand on Monte's shoulder, he said something that made Monte shout with joy and look over to where the Mason family, Daddy, and Irma were standing. He gave the thumbs-up, and the Mason girls and Irma cheered. Aunt Laura smiled and waved her approval.

Irma put her gloved hand on Uncle Charlie's arm and pointed. "Is that—"

Uncle Charlie nodded. "Must be. Shep Sterling in the flesh."

He was handsome. Broad shoulders. Nice eyes. Scruffy beard. Irma couldn't tell if he was still wearing the new boots or not, but the ridiculously large buckle was evident. Watching Hank Mortimer—who apparently really was Shep Sterling—saunter back to his spot just outside the corral, Irma wondered if he still smelled of bay rum cologne. And she blushed.

CHAPTER 5

Shouts and whistles sounded in the distance as part of Buffalo Bill's crowd of guests, the Mason girls among them, watched the ongoing action. Daddy, Uncle Charlie, and a half dozen other guests were among those challenging fifteen-year-old sharpshooter Lillian Smith at the shooting range. Irma and Monte watched for a few minutes before ducking through the crowd and making their way toward a smaller corral behind the bunkhouse. As they approached, Irma— who had misplaced her parasol hours ago—shaded her eyes with one hand to watch the small herd biting, snorting, half-rearing, and kicking its way through the equine ritual that would eventually decide the pecking order by which the herd would function.

"Looks like the chestnut with the blaze is vying with that roan to be lead mare," Irma said as they neared the corral fence.

Monte nodded "She's a feisty one. The roan doesn't stand a chance."

Irma gripped the top pole of the corral fence with her gloved hands and watched the horses mill about. After a few minutes she wondered aloud, "Isn't she just about the most beautiful thing you've ever seen?"

"I do believe she is."

Irma started at the sound of the voice behind them. She didn't have to look to know who it was. She'd been trying to avoid Shep Sterling for most of the day. First of all, she was embarrassed that she'd refused to believe him when he'd introduced himself after finding her asleep in the barn. And second, if Momma ever learned that Irma had been alone with a stranger in Bill Cody's barn . . . Whew.

Sterling spoke over her head to Monte. "Aren't you gonna introduce your little lady?"

"Sure," Monte said with a grin and nodded toward the mare. "Go get your rope and we'll reel her in."

"I don't believe in using a rope, pardner," Shep said, grinning down at Irma. "At least not until we've been properly introduced."

"Shep Sterling," Monte held out a hand toward Irma, "Irmagard Friedrich. Irmagard—"he motioned toward Sterling—"Shep."

"*Friedrich?*" Sterling repeated, cocking his head as he looked down at Irma. "As in Otto Friedrich—the banker from North Platte?"

"As in," Monte nodded. "He's my uncle. Irma's my cousin. My *favorite* cousin, as she so often reminds me. Also my *only* cousin."

How does Shep Sterling know about Daddy? And when, exactly, did he and Monte get to be on such friendly terms? Irma didn't remember Monte saying all that much about the cowboy, even though Sterling and a few of the wranglers from the Wild West had participated in the spring roundup last year before the show season started. Monte had said almost nothing about the event—mostly, she thought, because he'd known how badly she wanted to be part of it and just how insistent Momma had been to prevent it. But if Monte and Sterling were friends—Irma could just hear the teasing she'd have to endure if he learned about this morning. And Monte wasn't above blackmail, either.

Irma met Sterling's gaze with a silent plea *Please . . . please . . . please don't say anything about this morning.* Sterling smiled a conspiratorial smile even as his gaze followed the line of lace spilling out of her jacket down to her waist and back up again. Irma could feel her cheeks growing warm.

There was a decided twinkle in the man's eyes as he touched the brim of his hat before asking, "Could we possibly have met before, Miss Friedrich? You look somewhat familiar."

"I suppose it's possible," Irma said. "My father and Bill Cody have been friends for years. Although I can't say that I recall our being introduced before." It wasn't a lie. They hadn't been introduced by anyone else. She did what she could to intensify the unspoken plea in her expression.

Sterling nodded. He was clearly enjoying her discomfort, and it made Irma want to— Well, she didn't quite know what she wanted other than to catch her breath and change the subject. She cleared her throat and nodded toward the horses. "Monte brought me over to see the chestnut mare with the blaze. He's been talking about her ever since he and my Uncle Charlie sorted some of the prime stock out." *Finally.* Finally the man stopped staring at her and looked at the horses. "I don't know when I've seen movement like that. She's going to be something special."

"She's nice," Sterling agreed. "Although I usually reserve my judgments until after I've ridden 'em. Sometimes they look like silk and ride like a sack of rocks."

"Irma's got an uncanny way about her with horses," Monte said. "I'll wager the mare glides like a rocking chair."

Irma smiled at him. "Why, Monte Mason, I do believe you're *my* favorite cousin, too."

Monte nudged her. "Aw, you're just saying that because I think your parents ought to back off and let you 'Wild West' all you want."

"This is *that* cousin?" Sterling asked, looking at Irma with feigned surprise. "The one you told me about during roundup?"

"Yep," Monte said.

Shep swept his hat off and bowed.

What on earth had Monte said about her? Sterling must have barely managed not to laugh in her face this morning while she went on about being Liberty Belle.

"I don't quite recall," Sterling said with a little smile. "What was it Monte said you were working up as an act?"

He was enjoying this way too much. Well, he wasn't the only one who could pretend. Irma decided to give Shep Sterling/Henry-Hank Mortimer a dose of his own medicine. "Oh, nothing that would impress someone like you," she simpered. "I mean—you being a headliner for Buffalo Bill and all. I'm just a little old country girl with a lot to learn."

"You don't say?" Sterling looked past her to Monte and then back again. "You didn't sound like some 'country girl with a lot to learn' this morning in Bill's barn."

Irma let out a protest just as Sterling ducked between the corral poles and, retrieving a rope looped over a fence post a few feet away, tied a knot to form a noose as he walked toward the horses.

Monte looked down at her. "Did he just say 'this morning in Bill's barn'?"

Irma shook her head.

"Yes," Monte insisted. "He did." He turned his back on the corral and folded both arms. "Is there something you forgot to tell me about your little adventure getting lost out on the big wide prairie. . . . *cousin?*"

Annoyance sounded in her voice as Irma confessed. "Oh, all right." She pointed toward Sterling. "*He* found me sleeping in one of the empty stalls. Said his name was *Henry Mortimer*. The varmint."

She groaned. "He actually told me his name was Shep Sterling at first. But I didn't believe him. I called him a drugstore cowboy."

"You did?" Monte smiled, clearly enjoying her embarrassment.

"Well, he . . . he had that belt buckle on and shiny boots, and he—" She waved her arm toward Sterling. "He just looked too fine to be a real cowboy. And he let me go on and on about how I was going to be Liberty Belle, a headliner for the Wild West. And all the while he didn't say one word about knowing you."

"You went on and on? Why, I'm . . . so surprised, Irma. Shocked, really. You're usually so shy . . . so reluctant to speak up."

"You," Irma said, as she punched his arm, "are having entirely too much fun with this."

Sterling had roped the chestnut mare. Irma put a hand on Monte's shoulder and pressured him to turn around. "Pay attention while he works. You might learn something. After all, he's the King of the Cowboys."

Together Monte and Irma watched Sterling handle the mare. Bracing himself against the inevitable fight, he held on, all the while talking in a low, calm voice. In record time he was standing next to the horse rubbing her neck while she bobbed her head up and down, nervous but apparently willing to give the stranger a chance.

"Would you look at that," Monte said with a low whistle.

"I can't believe it," Irma said. "The way she was rolling her eyes and dancing around, I expected she'd put up a fight." She shook her head. "Maybe the man actually *earned* his royal title." She paused. "But I'm still not forgiving him for not telling me who he was."

"He *did* tell you." Monte nudged her shoulder. "You wouldn't believe him."

"He should have made me believe him," Irma said.

"He doesn't exactly have the title branded on his backside," Monte blurted out, then gulped. "Oh, Irm . . . I'm sorry."

"For what?" Irma giggled. "*Backside* is a perfectly accurate anatomical term." She glanced past Monte to where Sterling was standing, quietly talking to the mare. The horse was almost eating out of his hand. *How did he do that?* As she watched, Sterling began to stroke the mare's head. Slowly, he moved his hands up to her ears, down her sleek neck, across the withers. The mare shivered and took a step away. Sterling went back to her head and talked some more. Finally he took a step toward Irma and Monte. The horse followed. He took another step. So did she.

"I believe," Sterling said to Irma, when he got within earshot, "this fine lady was hoping to make your acquaintance."

Irma reached up to pull her hatpins out, then took off the hat and handed it to Monte along with her dress gloves. Ever so slowly, she bent down and slipped between the corral poles and stood with her hands at her sides. "Hello, beautiful," she said.

"Thank you very kindly, ma'am," Sterling teased, "but I believe her name is Blaze. Or Lady Blaze, if you prefer."

Without taking her eyes off the horse, Irma said, "And how would you know that?"

"I asked her," Sterling said. He seemed half serious.

"Well then, Lady Blaze," Irma said gently, "I am more than pleased to meet you." Slowly, continuing to talk to the horse as she moved, Irma raised her right hand. When the mare rolled her eyes and tossed her head, Irma stood still, her hand poised in midair. "Sshh, sshhh," she said. "Now, what are you afraid of? Nobody here's gonna hurt you. Nobody, nobody." As she talked, Irma took first one step and then another toward the trembling horse that, in spite of flaring nostrils and an occasional snort, was staying put. Until, that is, someone screamed.

———

The first thing Irma noticed was that she was no longer out-of-doors. The second was pain—a lot of pain every time she tried to take a breath. Her hands slid to her midsection. There was no corset restricting her, so why was it so hard to breathe? She inhaled again, this time more slowly. There. Not so agonizing. Opening her eyes, she stared up at the ceiling. At the sound of Momma's exclamations of joy, Irma remembered. A human scream followed by an equine scream and then a flash of white as Blaze's head went up, and then, as the mare spun around to flee, a hoof lashed out. *How embarrassing.* She'd been kicked while two expert horsemen looked on, all thanks to the infernal petticoats and the whalebone corset that kept her from being able to move quickly. This *never* would have happened if—

"Oh thank God, thank God," Momma said. She was sitting beside the narrow bed where Irma lay. It was a small room with simple furniture and only one window obscured by plain muslin curtains. A Wild West broadside hung on the otherwise bare wall, a gingham apron on a hook beside the door. With a little grunt, Irma tried to sit up.

Momma's hand pressed her back down. "No. Don't move. Not a muscle. Not until Dr. Sheridan has a chance to examine you."

Beneath the covers, Irma slid her right hand up under her chemise. She could feel an especially tender spot. Some swelling. No . . . a *lot* of swelling. Had she broken a rib? And how many shades of green and purple would she be in a day or so? "I'm fine," Irma protested and tried to ignore the pain and force herself to sit up. "Just a little kick—nothing serious." But her best intentions meant nothing. As pain rocketed through her body, she gasped and lay back.

"I don't know what he could have been thinking, letting you in a corral with a wild animal!" Momma dipped a cloth in a bowl and, wringing it out, laid it across Irma's forehead.

"She wasn't completely wild, Momma. And I'm the one who got in the corral. There wasn't any reason to think anything would happen." Irma puzzled for a moment. "What *did* happen, anyway? What was all that screaming about?"

Her eyes snapping with anger, Momma said, "Well, apparently

Mollie was coming to find you and Monte when Jason Zigler dropped a garter snake down her dress."

Irma closed her eyes and stifled a smile. "He did?" She put her hand over her mouth.

"It isn't funny," Momma said.

Irma shook her head. "It's just that you'd think Mollie would know to watch out for Jason by now." Jason Zigler had had a crush on Mollie Mason since the two of them were eight years old. The last seven years had been one long prank that included all kinds of critters. But to Irma's knowledge the garter snake approach was new. "He must really love her," Irma said, grinning.

"If that's love, heaven help Mollie if the boy ever decides he hates her!" Momma almost smiled, then recovered her indignance. "You could have been killed," she insisted. "This is no laughing matter, Irmagard. I hope you've learned your lesson."

"And what lesson would that be?" She would have sighed if inhaling didn't hurt so much.

"That associating with those Wild West people is more than just unwise. It's dangerous."

"Perfectly nice people get kicked by horses all the time, Momma. I hardly think the fact that Shep Sterling was there when this happened justifies a character judgment on the entire Wild West troupe. And besides that, from what I saw before I got kicked, the man is flat-out amazing with horses."

Momma got up. "I'll get your father. He's been pacing back and forth outside like a crazed man." Taking the cloth from Irma's forehead, she grabbed up the basin of water she'd been using and bustled out of the room.

Daddy came in. Alone. "Your Momma's gone outside to wait for the doctor with the others."

"The others?"

"Aunt Laura, Uncle Charlie. Monte. Minnie. And Shep

Sterling—although now that Momma's outside I expect he'll high-tail it. Even Ned Bishop came running when he heard what happened."

"Ned? How long have I been in here? Did I miss the last of the auditions? Did they get hired on?"

Daddy cleared his throat. "Yes, yes." He waved one hand in the air. "Monte and Ned both got hired. I can't believe you're asking about them when—"

Irma noticed his eyes were red. And watering. "Hey," she said, holding out her hand. "You don't have to look so worried. It's not that bad."

Daddy dropped into the rocking chair beside the bed. "I will never forget the sight of you being carried unconscious—"

Whoa? Carried unconscious? "Carried?"

Daddy nodded. "Apparently Shep Sterling had you scooped up before Monte could so much as blink. Monte opened the gate and Sterling carried you up to the house bellowing for a doctor at the top of his lungs. I'd just come to the house to check in with your mother." He brushed his forehead with a trembling hand. "You were so pale when Sterling laid you down on this bed. I thought . . . I thought . . ." He gulped and covered his eyes with his hand.

"I'm so sorry, Daddy. I never meant to cause so much trouble. I just didn't think. Mr. Sterling had Lady Blaze calmed down and she's so . . . so beautiful, Daddy. Did you see her? Don't you think she's the most beautiful thing you've ever seen?" The phrase echoed in her head and, remembering her introduction to Shep, she felt her cheeks warm with color. *Shep carried me up to the house?* And when had he become *Shep* instead of *Mr. Sterling* in her mind?

Daddy forced a smile. "I suppose if you're wanting to talk horses you can't be hurt all that badly."

"I'm just sore where Lady Blaze kicked me," Irma said. "It was an accident," she added quickly. "She spooked when Mollie screamed. You heard about that, right?"

He nodded. "So the mare already has a name, does she?"

"Riding her would be like riding a cloud. I just know it." She was just getting up courage to ask Daddy to buy Lady Blaze when Momma's voice sounded just outside the door, and in she came with Dr. Sheridan in tow.

"Well now," the doctor said, "from the crowd that's gathered and what your mother said, I expected you to be on the edge of the great divide." He set his black bag down at the foot of the bed.

"Not nearly," Irma said, wincing as she moved. "But I caught a real wallop in the ribs. And it hurts. A lot."

"What if it's more serious than broken ribs? Can we move her?" Momma clasped her hands before her. "Oh, I do hope we can take her home."

"If I can examine the patient," Dr. Sheridan said, then shepherded Daddy and Momma out of the room, returning with Aunt Laura in tow. "All right if your aunt assists me?"

Irma nodded, grateful that Momma wasn't going to be here to see the result of Lady Blaze's frenzied kick. While the doctor opened his bag and put on his stethoscope, Aunt Laura removed the pillows from behind Irma so that she lay flat. When Dr. Sheridan was ready, Irma folded down the comforter and Aunt Laura raised her chemise.

"Hmmm," Dr. Sheridan said, peering at Irma's midsection.

"Probably the shape of a hoof," Irma joked.

Dr. Sheridan nodded. "I'll make it as quick as I can, but I need to be thorough. And it's going to hurt more than ever."

Irma nodded. A few minutes later she was once again propped up on a pillow, her tousled hair damp with sweat from the effort not to yell as the doctor examined her. "I guess," she sighed, "corsets are good for something after all. It would probably be a lot worse if it hadn't been for the whalebone."

Dr. Sheridan chuckled. "I'll have to start prescribing them as rib protectors, although I personally would clarify that they must not be adjusted any smaller than the owner's natural waist measurement. I have this unshakeable belief in the benefits of breathing."

"You'll never get the ladies to agree to that," Aunt Laura said.

"Can I get you to agree to it?" the doctor asked Irma. "I don't think anything is broken, but I suspect you have a cracked rib or two. It's hard to tell. Happily nothing is out of place, so there's little to do but prevent further damage while it heals. If you'll be sensible about lacing the corset—which means *snug* but not *tight*— I think you'll find it helps you bear up under the pain." He peered over his glasses. "I'm sorry, dear girl, but the next week or so may be very unpleasant for you."

Irma smiled a lopsided smile. "Well, that's not entirely bad news." She glanced at Aunt Laura. "Especially if it gets me out of a certain luncheon."

Aunt Laura waggled her finger in the air. "Oh, no you don't, young lady. I'm not going to conspire with you on that one. Your mother's been planning that for weeks. She'll want to prop you up on the horsehair fainting couch and carry on with the show. And besides that, Minnie is really looking forward to a fancy day in town."

"What good is a kick in the ribs if it can't get me out of that ridiculous party," Irma whined.

Dr. Sheridan cleared his throat. "If you have no further questions for me, I'll be going." He looked over his glasses at Irma. "My medical opinion is that you can do whatever you feel like doing. It's what we call a self-limiting injury. When you're doing too much, you'll know it." He patted Irma's shoulder. "I'll check in on you this evening." He looked at Aunt Laura, "I'll tell Otto and Mrs. Friedrich what I've just said. I expect they'll want to take the patient home." He glanced back at Irma. "And I'll tell your crowd of admirers they can call on you in a few days."

Irma shrugged. "That'll be up to Momma." She frowned a little. "I really wanted to see the broncobuster that's challenging Buffalo Bill's champion. Who d'ya think it is?"

"Can't say that I'm up-to-date on that," Dr. Sheridan said, "but I'm sure a couple of the wranglers waiting outside would be more than happy to visit and tell you all about it." With a last pat on Irma's shoulder, Dr. Sheridan was gone.

The minute she closed the door behind the doctor, Aunt Laura whirled about and scolded, "It was thoughtless of you to step into that corral, young lady. You know better than to pull a stunt like that. You have just given the two people who love you most in the world—not to mention the rest of your family and friends—the fright of their lives. I hope you've learned your lesson."

Surprised at Aunt Laura's uncharacteristically stern tone, Irma swiped at a tear. "I'm sorry. But nothing's going right for me right now, Aunt Laura. *Nothing.*"

Instead of understanding, Aunt Laura kept scolding. "What do you mean *nothing* is going right for you? Have you noticed the envious stares you've gotten today over that gorgeous new ensemble? Do you have any idea how many young ladies from around here would kill to have their mothers plan formal socials? Do you know how much they'd love a chance to go to a nice school? Why can't you accept these things for what they are—outgrowths of your mother's love for you?"

"Why can't *she* see that the way she loves is smothering me? Why can't she understand what it's like to be forced into this—*mold* I just don't fit."

Aunt Laura pulled a hankie out of her pocket, passed it over, and while Irma dabbed at her tears, she said, "You might be surprised at just how much your mother understands about women being forced into molds that aren't necessarily of their choosing."

"If you're talking about how much Momma hated it here when I was little, I know all about that."

"Do you really?" Aunt Laura said, and tilted her head. "Do you really know *all about it?*"

"More than you realize," Irma murmured, thinking back to that evening when she saw Momma kiss a stranger.

"Do you know what it's like to be so homesick just to see a *tree* that you take a long ride every day just to cry in the shade of the only real tree in the county?"

Irma furrowed her brow. "Momma did that?"

Aunt Laura nodded.

"Weren't *you* lonely when you and Uncle Charlie first came west?"

"Of course. But it was different for Charlie and me. We—" Aunt Laura looked down at her weather beaten hands. "There's more to growing up than just breaking free from our parents, Irma. Grown-ups have learned that *ignoring* reality doesn't make it disappear."

"I don't know what you mean."

"You say your mother doesn't understand you. Well, dear girl, you don't understand her, either—not if you think she's going to change her mind about you being in the Wild West. Your Momma sincerely believes she *must* prevent you from making what she sees as disastrous choices—be that joining the Wild West or toiling away on a ranch."

"How can you sit here telling me to be nicer to Momma when you know how she feels about the life *you* chose?"

"Because we've found a way to accept our differences and to respect one another in spite of them." Aunt Laura paused, then said, "I would curl up and die if I had gone through some of the things your Momma has endured over the years."

"Oh yeah," Irma said. "She's had a hard life, what with deciding what Ella Jane should cook for supper every night. It's such a trial. And who *knows* where we'll find a new maid when Ella Jane and Sam get married. How *does* Momma bear up under all the stress."

Aunt Laura shook her head. "You don't know your mother at all, do you?" She looked away. She took a deep breath. Finally, she said, "Attending a good school and expanding your horizons is an *opportunity*, Irma, not a jail sentence."

She was too miserable to fight anymore. "I told them I would go and I will."

"That's more like it," Aunt Laura said. "And no more nonsense with wild horses in the meantime."

With that, Aunt Laura left Irma to her thoughts.

In spite of the small dose of laudanum Dr. Sheridan had given her for pain, Irma's ride home was miserable, both because she kept thinking about the things Aunt Laura had said, and because with every jolt pain shot across her middle. She did her best not to complain, but by the time the buggy rolled up under the portico that stretched away from the side of the house, Irma was glad to have Momma helping her navigate the stairs up to her room and thankful that Momma bustled about turning back the bed and helping her undress. When Momma tucked the covers under her chin, Irma smiled up at her. "Thank you, Momma," she said. "I'm sorry I've been so much trouble." And she meant it. She would take Aunt Laura's advice to heart. She would sincerely try to be the kind of daughter Momma wanted.

Her resolve lasted exactly one week.

CHAPTER 6

The next Saturday, from where she stood at the top of the stairs, Irma saw Momma hurry into the entryway at the first sound of the doorbell. Peering through the lace curtain mounted over the sidelights bordering the front door, Momma shooed Ella Jane away and opened the door herself. It wasn't hard to guess who owned the voice. The first thing he did was clear his throat.

"Ahem. I . . . uh . . . I thought the invitation read eleven o'clock." He took his bowler hat off. Irma started down the stairs. Orrin dropped his hat. Bending to pick up the hat, he dropped his walking stick. Muttering apologies, he handed over the hat and the walking stick to Momma and said again, "Hello. I . . . ahem . . . my invitation read eleven o'clock."

"No," Irma corrected him. "It was eleven thirty."

Orrin pulled the invitation out of his suit coat pocket and handed it over.

Miss Irma Friedrich
requests the honor of your presence
at a luncheon
eleven o'clock in the morning
Saturday, April 17, 1886

So, Irma thought, *Minnie was right all along.* This wasn't a simple gathering for Irma and a few of her friends. This was a web spun to trap Orrin Knox. And a thinly disguised one at that.

It was rumored that Knox was the sole heir of a considerable fortune. Daddy said all that was little more than gossip and that Orrin Knox was a fine young man perfectly capable of making his own way in the world, and hadn't he proven exactly that. Which made Irma even more determined to point Orrin Knox toward Minnie.

Extending her hand to her flustered guest, Irma smiled her most charming smile. "My mistake, Mr. Knox," she said. "You're the first to arrive. May I offer you some punch?"

"Ahem. You may. But only . . . ahem . . . if you'll join me."

Irma led the way to the dining room, where an elegant array of silver serving trays and cake stands bore an impressive weight of sandwiches, fruit salad, tarts, and chocolate cake. Momma's rushing about an hour ago made sense, now. The luncheon might be at eleven thirty, but the sideboard had to be ready for Mr. Knox's arrival a half hour early. Irma ladled punch into a crystal tumbler.

"Ahem. What a tantalizing array of temptations," Mr. Knox said.

"I hope you're hungry," Momma said. "But then you young men are always hungry."

"Well, I . . . ahem . . . expect I'll hold my own when the serving starts." Knox took a gulp of punch. And cleared his throat. Again.

A person gets used to things like that in time. At least that's what Momma said when Irma mentioned Mr. Knox's annoying habit. *Maybe so,* Irma thought, as she straightened the already straight row of napkins on the sideboard, but she was mentally counting *ahems*, and the man had been there for less than ten minutes. *Couldn't even one other person arrive early? And where is Minnie, anyway? She should have been here ages ago.*

Thanks be to heaven, someone rang the doorbell. Irma nearly beat Ella Jane to the front door. It was Shep Sterling—who had not been invited to the party—holding a massive bouquet of white roses.

"Oh . . . ahem . . . blast," Knox blurted out. He apologized quickly for his outburst and then apologized for not bringing the hostess a gift. He didn't know it was done in North Platte, he'd never been able to stay abreast of such things, and . . . ahem . . .

Ella Jane reached for the flowers, but Shep swept his hat off his head and waited. He was wearing brown work pants and a green shirt unbuttoned at the top to reveal a blue kerchief knotted around his neck. Hardly what one expected a man who was making calls to wear. And yet, whereas an impeccably dressed Orrin Knox standing in that very spot not ten minutes ago had looked about as comfortable as a man approaching the gallows, Shep Sterling looked like a man who would, at any minute, invite himself in for coffee. Irma thought she detected the faintest aroma of Bay Rum cologne.

"Mr. Sterling, I believe?" Momma said.

"Shep'll do, ma'am." He handed Irma the flowers before hooking one thumb through his belt loop in a gesture that said he was at ease and would not be intimidated by The Mother. His gaze glided from Momma to Irma. "Been worried about you," he said. "Thought I'd come and see for myself." He didn't look her up and down as he had at Scout's Rest last week. This time, Irma felt as if he were staring right through her to the place where her heart was thumping double-time. A slow smile spread across his face, crinkling up the corners of his eyes and inducing a wink. "I see there's no cause for worry." He gave a little nod. "You look just fine."

Irma supposed his eyes looked more green than hazel because of the green shirt. She ducked her head and inhaled the wonderful scent of the roses. He probably didn't know anything about the language of flowers. White roses meant *I am worthy of you*. The thought . . . Well, she'd better think about something else.

"As you say"—Momma stepped between Irma and Shep—"Irma is recovering nicely. She will, of course, be under the care of her physician for some time to come. And now, if you'll excuse us, we are entertaining guests."

Just when Irma thought Momma was actually going to close the door in Shep's face, Orrin Knox spoke up. "Ahem. I can't believe it. The very man I've been chasing over half the county."

Shep stepped unbidden through the doorway and extended his hand. "I don't believe we've met."

"Ahem. Orrin . . . ahem . . . Knox." Orrin swallowed and pumped Shep's hand. "Of the *Register*. The *North Platte Register*. I've been hoping to interview you . . . ahem . . . ever since you got to North Platte. Every time I got close, you were either surrounded by admirers or busy hiring wranglers, and I didn't want to intrude, but—"

Shep cocked his head. "You were at the ranch last Saturday?"

Knox nodded. "Of course. But I was hoping for a more personal . . . ahem. It's an honor, sir. An honor. I was in the audience last year in New Orleans. When you rode Old Steamboat." He grinned. "Never saw anything like it. Impressive. Don't know how you did it. All that mud, the horse slipping and sliding all over, and yet you stuck longer than anyone. Amazing."

"Well now," Shep corrected him. "You mighta seen me *try* to ride Old Steamboat. But it ain't been done yet."

Orrin Knox could talk without clearing his throat after every other word. As Irma watched the interchange between the two men, she smiled. *He just needs to be interested in the topic.* Which made her wonder if perhaps Mr. Knox felt the same way she did about Momma's matchmaking. The thought produced a distinct feeling of relief for about two heartbeats followed by a flash of *So what's wrong with me? Why am I not good enough for Orrin Knox?*

Irma forced her thoughts back to the conversation at hand. Shep was talking about the previous Wild West season, which had included an extended engagement at something called the World's Industrial and Cotton Centennial Exposition in New Orleans. "Forty four days of rain," he was saying. "Bill in the hospital after getting thrown by that bull—"

"I had the perfect headline for that one," Knox interjected, "but they wouldn't let me use it." With Irma and Shep and Ella Jane clearly waiting to hear it, he held up both hands and painted the air above them all with the words, 'Buffalo Bull triumphs over Buffalo Bill.' "

Shep admired the newspaperman's way with words before commenting, "If you saw me on Old Steamboat you must have been there that day—"

"Yep," Knox nodded his head. "There were exactly nine of us in the stands. I couldn't believe it when the band struck up 'The Star Spangled Banner.' We thought the show would surely be canceled."

"Bill left word that if people came out in all that rain, they deserved to see what they paid for." Shep paused. "When we left New Orleans he was so far in the red he could have painted every barn in the west with the ink. But he said it was worth it."

"Because of signing Miss Oakley?" Knox asked.

Shep nodded. "You guessed it."

"Is it true you ended up playing to a million people last year?"

"Can't say for sure," Shep replied. "But I can tell you that, after New Orleans, the stands were full at every stop—and a lot of it was thanks to Annie's shooting. She's a wonder."

"Is that why Mr. Cody is adding more ladies to the lineup? I met Miss Smith the other day, and she said something about female equestriennes joining the troupe in St. Louis later this month."

"Seems like you already know a lot about the Wild West," Shep commented.

"It's only right for me to keep up with Mr. Cody and his adventures. After all, his fame and fortunes mean a great deal to Lincoln County." Without a single *ahem*, Knox went on to expound on an idea he had for a series of newspaper articles featuring Nebraska ties to the Wild West. Irma was thinking she should invite Shep to stay when Knox turned to Momma and said, "I know this is rude of me, Mrs. Friedrich—Miss Friedrich—but would you ladies be terribly upset if I took this opportunity to speak with Mr. Sterling further about this idea?"

Glancing at her mother, Irma thought a man would have to be blind not to see that it was anything but all right, even though Momma managed to say, "Of course not," before snatching the flowers and saying, "I'll just put these in water."

"Thank you," Knox said, and practically dragged Shep toward the front porch.

With a silent plea for help in Irma's direction, Ella Jane followed Momma down the hall toward the kitchen. Irma excused herself and followed Ella Jane.

Momma had dropped the bouquet on the table, filled a vase with water and was now stabbing the flowers into place, one at a time.

"Let me do that," Irma said. "You're going to ruin it." *Uh oh. Wrong thing to say.*

"Ruin it? Ruin it you say? I'll tell you what's ruined—" Momma gestured toward the front of the house.

"I don't know what you're talking about," Irma said, and concentrated on the bouquet.

"With your permission, ma'am," Ella Jane said. "I'll just go wait by the door. For the rest of the guests."

"Fine," Momma snapped. "You do that."

Irma arranged the bouquet carefully, mindful of the raging silence in the room. Her side was beginning to throb. Funny how she hadn't noticed that until just now. Placing the last flower in the vase, she sighed. "They really are lovely." She winced a little as she picked up the vase.

"Where do you think you're going with that?!" Momma snapped.

"It'll look nice on the sideboard," Irma said.

"Put it down."

Irma frowned. "What?"

"I said, put it down." Momma touched one of the roses. "The man has no knowledge of social graces. I won't have your friends snickering about the hidden message in those." She pointed to the white roses.

"They won't snicker," Irma said. "They might be envious, but they won't snicker. And when it comes right down to it, Momma, I remember your saying that a real lady avoids needlessly hurting others' feelings. Shep Sterling may not know about the invisible language of flowers, but he will most certainly hear your message loud and clear if these are relegated to the kitchen table." Irma pleaded. "Please, Momma. He didn't know we had plans."

"It doesn't appear that we do, after all," Momma said.

"Why would you say that?"

"Have you heard the doorbell? Has anyone else graced us with their presence?" Momma's eyes glittered with unspilled tears.

Now this is embarrassing, Irma thought. A full-grown woman crying over a party. Just then Ella Jane and Minnie came rushing in. "We need a pitcher so I can take some punch out front," Ella Jane said.

At Momma's confused expression, Minnie said hello and pecked her on the cheek even as she gestured toward the front of the house. "I could see them on the front porch when I drove in. So I headed straight there after hitching Jerry out back. They're sprawled everywhere listening to Orrin, uh, Mr. Knox and Mr. Sterling talk about the Wild West."

"They?"

"All fifteen of 'em," Ella Jane said as she came out of the pantry, crystal pitcher in hand. She winked at Irma. "That cowboy of yours has 'em laughing and hanging on every word."

Cowboy of . . . mine? Irma concentrated on a single white rose in the bouquet.

Promising to refill the serving trays, Minnie grabbed a jar of cookies and followed Ella Jane toward the front of the house.

Momma cleared her throat. "Well, what are you waiting for, Irmagard? Join your guests. They'll be wondering where you are. And take the tray of sandwiches from the sideboard with you. I'll be out directly with the tarts. It's a lovely day. If your guests want to enjoy the sunshine on the veranda, there's no reason to make them stay cooped up inside."

Stifling a smile, Irma headed through the swinging door, up the hallway, past the empty dining room—where she positioned the roses on the sideboard and procured the sandwich tray—and onto the porch, where her "ruined" luncheon continued until nearly all the refreshments were consumed and Orrin Knox had wrangled a promise out of Shep Sterling to help him get an exclusive interview with the infamous Doc Middleton, who would tour with the coming season's Wild West.

It would have been a perfect party except for two things. Orrin Knox simply did not get Irma's hint about driving Minnie home, and Momma was just a hair shy of rude when Shep lingered after all the other guests save Minnie had gone home.

"Our best wishes for a successful season, Mr. Sterling," Momma said from the doorway. Clearly, she was waiting for Shep to leave.

Shep eased his way out of the chair where he'd been sitting and, pulling his hat on, nodded. "Thank you, ma'am." With an easy smile and a lingering glance in Irma's direction that set her cheeks aflame, he descended the front porch stairs and made his way down the path to the front gate, where he'd hitched a bay gelding.

Irma watched as he mounted up and rode away.

"Irmagard!" Momma said from where she stood waiting in the doorway. "Stop staring after him. I declare you're no better than that brazen Edna Hertz. That girl was practically *hanging* on the man's arm."

———

"The last thing I expected to see when I got home," Otto said, as he came through the back door, "was my wife up to her elbows in dirty dishes." He looked around the kitchen. "I see evidence of a successful party, but where's Irma? Why isn't she helping you?"

Before Willa could answer, Ella Jane came through the door that led to the front of the house with broom in hand and reported that the front porch had been swept within an inch of its life and all the dining room chairs brought back inside.

"Thank you," Willa said with a smile. "You've done excellent work today, and I know you're wanting to get ready for your afternoon out with Samuel. You may go."

"But the dishes—" Ella Jane protested. "Sam will wait."

"Well, he won't have to," Willa said. "I'm just as content as can be cleaning up at my own pace." She shooed Ella Jane toward her room.

Otto repeated his question. "Why isn't Irma helping you?"

Willa turned back to her dish washing. "Because I sent her home with Minnie."

"To the ranch?"

"I told her you and I will drive out tomorrow after church and bring her back to town. I hope you don't mind."

Otto shook his head. "Of course I don't mind. I'm surprised— that's all. I didn't expect you to willingly let Irma near the ranch for a long, long while."

"And I wouldn't have if it weren't for Minnie. Something happened at the party. I don't know what, but the dear girl was having a hard time keeping back the tears after everyone was gone. The girls were really very good about helping pick up, but poor Minnie—"

"You know something," Otto said. "I bet it was Edna Hertz. She was in the bank with her mother the other day, and I could not believe the way she spoke to Pauline."

Willa looked over her shoulder. "What did she say?"

"Acted as if she were the Queen of England and treated the best cashier I've ever had as if she were no more than a scullery maid. If someone was mean to our Minnie, I'll just bet it was Edna."

Willa washed another plate. "I'm hardly the confidante of choice for either of those girls, so I really can't say. But Irmagard's face lit up when I suggested maybe she'd want to spend the night with her cousin at the ranch. And Minnie actually gave me a grateful hug, so I gathered that for once I did and said the right thing."

Otto took off his suit coat, slung it over the back of a chair, picked up a dish towel, and began to dry plates as they talked. "Well, Minnie's upset aside, how did it go?"

"To tell you the truth, the entire event was nearly a debacle." Willa recounted Shep Sterling's most untimely arrival. "But Mr. Knox saved the day by heading him outside and steering the conversation to topics Mr. Sterling could discuss."

"Meaning?"

"All things Wild West," Willa said, regret sounding in her voice. "For a moment I had visions of our Irmagard being the brunt of gossip for weeks to come."

"Why?"

"Well, most young ladies don't talk about roundups and hoe-downs at luncheons," Willa said.

"Oh, Momma," Otto intoned, "will you never understand just how famous—and admired—Bill and his performers really are? Shep Sterling's being at Irma's party probably set all those feminine hearts to fluttering."

Willa ignored the comment. "Whatever the cause, everyone

lingered for hours. I could hear the laughter even from back here. As you can see, there's little that wasn't consumed—although I managed to save two pieces of chocolate cake."

Otto murmured his appreciation and Willa concluded. "Except for poor Minnie, I would say that, in spite of my reservations, a good time was had by all." She paused. "I do hope Irmagard can get to the bottom of what upset Minnie so. We must remember to see if there's anything *we* can do to help."

Sam arrived to claim Ella Jane. The couple had barely closed the back porch door when Otto laid aside his dish towel and said, "Sit down with me, dear. We've something to discuss."

"Is something the matter?"

Otto put water on to boil for coffee and served up the cake whistling softly as he worked. When the coffee was ready he sat down opposite Willa and asked, "Why is it, Mrs. Friedrich, that whenever I say there's something we need to discuss, your mind always assumes there's a problem."

"I don't," Willa protested.

Otto nodded. "Yes. You do. And it has ever been thus." He leaned over to kiss her cheek. "It's all right, dear. I've come to accept it as a charming idiosyncrasy."

"Please don't cry," Irma said as Minnie drove the buggy down the trail toward the Mason ranch. "He was just distracted with wanting to talk to Shep."

It was as if Irma's words had punched a hole in a dam. Dropping the reins, Minnie sank back and hid her face in her hands. The ancient gelding named Jerry—the only horse on the Mason ranch Uncle Charlie trusted to pull his daughters anywhere—stopped in his tracks. After a few minutes, Minnie quieted. Pulling a handkerchief from her dress pocket she mopped her tears and said, "It's very sweet of you to say that, but the truth is Orrin Knox just doesn't have any interest in me at all. It was as if I wasn't even there today. And if I'm honest, he's never given me any encouragement. I've been living in a stupid, romantic dream—with absolutely no anchor in reality. And frankly, I'm more embarrassed than I am brokenhearted." She sniffled.

"Orrin Knox didn't know *anyone* was there today except Shep Sterling. He was intent on getting the interview—just like any good newspaper reporter. And you're making entirely too much of one afternoon."

Minnie shook her head. "This isn't about just one afternoon. Mr. Knox and I have been in the same place dozens of times. Dances, the opera house—the traveling euchre party you invited me to last winter. And I was at Scout's Rest for the entire day. He never gave me a second glance."

"You can't count that day at Scout's Rest, either," Irma insisted. "There was too much going on. He was distracted."

"There wasn't too much going on to keep Shep Sterling from flirting with *you*," Minnie said. "And don't deny it because Monte told me all about it." She leaned closer and said quietly, "There wasn't too much going on to keep Jason Zigler from proposing to Mollie."

"What?!"

Minnie nodded. "I'm not supposed to tell anyone." She glared at Irma. "And you'd better not. But—"

"But Mollie's only . . . Jason can't possibly . . ."

Minnie nodded "I know. Mollie's only fifteen, and Jason can't possibly support her. But he got a job with Mr. Cody's cowboy band, and he's asked Pa for Mollie's hand. He says he'll have enough saved to get them a place in a couple of years, and Mollie's promised to wait." Minnie sighed. "So in no time at all I will be Mollie's old maid sister who can't get a husband." She swiped at fresh tears. "Which is probably the real reason I've been trying to talk myself into liking Orrin Knox. He's very . . . eligible."

"For heaven's sake, Minnie!" Irma scolded. "I don't know what you are in him." She mimicked Orrin. "Ahem. I . . . ahem . . . think . . . ahem . . ." She kept it up until Minnie smiled and flicked the reins so Jerry would start for home again. When the buggy topped the last rise and the Mason ranch came into view, Minnie said, "You know, Irma, in a way this restless feeling I have is your fault."

"*My* fault?"

Minnie nodded. "You've always had such grand ideas. I may not want to do a flying dismount off a horse in front of thousands of people, but you've got me thinking."

"Well, for heaven's sake, can't you dream any bigger than snagging a husband?" Irma stopped short. "I'm sorry. That came out wrong. There's nothing wrong with . . . if you really fall for someone . . . I'm not saying this right. I hope you know what I mean."

Minnie nodded toward the ranch. "I adore every single person who lives in that house," she said. "But I don't think I want to live out my life there."

"You're eighteen years old, and you're talking like your life is over."

"Well, give me a while," Minnie retorted. "I'm new at this dreaming stuff. And in case you haven't noticed, I'm not like you. My parents aren't rich, and I'm not going to finishing school. I can cook and sew, and that's about it."

"Too bad nobody in town needs any of *that*." Irma smirked.

"Hey. I may not have a plan to travel the world, but I have checked for help-wanted notices in the newspaper a time or two. At the moment the only people advertising for a housekeeper are the Hertz family. And I'd probably kill Edna Hertz inside of a week, so taking that job is probably not a good idea." Minnie chuckled. "Did you see the look on her face when Mr. Sterling said he'd show her around the Wild West grounds if she came to St. Louis?"

"I did," Irma said.

"Do you really think the Hertzes will take Edna to see the Wild West?"

Irma shrugged. "I suppose it could happen. I think they have family in St. Louis."

"Would Mr. Sterling really give her a *personal* tour?"

Jerry moved into a trot.

"Well, *he's* in a hurry to get home," Irma said.

Minnie let the reins go slack. Jerry kept going. With no further direction from Minnie, the horse pulled the buggy right to its usual spot just east of the older of the Masons' two barns. He tossed his head and whinnied.

"I do believe he's ordering up supper." Irma laughed as she climbed down and began to help undo the harness. Minnie led Jerry inside, and together the girls brushed him down. Diamond poked his head over the half door of his stall while they worked and, with a bobbing of his head and a little whinny, demanded attention.

As the girls headed for the house, Irma murmured, "You know, from the way Edna hung on Shep, I bet she'll do everything she can to talk her parents into taking her to St. Louis—whether they ever really said they would or not."

Minnie teased, "Irma Friedrich, I do believe you are jealous."

"Don't be ridiculous." Irma said as she stomped up the back porch steps. "Shep Sterling can *marry* Edna Hertz for all I care."

———

"I couldn't possibly," Willa said, trying to keep the excitement from her voice.

"And why not?" Otto took the last bite of cake and set his fork down.

"Well, for one thing . . . Irmagard isn't fully recovered yet."

"Irma just took off across the prairie in a buggy. She most certainly does not need you to stay home and play nursemaid. She'll be fine. And if her staying alone concerns you, we'll ask Minnie to come into town and stay with her."

"But you and I were supposed to have at least three dinner parties with investors in the next month."

Otto nodded. "That was before Mrs. Cody stopped by the bank with this." He tapped the elegantly scripted note that he'd brought home. "Think of it, Willa. *Chicago. Shopping.* The *theatre.*"

"Are you sure you wouldn't mind?"

"Not only do I not mind," Otto said, "I insist that you go. I know you, Mrs. Friedrich. At this very moment it is taking every ounce of your self-control to keep you in that seat. Your heart is dancing with joy. I can see it in your eyes." He stood up and drew her into his arms. "So . . ." He wheeled her around the kitchen in an exaggerated waltz. "SHOP-two-three-PLAYS-two-three-NOW-two-three PACK!"

Breathless with excitement, Willa laughed. "All right, all right. I'll go. But promise me one thing."

"I promise."

"You haven't heard what I want."

"It doesn't matter. If it will keep that smile on your lovely face, consider it done."

"Don't let Irmagard brood. Keep her busy."

"Done," Otto promised.

Willa smiled. "Do you suppose that little milliner's shop is still there? The one right up the street from Marshall Field's? Remember?"

"*Remember?!*" Otto sighed. "My dear, a man does not forget the day his honeymoon ended and the realities of married life set in."

"Was it that awful?"

"It was delightful. I wanted to buy you every hat in the place. But that was when reality set in."

"What reality was that, pray tell?"

"That I was going to have to make a *lot* of money to keep my beloved in hats."

They joked about a hat allowance for the upcoming trip as they cleared the dishes and finished tidying the kitchen.

Later that evening, with Otto snoring at her side, Willa lay awake as the moon climbed in the sky and cast silver shadows on the bedroom floor. When she finally drifted off to sleep it was to dream of owning one hat and living in a tiny house with a faithful husband named Otto who had no interest in an endless quest for more of everything.

CHAPTER 7

MAY HE KISS ME WITH THE KISSES OF HIS MOUTH!

Song of Songs 1:2 NASB

Not long after Minnie and Irma arrived at the ranch, eight-year-old Maggie Mason came bounding into the ranch house kitchen, her brown eyes wide with excitement. "He's here. He's here!"

"Who's here?" Irma asked as she put the roses she'd brought with her from home into fresh water and set them on the kitchen table.

"Buffalo Bill. Pa's gonna sell him some more horses."

"Hold on there," Irma said. "Uncle Charlie's selling off more horses?"

Maggie nodded. "Uh-huh. We don't need so many and we can use the money. That's what Pa said."

Irma frowned. Did Daddy know Uncle Charlie was pressed for funds? Maggie was still jabbering excitedly about Buffalo Bill's beautiful horse as Irma stepped to the door and looked toward the barn. Maggie was right. Bill Cody had ridden over on a sleek, well-muscled bay with a flowing mane and tail.

"You can come out to the barn," Maggie insisted. "All the other girls are helping in the garden. Ma has plenty of help. Isn't Mr.

Cody's horse beautiful? Do you think I could pet him? Ma won't mind if you come," Maggie insisted. "She knows you and me like horses better'n anything."

Irma followed Maggie out onto the porch just as Uncle Charlie and Monte and Ned Bishop converged on the showman from various points on the ranch. And then, just as Irma was reaching for a basket so she could head for the garden, Shep Sterling rode in.

"Oh . . . my . . . goodness," Maggie crowed as she grabbed Irma's hand. "Come *on*, Irma."

For some reason, Irma felt the need to catch her breath—and glance in a mirror before she left the house. Her heart thumped. "You go on," she said. "I'll check with your ma first." As Maggie charged out of the house and toward the visitors, Irma watched, thinking of her conversation with Minnie about Edna Hertz hanging on Shep's arm. She'd been a little dishonest. It really *had* bothered her to see Edna flirting with Shep. And the idea that Edna might get to tour the Wild West show grounds was absolutely maddening. She glanced over her shoulder at the roses sitting on Aunt Laura's kitchen table. And smiled. Edna might be a flirt, but Shep had brought white roses to Irma. Ducking into Miss Viola's room, Irma peered at herself in the mirror, despairing over what the wind had done to her hair on the way out to the ranch. *Momma was right. I should have worn a hat.*

"Hey, Irm," Monte called from the back door. Irma could hear his boots clomping as he crossed the kitchen toward the stairs leading to the second floor of the house.

"I'm here," Irma said, and ducked out of Miss Viola's room.

Monte turned around. "Thought you might want to come out and watch. Pa decided he could part with a few more of the stock, and Bill Cody and Shep are here to take a look." He nodded toward the upstairs with a grin. "Guess you could borrow my stuff again. If you want to change, that is."

She put her hand to her aching side. "Thanks, but truth is, the buggy ride out here was enough adventure for me for one day." She smiled. "And I promised to help in the garden. I'll have to check with your ma before I head out to the barns."

"She won't mind," Monte said. "And you know it. In fact, if you show up to garden when there's horse trading going on, she'll be wanting to send someone for the doc."

"What?"

"Well, if you choose picking peas over horse business, she's gonna think you're sick."

"Very funny," Irma said. "All right. But I have to . . . check on something first." There was no way on earth she was going to let Monte Mason know that she wanted to fix her hair before being seen by Shep Sterling.

Monte nodded at the bouquet on the table. "Does Minnie have an admirer in town we should know about?"

"Those are from Shep," Irma said. "I mean, he brought them to me. He stopped by the house before the luncheon." She could feel her cheeks turning red. "They're a peace offering directed at Momma more than anything."

"Did it work?"

Irma sighed. "Not really. When she said I could come home with Minnie, I figured she'd throw them out if I gave her half a chance, so I—" She was explaining too much.

Monte grinned. "When you're finished primping we'll be down at the south corral. And in case you're interested, Ma sent Mamie up from the garden with an invitation for Bill and Shep to stay to supper. And they accepted."

———

Someone rang the supper bell just as the sun closed in on the horizon and shadows lengthened. Shep Sterling went to look for Irma and found her in the stall with one of the horses Bill Cody had arranged to buy, braiding a hank of dark gray mane. "Seems I'm getting in the habit of finding you stowed away in one stall or another," he joked.

When Irma didn't respond to the teasing, he said, "In case you didn't hear it, the supper bell just rang. Everyone's headed for the house."

Irma nodded and swiped at her face. "Thanks," she said. "I'll be along directly."

She's been crying. Shep gentled his voice. "I gather this horse is special to you. If you want, I could probably talk Cody into taking him off the sale bill."

Irma shook her head. "Uncle Charlie already feels bad enough about it. He would never have sold Diamond unless he really needed the money. I'm not going to say a word." When she glanced up at Shep, her blue-gray eyes were brimming with tears. "And don't you, either."

"You mind telling me what's so special about him?" Shep nodded at the horse.

"He's my show partner." She blinked back tears. "He's kind and good and steady." She tried to chuckle, but it ended up sounding more like a sob. "And he's put up with more nonsense from me—bouncing, falling, making him misstep because I did something wrong—and all the time he just kept doing his best to be whatever it was I wanted him to be." She leaned into the horse and wrapped her arms around his neck, her shoulders shaking as she cried.

Shep opened the stall door. "Hey, now." He put a hand on her back. "Hey." Sliding his hand to her shoulder, he gently urged her into his arms. She curled against him crying like a brokenhearted child. He liked the way the top of her head tucked right beneath his chin, liked the faint scent of—roses?—in her hair.

All too soon, she stopped crying and pulled away. "Thanks," she said, and forced a smile as she looked back at the horse. "Stupid, huh."

"Not stupid at all. And I still think you oughta let me help figure a way to have this one left behind." Shep reached over and patted the horse's broad forehead, right where a patch of diamond-shaped white shone from beneath the forelock. "Why don't you ask your daddy to buy him for you? If Diamond already knows all that stuff about your act, he'd be a much better horse for you than Lady Blaze." He smiled when Irma looked surprised. "It doesn't take a mind reader to know you wanted that mare. I imagine you had a speech all planned for your daddy just about the time she let that kick fly."

Irma sighed. "It's for the best. I've been in a lot of trouble lately over my trick riding," she said. "Momma hates it."

Shep leaned back against the side of the stall and pushed his hat back on his head. "I gathered as much. What I don't understand is why."

"It isn't ladylike. And it scares her. She saw me fall the other day and nearly fainted."

"Maybe if she saw your act when you *don't* fall—"

Irma shook her head. "It wouldn't make any difference. She'll never change." She moved toward the wide aisle that ran down the center of the barn and, motioning for Shep to come out of the stall, closed the door behind them. Diamond stepped forward and snuffled the sleeve of her dress. "Sorry, old friend. No sugar today." She tugged on the horse's forelock, then brushed off her hands and, reaching up to smooth her hair back into place, headed toward the double-wide barn door. "I always knew I'd have to give it up someday." She blinked rapidly. "I just never thought it would come so soon."

When she said the word *soon,* her voice dipped. Shep reached out and touched her arm, thinking he might be needed to comfort another spell of crying. Hoping, actually. But Irma just cleared her throat and forced a smile. "I'll be all right," she said. "I've promised Momma to do things her way for the next year. I guess Diamond's going away is God telling me I'm doing the right thing."

"What exactly—if you don't mind my asking—is your momma's way of doing things?"

"There's a school in Omaha where all the high-society girls go. It's called Brownell Hall. Arta Cody already graduated from there. I'm her age, but Momma and Daddy got some special dispensation so I could follow in her hallowed steps." She corrected herself. "I didn't mean that the way it sounded. Arta's a friend of mine. I just . . . I'm not like her, is all. But Momma has always dreamed of having a daughter who makes her proud."

They were almost at the ranch house. The sound of chairs scraping against the floor and people talking and laughing floated toward them. Shep persisted. "Seems like she *would* be proud if she only understood just how few women are good enough to be part of the Wild West."

Irma shook her head. "Nope. She's embarrassed by the whole idea. And she'll never change."

"You might be surprised," Shep said, and led the way inside.

First white roses. Now this. Willa didn't know what Shep Sterling was up to, but she was not about to be charmed just because a man showed up at church. Let the rest of the congregation titter and whisper about the presence of the Wild West star as he made his way up the aisle and slid into the second pew from the front. Why did he have to go and sit there? It was going to be a distraction, what with him right in her line of sight. *Honestly.* Willa glanced at Edna Hertz, who had practically dragged her mother up the aisle to where they could sit right behind Mr. Sterling. She had to know she was being obvious. Why didn't she behave? And if Edna couldn't behave, why didn't her mother take her in hand?

Thank heavens Irmagard isn't here. While she hoped her daughter would never engage in such outlandish behavior as Edna Hertz, Willa had detected *something* in the air whenever Shep Sterling was around. Oh, the man had been gallant enough that day at Scout's Rest, rushing for help with Irmagard in his arms. And the roses—while entirely inappropriate—were an indication that he could at least try to be a gentleman. But for all of Shep Sterling's heroic ways and handsome smiles, Willa was grateful the Wild West train would be leaving the

North Platte station day after tomorrow. And that, she thought, would be that. Irmagard could turn her attentions toward the preparatory reading the headmaster at Brownell had suggested.

When Mr. Sterling glanced around and nodded a greeting, Willa nodded back, grateful that the Masons no longer made the long drive into North Platte every Sunday morning—and that at that very moment Irmagard was lined up with the Mason girls on a pew miles away. Charlie had donated land for a cemetery and a little church back when Laura lost their first baby, and just last year the small congregation had seen fit to hire an aging circuit rider as their full-time pastor. Preacher Daniels thumped the pulpit a bit too often for Willa's taste, but he loved the Lord God.

Willa reached for a hymnal just as Otto slid into the pew next to her. She looked up, surprised but pleased. Otto's church attendance had waned in recent months. More often than not he dropped Willa and Irmagard at the door and then remembered some pressing matter of business or some correspondence that needed answering. "I can get so much more done when the bank is closed," he would say. Tempted to despair over her husband's spiritual life, Willa did the only thing she knew to do—remained faithful in her own attendance, prayed for her husband, and did her best not to nag.

Otto winked as he took the hymnal from her hand. "I realized this is my last chance to escort my bride to church before she leaves for her holiday."

"But your business?"

"Concluded," Otto said.

And at that exact moment Shep Sterling glanced over his shoulder and nodded. At Otto.

Just seeing the twenty-six-car Wild West train would have made attending the send-off celebration on Tuesday worthwhile for Irma. Every car was painted to re-create a scene from the performance.

While Momma called it garish and in poor taste and said she would stay in the buggy, Daddy agreed with Irma. It was brilliant to turn the entire train into one long moving advertisement for the Wild West. Who could resist such a spectacular invitation to see Indians hunting buffalo or cowboys riding bucking broncos?

Monte said they'd be going through Indiana and Ohio, Pennsylvania and Maryland, New York and the nation's capital. Every state evoked images of places Irma longed to see. Wouldn't it be perfect for Liberty Belle to debut in Philadelphia? What would it be like to parade past the White House? And who knew what famous people would be in the audience during the months the Wild West would camp on Staten Island, just across from the city of New York?

It was almost more than Irma could stand to look at that train and know she wouldn't be on it when it left North Platte. On the car that advertised the cowgirls Buffalo Bill called his Beautiful Rancheras, a female rider stood atop her saddle, her reins in her teeth as she waved her hat in the air. Yet another leaned to the side of her galloping mount as she snatched a hat off the ground. A third *ranchera* sat astride a rearing chestnut horse with four white socks. It was, of course, a coincidence, but Irma thought the horse looked a lot like Lady Blaze. *I can do that,* she thought. *I can do all of it.*

As Daddy positioned the buggy near the station platform, Momma called out to one of her friends and waved her over. Mrs. Canfield's husband owned the hotel whose restaurant Daddy frequented for business dinners and investors' meetings. An elegant woman, she moved through the gathering crowd with grace. Momma invited her to climb up and watch the festivities without getting crushed in the crowd. Mrs. Canfield accepted, and as Irma climbed down, Daddy assisted Mrs. Canfield in climbing up.

Uncle Charlie and Aunt Laura and the girls joined Irma and Daddy just as they made their way alongside the train toward the stock cars.

"Do you think they'd let us look inside?" Aunt Laura wondered as they passed one of the passenger cars.

"I don't know why not," Daddy said. "After all, my bank helped pay for it." When he motioned for Aunt Laura and the girls to climb aboard, Irma hesitated. Daddy read her mind. "You know Monte and Ned will see that both Diamond *and* Lady Blaze are treated well," he said. "But come along. We'll see what we can see."

The crowd prevented Irma's seeing anything beyond the tips of antlers as two tame elk and the rest of the Wild West menagerie were loaded. However, once "only the horses" were left, most people headed back to the station to wait for Bill Cody's arrival. In spite of her obvious nervousness about walking up a gangplank, Lady Blaze followed Diamond without putting up a fuss. The stock car doors clicked shut. It was done. Lady Blaze was beyond her reach and Diamond was gone. Forever. Irma fought back tears.

Daddy put his arm around her. "It's going to be all right, Irma. I know this is hard for you. But it's going to be all right. You'll see." He hugged her and then pointed toward Bill Cody's private car. "Even your Momma would live on a train if she got a glimpse inside that car." He pointed at the members of the cowboy band standing near the front of the train. "Look there. Isn't that Jason and Jonathan Zigler? The band's starting to gather. If you want to inspect the troupe's living quarters, you'd better hurry." Irma shook her head. It would only make her feel worse to see where Monte and Ned Bishop would be living for the next few weeks. She couldn't imagine being at the ranch without Monte. She might even miss Bishop.

Glancing around her, Irma realized she wasn't the only one struggling with her emotions. Most of the people still at the station were saying good-bye to someone they loved. She wondered how Mollie Mason was holding up, how Aunt Laura and Uncle Charlie were feeling.

"Think I'll go check on your momma," Daddy said.

"I'll wait here and watch for the girls to finish touring the train,"

Irma said. She quickly regretted that decision, however, when Edna
Hertz sidled up.

"Have you seen Mr. Sterling?"

Irma shook her head.

"I promised to give him the dates I'll be in St. Louis." She pulled
a note from the pink silk bag dangling from her wrist.

"I haven't seen him." Irma stood on tiptoe and gazed toward
the train. "I'm waiting for my aunt and cousins. They went to tour
the train."

"We're staying for an entire week," Edna persisted. "Daddy says
I can go see the Wild West every day if I want."

Irma did her best to look disinterested. "Excuse me. I really do
need to find my family." She turned her back on Edna and walked
away. The cowboy band began to play "The Girl I Left Behind
Me." Finally she located Uncle Charlie and Aunt Laura, Monte and
the girls. Poor Mollie looked almost as miserable as Irma felt. Aunt
Laura was saying something and patting her on the shoulder while
she nodded. And Minnie was talking to . . . *Orrin Knox* . . . who
appeared to be fascinated by whatever Minnie was saying.

The crowd began to applaud. Shep Sterling and Lillian Smith were
the bookends to Buffalo Bill's Grand Entrance. All three were riding
horses adorned with show saddles and bridles. Silver discs reflected
in the sun. Fringe on the performers' costumes swayed as the parade
horses pranced toward the train. All three stars dismounted straight
onto the observation platform at the back of Cody's car. Wranglers
led the horses away, the band stopped playing, and Cody motioned
for silence. He waxed eloquent about how it was an honor to be able
to present a true picture of life on the frontier to the rest of the world.
He reintroduced Lillian Smith, the Champion Rifle Shot of the World,
and Shep Sterling, the renowned King of the Cowboys. Finally, Cody
thanked the people of the great state of Nebraska for sharing their
sons to make the West come alive for thousands, perhaps millions, of

easterners. With a last flourish of his hat and a theatrical bow, Cody ducked inside his private car. Shep and Miss Smith followed.

Irma's heart sank. That was *it?* Shep was *gone?* Without so much as saying . . . *What? What did you expect him to say?* Something. Something sweet. Something . . . personal. A man didn't just give a girl white roses and hold her while she cried and then just . . . leave. Did he? Apparently this one did. The varmint. Irma glowered at the train.

Monte and Ned strode up. While Ned shook Uncle Charlie's hand, Monte hugged his sisters and parents and promised to write. He smiled at Aunt Laura. "And I'll go to church every Sunday, Ma."

In spite of her sore ribs, Irma hugged him. Her tears flowed freely as Monte picked her up and swung her around. Every single Mason was crying, too. Even Uncle Charlie's eyes were red. With a nod and a tip of his hat, Ned said a quick good-bye and made a dash for the train.

Finally, with one last round of hugs, Monte headed for the train, but Orrin Knox intercepted him. Daddy joined them both train-side and there was more conversation until the whistle sounded and Monte climbed aboard. Members of the troupe appeared on the platform at the back of every car, waving and laughing. Shep really was leaving without saying good-bye. Irma turned away.

"A-hem." Orrin Knox was standing so close she could feel his breath as he whispered in her ear, "Mr. Sterling asked if you'd come with me, please." He touched her elbow and motioned for her to follow him. At the far corner of the station, he stopped. "I'll . . . ahem . . . wait here. You . . . ahem . . ." He motioned her around the corner, where Shep waited, his hat in his hands.

"You didn't think I was going to leave without saying good-bye, did you?"

His smile made her feel . . . *fluttery.* "I honestly didn't know what to think when you ducked into Mr. Cody's car. It made me feel—"

"What?" He moved closer. "What do you feel, Belle?" He traced the line of her jaw.

Belle. She'd never forget the sound of his voice saying that name. Never.

Irma nodded. "You'd better go," she said.

He put his hat back on and bent to kiss her. It was gentle and not really all that passionate, at least not in the way Irma had dreamed of passion. When the train whistle blew, he kissed her again, and this time he wasn't as gentle. The second kiss in her life set Irma to trembling all the way down to the tips of her toes. She clung to him as he smiled down at her and said, "I'm glad we got that settled."

The train began to pull out. After a quick hug, Shep charged across the platform. Jumping down, he sprinted after the last car. If it hadn't been for the wranglers grabbing him and hauling him up, Shep Sterling would have missed the Wild West train.

Her heart pounding as if she'd just bulldogged a calf, Irma watched until the train was out of sight before looking for the rest of the family. And that was when she realized that Momma was no longer waiting in the buggy.

CHAPTER 8

❖⟫═⟩ ⟨═⟪❖

THE FOLLY OF FOOLS IS DECEIT.

Proverbs 14:8 KJV

"There you are," Momma said as she bustled toward them. "Whatever are you doing hiding all alone over here by the shipping department?"

Irma steadied herself. *You can breathe now. She obviously didn't see anything.*

"Tut-tut now, dear," Momma said, and slipped her arm around Irma's waist. "I know it's all very difficult for you saying good-bye to Monte. But you mustn't cry. Things are going to be fine. He will write. And you know he'll take very good care of Diamond. And in time you'll see that it was all for the best. Now come along home."

Was it Irma's imagination or was Edna Hertz eyeing her? Was that a smirk? Or something more sinister? Irma watched with trepidation as Edna sashayed toward them.

"Were you able to give Mr. Sterling my message, Miss Friedrich? I saw the two of you . . . *talking.*"

Orrin Knox planted himself between the Friedrich women and Edna. Without giving Irma a chance to answer his question, he cleared his throat and said something to Momma about "asking Miss Friedrich for her assistance in arranging a future interview with Mr. Sterling—since Mr. Sterling had been to the house and seemed to be a particular friend of the family." He continued, saying that he hoped Mrs. Friedrich didn't mind that he had made the request of her, and that he would certainly never have done such a thing without asking permission under normal circumstances. . . . He blathered on and on until, out of the corner of her eye, Irma saw Edna Hertz roll her eyes and shrug, then retreat.

"Goodness, Mr. Knox," Momma said, "there's no need to explain so . . . thoroughly. Nothing could please me more than to learn that Irmagard has been of assistance to you and the newspaper." Momma nodded at Irma. "And I'm certain she was happy to help you. Weren't you, dear?"

Irma nodded. "I was."

"Well then," Momma said. "Go on, dear. Tell him."

"Tell him what?"

"What Mr. Sterling said. Whatever it was you asked on Mr. Knox's behalf."

Irma could not think of one thing to say.

"Might I walk you home, Miss Friedrich—so that we might . . . ahem . . . discuss matters further?" Mr. Knox glanced at Momma. "With your permission of course, Mrs. Friedrich."

Thirty-seven times. Orrin Knox had effectively ruined what could have been a nice walk on a nearly perfect spring day.

"Ahem."

Thirty-eight. How did he stand it? Didn't his throat feel like sandpaper by now? Couldn't he just swallow instead of making that awful sound? Why didn't he fiddle with his fob chain when he was nervous, or twirl his walking stick, or acquire any number of other less annoying habits. How did the other men in the newspaper office stand working with him? *That's probably why he gets all the traveling assignments*. Irma had given up trying to make pleasant conversation a few minutes into the walk home. She'd begun to walk faster, honing in on the gate in the picket fence. It was in view now, just a little—

"Ahem. I . . . ahem . . . I hope you know I can be trusted to keep a confidence, Miss Friedrich. That is if . . . if there's anything— anything at all. A journalist prides himself on being trustworthy. At least . . . ahem . . . *this* journalist does."

Irma lowered her parasol and, closing it, rested the shaft on one shoulder. She could feel a bead of sweat trickle down her spine. Having been her defender at the train station, was Orrin Knox about to use what he knew against her? What did he expect her to say?

Knox took his hat off. He cleared his throat. Again. "What I mean is . . . ahem . . . any fool could see that Shep Sterling finds you very attractive. Of course . . . ahem . . . anyone would see . . . I mean, any man in his right mind would see . . . Ahem."

If the man cleared his throat one more time she was going to brain him with her parasol. "Get to the point, Mr. Knox. What is it you have to say about Mr. Sterling and me?"

"Did he say anything about England?"

"*England?*"

"Yes. England." Knox looked around them and leaned closer. "I assume he had something very important—something special—to tell you. That's why he asked me to . . . ahem . . . stand guard. But of course I didn't eavesdrop. So I was wondering—is it official? Is the contract signed for the Wild West to go to England?"

"The Wild West is going to *England*?!"

"That's what I'm hoping you can tell me—whether they are. Ahem. Or aren't, that is." He paused. "I know for a fact that when they were forming their partnership, Mr. Cody's partner, Mr. Salsbury, said that he would one day get the Wild West to Europe. And with Queen Victoria's Jubilee next year and the exposition planned there, the timing would be perfect. I thought maybe Mr. Sterling had said something to you right before he . . . uh . . ."

"I'm sorry to disappoint you, Mr. Knox, but the subject of the Wild West itinerary did not come up when Shep was saying good-bye."

"You would tell me, wouldn't you? Ahem. I mean about England."

"What possible reason would I have to keep news like that to myself?"

"If he writes you—when he writes—and there's news of England . . . will you tell me? Please? It's very important. To be the first journalist to report such big news—it would mean . . . ever so much." He cleared his throat. "And in case you were wondering, I did see the kiss—but that secret is safe with me. I was only interested in the story. Of England."

They were at the front gate. Irma put her hand on his arm. "Thank you, Mr. Knox. Sincerely."

"Why, uh . . . ahem." He blushed furiously and bobbed his head. "Of course. I . . . ahem. I would never want to cause you any difficulty. That's why I stepped in when Edna Hertz . . . She may have seen—that's why I stepped in." He paused to take a breath. "I like you, Miss Friedrich. Not . . . not the way . . . ahem. As a friend. Not that you aren't a lovely . . . ahem."

"I'd like to be your friend, too, Mr. Knox. And please call me Irma."

He cleared his throat and bobbed his head. "Yes. Well. Ahem." He sighed and mopped his forehead again. "I'm sorry I'm so . . . ahem . . . awkward. I've always been this way with girls. Women. Females."

Irma smiled. "And yet that day at my party you talked to Shep Sterling for nearly an hour in the presence of many women, and I didn't hear one *ahem.*"

He shrugged. "I can't explain it. I only have this trouble when I'm put on the spot with a girl. Ahem. Woman."

"You aren't in the least bit interested in me as a woman, are you?"

"I . . . ahem. I'm not certain I understand. Ahem." Knox mopped his face again.

"Of course you do," Irma said. "You understand perfectly. You're just too shy to say it. It's all right. I'm not in the least bit interested in you, either."

He smiled. "Well, I, uh . . . ahem . . . guess I knew that. Even before today, I mean. Anyone could tell that. From the way you look when he's around. Mr. Sterling, that is."

"So why are you still so nervous around me?"

He shrugged.

"Is it Momma? She can be determined. Hard to convince to give up on things she wants."

He glanced toward the house. "It wouldn't do for me to offend the wife of one of the most powerful men in town by appearing to refuse to court her daughter."

Irma didn't know what to say to that. She hadn't really ever considered Daddy as being powerful or that people might be afraid to offend Momma—because of Daddy. Surely Mr. Knox was over-reacting. She patted his arm again. "It's all right. Really. Thank you for rescuing me earlier and for walking me home. I'll be happy to let you know if I learn some inside news about the Wild West's schedule. And now"—she motioned toward the house—"I imagine we're fueling Momma's matchmaking fires by standing out here so long. So"—she held out her hand—"to friendship."

"To friendship." They shook hands. "And please call me Orrin."

Irma was halfway to the front door when Orrin called her name. When she turned back around he was tucking his handkerchief in his pocket. He adjusted the glasses on his nose and tilted his hat until it looked positively stylish.

"Would you give my regards to Miss Mason—Miss Minnie Mason—the next time you see her?"

———

A few days after the Wild West train left North Platte, Otto walked into the parlor and settled into his chair, newspaper in hand. "Where's Irma?" he asked. "She'll want to hear this." He held up the newspaper. "Orrin Knox has written an article on suffrage." Otto chuckled, "And he's *for* it."

"She's gone up to her room to write Monte," Willa said, and picked up her needlework. "She said she was feeling tired and wanted to turn in early." Otto only nodded and opened the paper and began to read aloud. It was maddening how oblivious the man could be to trouble. Leaning her head back for a moment, Willa closed her eyes and tried to listen. If he asked her opinion—which he would not—temperance was a far more critical cause than getting women the vote. No self-respecting lady would go anywhere near the polls unless something was done to end the disgusting amount of public drunkenness that plagued Election Day.

As Otto droned on, Willa turned her attention to her needlework. She loved doing needlepoint, but this new fad of decorating patchwork with countless embroidery stitches in endless designs was more than a little taxing. It was called "crazy work," and Willa suspected she knew the reason. A woman could go crazy before she finished even a small sample. She'd been working on the same section of her mantel scarf for weeks.

As the sun went down and flickering lamplight replaced the light of day, Otto finished reading aloud, laid the newspaper aside, and buried his nose in a book. Willa pondered how to broach the topic she'd been worrying over for most of the day. The opportunity arose when Otto stopped reading and reached for his pipe.

"I've been thinking," Willa said, "that perhaps I should tell Louisa I can't go with her to Chicago after all."

Otto frowned. "Why on earth would you do that?"

Willa nodded her head toward the upper level. "It's been several days since that train left, and I don't think Irmagard has eaten a decent meal once. She simply isn't herself. She says she's tired almost every afternoon. She's taking *naps*."

"I agree that Irma's been a little quieter than usual these past few days. But when you consider that her best friend left on an adventure she's long wanted for herself, that's understandable. I also think the reality that neither Monte nor Diamond will be on the ranch this summer is just now beginning to sink in. I'd think it odd if she weren't a little depressed." Otto shrugged as he tamped the tobacco in his pipe. "She'll come around."

"I'm afraid it's more than 'a little' depression. You haven't witnessed her attitude toward me."

Otto paused midpuff. He frowned. "If she's been disrespectful, I'll—"

"No." Willa shook her head. "It's nothing like that. She hasn't complained about anything. She's been . . . agreeable."

Otto gave a little half-barking laugh. "Well, there's a sure sign there's something seriously wrong." He finished lighting his pipe.

"Don't joke." Willa got up and crossed to the window seat, where she perched in profile to her husband and stared out the window. "If she says 'Whatever you want, Momma' one more time, I think I may burst into tears." She looked back at her husband. "I'm worried. Truly, seriously worried." She paused. "She's beginning to remind me of Olive—toward the end."

"Don't be ridiculous. Irma's nothing like your sister—may her dear, tormented soul rest in peace."

"She is *very much* like my sister," Willa insisted. "The hair . . . the eyes . . . and, what frightens me most . . . the tendency toward moodiness." She blinked her tears away. She would not cry. Otto hated it when she cried. Worse than that, he never listened to what she was *saying* if she cried. Willa once again looked back outside at the piece of ground they called the yard—although it was little more than a picket-fence-bordered pasture.

Otto set his pipe down. He got up and crossed the room. Sitting beside her on the window seat, he put his arms around her. "Now, Momma," he said gently, and kissed her hair. "You must not let memories haunt you this way. It happens every April around the anniversary of Olive's death. You remember that, don't you? It's unfortunate that Irma's in one of her moods, but let's not blow it out of proportion. And let us also remember that your sister was a delightful woman in many ways. Her tragic end doesn't negate the fact that her stage career gave great joy to many, many people. To quote the Good Book you are so fond of reading, my dear . . . think on *those* things."

Willa shook her head. "You didn't see her in those final weeks. She stopped caring about her wardrobe. She let others make decisions for her. She complained of being tired all the time. And all the while she was sinking deeper and deeper until—" Burying her face in her hands, Willa began to cry as old wounds wrapped themselves around present fears.

Otto held her tight. "*You* are overreacting. *Irma* is going to be *fine.*" While Willa cried, he kept talking. "The past is past. We cannot change it. It can only harm us if we choose to let it do harm. You *can* choose what you think on. Doesn't the Bible say that?"

Willa blanched. He was right of course. Philippians chapter four, verse eight gave a long list of things a person should think about—and none of them had anything to do with mucking around in the past. Willa nodded.

He gripped her by the shoulders and pretended to scold. "Then think on those things. The good things. Because you *are* going on this trip with Louisa Cody, Mrs. Friedrich. You are going to buy at least a dozen new hats and indulge every whim and—" he lifted her chin and made her look him in the eye—"you are going to trust Irma to me."

Doing her best not to sound disbelieving or challenging, Willa asked, "Are you certain you can manage such a thing? The bank demands so much of you. Such long hours."

It was a while before Otto answered, and when he did it wasn't much of an answer. "I'll take Irma to eat at the hotel on Monday. On Tuesday she and I will escort you to the train. Then we'll drive out to the ranch for supper. And by Wednesday, I'll wager Irma will be writing you about how much fun she's having." He paused. "Trust me, Willa. Everything will be fine." He pulled her into his arms.

Trust him. How could she. How many times had she done so and been hurt. But she returned his embrace. Whatever his character flaws, Otto Friedrich adored his daughter. That, Willa realized, she *could* trust.

Saturday evening, April 24, 1886
Dear Monte,

Happy May Day! I suppose this letter will arrive about the time Minnie and I are making the rounds in town with our silly little bouquets. In case she didn't tell you, Minnie is coming to stay with me while Momma is gone. I will write more of that later.

How is Diamond? Is Lady Blaze turning out as I predicted? Do you think you will like living on a train? You must write and tell me every detail of what you are doing. You said there are no performances on Sunday, so I expect a letter to arrive here no later than the fifth of May. That will give you TWO Sundays to get one written. That should be more than enough time.

I am trying to be patient while Momma goes on and on about how wonderful it's going to be for me in Omaha this fall. I ask you, Monte, what am I going to learn at a "finishing school" anyway? Don't you think I'm "finished" quite well enough?

I clipped the latest headline and article so you could read the big news from at home, which is: people are finally going to have to stop letting their pigs run free in the streets or be fined. Orrin Knox is being credited with beginning a successful campaign to clean up our fair city. He has also suggested an ordinance requiring the burying of kitchen scraps—a good idea in my opinion, if the pigs are no longer to be allowed to run free and gobble them up. There has been talk of his running for mayor in the next election. The whole thing must seem very trite to you now that you've visited REAL cities. (I will admit, though, that Orrin's campaign has done a great deal to make a stroll along the boardwalks less odiferous.)

Does Helen Keen really ride sidesaddle in the production? Are you in any acts with Shep Sterling?

Irma stopping writing. She had promised herself not to ask about Shep at all. At least not until he wrote to her. To keep that promise she was going to have to rewrite the entire letter. With a sigh, she stood up, pleasantly surprised when the effort produced not even one twinge from her injured ribs. Dr. Sheridan had said it would take a few weeks for her to be back to normal, but she was already feeling much better.

Tomorrow was Sunday, and as Irma turned out her lamp and slid into bed, she wondered what the Sabbath was like for the Wild West performers. She wondered if Monte really was going to church as promised. Did Shep go to hear the cowboy preacher, too? Did he miss her? Why hadn't he written? And would she ever stop daydreaming about those kisses?

―――――

"It's nice of you to take me out," Irma said on Monday as her father pulled a chair out for her in the dining room at the Mayfair Hotel. As Irma spread her napkin on her lap, her stomach growled. She laughed. "I don't know if you heard that, but my stomach definitely approves."

"Good," Daddy said. "You haven't been eating well. Your mother and I—especially your mother—have been a little concerned about you."

"I'm sorry."

"Your mother says you haven't been yourself. She says"—Daddy grinned as he snapped his napkin open and, with a flourish, tucked it into his collar—"that you've been *agreeable*." He chuckled. "It's most disturbing."

Irma frowned a little. "Momma is worried because I'm . . . agreeable?"

"You must admit," Daddy said, as he signaled for a waitress, "it's not quite normal for you to get along with your mother." As the waitress approached he asked, "Do you want coffee?"

Irma nodded and Daddy ordered them each a cup. When the waitress was out of earshot she said, "I don't suppose I have been myself. Everything's changed so much." She bit her lip. "And I don't like most of the changes."

"Your mother's been so worried that this past weekend she very nearly cancelled her trip to Chicago."

"Well, that's ridiculous," Irma sat up straighter. "Minnie and I are going to have a nice time together." She added cream and sugar to her coffee. "Which reminds me. I wanted to ask you if I might have a luncheon while Momma is gone."

Daddy frowned. "I don't think that's a very good idea."

"Why not? We'll do all the work. You won't even know it happened. I'm not talking about one of mother's productions. This would only be Minnie, Edd Peterson, Orrin Knox, and me. And maybe Violet Dawson. She likes Edd."

"Could we please get back to the topic at hand?" Daddy said. He smoothed his mustache and goatee, then leaned forward and said quietly, "You must make every effort to show Momma that you are going to be just fine."

Was he really going to blame her for Momma's mood? Irma looked down at the scroll design around the edge of the hotel china. She was doing the best she could. She and Momma had talked for nearly half an hour yesterday about Reverend Coe's sermon. And she'd helped with dishes and even asked Momma to show her how to do that fancy embroidery stitch she was doing on her mantel scarf. And this morning at breakfast she had—

"You can look up, Irma," Daddy said. "I'm not scolding you. I'm only trying to help you understand that it helps no one for your mother to worry to the point she considers canceling her own holiday."

"What does she think I'm going to do?" Irma said. "Throw myself off a cliff because I didn't get my way? I'm not a child. I'll be fine. And could you please give your permission for the luncheon?"

Daddy dropped his spoon. When he bent to retrieve it, something fell out of his pocket. It was a train ticket. He laid it on the tabletop, then reached into his pocket and took out two more. When Irma didn't look at them, he pushed them toward her as he said, "I think it would be very reassuring for your mother if she heard you and Minnie wanted to *have* a luncheon. Tell her all about it. It'll put her mind at ease." He took a gulp of coffee. "Just last night I promised Momma that I would take a personal interest in doing everything possible to cheer you up," Daddy said, and tapped the tickets with his index finger. "She and I both know what it's like to be young and to have more than one disappointment come all at once." He leaned back as the waitress delivered plates of roast beef and potatoes swimming in gravy. "When Momma said that Minnie was coming to stay with you, I had the idea that perhaps you girls would enjoy your own little holiday—say for May Day? Something special." He looked pointedly at the tickets. "Of course you can choose to have a luncheon instead. If that's really what you want."

Irma looked more closely at the three tickets. *To St. Louis.* She could feel the goose bumps as she began to realize what Daddy wasn't saying. And he kept not saying it as he buttered a dinner roll.

"Of course we'll need *other* tickets to make it a perfect May Day, but I have it on good authority—I telegraphed a friend named Bill—that those tickets will be waiting for us once we arrive at our destination. Which," he said, "is a *secret*. And not to be discussed with *anyone*."

Irma nodded.

"So the question is: Can you put your mother's concerns about you to rest? Can you reassure her that you are feeling *much better* so that she can go to Chicago as planned?"

"Of course, Daddy." Irma nodded. "I understand. And . . . never mind about the luncheon I wanted to have. We'll do it another time."

Daddy gestured at her plate. "I'm sure it would help put your momma's mind at ease if I could go on and on about how much you ate today."

Irma slathered butter on a roll as she asked, "May I have dessert?"

Chapter 9

Bread of deceit is sweet to a man;
but afterwards his mouth shall
be filled with gravel.
Proverbs 20:17 KJV

She'd been here before, but it had always been in a dream, and something always happened to pull her out of the scene and down a tunnel into other places where dissonance and the absurd reigned supreme. But tonight the aroma of freshly graded earth was real. Her seat was solid, just like the thousands of other seats rising in stair-step fashion away from the Wild West arena. Irma closed her eyes and listened. *Footsteps.* Boots clunked and shoes scuffed as people clamored to their seats. *Laughter* as ticket-holders shared their anticipation. And, every now and then, a whinny or a snort—faint because the sounds came from behind the curtain and past the performers' tents, where temporary corrals and stalls housed buffalo and bucking broncs, tame elk and horses.

Opening her eyes, Irma looked down at the Wild West program in her lap. Large letters across the top proclaimed *Buffalo Bill's Wild West.* A pen-and-ink profile of Bill Cody dominated the center, but it was flanked on one side by a mounted Indian chief and tepees, and on the other by a cowboy and covered wagons. *"America's National Entertainment,"* the program heralded in inch-high letters, *"led by the famed scout and guide Buffalo Bill."* As Irma traced the images and letters with her gloved fingers, goose bumps crawled up her arms and across the back of her neck.

The Wild West program was more than a printed order of events. Irma paged through it slowly, scanning the historical profiles of great Civil War scouts and frontiersmen and the notes about the various Indian races as well as the *vaqueros.* She would keep it forever, and when she was old she would tell children stories about the day a girl's dream came true. She would talk about the train ride across the prairie and how they changed trains in the vast station in Omaha and then arrived in the even more vast station in St. Louis. She would describe the excitement she felt when she and Minnie followed Daddy out of the Laclede Hotel and climbed aboard a cable car to cross St. Louis en route to the fairgrounds. And she would speak of almost crying with joy when finally, after descending from the cable car, she caught sight of the canvas arena cover announcing *Buffalo Bill's Wild West* in foot-high letters. She would do her best to tell these stories, but it would be nearly impossible to find words to describe exactly how she felt sitting here in the stands waiting for the performance to begin; waiting to see Monte and Ned Bishop ride into the arena; waiting, too, to see Shep Sterling in all his Wild West glory; and waiting for the moment when the performance was over and she and Minnie would follow Daddy onto the back lot and surprise all three cowboys.

The Wild West Irma had seen with Uncle Charlie and Aunt Laura in Omaha was nothing compared to this. This Wild West boasted a twenty-member band and concession stands serving popcorn and fresh-squeezed lemonade. Monte had told her the stands in St. Louis would seat about twenty thousand people. Tonight they were full. *Night.* As she looked around her, Irma thought that might be the most amazing thing of all. Light fixtures mounted high on poles anchored to the front of the grandstand illuminated the entire arena. More lights focused on the scenic canvas backdrop painted to suggest a wide open prairie and vast blue sky. It was as close as a person could come to being magically transported into the West.

Minnie had been poring over her own program, but when a band member dropped something, she started and looked up. She pointed. "Is that Jason and Jonathan? Oh, look—they're wearing holsters. With guns!" She laughed aloud. "Imagine that. Growing up out west and the first time you strap on a gun it's to play your trumpet in a band."

"Ah," Daddy said, "but don't they look the part of rough and ready cowboys? And *looking* the part is important in show business. At least that's what Bill told me when we had our last meeting about the money end of this production."

Irma tapped the cover of her program. "Did you see the page about the band? They make them sound like world-renowned musicians."

"Mollie will be so proud," Minnie said. She beamed up at her uncle. "Thank you, Uncle Otto. I'll treasure the memory of this weekend forever. I don't know how you convinced Aunt Willa to let us come, but I'm so glad you did."

Irma went back to reading her program—or at least pretending to read it. It was only natural for Minnie to assume Daddy had told Momma all about this trip and convinced her to agree to it. After all, Uncle Charlie and Aunt Laura never disagreed about anything. At least not in front of their children as far as Irma knew. But whatever Minnie might believe, Irma was fairly certain that when it came to this trip, things weren't settled at all between her parents. She was almost tempted to feel guilty. Or to worry. But then she reminded herself that Daddy could handle Momma. He always had. And besides, when Momma got back home and realized how much it had meant to Irma, she wouldn't be able to stay mad for long. Eventually she would have to forgive them all, just as the Bible said. *Seventy times seven.*

"Your Aunt Willa and I want you both to have the time of your lives this weekend," Daddy was saying. "If it is in my power to provide it, I'll do it. In fact, you should be thinking about which of those stores along Broadway you want to go in tomorrow morning. I know better than to take a woman to St. Louis and not allow time for shopping."

As the stands continued to fill Irma nodded at the scenic backdrop. "That obnoxious reporter who was on the cable car with us is going to have a time of it proving his theory about Annie Oakley hiding behind there to do all of Bill Cody's shooting."

Minnie laughed. "Especially when you consider he said the whole thing worked because the hole Miss Oakley used was camouflaged inside a knothole in a painted tree." She motioned toward the backdrop. "No trees. No knotholes."

Irma looked at her father. "I still don't understand why you didn't tell him you know Buffalo Bill—and that everything he was saying was just so much . . . bull." Momma would have scolded her for using the word, but Mr. Gregory Harrison's ridiculous claim deserved even stronger language. "He was more than just pompous and annoying, Daddy. He was *lying*. You should have defended Mr. Cody."

Daddy shrugged. "I was enjoying listening to all his balderdash. Just think how embarrassed Mr. Harrison is going to be when he watches tonight and realizes Bill really is a good shot."

"Well, I hope wherever he's sitting he *can* see," Irma said.

Daddy pointed above them. "There are two searchlights up there," he said. "Nate Salsbury told me the operators will hone in on the sharpshooters and there will be no doubt when they hit their glass balls or clay pigeons. If he's watching, Mr. Harrison will see irrefutable evidence that William F. Cody does his own shooting."

"Even so," Irma sniffed, "he was rude. I hope we never see him again."

A blue-eyed boy about Maggie Mason's age slid in next to her. "I'm Jack Payne," he said, and put out his hand. "Have you ever been to the Wild West before?"

"Not like this one," Irma said as she shook the boy's hand.

"I've been waiting ever so long to come," he said and looked up at the prim-faced woman with him. "Father's been too busy, but it's my birthday in a few days, and so he finally gave Miss Farnham permission to bring me."

Miss Farnham, who introduced herself as Jack's governess, motioned for Jack to sit down. The woman seemed disinclined to talk very much, and Irma decided Jack must be used to entertaining himself, for the moment he sat down he began to leaf through his program.

"Miss Farnham," he said after a few minutes, "it says here that Colonel Cody knew General Custer, too. Do you think Father could have met Colonel Cody? Perhaps he has and he just doesn't remember. He doesn't seem to remember very much about being in the army."

Miss Farnham muttered something Irma couldn't quite decipher, although it was clear the woman had very little interest in engaging her charge in conversation. She was sitting ramrod stiff, her hands folded in her lap. Irma could almost imagine the woman mentally ticking off the minutes until she could leave.

"You read very well," Irma said.

"Thank you," the boy said. "Mama taught me before she died. She said I learned very quickly."

"Well, I think you are very clever," Irma said. "And I'm sorry about your mama."

Miss Farnham patted Jack's knee. It must have meant "be quiet," for Jack thanked Irma and then immersed himself in the page of the Wild West program showing a biography of Shep Sterling. Irma found the page in her own program and read about Shep's exploits in Texas. *"Audience members will be grateful for Shep Sterling's introducing the management to long-time friend and fellow Texan, Miss Helen Keen, who will delight crowds with her fearless riding and winsome smile." Long-time friend? Winsome smile?* Irma closed her program. Maybe it was better to *experience* the Wild West before reading about it.

When the band began to play the "The Star Spangled Banner," Jack Payne was immediately transformed from bookworm to wiggle worm. Clutching his program to his chest, he scooted to the edge of his seat and began to rock back and forth and chant softly, "Here they come . . . here they come . . . here they come."

Irma leaned forward, too, internally joining the boy's singsong chanting.

Sadly—at least in Irma's opinion—no "they" appeared at the conclusion of the first song. Instead, a lone man dressed in black, except for a huge white sombrero and a red kerchief knotted around his neck, stepped out from behind the backdrop. Quiet descended on the arena. A spotlight followed his progress as he strode toward his rostrum, his spurs rattling with every step. In a golden voice, he welcomed the crowd to the evening's "exhibition of skill, tact, and endurance created by men who have gained their livelihood on the plains." Anticipation hung in the air, a taut wire of expectation waiting to be strummed by the Grand Entry. Finally, the announcer took the red kerchief from around his neck and waved it in the air.

Jack couldn't stand it. "Here they come!" he hollered and stood up on his chair. Laughter erupted as everyone else got to their feet. Irma stood on tiptoe as mounted Indians, cowboys, and vaqueros marched single file into the arena. "Do you see them?" she asked Minnie. "Do you see any of them?" Her heart pounded as the line grew longer and the performers moved their horses into a trot. Still, Irma couldn't find Shep. Or Monte. Not even Ned Bishop. The applause got louder, transforming into cheers when the horses began to gallop.

Finally, when the Wild West troupe had formed a long line stretching across the wide end of the horseshoe-shaped arena, Minnie located her brother in the lineup. "There's Monte!" she said, pointing. "And there! There's Mr. Sterling!"

Monte looked wonderful in a bright blue shirt with a kerchief knotted at his neck. Shep Sterling smiled and waved his white Stetson while his palomino gelding danced in the spotlight. A gleaming golden coat, four dazzling white socks, and a silken tail that literally touched the ground would have been enough to dazzle any horse-loving girl,

but there was more: a black leather show saddle and bridle deco-
rated with silver that flashed in the lights. The sight of Monte had
thrilled Irma's heart, but Shep Sterling on his palomino took her
breath away.

Irma could sense Minnie watching her reaction when Buffalo
Bill's beautiful rancheras finally came into view. All Irma could
muster was disappointment. Not one wore anything like Liberty
Belle's imagined finery. One woman's butternut-colored skirt and
waist reminded Irma more of her own walking suit than something
designed for performing. Other than an abundance of fringe, the
costume's only decoration was an ivory scarf.

"What's wrong?" Minnie asked.

"They're so . . . plain," Irma answered. "And look at that," she
said, pointing to the woman riding sidesaddle. "I didn't think it
could be true. Why would she do that? It's the Wild West, not a
ride in the park."

Minnie shrugged. "Wait until we see the act. Maybe this is for
the parade."

Irma hoped she was right. While the other two rancheras rode
astride, their saddles looked positively timeworn. The only thing
fancy about their costumes was a little beading on their leather vests.
And their horses were nothing special either—a rangy bay, a bald-
faced pinto, and a positively ugly gelding with a spotted rear and a
scraggly tail reminiscent of a worn-out broom. Maybe Minnie was
right. Maybe everything would be different when they came back
into the arena during the performance. Maybe the cowgirls saved
their show costumes and better horses for later in the evening so
that nothing would compete with the headliners for attention. Irma
sincerely hoped that was the case.

"Ladies and gentlemen," the announcer boomed, "Buffalo Bill . . .
the chief scout of the United States Army and the avenger of Custer."
As the crowd roared approval, Bill Cody, mounted on his famous
white horse, Isham, charged into the arena and into the spotlight.

Here, Irma thought, was a man who knew how to dazzle. Cody wore a fringed and beaded buckskin coat and thigh-high leather boots. People had always said that Bill Cody sat a horse like royalty. Irma didn't know how royalty rode, but she marveled at the partnership between horse and rider as Isham skidded to a halt in front of the long row of performers and reared up while Cody waved his hat to the crowd and shouted, "Are you *ready?*" When the crowd yelled "Yes!" Cody whirled Isham around to face his company and hollered "Go!" and then charged back across the arena and out of sight.

Isham and his rider had barely disappeared behind the backdrop when the Wild West lineup transformed itself into an animated patchwork of whooping Indians charging one way, and cowboys firing revolvers and carbines going the other. It was choreography at its best, and as Irma watched the formations weave in and out of one another, the flames of her ambition flickered anew.

Monte dashed by. Irma and Minnie waved their lace-edged handkerchiefs and screamed his name. For a moment Irma thought she might cry from excitement and pride and bittersweet longing to be part of it all. Surely if Momma could see this for herself she would finally realize it wasn't some second-rate circus. The Wild West was one of America's greatest products, unforgettable to those who saw it and something to boast about for those lucky enough to perform in it. Why couldn't Momma understand that?

The crowd sat down as the Grand Entry concluded. Irma opened her program to the page listing what was to come. She glanced at the boy seated next to her. "Well, here we go, Jack," she said. "What are you most excited to see?"

Jack seemed to be thinking it over, but finally he said, "All of it," he said.

Irma smiled. "Me too."

As the evening unfolded, the band's music and the announcer's voice were the constants in an ever-changing drama unfolding in the arena. The announcer not only explained all sorts of things about

the West but also made certain the audience's attention was focused
in just the right place, so they didn't miss anything important. He
delivered well-timed anecdotes, and once, when a rider took a tumble,
the narrator eased everyone's fears and soon had them all laughing
at the antics of a cowboy clown who hurried into the arena while the
fallen rider was helped out of sight. Later, the narrator pointed out
that the rider who had fallen in an earlier act was back in the arena—
proof that he wasn't badly hurt. The band played tunes selected to
make things either more dramatic or more hilarious, and by the
third act Irma decided they more than deserved the praise given in
the program.

For all of Irma's daydreaming in recent years, she had not come
close to imagining the actual performances of the improved Wild
West. Diminutive Miss Annie Oakley fired rifles at glass balls and
vaulted her gun stand to shatter yet more targets, among them a
playing card held in her husband's hand. She moved with amazing
swiftness, agility, and a grace Irma believed even Momma would
find admirable.

"He's wonderful," Minnie exclaimed when Shep Sterling displayed his myriad of talents.

Irma nodded agreement, following Shep's every move and blushing furiously when he took a bow and seemed to be looking right at
her—which was, Irma knew, impossible. Shep didn't even know she
was there. Yet. She wondered how he would react when he first saw
her—and felt her cheeks grow hot again.

When the Deadwood mail coach came lumbering into view and
a half-dozen Sioux sporting war paint and feathers filled the air with
their cries, Irma shivered. At her side, Jack hid his face, and even the
stony-faced Miss Farnham seemed to be affected as she covered her
mouth with one hand. But then with a chorus of yips the cowboys
came charging to the rescue. Monte was among them, and Irma and
Minnie cheered right along with young Jack—louder, in fact, than
anyone around them. Miss Farnham did not cheer, but she did look

down at Jack and smile with what Irma thought looked like genuine enjoyment.

During one of the interludes a clown the announcer introduced as Hidalgo entered the arena mounted on a mule about the size of a large dog. Everyone—including Miss Farnham—burst out laughing. Hidalgo wore an enormous sombrero and winter chaps sporting long fur. He bumped along astride his little mule with exaggerated movements, and when he stood up and the mule walked out from under him and gave a happy little kick of freedom, the crowd applauded approval. Hidalgo spent the next few minutes chasing his mount around the arena and alternately being nipped or otherwise outsmarted. When Hidalgo swept his sombrero off his head to take a bow, the mule bowed alongside him—and then took the sombrero in his hand and charged away. Irma and Minnie laughed until tears were streaming down their cheeks.

As for the women of the Wild West, they raced one another and occasionally exhibited a skill that Irma had mastered. But no one female rider did *everything* Irma had worked into her routine. Two of the beautiful rancheras doubled as the homesteader's terrified wife in one act and a maiden in distress on the hijacked mail coach in another. That, Irma thought, would *not* be something Liberty Belle would care to do. But then a cowgirl retrieved a kerchief from the arena floor as her black-and-white pony charged by it at a dead run. Irma could pick up a Stetson, but a kerchief would be much more difficult. She'd need a few days' practice before she would be able to do that.

As soon as the Final Salute concluded, Miss Farnham grabbed Jack's hand and hurried for the exit. Irma watched Jack depart with a feeling of sadness for the boy being swept away without a chance to tour the grounds or meet any of the performers while she and Minnie and Daddy followed the dozens of spectators who, in spite of the late hour, streamed toward the back lot. This area was lighted, as well, although Daddy said those lights would be going out soon, which was why performers were hurrying to get horses and mules stabled, wagons unhitched, and countless other chores accomplished. Much to Minnie and Irma's disappointment, neither Monte, Ned, nor Shep Sterling were anywhere in sight. Buffalo Bill, on the other hand, was easy to find, standing just outside his private tent surrounded by at least two dozen admirers.

"Oh, no. . . ." Irma said, and grabbed Daddy's arm. "There's the man from the trolley. Do you suppose he's going to challenge Mr. Cody?"

"Either way, we should say hello to Bill," Daddy said, and led the girls in that direction.

Expecting a confrontation between the aggressive reporter and the famous scout, Irma was surprised when the recently obnoxious Mr. Harrison removed his hat and blathered energetically about how he'd been convinced no one could shoot well enough to accomplish the feats that he'd heard about. And then he apologized to Cody for his part in spreading a false rumor.

"Apology accepted," Cody said with a smile and a wink. He went on to invite Harrison to join him and a few friends at the Laclede Hotel for a late supper. He caught sight of Daddy and nodded before saying, "And here they are now."

"I can't decide," Irma said, and laid the dress she'd been holding up to herself atop the growing pile of other dresses recently "auditioned" in front of the dressing mirror in the elegant hotel room she and Minnie were sharing.

"It doesn't *matter* which one," Minnie said from where she sat in an emerald-upholstered chair by the window. "They're all lovely."

"But this one," Irma picked the most recent reject up, "makes me look too young."

"You *are* young," Minnie said. "We'll be the youngest ladies there."

"And this one," Irma continued, reaching for a soft blue sateen gown, "is probably too fancy."

"Indeed." Minnie lifted her chin and looked down her nose, pretending to be an elegant lady. "Unless, of course, there is a ball planned for the rest of the evening." She pointed to the clock on the mantel. "But then the evening is likely to be over before you're even dressed if you don't make a decision before long." She leaned back in the chair. "There's something to be said for being the poor cousin. At least I don't have a nervous breakdown trying to decide what to wear to supper."

Irma glanced up and, with a little frown, apologized. "I'm sorry," she said. "I . . ." She looked at the pile of dresses. "I didn't mean to make you feel—"

"Oh, hush," Minnie said and jumped up. "The only way you're making me feel is frustrated. For goodness' sake, Irma. Pick one and put it on! You've nothing to worry about."

"I'm not worried," Irma said. "I just . . . I want to make a good impression."

"On who? Or is it *whom*? Mr. Cody thinks you're adorable. Your father would be proud of you if you showed up in boots, jeans, and a flannel shirt. And as for Shep Sterling—he's not going to care what you have on, either." She teased, "Although, perhaps *he'd* prefer the nightgown with the blue satin bows."

"Minnie Mason!" Irma spun around to stare at her cousin with mock horror.

"Sorry," Minnie said. "I keep forgetting you're one of those modern women who has no plans to get married." She arched one eyebrow and gazed at the pile of discarded dresses. "Although you must admit there's some fairly contradictory evidence hereabouts."

"Don't be silly," Irma protested. "Shep Sterling doesn't care about me. He hasn't written once since he left."

Minnie reached for one of the dresses and began to hang it back up. "It hasn't even been two weeks, *Irmagard*. And besides, he wrote several volumes with his eyes the day of your luncheon. And later that day at the ranch. And let us not forget his good-bye." She made kissing noises.

"Whatever are you talking about?"

"I'm talking about his nearly missing the train." When Irma looked surprised, Minnie explained. "I—old-fashioned as it is to be interested in marriage—was making a last pathetic effort to get something besides an *ahem* from Mr. Knox. When I saw that he was headed around the corner of the train depot, I sort of . . . followed him." She shrugged. "So I saw what he saw. And, I might add, what Edna Hertz saw. Although you don't have anything to fear from *her*."

"How can you be sure of that?" Irma worried aloud. "She's had it in for me ever since Shep brought me those roses."

"Because when I saw Mr. Knox rescue you from a potentially dangerous encounter with your mother, I did my part." She shrugged. "I hinted to Edna Hertz that people who messed with you were inviting all kinds of unwelcome attention from the Mason family. The *entire* family. All *seven* of us. And I hinted how one or the other of us might know one story or another involving Edna and this or that boy from town. Stories Edna's mother would find . . . enlightening."

"You've never told *me* any of those stories," Irma said. Minnie tilted her head and raised both eyebrows. Irma grinned. "Minnie Mason, that was just evil. To make poor Edna Hertz think you were going to tell on her."

"I didn't actually say we would tell. It was more . . . hinting. But girls like Edna usually have lots of things they don't want their mothers knowing. Whatever secrets Edna has, thinking we Masons knew them made her incredibly agreeable to forgetting all about your one little moment with Mr. Sterling." Minnie abruptly changed the subject and motioned to a pale blue dress Irma had already ruled out as being too plain. "That really does make your eyes look blue. And in the candlelight downstairs . . ." She picked the dress up. "This is the one."

"Are you sure?" Irma looked doubtful.

"I'm sure," Minnie shoved the dress into her hands. "Now get it on, because Uncle Otto is going to be pounding on that door any minute now, and *you* might be too nervous to be hungry but *I*, dear cousin, am *not*."

———

When Shep finally walked through the door to the private dining room and smiled at her, Irma forgot about everyone else in the room. Her heart began to pound. He headed her way. But then Irma saw Helen Keen tagging along; Helen Keen wearing a simply tailored skirt and waist that showed off her lovely figure. Helen Keen, who was smiling at Irma and reaching out to her with hands Momma would approve. There was nothing masculine about Helen Keen's small, long-fingered, delicate hands.

"So here she is in the flesh," Miss Keen said, squeezing both Irma's hands and smiling warmly. "The Nebraska gal planning for glory in the Wild West." Before Irma could say a thing, Miss Keen nudged Shep. "Now don't be upset with him for telling me about your dream, honey. This big galoot can't keep a secret from me." She grinned up at Shep. "We go back almost as far as the Alamo. In fact, I taught him everything he knows." Laughing, she let go of Irma's hands and turned to Minnie, giving her the same enthusiastic double-handed greeting. "And you're Monte's sister?" When Minnie nodded, Helen said, "Well, I'd say the two of you are off to a good start with the Wild West. You already know the handsomest men on the grounds." She winked and then leaned close to say—in a stage whisper—"Although I shouldn't admit that right now. The Shepherd's head is so big already, his hat barely fits."

Shep smiled at Miss Keen with entirely too much affection just as Buffalo Bill motioned both him and Miss Keen over to meet the mayor. Minnie looked longingly at the candlelit dining table at the far end of the room. "Do you suppose we'll actually get to eat before next year?"

Monte finally arrived.

"You were wonderful," Minnie said and hugged him.

"Incredible," Irma agreed.

"Aw shucks," Monte said with mock humility. "It was nuthin'." He grinned.

While Minnie shared the news from home, Irma's gaze wandered, first to Shep and Miss Keen, then to a corner of the room where Daddy was engaged in an intense conversation with Nate Salsbury. "What do you suppose that's all about?" she murmured to Minnie.

"It's a banker and the Wild West business manager," Monte said matter-of-factly. "They're talking money."

In spite of being part of a gathering of famous people, Irma realized she cared about only one thing, and as Shep continued to squire Miss Keen around the room, Irma's excitement and appetite dissolved. Just when she was about to plead exhaustion and head upstairs, Bill Cody walked over to the dining table and used a knife to tap on a crystal water glass and call everyone to supper.

The place cards at the table put Minnie and Irma at the far end of the table from Buffalo Bill, opposite Daddy and—*oh no*—the reporter. Shep and Miss Keen sat to the left of Bill Cody, with Annie Oakley and her husband on his right. Mr. Salsbury came to sit at their end of the table. After all the guests sat down, Cody made a short welcoming speech—and thus began a parade of food like nothing Irma had ever seen. Her stomach growled and she took a sip of water. It was good to realize that she could be mature about things. Just because Shep Sterling was attached to another woman was no reason Irmagard Friedrich couldn't enjoy herself.

It was long after midnight when Buffalo Bill stood up and invited the gentlemen to join him for brandy and cigars. Shep bent to say something to Miss Keen but only gave Irma the slightest nod and a faint smile before following Cody and the other men across the hall. Only Daddy and Mr. Salsbury stayed behind with the ladies. Assuming the two men hadn't finished the private conversation begun before supper, Irma bade Miss Keen good-night, linked arms with Minnie, blew Daddy a kiss, and headed for the stairs.

But Daddy motioned for them both to linger with him and Mr. Salsbury. Miss Keen departed for the Wild West grounds with Annie Oakley and her husband, and when the last guest had left the dining room, Mr. Salsbury spoke up. "While we may not have been formally introduced until tonight, Miss Friedrich, in many ways I feel as though I know you. My partner speaks fondly of your camping with his daughter years ago. He says you were already quite a cowgirl back then. I've also heard about your summers on the Mason ranch."

Minnie chimed in. "Irma worked right alongside my pa and the other wranglers. She can rope and bulldog with the best of 'em."

Salsbury nodded. "And your father tells me you were planning to audition for the Wild West a few weeks ago, but that an injury prevented it."

"I've wanted to be with the Wild West ever since my Uncle Charlie and Aunt Laura took me to see the very first performance in Omaha."

Salsbury nodded. "Your father says you've put together an act. He seems to think it's something that would enhance the experience for our audience." He smiled. "We'd like to see it. I understand we have the horse you trained with. What do you say, Miss Friedrich? Would you and Diamond do us the honor, say, on Sunday afternoon?"

Say something, you idiot. She could only nod.

"She's just surprised," Minnie chimed in. "Dumbstruck would be the word, sir. Doesn't happen very often. But she definitely wants to audition."

Salsbury glanced from Daddy to Irma and back again. He glanced down at his watch. "Good. Sunday, then?"

"Sunday," Irma croaked.

Daddy clapped his hand on Mr. Salsbury's shoulder. "Thank you, Nate. You won't be sorry."

It was too much. A late supper, Shep's being more interested in Helen Keen than in the girl he'd kissed less than two weeks ago, and an *audition*?! Irma's head hurt, her heart pounded, and she thought she might just have to give up the late supper if she didn't calm down or catch her breath or . . . something. She didn't know whether to cry or laugh. At first she did a little of both.

Daddy grabbed her arm and guided her to a chair. "Breathe, Irmagard," he said, putting his hand on her back. "Slow, even breaths." He watched her face with concern, then smiled and finally chuckled. "I'm going to interpret all of this as joy," he said.

Irma nodded. Sucked in air. Glanced from Daddy to Minnie and back and then finally blurted out, "What about Momma? I promised I'd go to Brownell."

"If you'll give me the room key," Minnie said, "I'll head upstairs and give you two some privacy."

"Thank you, dear." As soon as Minnie was gone, Daddy said, "You must trust me when I say I've worked it out. I was feeling sad about how different things would be for you this summer out at the ranch with Monte and Diamond both gone. And then it dawned on me. The Wild West's summer season concludes in August." He smiled. "It's perfect, really. You have a summer with the Wild West, and Momma still gets her Brownell graduate."

"It *isn't* perfect," Irma insisted. "Brownell notwithstanding, she'll never forgive us for doing this behind her back."

"She'll be upset," Daddy agreed. "But eventually she'll see I did the right thing." He reached out and took both Irma's hands in his. "I am so proud of you. Proud of your determination to be what you want to be—to let the rest of the world think what they will think and to forge ahead into new adventures. I understand that kind of drive because you got it from me." He stared intently into her eyes. "I want you to have this, Irma. You must trust me to handle Momma."

How she wanted to believe him. But Momma wasn't the only obstacle. "I don't have the right clothes, Daddy. Without boots that fit, I won't be able to do a thing, and I don't think they sell work boots at any of those fancy stores on Broadway. Even if they do, I'm used to the saddle at home. I know just where to balance when I stand atop it and just where to grip when I'm doing a handstand."

"Surely you didn't think I'd go to all the trouble to plan this and not consider the details." Daddy stood up. "Come upstairs with me. I've a package for you." He winked and took her arm. As they mounted the stairs he explained. "I drove out to the ranch before we left. Your Aunt Laura helped me pack boots and clothes, and I packed them with my things. As for the saddle, your Uncle Charlie brought it into town and shipped it to Monte here at the fairgrounds. I checked with Monte earlier. It arrived a couple of days ago." At the top of the stairs he paused and put his hand on his heart. "In here, Irma, your mother and I both want the same thing. We want you to be happy and fulfilled." He gave Irma a fierce hug. "Now, let's get those clothes and get you to bed. It's already Saturday by the clock. You have a lot of work to do today, besides attending two more performances. And we'll want to rise early on Sunday and get over to the fairgrounds in time for church."

"Church?" Daddy rarely attended church in North Platte.

"It'll help your mother feel better about things if I can describe the Wild West church service to her. And tell her that you'll be attending every Sunday while you're gone."

By the time Irma had retrieved the package of riding gear and gone back to her room, Minnie was sound asleep. Snuggled beneath the luxurious comforters, Irma eventually convinced herself that what Daddy said about Momma was true. She would be angry. She would get over it. Eventually.

CHAPTER 10

Be kind to one another, tender-hearted,
forgiving each other, just as God in Christ
also has forgiven you.

Ephesians 4:32 NASB

From where she sat in the green chair by the hotel room window early Sunday morning, Irma focused on the mop of dark curls just visible in the bed across the room. She cleared her throat—just a little louder than usual. She didn't want to be rude, but she couldn't sleep, and if Minnie would only wake up, maybe between the two of them they could solve some of the problems swirling around in Irma's mind. Minnie stirred, then snuggled deeper beneath the peach-colored satin comforter and began to snore. With a sigh, Irma slid to the edge of the cushioned chair and pretended to hold Diamond's reins. Closing her eyes, she mentally re-created her routine—for probably the hundredth time since giving up on sleep and climbing out of bed. When she visualized failure—again—she sighed and sank back into the chair.

I can't do it. It's been too long. Diamond and I worked hard yesterday, but I still only landed that dismount one time. Daddy will be embarrassed.

Bill Cody and Mr. Salsbury will think their time's been wasted. Helen Keen will laugh out loud. And Shep— Who knew what Shep would do? She was thinking entirely too much about Shep Sterling. *This has to stop.* There were too many other things to worry about. "I can't do this," she murmured aloud. "I just can't, and that's that."

Minnie turned over. She tucked the comforter beneath her chin and said, "You can and you will."

"I've been sitting here going over and over it in my mind, and—" Irma got up and crossed to the washstand. Pouring cool water into the bowl, she scrubbed her face to keep from bursting into tears. As she turned to face Minnie she put her palm to her midsection. "I've never been this terrified in my life. I'll fall. I'll be the laughingstock of every single person in the Wild West."

"I hardly think *every single person* in the Wild West cares one way or the other about one more trick rider or one less," Minnie said. "Most of them probably won't even come to watch. Sunday's the only day they have to themselves. It's not like they haven't seen female trick riders before. And you said it yourself yesterday after seeing two more performances: Except for the handkerchief trick, you can do everything those rancheras do—and then some."

"Well, I was being . . . snooty," Irma said. "Did you hear what Miss Keen said about her riding sidesaddle?"

"I was standing right there. And she's right. Take away the saddle horn and a cowboy's ability to grip with his legs and most of 'em wouldn't last five minutes in the arena."

Irma nodded. "Exactly. Miss Keen is a better rider than I'll ever be." She sighed. "Which leads me back to my initial point: I can't do this."

"Stop saying that." Minnie tossed her dark curls as she slid out of bed. "Because you're going to *try,* even if I have to drag you bodily across town and tie you to the saddle." She pulled her dress over her head and began to button the waist. "What time did Uncle Otto say he'd come for us? I'd like to have some breakfast before we leave."

"Breakfast?" Irma moaned. "How can you even think of breakfast? I still haven't digested the seven courses from Friday night." She undid her braid and began to brush her hair.

"Do you think Mr. Cody and his stars have a party like that every night?" Minnie asked.

"I don't know about everyone, but I think Bill Cody might. Apparently one of the issues between Arta's parents is her father's penchant for socializing."

Minnie interrupted as she twisted her hair into a bun. "It's good that we're starting the Sabbath by going to church. Uncle Otto will be able to talk about *that* instead of midnight parties that might start more *gossip* when he gets back home." Her hair finished, Minnie perched on the edge of the bed. "If you end up signing on with the Wild West, I'm going to miss you. You have no idea how I've relied on you over the years to be the one always getting in trouble so no one notices when I make a mistake."

Irma chuckled. "It won't take you long to find a new scapegoat. I'd say Maggie has real potential for stepping right into my shoes." She frowned into the mirror. "Look at this." She pointed to her hair. "I'm shaking so hard from nerves I can't even put my own hair up."

"Give me that," Minnie said, and took the brush out of Irma's hand. Motioning for her to sit down, Minnie started over. "We'll do a braid. I'll pin it up for church, and you can just let the braid down for your audition."

Irma peered in the mirror while Minnie worked. When she put in the last hairpin, Irma nodded. "Very nice. Even Momma would approve."

"Which brings me to the question that *I've* been thinking about while you were doing imaginary gymnastics over there in that chair." Minnie handed Irma her brush. "What's Aunt Willa going to say when she gets home and you aren't there?"

Irma got up and began to pack her things into a small carpetbag. "She's going to be upset."

"I'd say that's something of an understatement. You and I both know that when Uncle Otto talked her into letting him bring us to St. Louis, he didn't say one word about an audition. In fact, I bet he had to promise he'd do no such thing just to keep her from throwing a fit about our coming at all."

Irma shrugged. Minnie still believed Momma had agreed to this outing. Opening the wardrobe door she reached for a white waist. "Daddy said I should trust him to handle things." Taking the waist off the hanger she put it on, talking as she buttoned up. "He told me to write long letters about how wonderful everything is, and that by the time I get home for school in the fall, Momma will have realized Daddy was right to let me have my last summer as a cowgirl."

"Right," Minnie said. "I'm sure that's exactly what will happen." She began to make up the bed. "Just about the same time Diamond sprouts wings and flies you into the arena for a performance."

"I have enough to be nervous about today without worrying about Momma," Irma stuffed her audition clothes and boots into her carpetbag. "Daddy said I should trust him to handle things, and that's what I'm going to do." She inspected herself in the mirror. "How bad could it be?"

Shep was in one of the canvas "barns" brushing down Diamond when Helen sauntered up.

"Hey, cowboy," she teased, "you keep brushing and pretty soon we'll be able to use that gray coat as a mirror. What's going on with you, anyway? Dora said you shoveled breakfast in and sprinted out of the dining tent like you were trying to catch a fast moving train."

Shep patted Diamond's broad back. "Just sprucing him up a little." When he ran his hand down a foreleg, Diamond picked up his foot. Hoof pick in hand, Shep bent to grasp the hoof, balanced it on his knee, and went to work.

"You goin' to church this morning?"

Shep shook his head. "Thought I'd polish her saddle a little after I finish with Diamond. Monte pulled it out a while ago, and it's real beat up. Stiff. Could use a good going over."

"You know," Helen said, "a shiny saddle isn't going to win your girl a spot."

"She's not 'my girl.' " Shep checked Diamond's other feet. Helen wasn't leaving. "You need something?"

"No, but I think you might."

"What d'ya think I need?"

"A listening ear," Helen looked up at him. "Come on. Remember me? The sister you never had?" She punched him in the shoulder. "I know a lovesick cowboy when I see one, Shepherd. So tell me about it. You been writing her?"

Shep shrugged as he reached for a body brush. "Nothing to write about."

Grabbing another brush, Helen began working the other side of the horse. "I know you may not remember this, but from time to time I've been known to have feminine emotions. So you can believe me when I tell you that two weeks can be a very long time to a girl. And if you ask me—which I realize you haven't—that little gal was a mite standoffish on Friday. And I know that bothered you. So what I'm saying is, if you haven't written her, that's probably why."

"If I wrote Irma, her momma would have a fit." While they worked, Shep told Helen about the incident with Blaze. "Mrs. Friedrich blamed me for that—which I can understand. And then . . ." He went on to relate his taking Irma flowers and arriving at the house just in time for a party—to which he wasn't invited.

"Well, you just charmed the socks right off the grand dame," Helen teased. "What about *Mr.* Friedrich? What's he think about his daughter's feelings for you?" She held up one hand. "And don't argue with me about that, because the little gal has feelings for you even if you are too obtuse to see the signs."

"If Irma said she wanted to fly to the moon, her daddy would try to build a set of wings."

"So Daddy would have given permission for you to write," Helen said, nodding. "But you clearly didn't ask. Why not?"

"Because I didn't want to make trouble for anyone by causing even more conflict between Irma's parents." He paused. "I can't explain it. There's just an undercurrent of . . . something between them. I'm not sure they get along all that well."

"You've never let parents stop you from flirting before," Helen said. Understanding dawned on her face. "You're *serious* about that little gal."

Shep traded the body brush for a mane comb. "She's seriously young. And seriously spoiled."

"And seriously attracted to you," Helen countered as she went back to brushing the horse down. "And beautiful. And apparently quite the talented horsewoman."

"She's also willful and temperamental," Shep said.

Finishing with the brush, Helen walked to the box of grooming tools, took out a comb, and went to work on Diamond's tangled tail. "What one person calls 'willful' and 'temperamental' can also be described as 'determined' and 'passionate.' Sometimes it's all in the way you look at it."

"Maybe," Shep said. "But even if that's true, she's still young and spoiled. And the only thing I know can fix that is *time.*" He and Helen worked for a while in silence. Finally, Shep said, "She wants to become Liberty Belle. She doesn't need me complicating her life."

"That's a great name, by the way," Helen murmured. "I hope she can live up to it."

"So do I," Shep agreed, "because it'll break her heart if she can't."

Helen ducked beneath Diamond's neck and nudged Shep out of the way. "Get to work on that saddle, Shepherd. I'll take care of the mane and tail. Although it's the most tangled mess I've seen in a long time."

Shep reached for the saddle and, settling on an empty crate nearby, opened a tin of saddle soap and went to work. If Helen was right and Irma was upset with him for not writing, he was going to have to explain himself. But how did a man tell a girl he was giving her time to live her dream before moving in to sweep her off her feet? And what if she refused to be swept? Maybe those stolen kisses didn't mean anything. Maybe she'd only been playing the age-old game of cat and mouse, dancing the timeless dance of "boy meets girl, takes her flowers, steals a kiss." Pondering that, Shep realized there was a problem with that scenario. He wasn't playing a game.

"I didn't expect it to be so deserted," Irma said, as Monte led them past the Wild West ticket wagon and onto the grounds.

"Most of the performers are just now getting around to doing chores on the back lot," Monte explained. "Today's the one day we don't all have to get up while it's still dark." Once they were past the arena, he began pointing to various tents and describing what was what. "That big tent over there is the dining hall. And next to that is wardrobe tent, where everybody gets dressed before a performance. Those smaller tents are where the cowgirls bunk. Of course, once we start the road tour, we'll all just live on the train until we get to Staten Island. Shep said that will be a more permanent camp."

As they walked past the Indian camp with its open campfires and cooking pots, Irma said, "I can see why the Wild West is the talk of St. Louis. How many have ever seen that? Goodness, I *live* in the West and I've never seen a real Indian camp until now."

"Well," Monte said, "it's not *exactly* the same. The tepees are canvas now, thanks to Buffalo Bill's compatriots and their success at killing off the big herds."

Daddy spoke up. "You taking the Indians' side in that discussion?"

Monte shrugged. "Not taking sides. Just saying what is. Been talking to one of the braves some. Name of Macawi. It means 'generous.'"

"Is he?" Daddy asked.

"Well, he invited me to share supper the other night. I think he enjoyed having a white boy to tease. While we were eating, Macawi and a couple of the others began talking about the old ways—sort of hinting we might be eating dog meat stew." He grinned at his uncle. "You ever had that?"

Daddy nodded. "Had it and loved it. A very long time ago." He winked at Irma.

They ended up at a spot beneath a towering oak tree where a collection of crates and boxes provided seating. "Welcome to First Church of the Wild West," Monte said, and nodded toward a tall cowboy walking out of the dining tent. "That's our preacher, Sunday Joe Cooper."

Sunday Joe welcomed Monte's family with a strong handshake and a warm smile. "Just make yerselves ta home. We'll get started directly." He turned back to Monte. "No Ned today?"

Monte shook his head. "Afraid not," he said. "I'll tell him you asked after him."

"No need," the preacher smiled. "I'll catch up with him later today."

They sat halfway back from the front, and as people began to arrive, Irma realized she was watching for Shep. She hoped he went to church, although she didn't take time to think through exactly why that mattered. Leaning toward Minnie, she said, "I wonder if this will be anything like the revival meetings at home." She wondered what Momma, who had always called revivals undignified and kept her family at home, would think of this "church" of wranglers and roustabouts and even, it would seem, a few Indians.

When the church bells of St. Louis began to toll, Sunday Joe stood up and welcomed everyone. "My name is Sunday Joe Cooper. And if you don't already know, I ride broncs and buffalo to put clothes on my back and food in my mouth and speak for the Lord God Almighty to do what I can to help others along the way. I am grateful to William F. Cody for giving me the job that feeds my body and to the Lord God for reaching into a saloon in West Texas a few years back and dragging me into the kingdom. I kicked and I screamed but He didn't let go. And if you are the sort who doesn't want nothin' to do with religion, you have come to the right place, folks, because this here ain't about religion. It's about relatin'—first to the God who made us and then to one another." He paused. "And now we'll just bow our heads and say thanks.

"Lord," Sunday Joe said, "we want to say thank you that when Rocky Bear got throwed by that buffalo the other day he didn't get hurt bad. And we thank you for bringin' folks to see our Wild West show so's we can earn our keep on this earth. Thank you for givin' us friends and for blue skies and good horses. Thank you for the strength to shovel manure and the peace that comes from knowin' you. Thanks for not givin' up on us when we fail and for tellin' us about heaven. Thanks that most of us can read your book and help us to share it with them that can't read. Now we want to ask you to please watch over us all when we start to travel. Please keep the train on the rails, and if you'd see your way to give us sunshine and good crowds, why, we'd like that and we'd be sure to say thanks."

Once he'd said amen, Sunday Joe stepped aside to make way for what he called the Wild West Choir. Their singing was off-key, but no one seemed to mind. Irma didn't think much of the sound, but she had to admit they seemed sincere. One white-haired old woman even swiped away a tear while she was singing the chorus about "living for Him who died for me."

Once the singing was over, Sunday Joe pulled a small black testament out of his back pocket. "Now we will be reading from Matthew chapter 18, because what it says should help us all." He looked around the crowd. "Living like we do, we can't hardly keep from stompin' on each others' toes from time to time. And I've been upset a time or two with some of you this past week. So I reckon I'm not the only one who's been feelin' that way." He held up the testament. "And the Good Lord has somethin' to say to that." He read:

> "Then came Peter to him, and said, Lord, how oft shall my brother sin against me, and I forgive him? till seven times? Jesus saith unto him, I say not unto thee, until seven times: but, until seventy times seven."

The reading went on and on. It involved kings and servants and debts and paying back what was owed, and Irma's mind wandered. She looked around her at the setting, at the people in attendance. She thought about church at home and how different this was.

And then the preacher raised his voice—almost as if he knew some folks weren't listening very well—and Irma sat up straighter and made herself pay attention as he finished reading.

> "O thou wicked servant, I forgave thee all that debt, because thou desiredst me: Shouldest not thou also have had compassion on thy fellow servant, even as I had pity on thee? And his lord was wroth, and delivered him to the tormentors, till he should pay all that was due unto him. So likewise shall my heavenly Father do also unto you, if ye from your hearts forgive not every one his brother their trespasses."

Sunday Joe closed his testament and bowed his head for a minute before looking up at his congregation. "So here's the point of what we just heard: Before I hold a grudge against someone else, I got to think on what the Lord has forgiven me." Joe went on to talk about his life before he "saw the light" and "came to Christ." Irma had never heard a personal conversion story like Sunday Joe's.

"So that's it, folks," he concluded. "When you're aimin' to carry a grudge, just remember what Jesus done for you. He forgave it all." Joe held out his hand and swept it across the crowd. "All the past, all the present, and all the future, all in one speck of time. And all you got to do to get that forgiveness is ask for it. So let's all ponder what Jesus done for us before we harbor a grudge against the cowboy that borrowed our favorite bridle or the cowgirl that said somethin' unkind." Sunday Joe tucked his testament in his pocket as he said, "Forgiveness, folks. Seventy times seven. Amen." He smiled and nodded. "Now I'd like for you to just sit quiet and let the words of this song speak to you." From behind them came a clear soprano voice.

> "My life, my love I give to Thee, Thou Lamb of God, who died for me;
> Oh, may I ever faithful be, My Savior and my God!
> I'll live for Him who died for me, How happy then my life shall be!
> I'll live for Him who died for me, My Savior and my God!"

Sunday Joe motioned for everyone to sing along. Between Daddy's booming voice on one side and Minnie's nice alto on the other, Irma gave in and sang in spite of the fact she really didn't have any idea what "living for Jesus" meant. The concept made her uncomfortable. What if a person promised that and found out Jesus didn't approve of their plans? What if Jesus wanted a person to give up a dream?

Church at the Wild West took less than an hour. There was no offering taken, and once Sunday Joe had said his final amen, he hurried off instead of staying around to hear everyone tell him what a wonderful message he'd given. All in all, Irma would have said church was enjoyable except for two things: it was hard to sit still when her entire future was about to be decided just a short distance away and Shep never did come.

CHAPTER 11

❖⟫══⟩ ⟨══⟪❖

HOW BLESSED IS THE MAN . . .
IN WHOSE SPIRIT THERE IS NO DECEIT!

Psalm 32:2 NASB

Irma stood in the Wild West arena with Diamond at her side, gazing up at the empty stands. Empty, that is, except for a few dozen of the Wild West troupe scattered in small groups here and there. As she watched, Helen Keen sidled up to Shep. Did the woman have to follow him everywhere? *Don't be that way. She helped him get Diamond ready.* Irma touched the newly oiled and cleaned saddle. *And Shep went to a lot of trouble for you.*

Diamond tossed his head and began to paw the loose earth. Taking a deep breath, Irma murmured, "Okay, boy. Here we go." Gathering the reins, she reached for the saddle horn at the same time as she put her left foot in the stirrup. The saddle slipped and Diamond danced away.

She could imagine the few cowboys sitting up in the stands laughing at her. Anyone knew to check a girth strap before they mounted up. Horses had a way of sucking in air just before a rider tightened it and then letting it out so the strap wouldn't be so tight. "You

147

brat," Irma scolded as she righted the saddle and tightened the strap. Diamond turned his head and looked her over. He whickered and tossed his head.

"All right, all right," Irma answered. *"Now* we can get started." Taking a deep breath she mounted up for the second time. She tugged on Diamond's mane. "You do remember how we do this, right?" One velvety ear turned to listen to her. "All right, then." Irma gathered the reins and took a deep breath. "Let's get this over with."

"Ride 'em, cowgirl!"

It was Helen Keen hollering, and when Irma looked over to where she stood next to Shep, Helen waved. The woman was almost too nice to be real. The other two cowgirls Helen had introduced Irma to just yesterday weren't waving, though. Mabel Douglas looked positively sullen. Dora Spurgeon, who hadn't said more than two words when she showed Irma where to change after church, wasn't even watching. She was talking to Monte. Ned Bishop had ambled up just as everyone headed for the arena. He'd wished her luck. The way he'd said it made Irma think he was just being polite. No way did he think she had a chance of being part of the Wild West.

Irma closed her eyes. *Please, God. I know you and I don't have a real close relationship, but if you could help me out I'd be grateful.* It wasn't much of a prayer, but maybe it would make a difference. Preacher Joe seemed to think someone was listening when he prayed. It couldn't hurt to try.

She nudged Diamond into an easy lope and made a couple of laps of the arena, hoping to regain her composure. All she managed was to loosen her white-knuckled grasp on the reins a little. Movement high up in the stands caught her attention. A few wranglers were leaving. She couldn't blame them. What was there to see? Taking a deep breath, she looped the reins over the saddle horn, then gripped the horn with one hand and the cantle with the other to leverage her weight so she could balance on her knees. Diamond continued his steady lope around the perimeter of the arena, but when she moved to stand up, she lost her balance and almost did a nose dive into the dirt.

Great. Just great. I look more like Lula Belle the Clown than Liberty Belle the Star. Sweat was beginning to trickle down her back. She tried again. This time, with Diamond gliding along in a smooth lope, she managed an entire lap of the arena while standing. She stole a glance at Bill Cody. He wasn't even watching. In fact, he was talking to Daddy. Almost as if he was bored. And why shouldn't he be? Helen Keen and Dora Spurgeon could both ride standing up.

Taking her seat again she jerked Monte's hat off her head and sent it flying. It soared halfway across the arena before settling. Irma pressured Diamond with her knee just as they rounded the narrow end of the horseshoe-shaped arena. In answer to the signal, Diamond executed a flying change of lead and moved into a gallop. Horse and rider charged past the hat, and at the last possible second Irma took one foot out of the stirrup and swooped down to pick up the hat. Guiding Diamond toward the edge of the arena, she tossed the hat at Monte and raced away. Pulling both feet out of the stirrups, she slid behind the saddle and stretched out prone before holding both arms out like a bird soaring around the arena.

Regaining her normal seat, Irma grasped the saddle horn with both hands and dropped to the ground, springing back into the saddle the instant both feet landed in the dirt. When she repeated the move on Diamond's offside, someone let out a "yee-haw." Irma felt a surge of confidence. It was a good move, and none of the cowgirls had done it in yesterday's performances. Feeling more sure of herself, Irma decided to repeat the trick, but this time she lost her grip on the saddle horn and when her feet touched the ground she was left without a horse. Diamond was halfway down the length of the arena before he realized he no longer had a rider and stopped, looking back as if to say, "What happened to you?"

Laughter broke out in the smattering of spectators. Her face red from a combination of physical exertion and embarrassment, Irma ran to catch up with Diamond and climbed back aboard. She repeated the trick to show everyone she could do it, but when she tried to execute a handstand moments later, a combination of fatigue and sweaty palms sent her scrambling to keep from falling. After that, everything she tried either didn't work at all or had to be adjusted. She tried to cover up her mistakes but doubted anyone was really fooled.

By the time she had gone through every trick she knew twice to prove she could do them without falling, her sore ribs were complaining and Monte's borrowed shirt was damp with perspiration. Tempted to forego her flying dismount, she told herself it was no time to hold back. And so she hollered "go-go-go" and kicked Diamond into a gallop, hoping the horse remembered what the short burst of sounds signaled. She had just gone into a handstand when Diamond gave a little buck and stopped in his tracks. The move was designed to make it look like Diamond had balked and thrown her over his head. What really happened was the little buck created just enough extra thrust for Irma to be thrown high enough into the air so she could theoretically tuck in midair and still have time to end up on her feet. Theoretically. This time, there was no tuck. This time, Irma was going to land headfirst. By putting her hands above her head she broke the impact and managed a somersault. Instantly, she sprang to her feet and pretended to wave to an imaginary crowd. *Stupid. There's no crowd. And if there was, they wouldn't be applauding. Stupid, stupid girl.*

Ducking her head, Irma walked to where Diamond waited, his nostrils flared, his sides heaving. She leaned close and patted his neck. "I messed up," she said, "but you—you were perfect." It was all she could do not to burst into tears.

"I'll see to Diamond for you," Shep said, and reached for the horse's reins. He put his hand on Irma's shoulder. "Bill and Nate want to see you right away—over in the office by the entrance."

Irma looked toward where Cody and Salsbury and Daddy had been standing to watch her routine. The Wild West partners were in what appeared to be a heated conversation with Daddy. While she watched, the men shook hands. With barely a nod in Irma's direction, Cody and Salsbury left. Daddy took off his hat and ran his hand over his mustache and goatee—a gesture of his that always telegraphed a nervous state of mind.

Irma looked down, scraping at the arena dirt with the toe of her right boot, while she tried not to cry. She wished everything around her and Shep would just fall away so she could lean into him and be comforted.

"It wasn't so bad," Shep said. Maybe he read her mind, because he put one arm around her and gave her a quick, half hug followed by a friendly little shake—the kind of thing Monte would have done if Shep hadn't beat him to it. "Come on, now," he teased. "Chin up. Those two showmen know how hard it is to do those tricks you tried."

"*Tried*," Irma muttered. "That's a nice way to put it."

"And," Shep continued as Monte and Minnie and Helen Keen walked up, "they know you haven't had a chance to practice much. It'll be all right, Belle. You'll see."

Was he trying to cheer her up or convince himself? Irma sighed and said nothing. She was relieved when Ned, Dora, and Mabel mumbled "good job" and then excused themselves to do chores.

"I know you're thinking about all the mistakes," Miss Keen said, "but, honey, it wasn't that bad. You showed you're a born performer out there. You *kept going*. And honey, city folks wouldn't have known the difference. They're gonna love Liberty Belle." She nudged Shep. "Tell her, Shepherd. You know I'm right."

Shep smiled and agreed. Irma didn't think he really meant it. When Monte and Minnie offered similar comments, she shrugged. Her voice wobbled as she said, "At least I tried."

She swiped a tear away. "But no matter what you all say, we all know I messed up. And not just once but over and over again."

Thankfully, Daddy came to the rescue before her tears erupted in earnest. "Bill's got an appointment with a newspaperman in a few minutes. We've got to get over to the Wild West offices right away." Taking Irma's arm, he led her away.

It was the longest walk of her life. Worse even than the walk from the corral at Uncle Charlie's to the back porch that day when Momma fainted and Daddy was so angry.

"Calm down, sweetheart," Daddy said halfway to the office. "I can feel your hand trembling." He covered her hand with his own as they walked along.

Irma sighed. "Well, at least I'll be out of my misery sooner rather than later."

Daddy paused just long enough to glance down at her. "For heaven's sake, child. It's *your* dream. Don't tell me that after all the trouble I've gone to you're going to just give it up without a fight."

"I came, I fought . . . I lost."

"You haven't lost yet," Daddy snapped. He stopped in his tracks and, turning toward her, gripped both her forearms with his hands. "Dreams do not come true for those who give up. Do you really think you can win a spot with this attitude? Our friendship with the Cody family may have been a factor in this audition, but I can assure you that no amount of friendship with *anyone* is going to get Liberty Belle into the Wild West arena. Everyone knows you weren't at your best just now. I refuse to believe that means only one thing." He frowned. "Why, if I'd had this attitude when I first arrived in Nebraska—" He gave her a little shake. "Friedrichs do not wave white flags, Irmagard." He turned her back toward the offices. "Now, walk into that office and convince Bill Cody and Nate Salsbury that they'd be fools to turn you down based on half a performance on a Sunday afternoon when neither you nor your horse are in anything approaching prime condition."

Irma began to talk the second she and Daddy sat down opposite
Bill Cody and Nate Salsbury. "I know what you just saw was a mess.
It wasn't worthy of the Wild West. But if you'll give me a chance—if
you'll let me stay—I'll work harder than anyone. I'll give you your
money's worth and then some. You won't regret it. I promise."

When Mr. Salsbury seemed about to speak, Irma pressed on. She
pleaded with Cody. "You don't know what it's like for a girl like me.
My momma wants a daughter like yours—a beautiful accomplished
lady. But I've never wanted that. Never ever. And here—for the first
time in my whole life—I'm around dozens of people who don't think
it's strange for a girl to prefer corrals to drawing rooms and stables to
afternoon tea. You can't send me back home. You just can't."

Irma stopped abruptly. How had Momma gotten all tangled up
in what she was saying? Men like Bill Cody and Nate Salsbury didn't
care about some girl's whining about being misunderstood. Here she
had a last chance and she'd bumbled it.

It seemed to take years for Cody to say anything at all. Finally,
he spoke up. "My dear girl, who said anything about sending you
home?"

Irma looked at him in disbelief. "You . . . you aren't sending me
away?"

"Certainly not." Cody nodded at Mr. Salsbury.

Salsbury spoke up. "How much do you know about the city of
New York, Miss Friedrich?"

"Only what Monte's told me. That the Wild West arrives in
June and will be there for some weeks."

Salsbury nodded. "What Monte does not know is that we are in
negotiations right now to remain in New York for an unprecedented
winter performance—indoors—at a venue called Madison Square
Garden." He continued, "The last time I was in New York, I took the
ferry across from the city to Staten Island to check on the progress of

track we're having built to transport our audience from the ferry landing to the Wild West grounds. Now the ferry passes near Bledsoe's Island, soon to be graced by a very significant monument. Have you heard anything about that monument, Miss Friedrich?"

Daddy spoke up. "I have. In fact, now that you mention it, I believe Mrs. Friedrich and I saw an exhibit intended to raise support for that project at the Centennial Exhibition in Philadelphia ten years ago. Something about celebrating the friendship between France and the United States?"

Salsbury nodded. "Exactly. It's over three hundred feet high. Named 'Liberty Enlightening the World,' the figure of a woman holding high a lighted torch. They expect the light to be visible from fifty miles at sea."

"That's what we saw at the Centennial," Daddy said. "The hand and the torch. Impressive."

"Indeed," Salsbury said. "The dedication ceremony is sure to be a historic occasion. President Cleveland himself is giving the official acceptance speech. There will of course be a parade. And fireworks." Salsbury smiled at Irma. "People will be telling their grandchildren about that day, Miss Friedrich."

"I expect so." Irma agreed. *What did any of this have to do with her?*

"Which brings us to the topic of Liberty Belle," Cody said, folding his hands atop the desk and leaning forward, "who we see as the perfect Wild West contribution to a momentous event in American history." He smiled. "Thanks to you, Irmagard, the Wild West can have a living, breathing Liberty, not only to perform on Staten Island while the statue goes up on Bledsoe's Island nearby, but also to ride in the parade on the day the Statue of Liberty is dedicated." He winked at Irma and sat back. "Thanks to Liberty Belle, every single person who witnesses that parade will remember the Wild West." He smiled. "They'll come in droves, my dear." He nodded at Daddy and then looked back to Irma. "It's really perfect for us. And hopefully, acceptable to you."

"You're . . . you're *hiring* me? After—" Irma motioned toward the arena. "After that pathetic excuse for an audition?"

"It wasn't pathetic," Cody said. "It was . . . imperfect. You were out of practice."

Mr. Salsbury chimed in. "But you never gave up. You covered your mistakes. And you kept that dazzling smile on your lovely face." He nodded. "You're a born performer, Miss Friedrich."

"I-I am?"

"You are," Cody nodded as he stood up. "And now if you will excuse me, I try never to keep a journalist waiting." He shook Daddy's hand and then stepped out from behind the desk. "My partner has the contract for you both to look over." He glanced at Daddy. "I don't want anyone to question whether or not we are treating her fairly," he said. "*Anyone.*"

He was talking about Momma, of course. Irma glanced at Daddy, who nodded and said something about being grateful that Louisa Cody and Willa were friends.

"You can assure Mrs. Friedrich that we will take very good care of her daughter," Cody promised. "If it will comfort rather than upset her by encouraging imagined tragic scenarios, you might mention that we'll have our own physician on staff throughout the tour. Dr. Miller comes highly recommended."

Salsbury spoke up. "And he's ordered supplies enough to stock a small hospital."

Cody agreed before adding, "And should she decide to visit the Wild West, be certain to let us know so we can make proper arrangements." He turned to Irma. "Now you, my dear, must promise that you will work very hard to perfect moves worthy of Liberty Belle, both for her debut this summer and in the October parade."

"I will," Irma croaked. "I promise." She wasn't sure which had given her a bigger knot in her stomach, failing in the audition or succeeding in getting hired for . . . *October?! But*—

"And I have one more request," Cody said.

"Whatever you say, sir," Irma replied. *Maybe she misunderstood about October.*

Cody laughed and nodded to where his partner stood, contract in hand. "If only we could get everyone else on our staff to learn that phrase." He looked at Daddy. "Irmagard Friedrich is a perfectly fine name for a girl from North Platte. But I think we all agree that Liberty Belle is a better one for the Wild West. With both your permissions, that's how we'll introduce our new ranchera to the rest of the troupe."

"As my daughter so eloquently stated just now," Daddy said, with a little nod, "whatever you say."

"Well then"—Cody swept his hat off his head and gave an elegant bow—"welcome to the Wild West, Miss Belle."

"Did he say *October?*" Irma asked as soon as Bill Cody was gone.

"He did," Mr. Salsbury replied. "I believe the exact date is October 26. Which is why it's so perfect for Liberty Belle to be part of that event. We open in Madison Square Garden in November."

Irma stared at her father. "But I can't still be here in *October.*"

Salsbury frowned. "I beg your pardon?"

Daddy cleared his throat. "If you'll excuse my daughter and me for a few moments, Nate—" He reached for the contract.

Salsbury handed it over. "Of course." He paused. "I need to speak to a few people about where we'll house our new performer." He looked at Daddy. "We do *have* a new performer?"

"You do," Daddy said. "Irma and I just need to have a little talk is all. She was hoping to be hired on for the summer. This new information—" He cleared his throat. "We just need a few minutes."

As soon as Salsbury was gone, Daddy laid the contract before

Irma and pointed to the signature line. "Trust me," he said. When
Irma hesitated, he said, "Or shall I telegraph your mother in Chicago
and ask her permission? I could do that. If you want me to."

"She'd say no." Irma groaned with frustration "She'd *scream* no."
She took a deep breath. "You really did have me convinced that it
would be all right—that Momma would eventually come around. But
that was when I was only going to be gone for the summer. This—"
She gestured at the contract. "This is another animal entirely."

Daddy nodded agreement. "Indeed it is. But look at this way.
Why did Momma want you to go to Brownell? *Education.* What better education could you have than to travel and meet people? And I
don't mean the other performers. Why, you've already met the mayor
of St. Louis. If you make yourself a student of the people you meet
and the places you visit, you could end up with an education that the
best schools in the country could not rival. If you remain with the
Wild West beyond this first season, you'll be going to *Europe* next
year. Nate told me—in confidence, of course— that the negotiations
are nearly finished. I only know about it because the bank is going
to help with the financing." He smiled. "Now, what parent would
stand in the way of their child meeting the Queen?"

"I hardly think I'd meet the Queen."

"Who's to say?" Daddy shrugged. "Either way, it looks to me
like being with the Wild West will provide you life experience that
will trump anything Brownell Hall could offer." He reached for her
hand and squeezed it. "Sign the contract, Irma. Your momma loves
you. When you're settled in New York, I'll bring her for a visit. By
then you'll be a well-traveled and mature young woman who will, I
am certain, take great pains to treat her mother to a tour of the city
of New York that will impress even her."

Still doubting, Irma looked down and began to read through the
contract that stated Liberty Belle agreed to perform twice a day, six
days a week "as soon as competence is demonstrated." She would be
paid thirty dollars a month. Three meals a day and lodging would be

provided. Additional responsibilities and performing wardrobe were "to be arranged." She was required to keep herself and her equipment and costumes clean. She had to be "orderly, quiet, and gentlemanly." Irma forced a laugh at that last requirement before reading, *"Each cast member is allowed one dressing trunk 18 inches by 18 inches by 24 inches and one personal trunk the same size, but only if absolutely necessary."* Her trunk was much larger than that.

"We'll get a smaller one as soon as the stores open Monday morning," Daddy said as soon as Irma read him the rule.

She had just finished reading the front page when Mr. Salsbury returned and asked, "Do you have any questions before you sign?"

Irma took a deep breath. She glanced at Daddy again. When it came right down to it, she realized there was no way she was going to walk away from this. And Momma would just have to learn to accept it. Or not. She picked up the fountain pen even as she asked Mr. Salsbury about her additional responsibilities and wardrobe.

"Ma Clemmons is our wardrobe mistress, and I think she'll be the one to see on both counts. As you get to know her and her staff better, you can begin to talk about a costume for Liberty Belle. For obvious reasons we'll want you thinking in terms of red, white, and blue. And I'll want to approve the final design before Ma Clemmons makes it. I just talked to her about you, and she's thrilled with the idea of having more help. If you can sew, that's where you'll be working."

Irma grimaced. "Can't I work with the stock?"

"You'll like Ma Clemmons, and working in wardrobe will also give you the opportunity to get to know some of the other girls."

"I said I'd work hard if you'd give me a chance. I meant it." *Of course I didn't think I'd be threading needles.* She squelched the inner voice and went back to reading while Mr. Salsbury gave his assurance about taking good care of Irma, and Daddy said Momma would especially appreciate Nate's promise. Irma very much doubted Momma would appreciate anything about this adventure, but she said nothing. She had made up her mind and there was no going back now.

"I just now talked with Miss Keen," Salsbury said, "and she's agreeable to sharing quarters with you. So if you have no questions and that's agreeable to you . . ." He pointed to the signature line at the bottom of the second page.

Irma hesitated when she read the last few lines of the contract. "It says I have to have my own horse." She glanced at Daddy.

"And you do," he said.

"I do?"

"What do you think the three of us were talking about over at the arena just now?" Daddy smiled. "Diamond belongs to you now—or should I say to Liberty Belle."

Irma jumped up and hugged him. She began to cry happy tears. Finally, she sat back down and signed her first Wild West contract.

Liberty Belle.

CHAPTER 12

You husbands, in the same way, live with your
wives in an understanding way . . .

1 Peter 3:7 NASB

Chicago taught Willa shocking things about herself. She, who had grown up reveling in the hustle and bustle of the tens of thousands of people living in her home city of Cleveland, found the endless traffic in the streets of Chicago positively unnerving. Crowded walkways and department stores that had once energized and excited her now induced something approaching claustrophobia. The noise in the streets below her hotel room window kept her awake. She missed the way people on the street at home always smiled and said hello. She missed Ella Jane's sense of humor and Irmagard's laughter. Staring at the far horizon across Lake Michigan made her homesick for the unobstructed view from her front porch. The aroma of cigar smoke that wafted out into the hall from the "gentleman's club" at the hotel reminded her of Otto. When she saw any young woman with red hair, Willa struggled most of that night worrying about Irmagard. Was she truly all right? Had Minnie come to stay? Would Otto take their daughter's depression seriously? When he failed to answer her first telegram, Willa worried aloud to Louisa. Together they agreed that no answer wasn't necessarily an indication of trouble. It could be anything. Certainly if there were a problem, Otto would have contacted her at once. But for all her logic, Willa finally gave in to the unshakeable longing for home.

"I'm so sorry," she said over an elegant supper with Louisa Cody, "but I simply cannot shake this *feeling* that I need to go home."

Louisa waved her hand in the air. "I understand your concerns completely. Just don't forget to mention Manitou Springs to Mr. Friedrich. It's lovely there in late July, and wouldn't it be nice to escape the heat in North Platte?"

It would, Willa agreed, but that evening as she lay in bed imagining surprising Otto and Irmagard with an early homecoming, Willa was not so certain she would go to Manitou Springs after all. It was an amazing thing to admit, even to herself, but after all these years, the prairie was *home*.

———

"Yee-haw, cowgirl!" Helen Keen called out as Irma and Daddy ducked out of the Wild West office. She was walking along with arms linked with Monte and Shep. As the trio approached, Miss Keen called out "Do-si-do," and both Irma and Daddy were swept into a two-step victory dance that ended with everyone laughing and Irma a little breathless because Shep had lifted her off the ground with a fierce hug as the moment of silliness ended.

Daddy beamed at them all and invited everyone to the hotel for an early supper, after which he and the men returned to the Wild West grounds, leaving Miss Keen behind to advise Irma on how to pack.

"You can have my trunk," Minnie offered as they headed upstairs to their room. "It's smaller than yours—probably about perfect." As she unlocked the hotel room door she teased, "I don't know if I'll ever learn to call you Belle." She led the way into the hotel room.

"Oh, I'll still be Irma at home," Irma said.

"Not for long," Minnie disagreed. "Orrin Knox is going to *love* hearing about this. Remember he wanted to do a feature on Monte? I bet it won't be long at all before he shows up at a performance to interview Liberty Belle." She smiled. "You could end up on the front page of the *Register*."

Irma crossed the room and opened the drapes. "Since you brought his name up, may I suggest that you pay a visit to Mr. Knox as soon as you get back to North Platte? If he really plans to do a series on Nebraskans in the Wild West, he'll be in your debt for telling him about Liberty Belle." She worked her eyebrows up and down and teased, "And you could collect on that debt in any number of ways."

Miss Keen laughed. "Sounds like you two are plotting to rope someone."

"Don't listen to her," Minnie said. "She doesn't know what she's talking about."

"Just tell me you'll do it," Irma said.

Minnie didn't answer. Instead, she slid her trunk into the middle of the room. "Isn't this about the right size?"

Miss Keen nodded. "It's perfect."

"Then let's get started outfitting my friend *Belle*." Minnie began to empty her trunk.

It didn't take Miss Keen long to look Irma's clothing over and say, "I hate to tell you this, but I don't see a thing that's gonna be of much use on tour." She reached for a hanger and held up a waist. "Here, for example. The fabric's just too flimsy. It'll never hold up." She looked at the rest of the dresses, shaking her head. "They're beautiful. They just aren't much use."

"What about for suppers in town?" Minnie asked.

"There honestly isn't much time for any of that for us lowly performers," Miss Keen replied and looked at Irma. "I only came along Friday night because the Shepherd wanted me to meet you. But even on the rare occasion when we *do* get invited to 'dine with the stars,' we're supposed to keep our western duds on."

"I assumed you just didn't have time to change after the show," Irma said.

"Doesn't it bother you the way people stare?" Minnie asked.

Miss Keen shrugged. "Doesn't matter if it bothers us or not. It's free advertising for the Wild West if we wear our show duds around town."

"Well," Irma said, taking the waist out of Miss Keen's hand and hanging it up again. "I guess that simplifies packing." She gathered a few toiletries, her brush and comb, hairpins and jewelry, and laid them in Minnie's trunk tray. With the addition of two nightgowns and her unmentionables, she was finished.

"We'll go see Ma Clemmons first thing when we get back," Miss Keen said. "She'll know what to do."

"I thought everyone had the day off on Sunday."

"Oh, everyone does, but Ma and Pa Clemmons sorta hold court on Sunday evenin' for anybody needing a listening ear. I guess you could say they're everyone's honorary grandparents." She smiled. "Since packing's finished, how'd you two feel about headin' back over and taking a real tour of the back lot before we talk to Ma?" She glanced at Irma. "You might as well get started settling in."

Just inside the gate, Miss Keen motioned toward the deserted midway. "I assume you got a good look at the concessions and the souvenir stands yesterday?" Irma and Minnie nodded. "All right, then." She led the way across the grassy area just south of the arena and past the tent where Liberty Belle had signed her contract. She pointed toward a roped-off shop. "It takes four blacksmiths to keep all the horses shod and machinery repaired," she said before leading the way toward the stables and corrals. "The buffalo are in the opposite corner at the far end of the midway," she explained. *"Everyone* wants to see the buffalo."

"And the elk?" Minnie chimed in.

"And the elk," Miss Keen agreed. "Probably the only thing that attracts more attention than the buffalo and the elk is the Indians." She nodded toward the Indian camp, where half a dozen women were gathered outside one tepee. "Last year we had Sitting Bull with us. This year it's American Horse and Rocky Bear."

She pointed toward the opposite side of the grounds at the largest tent in sight. "That's wardrobe. We'll head there later. This way for now." Miss Keen named names as they walked past a long row of tents, most of them with flaps closed because the occupants were away from the grounds enjoying their day off. "Bill Cody, Nate Salsbury, Shep Sterling, Mr. & Mrs. Gable"—she leaned close—"also known as Annie Oakley and Frank." She continued. "Lillian Smith . . . and various owners and management." She indicated the rest of the long row with one sweep of the hand. "Important, but you don't need a thousand names swimming around in your head right now. You'll meet them all soon enough."

At the far end of the row of larger tents, they turned left and stopped in front of two smaller tents pitched away from the others. "Dora and Mabel are in this one—they do the cowgirl race in the performance," Miss Keen explained as she looked toward the corrals. "I thought we might catch up with them." She turned back around and said to Irma, "You'll like Dora. Oh wait, you've already met her. She helped you get changed for the audition."

"She showed me *where* to change," Irma said. "She didn't say two words to me."

"Well, Dora's shy," Miss Keen said. "But you'll like her. She's very sweet. And this," she said, as she lifted the flap on the other tent and motioned Irma and Minnie inside, "will be our home sweet home for the next few nights—and again when we get to New York in a few weeks." She leaned close and teased, "As long as you don't snore, that is."

The tent was furnished with two beds and a table. It was smaller than Irma's room at home. When Minnie's trunk arrived, there would barely be room to move.

Miss Keen pointed to the cot made up with a feather bed and several quilts. "That's mine." She pointed to the empty cot. "This is yours. And don't worry, one of the porters will see that your bed's all made up before tomorrow night." She shrugged. "I know it seems really crowded, but the fact is, we work about sixteen hours a day, and by the time you get back here most nights you'll be asleep almost before your head hits the pillow." They went back outside and continued the tour. "Stay away from that," Miss Keen said, pointing to what she said was the ammunition wagon. "The burly guy with the blond moustache is Bud Kramer. He has absolutely no sense of humor, and I personally give him a very wide berth." She kept walking.

"What's he do?"

"What *doesn't* he do? He's in charge of all the guns and ammunition. Repairing, cleaning, loading the blanks, loading Bill's cartridges. And Bud makes all the glass balls for Bill, Miss Smith, and Annie." Miss Keen paused. "Which reminds me, we tend to be informal around here, so from now on, *please* stop calling me 'Miss Keen.' Miss Oakley will likely order you to call her Annie the second she realizes you've been promoted from spectator to troupe member. But there is an exception to this rule. *Never* call Miss Smith anything but just that. *Miss Smith.*"

Irma nodded. "Got it, *Helen.*"

"About time," Helen said with a nod. "*Belle.*"

As the trio walked toward the wardrobe tent, they passed another corral of sorts to one side of the backdrop where the covered wagons, the Deadwood coach, and various other props were stored behind ropes intended to keep the public from climbing on and around the equipment. "It may look haphazard," Helen said, "but believe me it's not. Dooley Parker is in charge of all that, and there's a place for everything and everything is in its place." She chortled. "And you do *not* want to encounter the wrath of Dooley Parker."

"Sounds like you learned that the hard way," Irma said.

Helen cleared her throat. "That," she said, "is a story that must be earned."

———

"You aren't having second thoughts, are you?" Minnie's expression was concerned as she and Irma settled in for their last night in the hotel. "You seem awful quiet."

Irma slid between the covers with a sigh. "I'm just distracted. Wondering what Daddy was up to while we were with Helen."

"Right," Minnie teased and nudged her playfully. "With not one thought to where Shep Sterling made off to."

"Guess I know the answer to that," Irma said. "Both he and Monte had to get ready for tomorrow." She paused, then murmured, "It's a lot of work, being part of that troupe."

Minnie propped herself up on one elbow and looked over at Irma. "You're going to be great, Belle. You've got nothing to be worried about."

Irma sighed. "I'm not worried—exactly." She paused, then decided to say it. "Truth be told, Minnie, I'm sorta scared."

"Scared? Of what?"

"I know Monte says they're just like family, but they aren't a family to me. Not yet. The grounds were practically deserted today. And the few people we saw were in no mood to chat."

"Mr. and Mrs. Clemmons *both* gave you a hug. Helen is as nice as they come. And you'll have Monte for family. Probably Shep Sterling, too—if you'll have him." She winked.

Irma didn't want to talk about Shep tonight. Her feelings about him were confused. Her heart skipped a beat every time she saw him, and when he smiled at her—a girl could almost forget her determination to be a Wild West star when a man smiled at her that way. Which was part of what was confusing her. Here she was making speeches to Momma about not wanting to get married, and meanwhile she was daydreaming about kisses. How was she going to be around Shep day in and day out and keep her head clear about what she really wanted in life?

Minnie lay back and stared up at the ceiling. "I'm really, really, really going to miss you. You'd better write."

"I will."

"Ma and Pa and everyone are going to be so proud. And Aunt Willa's going to be proud, too, someday. You may not believe it now, but I just know everything's going to be all right."

"I hope you're right," Irma said. "But I have my doubts."

"You know what my ma says about your momma?"

"What's she say?"

Minnie mimicked her mother's voice. "Your Aunt Willa is a complex woman, but underneath she's pure gold."

"Aunt Laura says that?"

"She does."

"Hmmm." Irma turned on her side and closed her eyes, but a torrent of conflicting emotions kept her awake long after Minnie started to snore.

———

Early Monday morning, Daddy hefted Minnie's trunk into place along the back wall of the tent Belle would share with Helen Keen. "Fits just fine," he said.

Irma nodded. "It does."

Helen ducked inside and set a pile of faded clothing on Irma's cot. "Ma Clemmons pulled these out of a mending basket after we left last night. She said to give you them for now and have you check in with her after the noon performance starts. By then she'll have some newer duds for you to try out."

Irma inspected a faded split skirt. "Whose are these?"

"Ma said Mabel's likely forgotten about them—Mabel being something of a clothes horse. There's a button needs sewing on, and the seat's about to give out, but they'll sure fit better than Monte's duds."

"I'll get some new boots ordered for you as soon as I get back to North Platte," Daddy said. He pulled out his money clip and counted off several bills. "They keep back the first two weeks' pay—remember?" He handed the money over. "I don't want you doing without."

Helen cleared her throat. "I don't know if you saw it," she said to Daddy, "but there's what we call a pie car over by the dining tent. Serves as a kind of company store." She glanced at Irma. "Carries real nice writing paper and other supplies, so you can write home. *Often.*" She grinned and nodded at Daddy. "Now, if y'all will excuse me, I need to get over to the stables and start getting my pony ready for the performance." She patted Daddy on the arm. "She'll be all right, Mr. Friedrich. Don't you worry. I'll take good care of her." She turned to Irma. "If I was you, I'd separate that wad of bills and tuck 'em in a couple of places folks wouldn't be so likely to look. But wait until I'm outta here 'cause I don't want to know where you keep your stash." She extended a hand to Minnie. "It'll be a good day for me when our trails cross again." With a reminder to Irma to get changed and meet her at the stables, Helen left.

Irma and Minnie hugged. Daddy swept her into his arms, holding her so tight she could scarcely breathe. When he finally let go, he looked down at her and said, "The stage is set, sweetheart. You've earned your spot. Now step into that spotlight you've always wanted and live your dream."

Irma stood at the entrance to her tent and watched until Minnie and Daddy disappeared into the growing crowd of Wild West spectators roaming the back lot. Once they were out of sight she stepped back inside the tent and muttered, "Welcome home, Liberty Belle." She lowered the flap so she could change. And burst into tears.

———

Hiring a boy to round up her trunks and bring them to the house, Willa set out on foot, reveling in the fresh air and the abundance of spring wild flowers blooming along the way. Her time with Louisa Cody had done more than reveal Willa's attachment to her adopted state. Louisa Cody was a woman on the cusp of divorce, and while Willa could understand her friend's feelings better than many women, she could also be thankful that Otto's wanderings had never been public knowledge and were now part of a private and distant past. The Friedrichs had faced their demons, fought their battles, and fallen in love all over again. Just thinking about it set Willa to counting her blessings. She quickened her pace. Oh, it was wonderful to be back home. In fact, as soon as she freshened up and said hello to the girls, she was going to surprise Otto at the bank.

Ella Jane answered the door. One look at Willa and the girl's face paled. Willa's heart skipped a beat. What was wrong? She brushed past Ella Jane, pausing in the hall to listen for voices before going in search of Irmagard and Minnie. She circled the main floor, going first through the dining room, then through the swinging door into the kitchen and onto the back porch before hurrying back up the hall and into the entryway. "Irmagard," she called up the stairs. "Minnie. I've come home."

They must have gone to the ranch. She should have known. Otto's business had taken increasing amounts of his time, and however well intentioned he'd been about helping, he'd obviously sent the girls to the ranch. Ah, well. Perhaps that was for the best after all. While Willa thought aloud, Ella Jane listened, nodding her head in what Willa assumed to be agreement.

"I'm going upstairs to freshen up and then over to the bank to surprise my husband," she said. "When Johnny Dolan arrives with my trunks, can you see to them for me?"

"Yes, ma'am," Ella Jane said, bobbing her head as she agreed. "Of course."

"And if Otto and I drive out to the ranch to see the girls, will that cause a problem with whatever you'd planned for supper?"

"No'm," Ella Jane shook her head. "Fact is, Mr. Friedrich hasn't been eating at home. He's been having supper at the hotel. Without Minnie and Miss Friedrich here, he just said it was too lonely."

Willa's heart warmed to the notion that Otto missed the women in his life so much he'd taken to eating at the hotel instead of alone at the dining table. The dear man. "Well, that's fine, then. Thank you." A few minutes later, as she headed out the door, Willa circled back to Otto's home office, scooped up the day's mail, and dropping it in her bag, set out for the bank.

CHAPTER 13

Instead of smiling and jumping up to give her a hug, Otto just sat there staring. The only emotion he seemed to be feeling was disappointment. It was downright hurtful.

"Is everything all right?" he sputtered. "You and Louisa haven't had a spat, I hope?"

"Good heavens no," Willa said. "I-I missed you. I missed Irmagard." She laughed at herself. "Good heavens, Otto, I even missed *North Platte*, if you can imagine that." She rubbed her arms and gave a little shiver. "All that traffic and noise in Chicago. All those people. And the longer I was there, the more I wondered about Irmagard."

"I told you I would see to Irmagard," he groused.

Was he angry? Or defensive? "I know you did. But when you didn't answer my telegram—"

"What telegram?" He almost barked it. "I didn't receive any telegram."

"I wired you a few days ago to see if everything was all right. And when you didn't answer, I realized that what I really wanted was to be at home with my family. And—" she blinked back tears—"to be quite honest, I'm more than a little hurt that you haven't so much as seen fit to get up from behind that desk and give me a kiss."

He got up then. Came around the desk. Kissed her on the cheek. It wasn't what she'd hoped for. Doing her best to scold herself into adjusting her expectations, Willa gave him a little smile. "That's better," she said. "Ella Jane tells me—"

"You've been to the *house?*"

Now what did *that* tone of voice mean? "Well, of course I've been to the *house*. Johnny Dolan's delivering my trunks. I told Ella Jane that you and I would probably drive out to the ranch for supper tonight. We can, can't we? I'm not upset with you for letting the girls go out there. In fact, it was probably the best thing. But I'd like to see Irma. To see for myself that she's all right."

"Willa." As he said her name, Otto grasped her hands in his. Sitting down in one of the chairs that faced his desk, he pulled her into the other. "We need to talk."

Willa's mind raced from who might have died to who might have been injured and landed at Irmagard. Her heart pounding, she stared into Otto's gray eyes. She should have known something was wrong. Ella Jane had been acting so— "What is it? What aren't you telling me?" She clung to Otto's strong hands.

"Irma's fine, Willa. Better than fine, really." He looked away. Then, with a sigh, he began to explain. "I'm deeply sorry that you've cut your holiday short and come home to find out about it this way. I had . . . I had plans to meet the train next week. Plans to try and—" Swearing softly, he let go of her and stood up. He began to pace back and forth between the oak bookcases on one wall and the filing cabinets on the other. Back and forth, back and forth. Finally, he shoved his hands in his pockets, planted his feet, and said, "I took her and Minnie on a little trip while you were gone. To see Monte in the Wild West in St. Louis. One thing led to another. . . . Bill invited her to audition . . . and . . ."

Willa held up both hands to signal him to hush. He did. When she didn't speak, he came back to sit in the chair beside her. He reached for her, but she pulled away. Swiping his hand across his mustache and goatee, Otto waited. It was amazing how the noises from beyond the office door seemed to reverberate in the silent room. The door to the street opened and closed a few times. Tellers called out greetings. Boots clunked as customers made their way toward the tellers' windows. And still, Willa could not speak as her mind and heart reduced a thousand thoughts and emotions to one painful realization—given the opportunity to choose between Irmagard and his own wife, Otto chose . . . Irmagard.

"She's happy, Willa," Otto said. "If you could have seen her face. You should see the rules Bill has in place to protect the girls' reputations. They never leave the grounds without an escort. And their privacy is absolutely sacrosanct. Think of it, dear—the education. The travel. When I arranged for the audition, I made it clear she could only be gone for the summer. But then . . ." He swept his hand across his forehead. "They're going to *England* next year, Willa. Can you imagine? Our daughter could meet the Queen." He cleared his throat. "I just couldn't let anything stand in the way of that."

Willa swallowed. Why, she wondered, did any of it surprise her. Otto never denied Irmagard anything. Still, he'd never gone so completely against what Willa wanted. At least not in such an overt manner. *Dear God in heaven, help. Please. Help me. Help me now.* She could feel herself trembling. In a moment she would be in tears, and she must not cry. She stood up. He did, too—and reached for her.

She stepped back. "Don't," she said. "Just don't."

"I didn't want to hurt you. But Irmagard—"

But Irmagard. As if that justified everything. He was blathering on, but she wasn't listening. She needed to get away from Otto so she could calm down. She needed a place where the storm of emotions inside her could wear themselves out without threatening her carefully reconstructed relationship with her husband. She interrupted him. "We'll talk later." She headed for the door.

"Wait," Otto said. "Please—darling. Let me explain."

She stopped in midstride. Lifting her chin, she said, "I'm certain you have a thousand reasons why you believe what you've done is right." She clutched her bag and motioned him aside. "Now let me out. I want to go home. I need to think."

She could hear the relief in his voice as he said, "I'll see you at home, then." She stole a glance at him. He wasn't even looking at her. *He was relieved to be rid of her.* In fact, he'd already shifted his attention to the piles of papers waiting atop his desk. Willa exited the bank and walked home.

"I didn't know what he was up to, ma'am," Ella Jane called after her as Willa headed upstairs.

She paused on the landing and gazed down at the worried housekeeper. "I'm not angry with you, Ella Jane. I'm just . . ." She sighed and shook her head. "I'm just tired."

"I'll make you some tea."

"No. Don't. I just . . . I'll call you if I need anything." Willa looked down at her. "Did you have plans to spend the evening with Samuel?"

"I did, ma'am. But I'll send him away."

"Don't. I won't be needing anything tonight."

"You're sure?"

"I'm sure." With a sigh, Willa put her hand on the banister and hauled herself up the stairs. Taking her hat off and unbuttoning the waist to her traveling suit, she retrieved the mail from her bag and headed downstairs to put it back on Otto's desk. She was in Otto's office before she noticed the flowery script on the second letter. Her heart pounding, Willa opened it. And her world fell apart.

At first she thought she was having a heart attack. Sinking into Otto's chair, she put her head in her hands and wept. It had been a

dozen years since Otto'd had an affair. At least that's what she had
believed. Of course things between them weren't perfect, but what
married couple achieved perfection these days? Willa had learned to
be content. Otto was a driven man, and living with him had never
been easy. Still, when he promised "never again," she'd believed him.
She did what she could to be a good wife. And now . . . this. She
closed her eyes and leaned back in Otto's chair.

The longer she sat there, the angrier she became. How long had
their marriage been a sham? How could she not have known? How
could she have been so stupid? Why hadn't she listened to Philip? If
she had, this wouldn't be happening. In fact, if she'd listened to Philip,
Irmagard wouldn't be off on some wild theatrical jaunt, either.

Back upstairs, Willa changed from her black silk traveling suit
into a simple calico frock and emptied the trunk Johnny Dolan had
delivered while she was at the bank. She refilled it with her simplest
dresses, a few toiletries, and her Bible. Where she was going, she
wouldn't need silks.

She wrote out a bank draft and then, sitting down at her writing
desk, scribbled a note.

> To Mr. Wilber Cranston
> From Mrs. Willa Friedrich
>
> Enclosed is a bank draft I wish to have converted to cash. I realize
> this is an unexpected and rather sizeable withdrawal requiring Mr.
> Friedrich's authorization. Please remind him that this bank draft
> represents only the principal amount of the personal funds I inherited
> from my brother. I do not at this time require that the interest on my
> investment be paid. I anticipate making this withdrawal in about
> half an hour and would appreciate the cash being assembled prior
> to my arrival.

Calling for Ella Jane, Willa handed her the note and sent her off
to deliver it, then sat back down to write the note she would leave
Otto.

Years ago when I learned that I couldn't trust you to be faithful in the way most women expect faithfulness, I made a conscious decision that, for the sake of our daughter, I would accept whatever love you could give me. I am proud of the fact that Irmagard has grown up in a family with two loving parents.

No. She didn't need to explain any of this. She should just get to the point. Laying that sheet of paper aside, Willa took another.

I stayed with you because of Irmagard. I thought we had rebuilt a life worth keeping. I was deluded. Given opportunity, you encouraged our daughter's most egregious foray into deceit in her eighteen years. You've shown her how to get her own way and how to manipulate circumstances to her liking. You've helped her ignore my wishes and allowed her to break her promises. But that is not all. It is not even the real reason I am leaving you. The real reason lies beneath this note. I have taken what I want from the house, and I have enough of my own money to live comfortably. Willa.

She began to weep as she wrote, but by the time Willa had rewritten the letter a fourth time and reduced it to one paragraph, she was past weeping. She got up, closed her trunk, and pushed it out into the hall. Downstairs she laid the day's mail and her note atop Otto's desk. Hearing Ella Jane's return she called for her to help her bring her travel trunk back downstairs.

After Ella Jane had helped her hitch up the buggy, Willa climbed aboard. "I'm going to the bank. I'll be back in a few minutes. There's a note in Mr. Friedrich's office that explains what's going on. You have my permission to read it." She drove away.

Hatless, his arms pumping, Otto came barreling down the road toward her. When Willa didn't slow the buggy, he called out for her to stop. Shaking her head, she flicked the reins, and Nellie moved into a trot. Once at the bank, she pulled up and climbed down with a glance behind her. There was Otto, fast on her heels. She ducked inside and headed for the teller's window. When she asked for her money, Wilber shook his head.

"Please, Mrs. Friedrich." His pained expression went from Willa's face to the bank entrance and back again. "You know I can't—" He cleared his throat. "I need to have Mr. Friedrich's authorization or—" He paused and leaned forward. Lowering his voice, he pleaded, "I'll lose my job, Mrs. Friedrich."

Just then Otto came storming through the door. He reached for the carpetbag Willa had tried to give Wilber.

"I insist that you stop causing a scene. This is ridiculous."

"*You* are the one causing the scene," Willa hissed. She shoved the carpetbag at Wilber. "It's my money. I want it. *Now.*"

"What, exactly, are you going to do?"

"First, I'm going to pay you for Nellie and the buggy. Then I'm going to drive back to the house and give Ella Jane a very generous wedding gift. And then I'm leaving you."

"Leaving me?" He lowered his voice. "You're blowing this all out of proportion. Irmagard is perfectly safe. She's going to have a wonderful education. If you don't believe me, I'll take you to see her." He put his hand on her arm and leaned close, "Please. Darling. Come into my office so we can talk in private."

She could barely look at him. She did, however, glance around the bank enough to realize that while Otto's employees were busily looking busy, they couldn't have avoided hearing at least part of the spat. She didn't want to be the topic of supper conversations that evening. She didn't want to be "that poor Willa Friedrich. Had no idea the old boy was playing the old game with a little hussy out Denver way."

"I don't want a scene, either," she said softly. "But I intend to finish this transaction one way or the other." She looked him in the eye. "And when I'm gone, you'll be free to attend to your little friend in Denver without my interference."

Otto went pale.

Willa nodded. She looked away.

After what seemed like an eternity, Otto ordered Wilber to "do what Mrs. Friedrich has requested." He touched her arm. "It isn't what you think," he croaked. When Willa didn't move, he crossed to his office. She heard his footsteps retreat. The door close. Once again she was aware of how quiet things were in the bank. Weariness descended. Wilber counted the money. Finally Willa composed herself enough to ask, "What's a good horse and buggy cost these days?"

The balding teller stammered, "I-I . . . about sixty dollars."

"Take sixty dollars off that pile of bills and hand it to me. With an envelope, please."

She scrawled Otto's name on the envelope, inserted the money, and handed it back. The door to Otto's office remained closed as she walked past.

Back at the house Willa spoke to Ella Jane. "I'm leaving now, and I won't be coming back. It comforts me to know that I can trust you to take good care of things until Mr. Friedrich decides what to do."

"Yes, ma'am," Ella Jane nodded. "Of course."

Willa peeled off several twenty-dollar bills and held them out. "This is for you."

The dark-haired girl stared at the pile of bills and backed away, shaking her head. "I can't, ma'am," she said. "It's too much."

"It's a rare young lady who can witness the things you've witnessed while working in this house over the years and keep from gossiping all over town, Ella Jane. You've been loyal and kind. And this doesn't even begin to be enough." Willa almost broke down. She cleared her throat. "You know, I doubt that Reverend Coe would want to know this, but your quiet faith has been more of an encouragement to me over the years than all his sermons combined."

Ella Jane started to cry. "Thank you, ma'am."

"Now you take this money, or I'm going to have to—" Willa changed her tone. "Please. Please take it. I need for you to take it."

Ella Jane looked up, her eyes luminous with tears. She took the money.

"There's a good girl," Willa said. "God bless you."

"I'll pray for you, ma'am," Ella Jane said. "I'll pray for you and I'll never stop."

The tears were spilling out of Willa's eyes now. She nodded toward the house. "Would you pray for him, too, dear? I don't think I can right now."

Willa's buggy topped the last rise just as the sun was setting. As she pulled up and looked down in the valley at the little ranch bathed in golden light, she wiped away the last of her tears. Here, she thought, was the ultimate irony. After spending years resenting Charlie Mason and blaming him for turning Irmagard into a cow-girl, after railing against what ranch life had done to Laura—when Wilhelmina Ludvik Friedrich needed sanctuary . . . here she was looking down on the Mason ranch.

Charlie and Laura Mason would be able to give her the quiet strength and faith-based wisdom she so desperately needed. But it wasn't just the Masons who brought her out here. Willa knew that the prairie itself had a role to play, too. It had happened in times past when she rode out to sit beneath a lone cottonwood tree. It would happen again. She reminded herself of the things she believed. The God who loved her and told her to cast her cares on Him was the Creator and Sustainer of everything stretched out before her. The God of this endless sky cared about her. The God of these seemingly empty plains knew what was going on in her life. She might not have always been able to live out those truths, but she believed them with all her heart. And she knew that if she would listen to His voice in the midst of the worst things, He would teach her eternally good things. Out here, she would be able to listen.

Looking down on the ranch, Willa prayed. The first word that came to mind after she'd said amen was the last word she wanted to hear. *Forgive.* She flicked the reins and headed the buggy down the trail. She didn't *want* to forgive Otto. She was *tired* of forgiving Otto.

Through the screen door Willa could see the Mason family gathered around the dinner table as she climbed down from the buggy. Laura and Charlie came out onto the porch, a combination of surprise and concern shining on their faces. They both spoke at once. What was wrong? Was Otto all right? Had something happened with Irma?

Willa stood quietly, her hands clasped in front of her. "Otto's fine. He, uh . . ." Her voice wobbled. "He was at the bank. I came back early. To surprise him. *Them.* But—" She swallowed. "Of course Minnie's told you. . . ."

An unspoken message passed between the Masons. Charlie went back inside and Laura came down the stairs. Taking Willa's hand, she said, "Let's walk." And she led the way right back up the trail Willa had just driven over. "Otto didn't say a word to anyone about his Wild West plans until after you were gone," Laura said. "Even when he asked Charlie and me about taking Minnie with them, he didn't mention that you didn't know about it." She shook her head. "I'm so sorry. I suspected. I should have pressed him for the truth." She sighed. "But Minnie's been unhappy, too." She explained Minnie's reaction to Mollie's engagement. "I owe you an apology. I chose to remain ignorant because I knew the trip would cheer Minnie up."

"You needn't apologize," Willa said. "It all falls squarely in Otto's lap. Even if you had said something, he wouldn't have changed his mind."

"If it means anything to you, since he's been back Otto has heard from me about involving Minnie in this latest deception—in not very calm terms." She paused before saying, "What Otto did was terrible. But the two of you have been through worse. What I meant is . . . I saw the trunk in the buggy. Are you sure about that?"

"Angry as I am about Irmagard and the Wild West," Willa said, "the trunk in the buggy isn't about that." Taking a deep breath, she told Laura about the letter from Denver.

Laura stopped walking. She shook her head and reached out to hug Willa. "I am so sorry."

Willa pulled away. "But you aren't surprised."

"I didn't know, if that's what you mean. But. . . Otto's. . ." She sighed. "Otto is Otto. I *hoped* he had changed."

"I couldn't stay in that house another moment. I hope it's all right that I came here. I suppose I've put you in a terrible position with Otto being your brother and all. But I didn't want to go to a hotel."

"I'm glad you came to us," Laura said. After a moment, she added, "Heaven help Otto when Charlie finds out about this."

"Charlie doesn't need to get involved," Willa said quickly. "I just didn't want the two of you to think I came running out here because I was throwing some childish fit over the Wild West." Her voice wavered. "I'd be grateful if I could stay until I know what I'm going to do."

"As long as you want," Laura said. "Now come back to the house with me and try to eat some supper. Charlie can bring your trunk up to Monte's room later."

CHAPTER 14

❖⟤⟤⊙⟢⟢❖

WHATEVER YOU DO, DO YOUR WORK HEARTILY,
AS FOR THE LORD RATHER THAN FOR MEN.

Colossian 3:23 NASB

Irma lay atop her cot and stared up at the canvas tent roof. "I don't know if I'll ever get used to being called Belle," she said.

From where she lay a few feet away, Helen answered. "That's the name on your contract, isn't it?"

"It still feels like I'm putting on airs to use it."

"Give it a few more days. And stop explaining. Annie Oakley used to be Annie Moses, and Shep Sterling's mama calls him Henry. Nobody thinks *they're* putting on airs. Belle's a fine name."

"Wh-what did you just say?" Irma sat up and looked across at Helen.

"I said," Helen repeated, "to forget about *Irmagard* and just be *Belle.*"

"No—not that. About Shep. You said his mama calls him—Henry?" *So he was telling the truth about that, too, back in Bill's barn. He was telling you the truth about everything, and you didn't believe him. You made fun of him. Oh, brother. Could it be more embarrassing?*

185

Helen cleared her throat. "I thought you knew that?"

"The program says he's from Texas. Is that really true?"

"If the program says Shep has punched cattle in Texas, then you can believe he's punched at least two cows in the state of Texas. Show names aside, Bill tries to be as accurate as he can about things like that."

"But I'm right, aren't I? Shep's not really *from* Texas. And his real name is Henry Mortimer."

"Which person are people going to talk about, read about, want to come and see at the Wild West? *Irmagard Friedrich* or *Liberty Belle*? A cowboy named *Henry* or *Shep*? It's not very hard to figure out, is it? And I'm no gossip, so that's all I've got to say on the subject of Henry Mortimer. But I'd love to know where you got Liberty Belle. Which is, as I said, a fine name."

"Did you ever play dress-up or pretend when you were little?"

"Honey, I started keeping house for my daddy and five brothers when I was ten years old. I didn't have time to play at much of anything. But I know what you mean. I used to pretend my mama was just outside in the garden. It got me through some awful times."

What must Helen think of her—a girl whose daddy essentially bought her an audition and a horse. "You must think I'm the world's most spoiled brat," she said.

"The Good Lord takes people down different trails, Belle," Helen said, her voice gentle. "He don't love me any less because He let me have a different childhood from you. Now hush up about all that and tell me where you got the name."

Irma took a deep breath. "I was about fourteen when I started trying to do a combination of things I'd seen at a traveling circus that came through town. And you know how they take off their hat and take a bow and pretend the announcer is calling their name? Well, I just could not imagine anyone hollering *Ladies and gentlemen . . . Irmagard Friedrich*."

When Helen chuckled, Irma said, "See? That's exactly what I

mean. So I decided to make up a name. July fourth is my birthday. So the *Liberty* part was easy." She smiled as she told the rest. "And Belle was the name of one of my Aunt Laura's favorite milk cows. Aunt Laura told me *Belle* was French for *beautiful,* and I decided Liberty Belle sounded nice."

Helen laughed out loud. "How can anyone who's named for a *heifer* feel like she's putting on airs?"

"You won't tell anyone that part—will you?"

"Of course not." She chuckled, "But it's gonna be hard."

"Thank you."

"You're welcome."

Belle was almost asleep when a very low *moo* sounded from the other side of the tent.

She laughed. And mooed back.

Liberty Belle's romantic dreams of the Wild West were challenged by several immediate and very strong doses of reality. Feeding several hundred people three meals a day was a complex task, and Belle soon learned that she was not the exception to any of the rules. When she first slept through the predawn clanking of the cook's triangle, Helen gave her a good-natured shake and helped her get up. A couple of days later, when Belle was still moaning about the predawn rising, Helen was still patient but obviously less amused. Finally, she shook Belle awake with a "Look, honey, if you want to skip breakfast, then skip breakfast. I'll see you later." And she left. Belle rolled over and fell back to sleep.

Anybody could oversleep. It didn't seem like anyone should care. But when Belle presented her first-shift breakfast ticket during third shift, the waiter said, "See you at dinner," turned his back, and walked away. Belle skittered out of the dining tent to a rousing chorus of snickers and jibes.

All right, she thought, *I'll just go over to the office and get new tickets for the later shift.* Except the clerk she talked to in the office laughed in her face. "If you can get someone to switch tickets with you, go right ahead, but this ain't no hotel, and I'm not your concierge."

That night, when she asked Helen to keep getting her up until she learned to hear the triangle, Belle promised not to moan and groan like a lazy child. The next morning Helen clanged a cowbell over Belle's cot. And mooed. Helen, it appeared, was one of those annoying people who had a sense of humor in the morning. Belle was not. But the threat of a cowbell must have shaken something loose, because in a couple of days Belle was hearing the cook's triangle. Helen hung the cowbell high up on the tent pole. Just in case, she said.

Another thing Belle had to learn was what it meant to work. Uncle Charlie might have let her be a ranch hand, but he'd also watched out for her. She had never realized just how much leeway she'd been granted—until now, when workdays were sixteen hours long and everyone had to do his or her part. With hundreds of animals to care for and two performances a day, there was no time for anyone to linger anywhere. Belle loved being part of it, but she'd never been so tired in her life. There was a rule against the performers sleeping with their boots on. If it hadn't been for Helen Keen pulling them off while Belle slept, she would have broken that one more than once.

And then there was Blaze. Some of the wranglers were using the time in St. Louis to check out the new horses Bill Cody had purchased in Nebraska, and as far as Belle was concerned, not a single one of them deserved a mare like Blaze. They handled her without giving any quarter to the mare's high-strung nature. By the end of Belle's first week in St. Louis, it was fairly common knowledge that the chestnut mare was a humdinger of a bucking bronc. Belle couldn't stand the idea. Of course no one would listen to her. Not even Shep.

"I hear what you're saying," he said one morning when Belle appealed to him for help. "And in a different world, maybe she *would* be a fine saddle mare. But the reality is, she's not in a different world— she's in the Wild West, and she's the perfect combination of kindness and spirit to make a great bronc. She doesn't pitch all over when the boys saddle her up, she leads well—and she can be counted on to tear up the place trying to unseat her rider. That makes her worth a lot more to Cody as a bronc than as an untrustworthy mount for one of the wranglers."

"She could be trusted if they'd quit sawing at her mouth like that." She waved toward where Ned Bishop was taking his turn trying to ride Blaze. Impulsively, she shouted to Ned. "Stop sawing on her mouth like that! She'll go easy if you just give her a minute!"

Bishop pretended not to hear her. He tugged on the brim of his hat and said something to the wrangler standing at Blaze's head. The wrangler stepped away. Blaze hesitated.

"See that?" Belle insisted. "She's just waiting for someone to treat her right. She's *not* a natural—" At that moment Nate pulled back on the reins even as he kicked Blaze in the side.

Belle grimaced. "Don't kick her like that," she yelled. "Just nudge her a little and—"

It was too late. Blaze exploded in a frenzy of bucking and twisting that unseated Bishop in less than half a minute. While other wranglers snagged Blaze, Bishop got up, dusted himself off, and lumbered across the corral. Ducking between the poles, he walked over to where Belle stood with Shep and said through clenched teeth, "Don't you *ever* tell me how to ride a horse again! I don't know who you think you are, Liberty Belle, but to me you're still a spoiled brat whose Daddy bought her a ride on the Wild West train. And—"

Bishop didn't finish whatever it was he was going to say, because Shep stepped between them, spread his hand across Bishop's chest, and propelled him backward away from Belle. Whatever Shep said took the spunk right out of Bishop, who glanced at Belle once and then turned around and strode away. The idea of Shep protecting her was nice . . . but every time Belle practiced her own routine in that corral she still thought about Blaze and wished things were different.

The long hours and the disappointment on behalf of Blaze were hard to take, but those were nothing compared to the frustration Belle felt as, day after day, she and Diamond went through a rigorous practice session that no one who mattered seemed to notice. Oh, once in a while a few watched, and once in a while they even shouted a "yee-hah" of approval. But no one said a thing about her actually riding into the arena for a performance. Neither Nate Salsbury nor Buffalo Bill seemed to have any interest in checking up on her. Apparently her most cherished dream was going to have to wait to come true.

For all her difficulty adjusting to her new life, Belle realized that if she made the effort to look for it, there was good even in the things she didn't like. Rising before dawn meant she was part of the early shift for breakfast, when the coffee was fresh and the bread still warm. The fatigue from working long hours meant she slept soundly instead of fretting over things like what was going on at home and what was going to happen to Lady Blaze. There was even one good thing about the encounter with Bishop, and that was the memory of Shep's inserting himself between the two of them so as to protect her. And if Salsbury and Cody weren't watching her progress with Diamond, at least that gave Belle freedom to avoid Salsbury's instructions about working in the wardrobe tent—which, Belle convinced herself, he never would have done if he truly understood how much she loved horses and hated sewing. After all, if Helen Keen could work in the stables, why couldn't Liberty Belle? It seemed a perfectly reasonable argument to her.

Belle was untangling Diamond's mane one day when Shep ambled up.

"I was over at wardrobe just now," he said. "Ma Clemmons mentioned you haven't checked in with her yet."

Belle shrugged. "I have to 'prove competence' before the boss lets me in that arena, and working in wardrobe isn't going to do a thing for my performance skills."

Shep nodded. "I understand how you could think that. The thing

190

is, your *act* isn't the only thing to be proven around here." He scratched his scruffy beard. "There's plenty of people in the troupe who agree with what Ned Bishop said the other day."

"And why should I care about that?" Belle said.

"Because it'll make for an easier time for everyone if we all get along."

"Ned Bishop can talk all he wants. I'll prove I deserve a spot. As of this morning I can do everything Helen and Dora and Mabel do in that arena. You can ask Monte if you don't believe me. He saw me pick this very kerchief up off the dirt from Diamond's back. At a gallop." She yanked on the red scarf knotted around her neck. "Of course, until Mr. Salsbury or Bill Cody see it, I don't suppose it will matter how hard I work."

"Just because they aren't baby-sitting you doesn't mean they don't know how you're getting along," Shep said. He took his hat off and raked his hand through his hair. "Guess you might as well know that before he left, Nate asked me what I thought about putting you in the show when we get to the next stop." He pretended to shape the crown of his Stetson as he said, "I told him I didn't think you were ready."

"Thanks for the vote of confidence," Belle snapped.

"Now calm down and just listen to me a minute." Shep put his hat back on. "I know how it feels to be trying to earn everyone's respect. I grew up reading dime novels and dreaming about the West. A little over four years ago I was in Ohio on a business trip when I learned that Buffalo Bill himself was in town performing on stage. Of course I had to go.

"From the second that man walked onto the stage until he took his last bow I was completely mesmerized. I had to meet him. When I finally got a chance to buy him dinner, he told me that being a cowboy was a learned skill, just like banking or building bridges or bookkeeping. I took that for encouragement. So I emptied my bank account and headed west, and for the first few months I was the laughingstock of every outfit I tried to join, but I kept at it for almost three years."

"And you punched cattle in Texas," Belle said with a smile.

"Oh, I punched cattle in several states."

"So while I was landing in the dust in my Uncle Charlie's corral—"

Shep nodded. "Yep. I was flying through the air after being thrown or bucked off or maybe just falling off a horse or a steer or, occasionally, an old buffalo." He looked down at her and smiled. "So when I tell you I understand how hard it is to keep waiting, I do understand. But there's more to being part of the Wild West than the skills you use in the arena. When I showed up to audition, I told Bill Cody I didn't care if he ever let me in the arena—I was willing to do anything to be part of his troupe."

"But he must have made you King of the Cowboys right away."

Shep scuffed at the ground with the toe of his boot. "Yep, some-times it's just a matter of being in the right place at the right time—but the point is, I didn't care what I did. I just wanted to be part of Buffalo Bill's Wild West."

"Well, I do care," Belle said. "I didn't join the Wild West to be a seamstress."

Later that night Belle poured out her frustrations over not being accepted by the troupe. "No matter what anyone thinks," she said, as she and Helen got ready to turn in, "I'm not just 'Daddy's little girl' who always gets what she wants. I *did* work on a ranch. I spent over two months every summer with Uncle Charlie. I know how to—"

"Two *months*? Every summer? Really?" Helen put her hands on her waist in mock amazement. "Well, sure as shootin' yer a real cowgirl now." She plopped down on her cot and began to pull off her boots. "I'd like to visit your Uncle Charlie's ranch sometime, by the way, 'cause he's figured out something I've never heard of before."

Belle frowned. "What's that?"

"How to run a ranch when your hands don't get up until mid-morning." Helen set her boots under her cot and let down the tent flap.

"All right," Belle confessed, as she pulled her own boots off. "So they didn't always get me up with everybody else. But I still worked hard."

Helen's voice gentled. "I'm just tryin' to help you understand what's going on here." She pointed out of the tent. "You're kind of a mystery woman to everyone. The boss man himself knows you and your family, and frankly that's not necessarily a plus."

"Why not? Is that why everyone's been so standoffish? Because I know Buffalo Bill?"

Helen hesitated. "You do know that most people in this country would rather meet the Honorable William F. Cody than President Cleveland? And not only are you invited to supper at the hotel on your first day in town, but then the great man himself and his partner schedule a special audition. And you don't do all that great in the arena, but they hire you anyway—with plans to put you in a special parade. And it doesn't take a genius to realize that, if she doesn't mess up, Liberty Belle will be a headliner when we open at that garden place in November."

Belle frowned. "I can't do anything about any of that." She snatched up her brush and ran it through her hair a couple of times, then gestured as she spoke. "I'm trying to be nice. Really, I am. I know I messed up asking to switch breakfast shifts. I just didn't think how that would look."

" 'Course you didn't," Helen said. "Because most of your life your little world has revolved around you." She began to change into her nightshirt. "And if all the special treatment with Buffalo Bill himself ain't enough to make folks a mite jealous, you've got the Shepherd jumping through hoops like nobody's ever seen."

"I do *not* have Shep Sterling jumping through hoops," Belle protested. "I've barely seen him since I've been here. Except for this morning when he delivered his version of the lecture you're giving right now."

"Excuse me, honey," Helen said as she slid beneath the covers, "but wasn't that Shep spending most of his day off polishing *your* saddle and grooming *your* ride before *your* audition? And if I'm not mistaken, wasn't that Shep sitting with you at supper every night this week? And didn't he sit with you in church Sunday?"

"He and Monte are friends," Belle said. "It's only natural he's around us a lot. Monte promised Daddy he'd watch out for me."

"Right," Helen nodded, then said, "Well, it's a good thing Shep isn't that nice to everybody. He'd never find time to actually ride a horse."

Belle sat back up. "It isn't fair for people to judge someone they don't even know."

"Last time I checked the real world, Miss Belle, it wasn't filled with justice and light. People aren't always fair. The Wild West is a small town of mostly frontier people plopped down right in the middle of what amounts to a foreign country, because, believe me, St. Louis and all the other big cities we're going to play are foreign countries to people like me."

"What d'you mean, 'people like you'?"

Helen sighed and lay back on her cot. Propping herself up on one elbow, she said, "I was eight years old when my mama died. It was Daddy and my five brothers and me on a spread that was about the size of a raindrop in the great ocean of Texas. Today that raindrop is a decent-sized pond. And it got that way because, in addition to cooking and mending and washing laundry, I spent a good part of every day baby-sitting orphaned calves and doing whatever I could to help my daddy hang on to his little piece of Texas. I rode spring roundup and dragged calves out of the mud and roped steers, and I did it when I was so tired I could hardly stay awake in the saddle. And you can be darned sure that if it would get me a little piece of this heaven called the Wild West, where all I have to do is look pretty when I ride my horse and peel potatoes or iron or mend or do laundry a few hours a day, I'd be willing to do it Any of it.

"I'm lucky enough to get to work in the stables, and I like that. But the truth is, if I couldn't work there, I'd sew until I was blind and never say a word against it." She lay back. "Most of the people outside this tent have stories a lot like mine. We're all waiting to see what's behind the fancy name and the pretty face of Liberty Belle."

"Well, look who's here." Ma Clemmons looked up from the wardrobe tent worktable.

Helen nudged Belle forward. "Nate said she should report to you once she got settled." She winked at Ma. "It took her a little longer than some. But she's settled." With an encouraging pat to Belle's backside, Helen left.

Ma tucked a wisp of white hair behind her ear as she said, "You like sewing?"

Belle shook her head. "No, ma'am. But I know how, and this is where Mr. Salsbury said I should work." She hesitated. "My momma was adamant that all ladies need to know how to sew. She started me on buttons when I was about four. Hemming at six. I made a nine-patch doll quilt when I was ten." Belle decided it best not to elaborate on the relative success of the quilt.

Ma unrolled a length of dark blue calico and cut off a piece. Smoothing it so it would lay flat, she positioned a pattern piece on the fabric before walking over to a cabinet standing at the end of a row of treadle sewing machines. Opening the cabinet, she pulled out a square black metal tin and handed it over. "Buttons," she said, and motioned to a basket of men's shirts. "Those are clean, but they all need one or two buttons sewed back on." She motioned toward a worktable piled high with the tools of her trade. "Take whatever tools you need, and if you have any questions, ask."

She went back to the worktable and, pulling some straight pins out of a little pin cushion she had strapped to her wrist, began to pin the paper pattern in place, talking as she worked. "You'll be less likely to go blind if you sit over where the tent flap's rolled up. If there's a ripped seam, go ahead and put the buttons on, but put it in . . ." She reached beneath the worktable and pulled out an empty basket. "Put it in here when you're done. Dora and Mabel can take it from there."

As if on cue, Dora Spurgeon and Mabel Douglas sauntered in and, with a disbelieving glance at Belle, took seats at the two sewing machines.

Ma Clemmons spoke up. "You ladies been introduced?"

"Yes, ma'am," Belle said and nodded at Dora and Mabel, who mumbled greetings and then turned their backs. After a couple of attempts at starting conversations wherein Dora seemed friendly enough but given to one-word answers or shrugs on any topic and Mabel refused to talk, Belle fell silent. For a while the only sounds in the tent were Ma Clemmons's humming as she worked. In an hour Belle had sewn on more buttons than she had in her entire life. Her neck and back were aching and her fingers smarting from needle pricks.

Ma Clemmons left on an errand. While she was gone a cowboy brought in a pair of torn britches. Mabel flirted shamelessly. Dora pedaled away at her sewing machine, not even looking up. As the cowboy made his way back toward the stables, Mabel watched from the opening near where Belle was sitting and muttered, "I'd like to be at the other end of that cowboy's rope sometime."

Dora scolded. "D-do you ever think of anything b-besides m-men?"

Mabel nudged her. "And I suppose you just normally skitter behind a tent flap to avoid talking to them." She smirked. "Oh, wait. I guess you do. Unless it's Monte Mason."

"SHHHH!" Dora said, with a glance in Belle's direction.

Belle smiled at Dora. "If you like my cousin you've got good taste in men," she said.

"*Like* isn't exactly the right word," Mabel said. "Dear little Lora Dora is *obsessed.*"

"I am n-not!" Dora protested.

Mabel didn't let up. "You are," she insisted. "She even talks about him in her sleep." Clasping her hands together and batting her eyelids, Mabel did an impression of a melodrama heroine. "Oh, M-Monte . . . s-save me . . . Oh, M-Monte . . ."

"I s-said be qu-quiet!" Dora said, jumping up and clenching her fists.

Just then Monte ducked beneath the tent flap. One look at Belle and he burst out laughing. "Helen said it was true, but I didn't believe her."

Belle sat up straighter. "Why not?"

"If Aunt Willa could see you now, she'd likely beg Bill Cody to keep you instead of telling him to send you home."

Belle glowered. "Did you come over here to make fun of me or did you actually have something to say?"

"Well, yeah. Actually, I did have something to say. It's time for supper."

Just at that moment Belle saw Mabel plant the flat of her hand between Dora's shoulder blades and give the smaller girl a shove so that she stumbled right into Monte.

"Whoa, there," Monte said and grabbed Dora's arm to keep her from falling.

"Th-thank you," Dora said, pulling away. With a hateful glance Mabel's way, her cheeks flaming red, Dora hurried back to one of the sewing machines, where she plopped down with her back to everyone before realizing there was nothing to work on. She sat still as a stone.

"So," Monte said to Belle. "You want to come eat with Shep and me or not?"

The look on Mabel's face when Monte mentioned Shep sent a chill up Belle's spine. Dora liked Monte and Mabel liked Shep. Raising her voice to include Mabel and Dora in the reply, Belle said, "Sure we would. Wouldn't we—Dora? Mabel?"

Dora shook her head. "N-no thanks." She didn't even turn around.

"Come on, Lora-Dora," Mabel urged, "Let's go have some supper."

Dora still shook her head.

"Suit yourself," Mabel said, rubbing her neck as she commented about how sewing was a literal pain in the neck. "Nice to be rescued," she said and looped her arm through Monte's and then Belle's. "Sure you don't want to c-come?" she called to Dora.

Ma Clemmons came back just in time to intervene. "Take it from an old lady, my dear," she said, laying her hand on Dora's arm. "Never refuse the invitation of a handsome gentleman." She squeezed Dora's shoulder even as her blue eyes sent Mabel an icy message.

"Come with us, Dora," Belle pleaded. "Please."

When Dora finally shrugged and got up, Belle inserted her into the space between herself and Monte.

Belle stayed in the wardrobe tent that evening during the Wild West performance. While the cheers and laughter of the thousands of spectators in the stands rang across the lot, she finished sewing on buttons. Once finished with that, she fired up the stove for heating Ma's flatirons, relieved when she remembered enough from watching Ella Jane iron Daddy's shirts to produce acceptable results.

After a while Belle decided it was better to be useful in the wardrobe tent with Ma Clemmons than to be wandering the back lot, miserable because she wasn't riding into the arena.

Ma showed her how the costume department was organized, with each performer assigned a hook and each one leaving their work clothes on the hook while they performed and changing back at the end of the evening. The ladies had a private area cordoned off by a thick canvas drape. Ma had helpers assigned to the various aspects of costume management from cleaning to mending to replacement to sorting for the laundry.

"How'd you learn to do all this?" Belle asked at one point. "I mean . . . did *you* figure out how to make it work?"

"Mr. Clemmons and I traveled with a circus for years before Mr. Cody hired us on," Ma said.

"I've never met a circus family before," Belle said.

Ma laughed. "Oh, we weren't a circus *family*. Not at all. In fact, when Grady asked me to marry him my family was outraged."

"But you did it anyway?"

Ma nodded. "He was the handsomest man I had ever seen. And the kindest. Completely swept me off my feet."

"What happened with your family?"

Ma shrugged. "Oh, they disowned me for a while. Although none of them were very sincere about it. Except for my dear mother—may she rest in peace."

"Did she ever change her mind?"

Ma sighed. "I hope so. If she did, I never knew about it."

Belle frowned. "My momma doesn't approve of my being here."

"I hope you can work that out," Ma Clemmons said.

Belle shook her head. "That would take a miracle."

Ma smiled. "Well then, we'll just have to pray one up."

CHAPTER 15

. . . PUT ON A HEART OF COMPASSION, KINDNESS,
HUMILITY, GENTLENESS, AND PATIENCE.

Colossians 3:12 NASB

Willa had been at the ranch for only a couple of days when Charlie
rode in from the range and knocked on the back door to ask if she
would "set a spell." When she came out onto the porch, Charlie
motioned her into a chair. He didn't sit down, but rather looped one
leg over the porch railing. Perched there, he took his hat off and set
it on his knee before saying in his gravelly voice, "Been workin' on
this speech all mornin', and I'd appreciate you hearing me out."

He's going to tell me to go home. She and Charlie had never gotten
along very well. She resented his encouraging Irmagard, and Charlie
knew it. They'd always been polite to each other, but it was a thin
veneer, and it was easy to peel away such things when situations
changed. She steeled herself against what she was about to hear.

"Fact is, Willa," Charlie began. "I didn't really care whether you
liked the idea of us having Irmagard out here during the summers
or not. I always knew you were only tolerating the idea. But that
was good enough for me. She loved it out here, and we love her. I

won't say I'm sorry for those summers because I'm not." He looked up. "But I'm not proud of the fact that part of the reason I liked her coming so much was because I knew it bothered you." He cleared his throat. "I had a wrong attitude, Willa. Plain and simple. And I'm askin' your forgiveness."

Willa nodded. "I'm sorry, too."

Charlie cleared his throat. He scratched his head. Took a deep breath and blew it out. "Now about this other. Otto didn't turn out to be quite what he seems to be." He twirled his hat nervously in his hands and didn't look up as he said, "I didn't know about this situation out Denver way." He looked up at her. "But I *did* know about that other time way back when. It was me who sent the telegram that brought Philip out here."

"You?!"

He nodded. "When you sent Philip away, I was plumb amazed. It wasn't any secret how much you hated it out here."

"I couldn't take Irmagard away from her father," Willa said. "I just couldn't."

Charlie nodded again. "So what I need to tell you is that, while I've been critical of some things as I saw them over the years, I've also learned there's plenty to respect about you."

"Thank you," Willa said.

"I've been thinking long and praying hard about what Laura and me are supposed to do about this latest thing. Well, I've decided, and that's mainly what I want to say this mornin'. Wanted you to know that I'm going to ride into town in a bit and have a talk with my brother-in-law. It was wrong for him to sneak off the way he done with our girls. I especially resent his involving Minnie in those doin's. And then, of course, I'll have to say somethin' about this other." He moistened his lips. "I'm going to tell him that you are with us and you are welcome for as long as you want to stay. And I'm also going to tell him that if it comes to taking sides in this mess he's created, he'd better not count on Laura or me to choose his side."

Willa blinked back her tears. She couldn't trust herself to speak, so she just nodded.

Charlie glanced across the yard toward the two-room cabin he and Laura had started out in. "Laura thought you might want more privacy than we can give you here at the house. If you want, we'll clean out the old place, and you can make it your own. That's only if you want it. Monte's room is fine, too. We'll do whatever's best for you. And I mean that."

Willa stared at the cabin. Over the years it had been everything from a playhouse for the girls to a storage shed. But they'd kept it in good repair. She began to cry grateful tears. "Thank you," she croaked. "I'd love the cabin."

Charlie put his hat on and, with a little nod, stepped down off the porch. "Things'll work out, Willa. You got to believe they will. The Good Lord's got a plan. We just have to find out what it is."

———

"Aunt Willa?"

Willa looked up from where she crouched on her hands and knees, scrubbing the cabin floor. Minnie looked like she'd seen a ghost. "Yes, Minnie," she said, and tucked an errant strand of hair behind her ear as she stood up.

"You're scrubbing the floor."

Willa supposed it was something of a shock for the girls to see her actually keeping house. She'd had a maid for as long as any of them could remember, and she hadn't exactly pitched in and helped in the kitchen when she and Otto visited over the years—the reason being she was completely inept in the kitchen, but of course the girls didn't know that. She dropped her scrub brush in the bucket of soapy water and dried her reddened hands on her apron. "Amazing, isn't it?" She forced a little laugh. "It seems I do remember how to do housework after all." She motioned toward the wood stove in the far corner of the room. "Although mastering that thing is another story."

"I can help you," Minnie blurted out, then bit her lip. "I mean, if you want." She shrugged. "It's not that hard."

"Did you walk over here to give cookstove lessons or to give me that?" Willa pointed to the envelope in Minnie's hand.

Minnie looked down at it. "It's from Irma. I thought you might like to read it. To see she's all right. Happy." She shrugged. "You know." She looked off toward the house.

If ever a girl were ready to take flight, Minnie was. She'd been avoiding Willa for most of the week, and Willa was too busy and too overwhelmed to know what to do about it beyond an occasional *Help me know what to say to Minnie* thrown in with her other disorganized prayers.

Apparently God thought it was time for their strained relationship to be restored. If only Willa knew how.

The stove.

"Could you make me some tea? I mean, show me how. On the stove? I've never been very good at keeping a fire going long enough to do much." She forced a little laugh. "Your poor Uncle Otto spent several years eating undercooked oatmeal and half-charred meat. He finally hired a cook."

Minnie tucked the envelope in her apron pocket and began to build a fire in the stove. "I bet you were relieved," she said.

"Actually," Willa said as she set two cups and saucers on the table, "I was more hurt than relieved. It was the first time I'd failed at anything really important to me." She looked over Minnie's shoulder as Minnie bent over the stove. "Why are you stacking the kindling that way?"

"I don't know," Minnie shrugged. "It's just the way you do it." She struck a match and, as the kindling began to smolder, she blew on it, adding more wood as the flames grew until, finally, she put the iron lid over the opening and slid the kettle in place. "It's easy," she said. "But if it doesn't work next time you want tea, just come and get me. I'll help until you can do it yourself."

Poor Minnie. So nervous. Self-conscious. And yet, she'd brought the letter. "I think," Willa finally said, "that you and I need to have a little talk."

Her hands clenched at her sides, Minnie blurted out an apology. "I'm sorry, Aunt Willa. I'm so sorry. I thought you'd agreed to the trip. Honestly, I did. Please believe me. I didn't know we were sneaking off like that. I didn't."

"Of course I believe you," Willa said.

"You do?" Minnie seemed surprised.

"I do. And therefore, there is no apology necessary. Is that why you've been avoiding me all week?" Willa sighed. "And all this time I thought it was because you girls just didn't want me staying here."

Minnie frowned. "Why wouldn't we want you?"

Willa smirked. "Well, let's see. For starters there's this nose of mine." She pointed at her nose. "The one your daddy says I carry too high in the air for his taste." She lifted her chin and stared down at Minnie.

Minnie blushed, then pulled out the letter and handed it over. "I'll make the tea while you read."

"Thank you," Willa said. "The only thing better than reading this would be if she'd written *me*." She sighed. "But I don't suppose I can blame her for not wanting to do that." She sat down and read while Minnie poured hot water into two china cups and dipped a tea ball in and out, watching as the clear water turned brown.

Dear Minnie,

This has been the hardest week of my life. I thought everything would be easy because I am so happy to be here, but it isn't. I alienated Ned Bishop the other day when I tried to get him to use a more gentle hand with Blaze, and I wouldn't be surprised if he never speaks to me again. I probably could have been a little more tactful in the way I did it, but he was being too rough with her, and I just couldn't stand by and watch without saying something. Shep stood up for me, but there were more wranglers upset with me than just Ned.

It's fairly obvious that most everyone thinks I am only here because Bill Cody owed Daddy a favor. To tell you the truth, if weren't for Monte and Shep and Helen, I don't know if I could have stayed. But I think I'm finally making some other friends. I'm working hard. Believe it or not, after I train with Diamond in the morning I am working in the wardrobe tent. I can hear you laughing already at the idea of me patching pants and sewing on buttons. Ma Clemmons is in charge of everything, and she's really nice. If I had a grandma, I would want her to be just like Ma.

Do you remember the two cowgirls on the program that did the race? I work with them. One is very sweet and one isn't. I try to get along. My bunkmate, Helen, would shock Momma with her bad grammar and her cowgirl ways, but she is truly the best friend I could have asked for.

I probably won't get to ride in the arena for a while. You can imagine my reaction when I realized that. But Shep says I have to be patient. I'm trying. We will be packing up in a few days. Here is our schedule: Terre Haute, Indiana, May 18–19; Dayton, Ohio, May 20–21; Wheeling, West Virginia, May 22–23; Cumberland, Ohio, May 24–25; Hagerstown, Maryland, May 26–27; Frederick City, Maryland, May 28–29; Washington, D.C., May 30–June 6; Philadelphia, Pennsylvania, June 7–21; and then finally New York, where we will put up a more permanent camp at a place called Erastina on Staten Island.

Shep says Liberty Belle will probably debut in New York, although he might talk to Mr. Salsbury about letting me ride in the parade in Washington. (Mr. Salsbury and Bill Cody have assigned Shep to watch me train and tell them when he thinks I am ready to perform. At first that made me angry, but now I understand they can't be baby-sitting me all the time, and it's not all bad. Shep doesn't seem to mind the job.)

If you see Momma, please try to make her understand that in spite of it being difficult here, I am happier than I have ever been in my whole life. I have tried to write her, but I just don't know what to say. I can't tell her I am sorry, because that would be a lie. Every time

*I get out a piece of notepaper and write the words "Dear Momma," I
stare at the paper and then I give up. I haven't written Daddy because
it would be mean not to include Momma, but she would be upset if I
just acted like nothing happened and wrote about the Wild West. I
don't know what to do.*

*I hope you remembered to tell Orrin Knox what I said. Did you?
Write me soon. Monte says hi. He just came by the tent. Some of us
are going over to Forest Park for the afternoon.*

*If you talk to Momma tell her I am going to church. Since you
have been here you can tell her what it is like. Sunday Joe's sermon
this morning was about being humble and taking the first steps toward
making up when you have a fight with someone. I thought about
Momma so much I almost cried. But I still don't know what to do.*

*Well, now here is Shep and Helen telling me to come on, so I
will close.*

Ever your faithful cousin and friend,
Liberty Belle

*P.S. You can write to me at the Wild West, General Delivery,
New York, New York. Helen says they do a good job of chasing us
down and delivering the mail.*

Willa got teary-eyed halfway through reading the letter. When
she finished she reached across the table and grasped Minnie's hand.
"Thank you," she said. "Both for having the courage to walk over
here and for letting me read this." She folded the letter and handed
it back. "Will you be writing her soon?"

"I write almost every day," Minnie said. "I just add a paragraph
or so—or one of the other girls does. Or Ma. When we get a few
pages, we send it off."

"And have you told her I'm staying out here?"

Minnie shook her head. "No, ma'am. That's not for any of us
to tell."

Willa smiled. "When you send off the next letter, would you tell
her that you and I had tea and that Momma sends her love."

CHAPTER 16

DO NOT BE DECEIVED, GOD IS NOT MOCKED; FOR
WHATEVER A MAN SOWS, THIS HE WILL ALSO REAP.
Galatians 6:7 NASB

At first she thought it was only her imagination, but within a week of Belle's setting foot in the wardrobe tent, things began to change. One of the surlier wranglers nodded and almost smiled when Belle walked by. The waiter in the dining tent refilled her coffee without her asking. The head trainer, Cy Matthews, showed her how to make an easy trick look more impressive. He even commiserated with her about Blaze's fate, although he insisted the mare was too flighty for regular arena work. More troupe members began to drift past the corral when she was practicing and to shout encouragement. Best of all, Belle began to be included in the inside jokes and banter about everything from tough beef to ignorant guests. She wasn't performing in the arena yet, but she was definitely beginning to be accepted as more than a visitor.

She wrote Minnie about how some folks returned to the show so often that troupe members began to call them by their first name.

You should have seen the look on Jack's face (remember the little boy who sat next to me at our first show?), when Shep called him "pardner" one day.

If I were Orrin Knox and writing an article for the Register, here's what I'd want people to know about the Wild West: The Wild West is the sweet scent of fresh hay and the not-so-sweet smells when the thermometer climbs and the crowds press in and the performers give their all and come out of the arena drenched in sweat. It's the smell of gunpowder wafting across the arena and the aroma of popcorn popping on the midway. It's the cowboy band striking up "The Star Spangled Banner" and the whinnies and whickers of the horses waiting to enter the arena. It's cowboy clowns and bucking broncos, buffalo hunts and horse races, trick roping and sharp shooting—and Bill Cody commands it all with such elegance and grace the ladies fairly swoon when he walks by.

It's nearly heaven—and if not exactly heaven, what with the mountains of manure and all, it's near enough to heaven that I don't want to be anywhere else.

Belle wrote of looking forward to the October parade in New York and performing at Madison Square Garden and of sailing for England the following spring.

She began to write home, too, although her letters to Momma and Daddy struck a different note. In these, Belle spoke of the work ethic required to be a success, the opportunities she had had to meet interesting people, and the time she spent in the company of Ma Clemmons, who was a devout Christian woman admired by all. She recounted Sunday Joe's sermons and did her best to paint the Wild West with hues designed to convince Momma that things with Irmagard Friedrich were, indeed, all right.

But still, she did not hear from Momma.

———

Helen and Belle readied their tent and its contents for moving between the afternoon and evening performances on May 17, their last day in St. Louis.

"Just set your trunk outside the tent flap," Helen directed. "Bedding atop the trunk. The boys'll load the tent and table onto another car since we won't be needing them again until New York." She reached up and took the cowbell down from where it had hung at the top of the tent pole. "What about this?" she said with a smile.

Belle grinned. "I hope you've noticed that once or twice I have actually managed to get up *before* the cook clangs that annoying triangle." She reached for the cowbell. "But let's keep this as a memento. I'll pack it with my things."

"I'm not sure about packing it away," Helen joked. "You get too big for your britches and a clang of that bell just might be the thing that brings you back to earth quick. Remindin' you of your roots and all." She mooed.

Belle laughed and mooed back. While Helen, Dora, and Mabel headed off to mount up for the last performance, Belle picked her way through the hoards of workers hurrying to dismantle everything on the back lot. She found Ma Clemmons busily folding up worktables and putting away bolts of cloth and sewing tools while performers changed into their costumes and staff members loaded Ma's equipment onto a wagon. Every department had its own wagons, and each wagon was specially designed to hold equipment. "A place for everything and everything in its place," Ma said.

"The wagons we'll need first at the next stop get loaded on the first car and so on down the line. I know it looks like chaos right now," Ma said, gesturing at the frenetic activity on the lot, "but it's not." She waved Belle toward the train. "You should go see how it all works while you got the chance," she said. "We've done what we can here until the Final Salute's over."

Belle made her way through the crowd and along the row of equipment wagons waiting to be loaded. Fascinated, Belle watched as, using a clever rigging of ropes and pulleys, the pull-up team walking alongside the train pulled the next equipment wagon up a long ramp and down the row of flat cars—connected into one long flat surface by the placing of iron plates across the gaps between cars. Once a wagon moved into place, the train crew put chock blocks before and behind the wagon wheels. And the process was repeated again for the next equipment wagon and the next.

Once Ma's equipment wagon was loaded, Belle went to check on Diamond. This time, when she offered to help with the animals, she was put right to work. Cy Matthews, the trainer who'd been watching her sessions, seemed to go out of his way to explain how things would work. "I know it looks like they're packed awful tight," he said, "but between that and the fact we load 'em in sideways, they help each other stay on their feet as the train moves." He let Belle lead Diamond up the gangplank herself, and when Ned Bishop grabbed Blaze's halter and went to haul her aboard and Blaze balked, Matthews sent Ned to do something else and then motioned for Belle to help. "See if you can calm her down," he said. Belle did, and in a few minutes Belle had loaded the "flighty" mare as if she'd been doing it all her life.

After the last performance, Belle helped the other cowgirls get their show animals ready for travel. When she and Helen finally climbed aboard the Pullman coach they would share with Dora Spurgeon and Mabel Douglas, Helen grabbed her stack of bedding and claimed a top bunk. "I expect you aren't used to a narrow berth on a moving train," she teased. "And if you was to fall out, it'd wake me up."

"Thanks," Belle laughed. "I appreciate your concern." When the train whistle finally blew its warning for everyone to climb aboard, Belle peered out the windows at the darkened and now empty fairgrounds. The eleven acres that had only hours ago been a slice of the Wild West was once again an expanse of grass and shade trees and an unimpressive empty grandstand.

The train headed east through the sleeping city of St. Louis and then across the Mississippi River by way of the Eads Bridge. Daddy had been impressed by the bridge, Belle remembered, calling it a marvel of engineering. As the train rattled along, the three cowgirls who'd performed that day fell asleep. But the rocking of the train car and the sound of the rails combined with other thoughts and worries to keep Belle awake far into the night. She didn't understand why she hadn't heard more from Daddy. She'd told him exactly how to address letters to the Wild West. And what was Momma thinking these days? Minnie had written that they had tea and that Momma said to send her love. That was something, but it wasn't enough. She wanted Momma to write.

Belle's mind wandered away from her parents and back to the Wild West. She wondered if Monte realized that Dora Spurgeon cared for him. Would Ned Bishop ever get over being mad at her? Did Shep know that Mabel Douglas watched his every move? Shep . . . Shep . . . Shep. His name was in her head so often lately. Something would have to be done about that. As Liberty Belle, she needed to be thinking more about perfecting an impressive act and less about Shep Sterling's smile. And much less about when he might kiss her again. With a sigh, Belle turned over. But she did not sleep.

Happiness could wear mighty thin when a person was forced to live in cramped quarters with someone who didn't like them. It seemed to Belle that when Mabel wasn't teasing Dora about Monte or her stutter, she was making sly remarks about Belle and Shep. Mabel Douglas just wasn't in the least bit friendly and it was getting increasingly hard to ignore.

Letters from home were very short. One of Daddy's recent notes was postmarked *Denver*. That helped some. Clearly Daddy was traveling for business. But Momma's wall of silence loomed ever higher. Belle's own letters home became less frequent. What was there to say, anyway? She helped unload. She sewed. She groomed horses. She helped pack up. And as far as she could tell she wasn't any nearer to actually performing. Shep kept saying she would ride Diamond in the parade in Washington, D.C., but that was weeks away. *Weeks.*

———

Willa was hoeing beans one morning when a rider approached from the direction of town. Laura, who had been thinning the dozen or so hills of squash at the far end of the garden, stood up and peered at the rider, then walked over and said, "Do you want me to send him away?"

With a sigh, Willa shook her head. "I have to face him sometime. It might as well be today." She reached for Laura's hand and gave it a squeeze. "Would you say a prayer for me?" Leaving the garden behind, she headed for her cabin even as she telegraphed a protest toward heaven. She did not want to see Otto today. It was too soon. But here he was, hitching his black gelding to a corral post next to the barn and striding toward her. Willa waited just beneath the overhang that created a small porch running the length of the rustic cabin.

"What's this?" Otto said abruptly, motioning at the cabin.

"Didn't Charlie mention this when he told you I'd be staying here?" Willa gestured around her. "The girls helped me clean it out."

He swiped an open hand over his mustache and goatee. "You can come home, Willa." He looked away. "I've already moved out. I'm living at the hotel now."

"I never wanted that house," Willa said. "A grandiose house was always your idea."

"I wanted you to have something nice."

She shook her head. "No you didn't. You wanted the biggest house in town. You wanted to impress everyone. If you'd wanted to give *me* something nice, you would have listened to what *I* wanted. We'd have built a smaller house and had money for gardens. And troon." She sighed. "But you never listened to me, and it doesn't really matter anymore. Irmagard is gone and there's no reason for me to live there." She gestured at the freshly turned earth that ran along the front of the porch. "I'm very content here. I've planted flowers. Daisies and larkspur. Charlie says they won't grow, but I'll keep them watered, and I bet he'll be surprised."

"Whatever you think you read in that letter," Otto blurted out, "I haven't betrayed you again. It isn't what you think."

"Really? How else should I have interpreted a letter from another woman that begins *My Dear Otto,* and goes on to express concern about a 'stipend' that hasn't arrived and then mentions how faithful you've been *over the years.*" Willa glared at him. "Exactly how many ways are there to think about a letter like that, Otto?"

He ran his hand over his mustache and goatee. "I am *not* keeping another woman. That money makes it possible for a promising young man to go to school."

Willa folded her arms and leaned against the door jamb. "And I suppose your relationship with the young man's mother is platonic?"

He looked away. Shook his head. "It wasn't at one time. But it has been for a long time. In fact, it isn't really even a relationship. I rarely see her." He gestured toward the cabin. "Could we please go inside?" When Willa hesitated, he reached into his coat and pulled out a bundle of letters. "From Irma," he said. "But there's something else I have to say, and I'd like to say it without several pairs of Mason eyes boring holes in me. Imaginary or not, I seem to sense that you and I are being watched."

Willa led him inside. Never had she seen Otto so flustered. He laid Irmagard's letters on the little kitchen table. "She's doing well," he said.

"I don't doubt that," Willa said. She was planning to visit Irmagard in New York, but it wasn't something she cared to discuss with him.

Otto took his hat off and set it on the table. He looked around him. "Please, Willa," he said. "I love you. I want you to come home." He took a deep breath. "You have to understand. It happened a long time ago. But I couldn't simply turn my back on my obligations. I couldn't just walk away and pretend he doesn't exist." He tugged on his goatee. "It would be different with a girl. A girl could make a good marriage and be all right. But a boy—a boy needs schooling. It isn't his fault the way he started out. Don't you see? He deserves a chance.

"His mother moved to Denver when he was little, and as far as everyone there is concerned, she's a widow. But I couldn't just turn my back on him. So I've sent money to a trustee. She never gets any of it. It's only for the boy." He sank onto the one chair in the tiny room and sat, fiddling with the stack of Irmagard's letters. Clearing his throat, he finally looked up at Willa. "He's twelve years old. And it was the last time I did anything like that. Do you hear me, Willa? It was *the last time*.

"I did a despicable thing to you, and I wouldn't have blamed you if you *had* left with Philip. But you didn't. You stayed with me. And we've built a good life together. I promised to be faithful to you if you'd stay, and I have kept that promise. With God as my witness, I have kept that promise. I love you, Willa. You and *only* you."

"He's twelve years old." As the reality of what Otto was confessing sunk in, Willa stopped listening. She lost the awareness of her surroundings, and when she regained her senses, she was sitting on the cot in the adjoining room trying to catch her breath—and trying not to vomit. Otto was still sitting at the kitchen table with his back to her and his head in his hands. If she hadn't known him better, she would have thought he was crying from the way his shoulders shook. It seemed to take hours for him to finally reach for his hat and turn around. He stood up and came to the doorway.

"Is there anything I can say, anything I can do that will convince you to forgive me and to come home?" His voice broke. "I am so sorry, Willa. So very sorry. I'll do anything. Anything you want. Just tell me what to do."

"Get out," Willa said. She was aware of him moving away from the door, but she didn't look at him. She heard the sound of his footsteps and then the squeaking of a hinge and the click of the latch as he pushed the screened door closed behind him. Finally the cadence of hoofbeats sounded as the great black horse took its rider away.

On the late-May morning when the Wild West set up in Hagerstown, Maryland, the sky was heavy with dark, billowing clouds. Thunder sounded in the distance as canvasmen and seat teams hurried to erect the grandstand. By the time the audience began to trickle in for the afternoon show, a fine mist had settled over the grounds.

Bill Cody had been confined to his parlor car ever since injuring his foot during the reenactment of his duel with Yellow Hand in Wheeling. Thanks to medicinal whiskey, Cody was managing to ride in the Grand Entry and at the head of the band of cowboys rescuing homesteaders from Indians on the warpath. Still, crowds were less than happy when they realized Cody wouldn't be presenting his famous target-shooting act, and they had ways of letting it be known. While Shep Sterling and Annie Oakley had received their usual ovations at the previous stop, when Cody rode out, things quieted down to what one reporter labeled, "merely polite." Things like that affected everyone's mood, and the gloomy weather was no help.

As the day wore on in Hagerstown and the mist evolved into bona fide drizzle, even Helen Keen, who could usually be counted on to keep friendly banter going as the cowgirls went through their preperformance routines, was in an off mood. When Mabel said something about Dora's "c-c-crush" on Monte, Helen grabbed her arm. "Shut up, Mabel. For once in your life, just shut up and leave Dora alone."

Belle excused herself and ducked into the wardrobe tent. Other than an occasional click of a belt buckle or the thud of a work boot dropping to the ground, the only sound in the tent was the patter of raindrops on the canvas overhead. When, with a clap of thunder and a flash of lightning, it began to rain in earnest, a collective moan went up.

For the first time since joining the Wild West, Belle was consciously grateful for Dr. Miller's presence with the troupe. She was also glad she wasn't performing. Riders would be soaked to the skin moments after shedding their slickers, and the arena would be a morass of slippery mud. Any act depending on quick maneuvers would take on an entirely new level of danger. Belle began to worry. She cared about these people and didn't want any of them getting hurt. Bill Cody might be calling his injured foot a "slight inconvenience," but it had sent ripples through the entire troupe and inspired a round of storytelling about past accidents. Shep said most of the tales were exaggerated. Belle hoped he was right.

The Grand Entry was finished before Belle donned her own slicker and headed toward the arena. The rules that forbade lingering backstage were strict, but surely no one would take issue with her being there to hold her friends' slickers while they were in the arena. That wasn't *loitering*. It was *helping out*.

Thunder rumbled and rolled across the sky just as Helen, Dora, and Mabel were getting ready to shrug out of their slickers and hand them over. Belle flattened herself against the false wall that blocked off the open end of the grandstand to get out of the way of Dora's roan as the horse did a little sideways crow hop. Even Helen's dependable pinto shook his head and danced about. Suddenly a bolt of lightning streaked out of the sky and hit a tree on the opposite side of the lot. With a tremendous pop the tree exploded into a ball of flames. Helen's pinto reared, striking out with his front hooves. For a fraction of a second, both horse and rider were outlined against the stormy sky. An expert horsewoman, Helen stayed with her mount, but the rain had dampened her saddle, and when the pinto slipped in the mud, Helen lost her seat and landed with a sickening thud.

While others grabbed the bay's reins to keep him from bolting, Belle fell to her knees beside her unconscious friend and tried to shield her from the rain. Shep ran up and, crouching down, laid two fingers alongside Helen's neck to check for a pulse. Satisfied, he ran his hands over her arms and legs. Apparently convinced there were no broken bones, he scooped her up and ran for the nearest shelter—the dressing tent.

Ma knelt over Helen, smoothing her pale forehead and murmuring comfort.

"I don't think anything's broken," Shep said. "Her pulse is strong. But—" He gulped. Belle glanced up at him. Was he really almost in tears?

Ma checked again for broken bones. When Helen inhaled sharply and let out a moan, Ma smiled. "I think she mostly just got the wind knocked out of her." She dabbed at a cut along Helen's hairline with a clean cloth. "She's gonna have a headache, though. Maybe a black eye."

Helen moaned again, then tried to sit up.

"Lie still," Shep said. He grabbed one of her hands and held on. "You're gonna be fine. Just lie still until Doc Miller gets here." He looked toward the grandstand. "Where is he, anyway?"

As if on cue, the doctor arrived, muttering while he worked. "She'll have quite the headache . . . doesn't needs stitches . . . no broken bones. . . . pulse is good . . ." Finally, he looked up. "She'll be fine," he said.

Belle reached for Shep. He pulled her close. Sighing with relief, they both looked down on Helen.

The arena manager came into the tent. "Thank God," he said when Doc Miller gave his report. He glanced at Shep. "We'll just skip the race in the second act tonight. Crowd's thin anyway."

"No need to do that," Helen protested. Wincing and rubbing her neck, she sat up.

"You are one crazy female if you think you're riding tonight," Shep said. Both the doctor and the arena manager nodded agreement.

"Not me," Helen said. Grimacing as she rubbed her shoulder, she pointed to Belle. "Her." She glanced from the arena manager to Shep and back again. "You know she can do it. It's just a little race. All she has to do is stay in the saddle." She nodded toward the outdoors. "And look. It's clearing up."

The arena manager stepped to where the wardrobe tent canvas had been rolled up to admit light near Ma's work area and peered up at the sky. He glanced back at Shep. "Blue sky peeking out. Bill had you keepin' an eye on her"—he nodded at Belle—"so I'll make this your decision."

Belle thought it took about ten years for Shep to finally look her way. "Take it nice and easy," he said. "Just get yourself and Diamond through the race in one piece. Let Dora take the lead."

Belle let out a whoop of joy and leaped into his arms.

Laughing, he returned the hug before pulling her arms from around his neck and saying, "And remember . . . let Dora *win*."

CHAPTER 17

THERE IS AN APPOINTED TIME FOR EVERYTHING. . . .
A TIME TO WEEP, AND A TIME TO LAUGH;
A TIME TO MOURN, AND A TIME TO DANCE.

Ecclesiastes 3:1,4 NASB

Belle was too worried about Diamond slipping and hurting himself to enjoy her debut. By the end of the race she was so covered with the mud flung into the air by Dora's mount she could hardly tell what color she was wearing. She could taste the arena dirt, and swiping at her face with the sleeve of her mud-caked shirt only made it worse, but as Belle sat astride Diamond and looked up into the smiling faces of the enthusiastic crowd and listened to the applause, she got goose bumps. "Good boy," she said to Diamond, and leaned down to pat his mud-caked neck. "Good boy."

Someone in the front row of the stands held something out as Dora took her victory lap. She accepted it, then trotted her pony to where Belle waited.

"W-wave," she said, and handed Belle the rose. "You d-did great."

Belle waved.

"Take a bow," Dora said.

Standing up in the stirrups, Belle took off her hat and waved it to the crowd. Together, the cowgirls wheeled their horses about and rode out of the arena. As far as any of the spectators knew, they had just watched Texan Helen Keen lose a race to Montana Girl Dora Spurgeon. Which was fine with Belle. She wanted Liberty Belle's first moment in the arena to be perfect. She wanted reporters watching her every move and writing articles about her. She wanted Bill Cody to be so glad he hired her that he offered her a raise. And she wanted to be among the chosen few who regularly entertained dignitaries visiting the Wild West. And so an incognito performance was just fine with Belle. For now.

While she might remain unknown among the spectators tonight, the wranglers on the back lot had no intention of ignoring Belle's debut. They hooted congratulations and joked about her "mud-mount" and her "fancy costume." They teased Dora about winning a fixed race and hollered for Belle to try harder next time. By the time Belle and Dora had ridden back to where they could dismount and get cleaned up, Belle was happier than she'd ever been. Sliding to the ground she reached for a hackamore just as Shep walked up.

"Thought you might be stuck to the saddle," he said with a grin. He picked a glob of mud off her hair. "You, Miss Belle, are a bona fide mess. Not to mention your horse. Didn't he used to be gray?"

Belle laughed and nodded. "He did. And I used to have red hair and freckles." She looked down at her mud-spattered clothes. "And we might be a mess, but we're happy messes." She patted Diamond's neck. "He knows he did good—don't you, boy?"

Diamond whickered and bobbed his head up and down.

"Well, you both did great," Shep said. "You even followed orders."

"I didn't have a choice," Belle retorted. "Diamond's no race-horse." She grinned. "Just be glad I wasn't riding Lady Blaze," she said. "I might not have been able to help myself. Not with that crowd cheering. It's amazing."

"As good as you imagined?"

"Better," Belle said.

Shep nodded. "I'm glad you had fun."

"Well, I did. Thank you for letting me ride tonight."

He squeezed her hand. "You earned it."

Was it her imagination, or was he leaning in to . . . Nope. He wasn't. Or, if he was leaning in to kiss her, he'd thought better of it. He let go of her hand. "Gotta get back over for the Final Salute," he said. Then he patted her shoulder. As if she were his kid sister. "You'll be riding in it before you know it."

"That she will." It was Helen, moving slower than normal but obviously feeling better. "Now git along, little doggie," she said to Shep. "You promised me a steak supper in town tonight, and I want it sooner rather than later."

Philadelphia
June 10, 1886
Dear Momma and Daddy,

I've had my debut! Not exactly the way I had planned, and no one knows it was me, but I took Helen Keen's place this past week in the pony race in the second half. I rode Diamond, and of course that means we lost every time, but the audiences don't care, and honestly, neither do I. Helen has been under the weather. But she's better now, so I doubt I'll have another chance to perform until after we settle on Staten Island and Cody, Salsbury, and Sterling finally agree that Liberty Belle and Diamond are ready.

Not long after I took Helen's place, they let me ride in the Decoration Day parade in Washington, D.C. Everyone seemed to think I should have the practice before we get to the big city of New York. I think they were testing how Diamond would react to street noise, but if they were worried, they aren't anymore because Diamond was perfect. He acted like he'd been doing parades all his life. And we rode right past the White House!

The crowds here in Philadelphia have been so big that right now as I am writing to you, I can hear the carpenters hammering away, adding more seats to the grandstand. People arrive via stage from three different parts of the city to see the Wild West, and in addition to the stages, the railroad is running special trains out to us. Shep says that if it keeps up at this pace the Wild West will play to over a hundred thousand people before we have moved on.

This past Sunday Shep took me into town. He said that Liberty Belle should see the Liberty Bell. Ha. It is hard to imagine that Benjamin Franklin once walked the very same streets. We saw where he used to live and then rode the ferry across to the zoo and ended our day in the city with the cyclorama of the Battle of Gettysburg. It made me cry to think of all those brave men dying in battle.

Daddy, did you remember to order new boots from Mr. Brady? I've had Monte's repaired twice. You can send them to me in care of the Wild West, Erastina, Staten Island, New York. Now that we are settled in, I am hoping to receive at least a dozen letters from home—letters I imagine following us across the country but arriving just after we've left a certain station. At least I hope that is why I haven't heard from you. I am not exactly homesick, but I do miss you. BOTH OF YOU.

> *Your affectionate daughter,*
> *Irmagard a.k.a. Belle*

As the evening sun dipped toward the horizon in the west, Willa dragged her kitchen chair outside and sat down to reread the letter Charlie had brought out from town. Irmagard "wasn't exactly homesick," but she missed. . . . *both of them.* Willa's eyes misted over when she read that. She folded the letter and tucked it back in its envelope.

She supposed it was understandable for Irmagard to be infatuated by someone like Shep Sterling. Still, the frequency of the man's name in all her letters was concerning. Willa wondered why Otto hadn't attended to shipping the boots. Irmagard obviously needed them. If he was going to support this phase of his daughter's life, the least he could do was follow through and see that she had the proper equip ment. As the sun sank behind the distant horizon, Willa decided it was time to go into town. Time to purchase train tickets. Time to visit Irmagard.

"Glad to see you still want them," Dan Brady said, as he set Irmagard's new boots on the counter. "I was beginning to wonder. They've been ready for a couple of weeks. I sent word over to the bank, but Mr. Friedrich hasn't been in."

"Would you have them shipped to this address, please," Willa said, and handed Dan a slip of paper on which she'd written Irmagard's address in New York.

Brady perused the address and whistled low. "Is she riding in the show?"

"She filled in for one of the other young women, who was indisposed," Willa said. "But I believe her own debut has yet to happen."

"Still," Brady said, "you should be proud. It's not every young woman who has that kind of grit and spunk."

Willa mumbled something noncommittal and left the store thinking that *grit* and *spunk* were not exactly the character qualities uppermost in her mind when she was raising her red-headed daughter. From Brady's she made her way to the dressmaker's.

"Have you begun the new ensemble I'd ordered for this fall yet?" she asked.

"I'm sorry, ma'am, but I—"

"Good," Willa interrupted. "I won't be needing it after all. I'd appreciate it if you could just carry the payment I made as a credit on your books. I'm certain I'll need some work done in coming weeks.

I'm just—well. Things are little uncertain at the moment regarding my plans for the fall.."

Miss Avery nodded. "Actually I'd thought that might be the case." she said. "When I saw that the house was closed up, I thought I should wait to begin until I'd heard from you again."

Closed up? The house has been closed up? Just because Ella Jane and Samuel married and left town is no reason— "Well then," Willa said, "I'll be in touch. Now if you'll excuse me."

She left the shop quickly, climbed into her buggy, and drove to the house. What was this nonsense Ellen Avery was spouting about her and Otto closing things up? Otto said he was living at the hotel, but she hadn't really taken that seriously. After all, he was the one who'd wanted the big house in the first place. She couldn't imagine him ever really giving it up.

She pulled the buggy beneath the portico and went to the side door, surprised when she could not look inside. Someone had drawn every drape in the house. Her heart pounding, Willa unlocked the door and let herself in. Every stick of furniture in the house had been covered with drop cloths. Ella Jane's room was empty. The kitchen was in order, but both icebox and pantry were empty. Someone had set a mousetrap beneath the kitchen table. *He'd really done it.* She let herself out and locked the door.

Willa drove to the bank. After all, Otto should know she'd been at the house in case someone reported seeing a woman snooping around. Of course everyone in North Platte recognized Willa Friedrich's horse and buggy. She didn't really believe anyone would report a "suspicious person" snooping around the house. But it wouldn't hurt for Otto to know that in spite of his betrayal, she could be civil. It also wouldn't hurt for everyone to see that the Friedrichs could effect a civilized separation.

"He's been staying over at the hotel since closing up the house," Wilber said.

Willa nodded. "I know." She paused. "I'll just wait in his office until he returns. If you don't think it'll be too long?"

"Well, ma'am, I couldn't say exactly. But you won't want to wait in there. Mr. Friedrich's in Denver. Didn't say when he'd be back."

The Wild West arrived in New York sometime during the night of June 25. Belle awoke the instant the train stopped moving. She lay for a few minutes listening to the now familiar sounds of pulleys and hammers, whinnies and hoofbeats, as supply wagons were unloaded and tents raised. When it was clear she wasn't going to be able to go back to sleep, she climbed out of her berth and began to dress.

"You've certainly come a long way since your cowbell days," Helen said from her upper berth. She reached down and ruffled Belle's hair. "In case you haven't noticed, it's still pitch-dark outside."

"But they're putting up the tents. *Our* tent. Aren't you sick of living on this train? And think of it—there's an ocean out there! And the city of New York! And the bridge! Who can sleep thinking about all of that?!"

"Apparently *no one* stuck in a Pullman with you," Mabel grumbled. With a dramatic sigh she turned over, telegraphing her intention to try.

Belle grabbed her boots. "Well, you three can sleep all day if you like. I'm going to go see if Diamond's unloaded yet. Maybe braid his mane for the parade. Do you think Ma would let me have some ribbon?"

"For crying out loud," Mabel said. "Will you *hush*?"

Rolling her eyes, Belle did an exaggerated tiptoe for the door, sitting on the bottom step to pull on her boots. Helen wasn't far behind.

The dressing tent was already up. Helen and Belle were among the first Wild Westers to arrive, but Shep and Monte soon popped in, and just as Belle was asking Ma Clemmons if there might be some red fabric she could tear into strips and braid into Diamond's mane and tail, Dora Spurgeon ducked inside, too.

"Nope," Ma shook her head. "I've got no red fabric to spare." She reached for a box. "But let's see what we can rustle up." She opened the box and with mock surprise said, "Well, lookee here." She pulled out a dark blue split skirt, matching vest, and a red shirt. Draping the vest and shirt over her arm, Ma held up the skirt. "Looks to be about your size, wouldn't you say?"

"It's perfect." Belle caressed the soft blue fabric, then held the skirt up to her waist.

Shep reached behind a folding screen and produced a hatbox holding a new fawn-colored Stetson with a scarlet hatband. "Approved by Mr. Salsbury as required," Shep said with a smile.

"And h-h-here," Dora said, and pulled a white kerchief out of her pocket. "I p-p-put those b-beads on the edge. S-s-ilver, so they shine in the l-lights."

Tears welled up as Belle looked at her circle of friends. "I don't know what to say."

"That's all right," Ma Clemmons said, "because there's no time for a speech anyway." She handed Belle a pile of red, white, and blue ribbons. "At least not if you're going to get that horse's mane braided in time for Liberty Belle's first official parade."

"Excited or scared?" Shep joined Belle at the ferry railing.

"A little of both," Belle said. She motioned toward the city. "That's an amazing sight for a girl from Nebraska."

"That's an amazing sight for anyone from anywhere," Shep said. He pointed across the water to a small island. "Bledsoe's Island.

Liberty Enlightening the World. Most of it still in crates around the base."

"Can we go over there sometime?"

"I'll take you first chance we get," Shep said.

Monte spoke up. "Too bad Orrin Knox won't be around for that." He held one hand up and swept it across an imaginary banner. "Liberty Belle meets Liberty."

They all laughed, then Shep nodded in the opposite direction of the New York and Brooklyn Bridge. "If you're *real* nice to me, I might even see my way clear to take you to see the bridge close up. But you got to be *real* nice. It costs three cents to cross it on the pedestrian walkway. I wouldn't want to waste my hard-earned money on just anyone."

Belle arched one eyebrow and looked up at him. "I'll have you know I'm not 'just anyone,' cowboy."

He smiled down at her. "Well, you're right about that, ma'am, and I do stand corrected."

Feeling herself begin to blush, Belle changed the subject, pointing to the ferry landing. "There's more people than in the whole of North Platte just right there at the landing."

Helen Keen shook her head. "I am gonna be more than ready to skedaddle straight to the train station and head for my wide-open spaces when this season is over and done."

Belle began to get nervous. "One thing's certain. I'm grateful for good old Diamond and his steady temperament today."

Helen patted Diamond's neck. "He's a good old boy. And you'll do fine. Just follow Dora and me, and don't try anything too flashy right away."

The ferry landed. Leading Diamond, Belle followed the other cowgirls ashore. Diamond's ears came forward. He began to dance around a bit. "It's all right," Belle said quietly. She put a hand on the horse's neck. "Just a waterfront. Different smells, I know. Not like back home. But see there up ahead? You know those other horses.

And there's Helen . . . and Dora . . . and grouchy old Mabel . . . and it's just another parade. Noisier than Washington, but still just a parade. We'll be fine." Whether she was talking to herself or the horse didn't really matter. Diamond calmed down a little and she began to feel better, too.

Helen led the way to where the troupe was forming a long line just outside the ferry station. Belle mounted up. Diamond flicked his silken tail and tossed his head as he danced into place.

"I think he likes it," Belle laughed as the old pony began to show more spirit than she'd ever seen.

"Of course he does, honey," Helen said. "The boys always like to strut their stuff." She nodded up ahead. "Look at the Shepherd. He's having the time of his life."

It was true. Shep hadn't even mounted up yet. Instead, he'd walked to where a group of New Yorkers—of the feminine variety—lined the curb. He was signing autographs and smiling and nodding, and if it hadn't been for Nate Salsbury's piercing whistle, Belle thought Shep might have just been swallowed up by the mass of ladies struggling to talk to him. When he tipped his hat and leaped into the saddle without using his stirrups, the ladies squealed with delight. Shep backed his palomino away from the curb and guided him into place just behind Buffalo Bill and alongside Annie Oakley and Lillian Smith. Cody stood up in his stirrups and, raising his arm like an army scout giving orders to a column of soldiers, motioned for everyone to move out. The band began to play, and off they went.

As the parade took shape, cowboys, vaqueros, and Indians fell in behind the Wild West stars, and Belle lost sight of Shep. Ma Clemmons's husband, Grady, followed the Indians, leading a pair of tame buffalo. Next came the Deadwood mail coach and mounted riders playing the part of the pony express charging up and down either side of the procession brandishing pistols as their ponies' hoofs clattered on the brick streets.

Finally, it was the women's turn to ride. Belle hadn't gone three city blocks before her face began to hurt from smiling and her shoulders to ache from waving.

"I can't feel my face anymore," Belle said at one point.

"The price of fame, honey," Helen replied without even looking over. She signaled her horse to rear up, and the crowd applauded and whistled. Diamond tossed his head and swished his tail. Helen laughed. "Go ahead," she said to Belle. "Give it a whirl. Just remember we're going to be doing this for about twice as long as we did in D.C., so pace yourself. And the horse."

In the next block Belle and Diamond put on the show. Then Mabel and Dora followed suit. Belle slipped behind her saddle and lay prone across Diamond's back. The reaction was so enthusiastic that Mabel and Dora began to show a few of their tricks, too. At one point, Belle took her feet out of the stirrups, turned around and, riding backward, bent her knees and positioned her feet atop Diamond's rump. Leaning back, she hoped she was giving the impression of a lady in repose. Apparently she was, because the crowd loved it. On impulse, she took her kerchief off and, waving it in the air, looked back at Dora. When Dora nodded, Belle tossed the kerchief. Dora caught it, then tossed it to Mabel. But Mabel didn't even try to toss it back. Instead, she twirled it in the air and then threw it down. Belle spun Diamond around and swooped down and picked the kerchief up off the pavement. Again, the crowd roared approval.

By the time the Wild West parade made the turn that would take them back down the length of Manhattan Island to the ferry landing, the four riders had repeated every trick over and over again. Muscles hurt that Belle didn't even know she had. She was exhausted, and she had never felt better in her life.

CHAPTER 18

✦✦═◎ ◎═✦✦

A TIME TO EMBRACE,
AND A TIME TO SHUN EMBRACING.
Ecclesiastes 3:5 NASB

June 28, 1886
Dear Minnie,

We have fifty acres here on Staten Island. FIFTY! There's an amphitheatre that was built especially for us. General Sherman himself was here for opening day. Mr. Mark Twain has been several times, and P. T. Barnum—who has foresworn any show but his own for forty years—came to ours, and had only words of praise.

It seems that some exciting bit of news makes the rounds here every single day. Bill Cody has hired a famous stage director to plan the indoor production opening at Madison Square Garden in November. I hope Liberty Belle is given a part. Monte tells me that cast members for that production will stay in rooming houses in the city. The Indians, however, will stay in camp here on Staten Island. Can you picture the Pawnee and Sioux, in full regalia, riding the Staten Island ferry every day and then making their way across Manhattan and up to the Garden for each performance?

Seventeen steamboats a day bring people out to see the Wild

West. *I haven't personally counted them, of course, but that's what the newspaper says. I am enclosing clippings from the New York Times and the Brooklyn Eagle. Please make sure that Momma and Daddy see them. I forgot to put the clippings in their letter.*

Tomorrow Shep and Helen, Monte and Dora and I are determined to go into the city. We invited Mabel Douglas, but she said she had other plans. I believe she has given up on Shep and may be working on Ned Bishop. Sunday Joe has been harping on forgiveness again, and this past Sunday he particularly stressed the necessity for the Christian to "bless those who curse them." Perhaps Mabel and Ned are God's way of seeing if I was listening.

In spite of not being universally loved by every single person in the troupe, at times I am so happy I could cry. Now that we are in a more permanent setting, I will be able to return to the practice ring with Diamond. If only Momma could see how the people of New York welcomed us, I know she would change her mind about what I am doing. I intend to write and try to get Daddy to bring her to New York.

Monte seems to be quite fond of a certain beautiful ranchera. Helen Keen is fast becoming my very good friend, and Shep Sterling proves in many ways the truth spoken in his gift of white roses. Please give my love to Uncle Charlie and Aunt Laura.

Ever your affectionate cousin,
Liberty Belle

Belle signed the letter with a flourish, smiling as she contemplated Minnie's reaction to the coded message about Shep Sterling and white roses. He might not have kissed her again, but it was uncanny how often he seemed to just turn up when Belle crossed the lot. If he was looking out for her, she didn't mind. And for a girl who'd scolded Minnie for not having a more worthy goal than simply getting married, Belle realized her own daydreams these days skirted dangerously close to similar themes, albeit with barbed wire and horses in place of picket fences and babies. Of course any of that would have to wait until she'd spent several years as Liberty Belle. Nothing was going to get in the way of that.

Folding her letter, Belle tucked it into an envelope and ducked out of her tent. After delivering it to the office for posting, she headed for the wardrobe tent, where she expected Ma Clemmons to put her to work. Halfway there she saw Shep smiling down at a young boy dressed in plaid wool knickers. There was nothing uncommon about an awestruck boy staring in openmouthed wonder at the King of the Cowboys. But there was nothing common about the woman holding the boy's hand. She was stunningly beautiful, with abundant blond hair, a radiant smile, and the bluest eyes Belle had ever seen.

"Worried?" Mabel Douglas, seated at a sewing machine a few feet away, glanced toward Shep and then back at Belle with a mean little smile.

Belle ignored the comment. "I was looking for Ma. To see what she needs me to do today."

Mabel smirked. She nodded toward where Shep was still talking to the woman and the boy. "*He* seems to be enjoying himself," she said.

"Where's Ma?" Belle repeated.

"Gone into the city. Meeting someone about the winter production."

The last thing Belle wanted to do was sit in this tent all afternoon without Ma—or someone else—to run interference between herself and Mabel Douglas. "Then I'm going over to the stables to longe Diamond. I'm thinking he's probably sore from all those miles on city streets yesterday. If Ma comes back, could you tell her I'll come back later and plan to work through tonight's performance?"

"I'm not your messenger girl," Mabel said. "And besides, I won't be here long. Unlike some people, *I've* got *two* performances today."

Belle found paper and a pencil and scribbled a note for Ma Clemmons. She left the dressing tent and picked her way behind some of the other tents so as to avoid seeing Shep—in case he was still talking to that gorgeous woman. Minutes later she was standing beside one of the newly erected corrals where Blaze and a couple of the other broncs had been turned out for exercise. But she couldn't get her mind off Shep.

———

"Mabel said you'd be over here," Shep said, and sidled up next to Belle as she stood by the corral. "I had someone I wanted you to meet."

"Mabel told you where to find me?" Of course she did. It was Shep asking. Mabel would turn a somersault for Shep.

"Why wouldn't she? You and Mabel have a falling out?"

"That woman has had a burr under her saddle about me ever since I joined up. Don't ask me why."

"Try to be patient with Mabel," Shep said. "Life hasn't been very good to her."

"Is that any reason for her to take it out on me? Believe me, if I knew what I'd done to rile her so, I'd ask forgiveness just to clear the air and hope life could be a little more pleasant for all of us. Problem is, I think it's the fact that I *breathe* she resents most, and I'm just not willing to stop that to please Mabel." Belle paused. "Who'd you want me to meet, anyway?"

"Another time," Shep said. He nodded at Blaze. "She's looking fit as a fiddle."

"I wish I had money. I'd buy her like that." Belle snapped her fingers. "It just kills me to see them using her this way."

"Cy doesn't think she has the temperament for the arena."

"I know," Belle said, "and I understand his reasoning. But that doesn't mean I have to like it. And I still say she'd never have thrown that fit if Ned had listened to me and used a lighter hand. I told him to stop sawing on her mouth." Just then Blaze reared up and pawed the air. Belle sighed. "Can't you just see her decked out in a show saddle?"

"Diamond's gonna get his feelings hurt if he hears you talking like that," Shep teased.

"I love Diamond," Belle protested. "It's not his fault that he's the apple pie while Blaze is the French pastry." She sighed. "Not that I'll need a French pastry anytime soon."

"Liberty Belle has a very bright future," Shep said. "She just needs to be patient."

"That's very sweet of you to say, but with all due respect, I don't think you really know that to be a fact."

"In case you haven't noticed, I sort of keep my eye on you."

"You have to," Belle teased. "It's your job, remember?"

"Now that hurts," Shep said, and put his hand on his heart and staggered back. "Give a girl roses and kiss her good-bye and she thinks it means nothing."

"Come on," Belle said. "I never would have heard from you again if I hadn't gotten hired."

"Do you really think that?"

She shrugged.

"I'll take that for a yes. Although I don't understand it."

"Forget it," Belle said. "I'm sorry I said anything."

"Don't be sorry. Just explain your line of reasoning."

Why had she brought it up? This was embarrassing. "I didn't hear from you." She shrugged again. "I mean you kissed me and then—"

"I kissed you and yelled at myself about it all the way to St. Louis," Shep said. "I was raised better than that. A gentleman shows respect for a lady by following the rules. Sneaking around like that was wrong."

"Rules?" Belle snorted. "I joined the Wild West to get away from rules."

"Don't ever run away from the rules created to protect you. I was wrong to kiss you that day. I knew your mother didn't approve of me."

"Well, if you need my momma's permission, you're off the hook completely, because even if she were talking to me—which she is not—she'd never give permission for you to so much as take me to dinner."

Shep grinned. "Ah, but you're not living under her roof anymore. So I don't figure I *need* her permission. But I do have every intention of winning her *approval*."

"You wanted to kiss me, and you did, but it was wrong. And now you don't need anyone's permission, but you're going for Momma's approval." Belle shook her head. "This game has too many rules. And they keep changing. I can't keep up."

He leaned close. "Allow me to clarify the situation for you, Miss Belle." He brushed his lips across her cheek and whispered in her ear, "This is no game . . . and I'm not playing." He walked away.

Belle folded her arms atop the corral fence and hid her face while she waited to catch her breath.

On Sunday after church, Helen and Monte, Dora and Belle and Shep flocked onto the Staten Island Ferry and headed for the city. As the ferry nosed its way into the bay, Helen nudged Shep. "I know you're dying to do it. So," she motioned, "let's hear it."

When the rest of the group began to badger him, Shep stood up and, taking his hat off, began a speech. "To the northeast, we have the New York and Brooklyn Bridge, spanning one of the busiest stretches of navigable salt water on the earth, first proposed as a way to prevent overcrowding in Manhattan by encouraging population growth in Brooklyn." He motioned toward the bridge. "The towers rise to the incredible height of 276 feet. Each of its four steel cables is fifteen inches in diameter. The foundations were constructed over a period of three years and an additional four years were required for the completion of the towers. The cost of the bridge? Fifteen *million* dollars—twice the original estimate. Pedestrians may enjoy the view from the walkway for the paltry sum of three pennies." Putting his hat back atop his head, Shep took a bow. Applause and hoots and catcalls erupted. Shep took a second bow, then settled next to Belle.

At the wharf, he took her hand as he led the way toward the new bridge. It seemed the most natural thing in the world to be walking hand-in-hand with him, and yet Belle could feel herself blushing as Shep paid the toll and led her onto the bridge. "You'll love this story," he said as they headed out across the water. "The chief engineer's wife had studied many of the topics related to civil engineering—with the idea that she could help her husband. A few years into the project, her husband was disabled by caisson disease."

"What's that?"

"It happens sometimes when the workers are deep in the earth digging the foundations. Something to do with the depth. It isn't understood very well, but it killed some of them. Roebling didn't die, but he was partially paralyzed, deaf, and dumb. Mrs. Roebling began to make daily trips in his place, and she did such a good job communicating with the contractors—and she knew so much about bridge building—that some of them actually thought *she* was the chief engineer. When the bridge finally opened, Mrs. Roebling was given the first ride across."

"For a cowboy, you certainly know a lot about the New York and Brooklyn Bridge," Belle said. She smiled up at him. "I'm thinking maybe you know all that because you were here when it happened."

He nodded. "Yes, ma'am. I was. You aren't the only rich kid to hightail it for parts unknown."

"How did *your* mother react?"

"She was fine with it. In fact, you'll likely meet her one of these days. She's out of the city right now, but she'll definitely come over when she gets back." He sighed. "In my case it was my father who protested long and loud."

"Is it any better now?"

"He passed away last year. But we had some good moments together before he died. He never understood me, but I never doubted that he loved me." He smiled. "I also have two sisters. One who won't have a thing to do with what she calls Shep's Folly, and the other who seems to think it's all right. She was actually on the grounds the other day. Her name's Marie. She has an eight-year-old son who really builds up my ego."

"The blonde with the boy dressed in plaid knickers?"

"So you *did* see them."

Belle nodded. "From the wardrobe tent. Mabel teased me about her. Said I should be worried."

"And were you?"

"A little," Belle admitted. "All right. More than a little. Your sister is one of the most beautiful women I've ever seen." She shrugged. "I actually skirted behind some tents to avoid you two. I thought—" She could feel herself turning red. "Never mind what I thought."

"No, please go on," Shep said. "I'm enjoying this."

Belle nudged him. "Well, stop it." She motioned to where a few of the Wild West crowd were gathered at the far end of the bridge. "We'd better get back. That's Dora and Monte waving for us." As Shep led the way back toward Manhattan, Belle said, "Do you think those two are unofficially courting?"

He nodded. "I do. And Monte could do a lot worse. Dora's a good woman."

"Mabel isn't very nice to her sometimes," Belle said. "She makes fun of her stutter. A lot. And I know you said Mabel's had a hard life, but that's no excuse to be mean. Especially to someone as sweet as Dora. Sometimes I wish Dora would just haul off and let Mabel have it. But most of the time she ignores the teasing. In fact, sometimes she even goes out of her way to be nice to Mabel, although Mabel never appreciates it." Belle shook her head. "I don't think I could ever forgive someone who was as mean to me as Mabel is to Dora."

"I don't know if I could, either," Shep agreed. "Which is one of the reasons I respect Dora so much. Her faith is quiet. She doesn't say much about it. She just lives it."

CHAPTER 19

REJOICE WITH THOSE WHO REJOICE . . .
Romans 12:15 NASB

All around her the camp had settled in for the night. Now that she
was used to working long days, Belle was beginning to have trouble
sleeping again. Her mind just wouldn't settle. There was so much
to think about, and everything she thought about had an element
of worry to it—from Mabel's being mean to Dora, to Dora's never
fighting back, to Daddy's goodness to her, to Momma's simmering
anger. As she wrestled with worry, Belle imagined her parents sitting out on the porch at home trying to catch a summer breeze while
Daddy read and Momma stitched on her mantel scarf. If she were
there right now, Belle knew she would be wondering why Momma
messed with fancy stitching and wishing she could saddle up and go
for a ride. Of course if she were back in Nebraska right now, she'd
be out at the ranch.

The Masons were likely gathered around the table for a late supper. More often than not during the summer, it was sundown before
anyone took time to eat. Belle pictured the family bowing their heads
while Uncle Charlie said grace. She imagined mounds of fresh-picked

green beans, sliced tomatoes, fresh-baked bread, and butter. Maybe Aunt Laura would have made a chokecherry pie. No . . . it was too early for chokecherries.

With a sigh, Belle turned over and tried to get comfortable. Though she was a thousand miles away from Nebraska, she was beginning to realize that she hadn't really changed all that much. She was still hankering for things she couldn't have. Still restless. Not exactly unhappy . . . but not content, either. Everyone said she and Diamond did a great job in the parades, but no one said a thing about her entering the arena. Lately she'd been thinking maybe it was Diamond. He was a steady and reliable horse, but there wasn't an ounce of flash in him. She hadn't liked the other cowgirls' horses at first, but over time she'd realized there was something to be said for Helen's brightly patterned pinto and the spotted rump on Mabel's horse. Such things made for better "costumes." Buffalo Bill's white horse was proof. So was Shep's palomino.

Shep. She could worry over him for half a night. He stole a kiss and then he backed off. He said he wanted her parents' approval for whatever it was he had planned and then he said he didn't need it anymore. He kissed her on the cheek and said he wasn't playing games, but then he seemed to hold her at arm's length the next time they saw each other. Last Sunday in the city he'd held her hand as they walked along. But then for most of the past week he was back to the arm's-length routine. What was going on? More important . . . why did she care? Because she did. She cared so much it frightened her.

Maybe romance had worked out all right for Uncle Charlie and Aunt Laura, but everywhere else Belle looked in the world the whole love and marriage thing turned out to be something of a mess. Everyone held up Ma and Pa Clemmons as paragons of marital devotion, but even they groused at one another from time to time. Working the wardrobe tent, Belle had seen it happen. As for Momma and Daddy, she wanted no part of a marriage like theirs. Oh, it might look great on the outside, but Belle knew that underneath the glossy surface of *dear*'s and *darling*'s there was all kinds of turmoil. And why did any of that matter to her? She was intent on staying single and being a star. Wasn't she?

With a sigh, Belle threw back the covers and sat up. Whatever she was intent on, it wasn't lying in bed thinking about things until she was wound up like a top. Tomorrow was her birthday. She'd be eighteen. And if she wanted to take a walk on a moonlit night without an escort, what was wrong with that? Some of the Wild West rules were just plain stupid.

Wiggling into her pants and pulling on her shirt, Belle grabbed her boots and ducked outside. The night air was cool. She felt better the minute she filled her lungs with it. Campfires burning over in the Indian village glimmered in the night. Moonlight reflected off the dozens of canvas "buildings," illuminating the grounds with a pale light. When her footsteps crunched on the gravel paths running between the tents, Belle stepped into the grass. She paused at the entrance to the arena and spent a few minutes visualizing the moment when Liberty Belle would gallop in.

Shep kept saying it would be soon. He kept telling her to be patient. Well, she'd been patient for the entire summer. Her patience was wearing thin. About a lot of things Shep said and did. Maybe he was just stringing her along. Men were like that. Weren't they? As if she knew anything about men. Momma had kept her on a very short leash. *Stop obsessing about all of that. You're on your own and you still aren't happy. What's wrong with you, anyway?*

With a sigh, Belle turned away from the arena and headed for the stables. If nothing else, she could give Diamond a treat or two and brush him down. He didn't need either, but he enjoyed both. As she walked past the bronc corral on her way to Diamond's stall, a horse's head came up.

"Hey, beautiful," Belle said.

Blaze snorted and tossed her head.

"You are *such* a show-off."

The mare pawed the earth and danced to the far side of the corral. Belle circled around. When she got close, she saw the first hints of scars on the mare's sleek shoulder. Of course that happened with all the broncs after being spurred over and over again, but seeing it on *this* horse? It wasn't right. Not for this mare. Not when she had so much promise—if only cowboys like Ned Bishop would back off and give her a chance to trust someone with a gentle hand.

It's none of your business. You can't afford to buy her, so let it go.

While Belle was arguing with herself, Blaze ducked her head and gave a little snort, then bucked a time or two.

"Ah, now," Belle said. "That's lovely, but it can't be any fun at all, not when there's a full-grown man flailing around on your back."

Blaze snorted and spun about, then stopped, her rear to Belle.

"I see that," Belle said. "And I see those ears. You're listening to every word I say, and we both know it. So why don't you just turn around and come over here and we'll have a little talk, woman to woman."

Blaze wheeled about. Instead of taking off again, she stood still and watched—albeit with the occasional tossing of the head and pawing of earth—as Belle ducked into the corral and, one step at a time, came within a few feet of her. *There's nothing wrong with giving her a lump of sugar. Shep said they like the idea of a bronc being easy to handle.* So Belle palmed the sugar and extended her hand. Nostrils flaring, the mare stayed put. Belle stepped closer until, finally, Blaze snatched the lump of sugar and took off.

Belle began to hum. The mare settled and looked her way, ears forward. Soon Belle was standing beside her, stroking her muzzle. "We're both nervous," she said, "but I don't think either one of us has anything to be afraid of, do we?" As she had seen Shep do back in Nebraska, Belle began to stroke the mare's neck, moving slowly toward her shoulders and then down her back. With a soft whicker, the mare turned her head and nuzzled Belle's arm.

"Don't bite now," Belle said.

The mare shook her head and snorted.

Belle laughed. "All right, so you don't bite. You can't blame me for mentioning it. You might remember that I'm the one you kicked—although I do believe that was unintentional." Even as she carried on the conversation, Belle was remembering Uncle Charlie's warnings about handling the barely broke ponies on the ranch. Blaze might be ready to make friends, but she was still a half-wild bucking bronco.

Someone had left a hackamore draped over a corral post. Without turning her back on the mare, Belle moved over to the post and retrieved it. In only a few minutes she had succeeded in slipping the hackamore over the mare's head. *This is good, but it's nothing new. The cowboys get a hackamore on her every time they move her. She's used to this.* It wasn't long before Belle was leading Blaze around the corral. *She knows all about this, too. You haven't done anything special.*

"So what d'ya think, lady?" Belle said aloud. "Would it be all right with you if I threw a leg over?"

"Absolutely not," a voice spoke from the darkness.

With a snort, the mare pulled free and charged to the opposite side of the corral. Belle spun around, ready to scold the owner of the voice—until she recognized Buffalo Bill.

"I-I was just . . ." Belle shrugged. "She shouldn't be a bronc. She deserves better." Cody was agonizingly quiet. Blaze bumped her from behind.

As Cody lit a cigar, a flash of light illuminated his face just long enough for Belle to realize she was in serious trouble. Cody motioned for her to get out of the corral. She obeyed and waited while he sauntered over. When he came to stand beside her, he still said nothing. Instead, he rested his arms atop the corral fence and watched Blaze while he smoked his cigar. Finally, he spoke up.

"When Irmagard Friedrich first arrived on the Wild West lot, I saw a spoiled young woman with a lot of potential and a ridiculous dream. Ridiculous, not because of any lack of talent, but because she'd been raised for a different kind of life. Now, I don't mind spoiled young women, Miss Belle. In fact, I have a great deal of affection for at least two such ladies by the name of Louisa and Arta Cody. And so I convinced my partner to see things my way. To decide there'd be no harm in doing an old friend a favor and seeing how the spoiled young lady with the dream would get on if we let her come along on the train." Bill drew on his cigar. "In spite of what you've interpreted as disinterest, I have kept up with what's been happening with you. Your road has taken its twists and turns."

"I've been working hard," Belle croaked.

"So I've heard," Cody agreed. "According to some, you've gone from thinking you *deserve* to be a star to realizing you have to *earn* it." He flicked ashes off the cigar. "You can be proud of that, Miss Belle."

"Thank you, sir," Belle croaked. He was pleased . . . right? Then why were those beads of sweat breaking out on her forehead?

Bill pulled his watch out of his vest pocket and held it up in the moonlight to read the time. Tucking it back into place he said quietly, "That being said, Miss Belle, I want you to understand something *very clearly*. If you weren't Otto Friedrich's daughter, you'd be packed up and on the train headed for home tomorrow morning."

Belle caught her breath.

Cody pointed toward the mare. "A good bronc—and by that I mean one that can be counted on to buck and still behave like something less than a son of Satan around its handlers—is worth about two thousand dollars to me." He paused. "Do you *have* two thousand dollars, Miss Belle?"

"N-no. Sir."

"I thought not." Cody nodded. "In the interest of making certain you understand what's just happened here, let me clarify something. I am looking forward to introducing Liberty Belle to my audience. I am hoping that she has a long and very successful career with the Wild West. As I see it, there are really only two things that will prevent that from happening. The first is beyond our control, the second is not." He paused. "Do you want to know what those two things are?"

Belle nodded.

Cody held up his index finger. "One. Injury. This Wild West business is dangerous. We do our best to make it as safe as possible, but horses slip, buffalo charge, and lightning strikes."

Belle nodded.

"Now, the second thing that will—and I urge you to understand just how distinctly I am saying that word *will*. The second thing that *will* prevent Liberty Belle's introduction to the Wild West audience—and is completely within her ability to control—is insubordination." He paused. "This Wild West I've created is a fine-tuned mechanism, Miss Belle, and I can't have my employees deciding they know better about this or that and straying from the fold." He nodded toward Blaze. "She's a fine horse, and I understand your attachment. But she's *my* horse. Now, you remember that and we won't have to have this conversation again." He tilted his head and stared down at her. "The fact is, Belle, we *won't* have this conversation again. Will we?"

Belle shook her head. She was too near tears to trust her voice.

Cody patted her shoulder. "So we both agree that when you take that hackamore off"—he nodded at Blaze—"that'll be the last contact you have with *my* mare."

Belle nodded again. She watched Cody walk away, his head held high, the tip of his cigar glowing orange in the dark.

Helen tucked her shirt in and sat down to pull on her boots, then looked at Belle. "How'd your little tea party with Blaze and Bill turn out last night—if you don't mind my asking."

Belle frowned. "You spied on me?"

"Honey, you have got to know by now that I am the worst mother hen on the lot. And in case you've forgotten, the female of the species wandering the back lot after dark alone is *strictly* against the rules on that contract you signed a couple months back. So yes, I spied on you and will continue to do so whenever and wherever I think you're fixing to get yourself fired." She stood up. "I assume from the fact you're getting dressed for breakfast and not packing your things that you aren't fired."

Belle pulled on a boot. "No. I'm not fired. Happy birthday to me. And I'd rather not talk about it."

Nodding, Helen bent down and pulled something wrapped in tissue from beneath her cot and plunked it on the table. "Happy birthday to you." Belle opened it and exclaimed over the beautifully beaded hatband. Helen grinned. "The Shepherd helped me decide on the design." She winked. "In case you need a reason to collect a birthday kiss or anything."

"Shep has made it very clear that he's a gentleman and that gentlemen don't do such things without the blessing of the parents." Belle rolled her eyes. "Or something like that. I don't remember his exact reasoning. Anyway, the gist of what he had to say pretty much guarantees there will be no kissing."

Helen chuckled a response and stepped to the tent entrance. As Belle sat down to put the new band on her hat, she saw Helen wave at someone, and just as she pulled her hat on, Shep showed up. "Happy birthday," he said, and handed her a copy of the Wild West program. He pointed to where a red bookmark showed. "Open it up."

Belle opened the program. Someone had written the name *Liberty Belle* in the lineup.

"Bill and Nate decided the Fourth of July was the perfect day to introduce Liberty Belle to the Wild West crowd."

Helen grinned. "What he ain't tellin' you is that Bill and Nate decided after this big galoot darned near threatened to quit if they didn't put you in on your birthday."

And I nearly ruined it all just last night. Clutching the program to her chest, Belle stood on tiptoe and kissed Shep on the cheek. "Thank you," she said. She kissed his other cheek. "Thank you."

"Don't mention it." He smiled down at her. "Just prove me right today by showin' 'em what you got."

———

"Ladies and Gentlemen . . . Miss . . . Liberty . . . Belle!"

Even Diamond seemed excited about the moment. Tossing his head, he gave a little half rear and charged into the arena. Belle gripped the flagpole holder tight and glanced up to see that the flag was unfurled as Diamond did first one, then two laps of the arena. They were in the spotlight the entire time, and while Belle couldn't see the crowd, she could hear them cheering and applauding. At the end of the second lap, Monte stepped out from behind the curtain just long enough to take the flagpole and holder from her. "You look great!" he shouted, and then he stepped behind the curtain, and Belle and Diamond were alone in the spotlight.

Her heart pounding, Belle stood up in the stirrups and waved her hat to the crowd. They responded with polite applause, then quieted again as Belle gathered the reins. Diamond tossed his head and whickered. *This is it. Here we are.* What was it Shep had said earlier? *Show 'em what you've got.* Belle leaned down and patted Diamond on the neck. "All right, old friend," she said. "Let's show 'em what we've got."

And they did. Belle couldn't remember a time when she and Diamond had been so in sync. It was as if the horse anticipated everything she wanted just a second before she asked it of him, and as a result, the entire routine was executed with a precision that had the crowd alternately cheering appreciation or gasping in amazement.

When the routine was finished, and she and Diamond whirled around in front of the curtain and Belle took off her hat and waved to the crowd, she thought her heart just might burst with joy.

As soon as she passed behind the curtain, the arena manager sent her back out to take another bow, and then another. Finally she was allowed to dismount, and as she slid to the ground, Shep came up behind her. When she turned around, he laughed aloud and picked her up and swung her around and for a brief moment forgot his own rules about kissing. And that was the best birthday gift of all.

CHAPTER 20

❖══◗ ◖══❖

IF POSSIBLE, SO FAR AS IT DEPENDS ON YOU,
BE AT PEACE WITH ALL MEN.

Romans 12:18 NASB

You'd think she could have at least been in the wardrobe tent sewing for Ma Clemmons on the day it happened. But no, it had to happen one of the times Ma had given all the girls a day off and they'd gone into the city. It had to happen on the one day Belle decided to hightail it over to the stables rather than going with the rest.

So there she was, knee deep in manure, her hair falling out of its braids, her boots caked with filth, with sweat rolling down her face as she shoveled refuse onto a wagon when Shep called, "Hey, Belle!" and Belle looked up and there was Momma, staring at her with the same old *What hath God wrought?* expression Belle had seen so many times before.

It figured. Just when she had decided to revel in her successful debut and stop worrying so much about what was going on back in North Platte; just when she had decided to stop obsessing over Blaze; just when she was beginning to feel all grown up and almost independent; just when she was beginning to be content—there was

Momma, her gloved hand holding a parasol at exactly the right angle to shield her face from the hot July sun, and her other hand on Orrin Knox's arm. *Orrin Knox?* What was *he* doing there? And where was Daddy?

Speechless, Belle stood openmouthed until a fly buzzed so close it nearly flew in. She waved her hand in front of her face, plunged the shovel deep into the mess at her feet, and stumbled forward. "Momma!" She pulled off a glove and wiped sweat off her forehead. "I . . . uh . . ." She gulped. "Hello."

Momma leaned in and kissed her on the cheek. She looked Belle up and down. "I'm glad to see you're well."

"Couldn't be better," Belle said. "Where's Daddy?"

"Your Father has pressing business. When I learned Orrin was planning a trip, I convinced him to let me come along."

Orrin cleared his throat and nodded, then reached out to shake Shep's hand.

As he returned the gesture, Shep nodded at Momma. "Ma'am."

Momma nodded back. She looked much older than Belle remembered. There was even a bit of silver showing at her temples. Was that new, or had Belle just never noticed before?

"Mr. Knox and I arrived in the city only a little while ago," she said. "As you are obviously busy"—she stared at the pile of manure with barely disguised repugnance—"I'll take the opportunity to get settled and perhaps rest a bit before this evening's performance."

Shep spoke up. "If you need a hotel recommendation—"

"We're at the Brunswick," Momma said, and looked at Belle. "On Fifth Avenue. Near—"

"Madison Square Park," Belle finished the sentence for her. She knew a few things about the city of New York. "You'll want to eat at Delmonico's," she said. "Delicious steak. Shep treated Helen and me to dinner there not too long ago." She enjoyed the surprise on Momma's face.

"The restaurant in yer hotel's good, too, ma'am. Stays open real late fer the theatre crowd." Shep laid on his cowboy accent. "I'll see to it the boys give ya' reserved seatin' t'night." He motioned at Orrin. "You, too."

"I don't want to be any trouble," Momma said.

"It won't be no trouble. People do it all the time fer fam'ly and special friends."

Momma said thank you, then turned to Belle. "Perhaps you and I can have a late supper. Unless you'll be too tired after the performance?"

"I'm not doing my act tonight. Diamond needed a rest. The last couple of weeks of two performances a day have taken their toll on the old boy."

Momma frowned. "But . . . you can't use another horse?"

Did she really think it was that easy? "It would take weeks— maybe months— for me to train another horse," Belle said. "And that assumes I could even find one suited for the act. Horses have different temperaments, different personalities. It's a lot more complicated than just roping one and riding into the arena."

"I didn't mean to imply . . . I mean . . . I suppose I should have realized." Momma took a deep breath. Almost a sigh. "If you aren't in the performance, perhaps we could have an earlier supper."

Belle pointed to the pile at her feet. "I have to finish this."

"I'll take care of it," Shep said, and reached for the shovel. Belle resisted. "No. *I'll* do it." She stared at him meaningfully, then forced a smile at Momma. "But I can finish up in plenty of time for us to eat early rather than later."

Momma nodded. Orrin Knox broke the next awkward silence by clearing his throat and pulling a piece of paper from his inside coat pocket. "I'm finally going to get to do some of those articles on Nebraskans in the Wild West. I've made a preliminary list of names, although I'm not certain how complete it is." He looked expectantly at Shep.

"Talk to Bill Riley," he said and pointed toward the Wild West office. "He's the contracts manager. He can get you a complete list."

"I'll do that," Orrin nodded. "Thank you."

"Well then," Momma said, "that's settled." She smiled at Belle. "Is five o'clock all right with you?"

"Fine. Whatever you want."

"Five o'clock it is, then." With a nod in Shep's direction she took Orrin's arm. Together they headed for the entrance.

Belle took a deep breath and blew it out. "Whew."

"That wasn't as bad as it could have been," Shep said.

Belle brushed hay off her sleeve. "Oh, no," she said. "I could have been . . . let's see . . . mud wrestling one of the Pawnee." She nodded. "Yeah. That would have definitely been worse." She looked down and pried a clod of mud off her pants. "Just look at me." A tear slipped out. She stomped her foot.

"Oh, come on," Shep said, and slung an arm around her shoulders. "All in all, it wasn't so bad. She didn't yell. It looked to me like she was doing her best to smooth things over with you."

"Momma doesn't have to raise her voice to yell." Belle sighed, then looked up at him. "And what's so funny about the Brunswick? I saw the look on your face when Momma mentioned where she was staying."

Shep grinned. He winked at her. "My uncle owns it."

———

Dear God in heaven, what am I doing here? Willa strengthened her hold on her parasol with one hand and Orrin Knox's arm with the other. She could sense Irmagard glaring at her as she and Orrin walked away.

What did you expect? You gave her no warning, and after all your objections to the Wild West you caught her at one of the worst possible moments. You can't blame her for being on edge. She said she'd come

*to supper with you. By then you'll be rested and she'll be prepared. It'll
go much better for both of you. Remember what Charlie said. "God
has a plan. We just have to figure out what it is." Stop panicking, and
pay attention to what's around you. It might help later when Irmagard
comes to supper.*

They walked past a large tent with a framed photograph of Annie
Oakley displayed on an easel. The tent floor was carpeted, the furnish-
ings much more elaborate than anything Willa would have expected.
Across the way, another equally large tent was obviously Buffalo
Bill's home away from home. Willa would have recognized the desk
Louisa had given Bill even if the place weren't the predictable "dead
zoo" with trophies hung from every available pole. She shuddered
inwardly, remembering Louisa telling her that Cody always hung
what he claimed to be Yellow Hand's scalp in his tent. She wondered
at the irony of Cody's reputation for treating the Indians he hired so
well and his hanging a scalp in his tent.

Two cowgirls walked by. One, a lovely brunette, made eye contact
right away and nodded. "Ma'am." The other girl mumbled "Howdy"
but made no eye contact. The brunette stopped. "Can we help you?"
she said and stuck out her hand. "Helen Keen. Welcome to the Wild
West."

Letting go of Orrin's arm, Willa switched the parasol to her left
hand and shook Miss Keen's hand. The girl had a strong grip and
a steady gaze. "How do you do," Willa said, without offering her
name. "Mr. Knox and I were just leaving."

Seemingly unaffected by Willa's icy demeanor, Miss Keen smiled
warmly and pointed toward a grove of trees. "If you walk that way,"
she said, "you'll go by the buffalo pens and the Indian village." She
grinned. "Makes for a more interesting exit."

Orrin tipped his hat and stumbled through "I . . . ahem . . . the
Register—my newspaper . . . I'm a reporter. Sent to . . . ahem . . .
report on—"

"Reporters are always welcome," Miss Keen said, "as long as they don't sling mud." She cocked her head and looked him over. "You aren't a mudslinger, are you?"

Orrin looked shocked. "Why . . . ahem . . . no. Of course not."

Miss Keen looped her arm through her friend's. "Dora and I have to get ready for the twelve thirty." She glanced at Willa and then looked back at Orrin. "Will you be in the stands?"

He shook his head. "Not until this evening."

"It was nice to meet you. If you stop in the office just inside the front gate as you leave, they'll help you arrange all the interviews you could want." Wishing them a good day, Miss Keen and her friend headed off toward—wherever it was they went to prepare for a performance. Willa wondered momentarily how one went about managing wardrobe for a troupe of this size. The thought of wardrobe drew her attention back to Irmagard dressed in filthy pants and mud-caked boots shoveling manure into a wagon. Shocked as the child had been to see her mother, two things had been abundantly clear. Irmagard was truly happy. And Shep Sterling was in love with her.

———

Dressed in the same ensemble she'd worn to St. Louis, Belle stood on the sidewalk staring up at the imposing entrance to the Brunswick. She was so nervous she almost felt sick. Were she and Momma really going to sit through a meal in the hotel's dining room and pretend everything was fine? Swallowing hard, Belle headed up the pink granite steps. A doorman bowed and opened the door, admitting her to an elegant lobby. For a moment she hesitated again, observing the soaring ceilings, crystal chandeliers, and highly polished mahogany walls. Taking a deep breath, she approached the hotel desk. "My mother is staying here," she said, "and I was to meet her for dinner."

"And her name would be . . .?"

"Mrs. Otto Friedrich."

The clerk referenced a massive leather-bound book, running his finger down the list of names, then checking the row of small boxes behind him. There was a note tucked into one. He opened it, read, then turned around and, with an ingratiating smile, waved a bellboy over. "Show this young lady up to the Rubens Suite, William."

Suite? Momma has a suite? Maybe Daddy was more successful than Belle realized. *Or maybe Momma is trying to impress everyone.*

William was leading the way to the ornate brass cage beside the grand staircase. Belle balked. Shep still teased her about it, but she couldn't bring herself to trust a fancy box to haul her around. "I'll use the stairs," she said. "You don't have to take me up."

William shrugged. "Suit yourself. It's 505."

———

Willa glanced at the clock on the mantel. *Four o'clock.* They would hardly have time to eat before it was time to leave for Staten Island. But then, perhaps less time was better. She gazed around her, once again marveling at the elegance of the suite. She still didn't quite understand exactly why she was here. The hotel manager had knocked on her door a couple of hours ago and said they wished to offer her a suite. When she declined, they insisted. Something about hotel capacity being lower than expected and a desire to be especially gracious to out-of-town guests. Her rate wouldn't change. And would madam care to dine *en suite* instead of keeping her reservation in the dining room?

Flustered, Willa had accepted the invitation, but as Irmagard's arrival grew near, she began to pace. Certainly a private discussion was warranted at some point. But here? The elegance was almost oppressive—heavy drapes, silk wallcoverings, plush carpets . . . and those flowers. Did hotels always grace their suites with such magnificent bouquets? Crossing the room, Willa cupped an open rose in her hand and leaned close, inhaling the fragrance.

Please, God, let this go well. Please help me control my emotions.

If Irmagard asked about Otto, Willa had already decided she

would tell the truth. Business had taken him to Denver. And then she would change the subject and ask about the boots he'd had made for his daughter. Did they fit? Was she pleased? Daddy would want to know.

Daddy. Otto. Without warning, Willa began to cry. Again. *Please God. I need things to be all right between Irmagard and me. I don't know what I'll do about anything else, but I do know there are worse things than having a daughter who wants to be a cowgirl. Please don't let me start a fight. Please help me understand her.*

When the knock finally came, Willa smoothed her gray skirt and glanced in the mirror. There was no hiding the stress she'd been under. Tension showed in every line of her face. Hopefully Irmagard wouldn't notice. With a last glance in the mirror to tuck up an errant strand of gray hair, Willa went to the door. She had practiced what she would say, but when she opened the door and Irmagard offered a hug, every word of it went out the window. Closing her eyes, Willa savored the hug before kissing her daughter on the cheek. "I am so *relieved* to see you." Her voice wobbled. "To see for myself that things are all right."

"Of course they're all right," Irmagard said and stepped into the suite. She looked around her.

"Yes," Willa said in agreement with Irmagard's unspoken comment. "Isn't it lovely? When I got back from Staten Island the manager had left a message. Something about special hospitality for out-of-state visitors." She laughed nervously. "I wouldn't have accepted, but they said the cost was the same and"—she gestured toward the table in the nook, already set for two diners—"it seemed a good idea." She paused. "I took the liberty of ordering for us. You still like roast chicken, I hope?"

Irmagard nodded.

"Well then," Willa said, "let's sit down. There's a lovely view of the park out that window."

Irmagard crossed the room and sat down, her back straight, her head held high.

"You wrote that you've been going to church," Willa said as she crossed the room to the table. "That's nice to hear."

"Sunday Joe preaches in the grove by the Indian camp every week. It's what I imagine the revival meetings in North Platte are like. He's very sincere. I like that about him. Sunday Joe lives his sermons right in front of us all every day of the week."

"Your father sends his love. As do your aunt and uncle and cousins." Willa smiled. "Did the boots fit?"

"Perfectly," Irmagard said. "They aren't quite broken in yet. I've been keeping them back. For performances only."

"And the first one was on your birthday?" Irmagard nodded, and Willa hurried to add, "I-I suppose you wondered why you didn't hear from me. Us." She looked away. "I thought I'd wait until I came to visit." She laughed nervously, "I hardly know what would be appropriate for your new life. But I'll make it up to you while I'm here."

Irmagard looked down at her plate. She fingered her napkin. She cleared her throat and looked up again. "I'm not coming home with you, Momma."

A knock at the door announced the arrival of dinner. Willa stood up. "I know that," she said. "I've accepted it." She held out her hand. "Truce?"

The shock on Irmagard's face transformed into surprise laced with a hint of suspicion. But to her credit, the child took her mother's hand and shook it. "Truce," she said.

CHAPTER 21

Belle and Momma had just stepped aboard the ferry headed back to Staten Island when a young boy pointed at her and said, "Daddy, it's her! The Liberty lady!"

Belle smiled and said hello. "I'm flattered to be recognized."

"It's the red hair," the boy's father said, and extended his hand. "David Carter." He smiled down at his son. "And this is George—whose mother had red hair."

Had. Past tense. Just like the boy in St. Louis. Ah, well. At least this boy had a father who made time for him—instead of sending him off with the governess. Belle sat down across from father and son. "This is *my* momma, Mrs. Friedrich," she said to the little boy. "She's never been to the Wild West before."

Things couldn't have gone better if Belle had hired someone and handed them a script. George struck up a conversation with

263

Momma that went from bucking broncos to the Deadwood stage, from sharpshooting to Indians and from trick riders to buffalo. He admired them "all to pieces," with special enthusiasm afforded the "Liberty Lady."

"My goodness," Momma finally said. "They should hire you to advertise for them."

"I hear nothing but talk of horses and cowboys and Indians these days," Mr. Carter said with a laugh. "George has a stick horse he rides all around the house, and his nanny has been startled more than once by a war whoop."

"My apologies," Belle said, laughing.

"No apology required," the man smiled. "George has almost convinced me we should heed Horace Greeley's advice and go west ourselves."

They chatted for a few moments, and when Mr. Carter learned that Momma had never been to New York before, he regaled her with what he called his "visitor's speech," sharing details about the Brooklyn Bridge, the statue going up on Bedloe's Island, and a dozen other topics Momma seemed to find fascinating.

When the ferry landed, the Carters escorted the ladies to the train, and it was during that part of the ride that Momma learned that David Carter was actually *Dr.* Carter, a widower, whose aunt was helping him raise George.

When conversation lapsed, George asked Belle a question about her horse, which he called a "dappered gray."

"My goodness." Belle smiled. "You really *did* pay attention."

"I liked the way the flag waved out," George said, gesturing as he spoke. "Did you have to teach your horse not to be afraid of that?"

Belle shook her head. "Not Diamond," she said. "He's very gentle."

George pulled a wad of peppermint candy out of his pocket. "Does he like candy? I could give him a piece."

"He likes sugar cubes," Belle said. "But he only gets a treat after he's worked hard. And Diamond is resting for a few days."

"Does that mean we won't have the pleasure of seeing Liberty Belle perform this evening?" Dr. Carter asked.

"I only have the one horse," Belle said. She glanced down at George. "So tell me, Master Carter, who *else* did you like watching in the Wild West?"

"The King," George said. "And the lady that shot the targets. And Hi-dalgo. And—"

"And as you can see," Dr. Carter said, "George and I will likely have to return many more times before he gets his fill." He looked at Momma. "Tell me, Mrs. Friedrich, do citizens of the West find Mr. Cody's production as fascinating as do we New Yorkers?"

"Some do," Belle interrupted. "But Momma doesn't care for it at all."

Momma spoke up. "I've voiced very strong objections to my daughter's involvement." She gave a nervous little laugh and shrugged. "A mother's concern over the inherent dangers to the participants."

"Understandable." Dr. Carter nodded. "Although I understand the Wild West travels with a very well-equipped medical department. Still, if it were George being tossed through the air by a wild horse, I'd probably be much less than enthusiastic about the whole thing myself."

"I wouldn't get *tossed*," George protested. "I'd *ride* 'em right into the ground!" He mimicked holding reins even as he slapped his back side with an open palm. All that was missing was the stick horse. The train pulled into the station at Erastina and as the crowd dispersed, Dr. Carter wished Belle and her mother a good day and headed off toward the stables, George in tow.

———

Things were going fine until the clouds rolled in.

"If it rains. . . then what?" Momma asked.

"Then everyone is even more careful than usual," Belle replied. She wasn't about to tell Momma about Helen Keen getting thrown because of lightning.

"Will people stay?"

Belle pointed to the canvas above them. "No reason not to. We won't get wet. And remember what Orrin said that day at my luncheon? They performed in New Orleans for a crowd of nine."

"Speaking of Orrin," Momma turned around and looked toward the stairs. "I would have expected him to join us by now."

Just a few minutes later, Orrin slid into a seat. He nodded toward the sky. "I hope it doesn't rain."

The cowboy band filed into place. "There's Jonathan and Jason," Belle said, and pointed out the boys from Nebraska. She leaned over and spoke to Orrin. "Did you remember to put them on your list?"

Orrin nodded. "Have a meeting scheduled with them for eight o'clock tomorrow morning."

"How long do you plan to stay?"

"Well," Momma said. "I thought at least through Tuesday. I'd like you to show me the grounds, and we'll have Monte to dinner, of course. And as long as I'm here, I might as well see what the Wild West church services are like." She glanced at Orrin with a smile. "I promised Orrin I wouldn't get in the way of his taking all the time he needs for his interviews. It's up to him, really."

Today is Friday. Four days, Belle thought. *Surely they could keep a truce for four days.*

Beneath the covered stands, the crowd stayed put, their enthusiasm undampened by the gentle rain that had begun to fall as the Grand Entry concluded. From time to time Belle glanced at Momma, whose expression remained polite but disengaged. She applauded at all the right places and even stood and clapped with the crowd. She sat up straighter when the cowgirls were in the arena and watched more intently, but overall Momma seemed distracted.

Disappointed by her lack of enthusiasm, Belle hopped up at intermission and, without waiting for Momma to react, said something about making sure Monte could find them after the Final Salute. Skittering down the stairs, she slipped in the mud. Lifting her skirt, she headed for the dressing tent and found Helen Keen and Dora— but no Monte—laughing with Shep about something.

"How's your mother enjoying the Wild West?" Ma Clemmons asked.

"Better yet, how was supper?" Shep added.

"She's doing her best. And who offered a truce."

Ma Clemmons chuckled. "I told you we'd pray one up."

Shep smiled. "How's the Rubens Suite?"

"That was you?"

He shrugged. "I made a phone call and asked if it was possible."

"Well, it was. The Queen of England would like that suite. To tell the truth, I think Momma's a little overwhelmed by it."

"I hope she's staying long enough to see a performance on a sunny day."

"They'll be here at least through Tuesday."

"That's great," Shep said, then frowned as he looked at Belle. "Isn't it?"

"I honestly don't know." She sighed. "It's so . . . awkward."

Dora spoke up. "She l-looks sad. You should b-be nice."

Belle mumbled a response, left a message for Monte, and ducked back out into the rain. In the grandstand, Orrin and Momma were drinking lemonade and talking to Dr. Carter while George leaned over the railing, his hand held out to catch raindrops.

"And here she is now," Dr. Carter said, looking up with a smile. "I've just convinced your mother to join me for a late supper at

Delmonico's after the performance. I'll need to drop George at home, of course. I hope we can convince you to join us?"

"I-I thought you wanted to have Monte to supper," Belle looked at Momma. "I left word for him to meet us up here. Shep and the others are going to tend to his horse for him so he can come."

"I take it Monte is a cowboy," Dr. Carter said, and when Belle nodded, he glanced down at George. "We'd be happy to have his company. In fact"—he patted George on the head—"perhaps I could make an exception and let George stay up."

George let out a "yee-haw" fit for any cowboy.

———

Rain continued to fall during the second half. As the mud in the arena got deeper, horses and broncs began to slip. Belle was thankful Blaze wasn't being used tonight and that Diamond was safe in his stall. The entire crowd gasped when, in one of the races, a mustang slipped and fell, throwing his rider and then rolling over him. Apparently cushioned by the mud, the Indian got back up, caught up with the pony, leaped on his back, and with a high-pitched war whoop, tore around the arena to the applause of the delighted and relieved crowd. Momma watched the entire thing with her hand at her throat and sat back with an audible sigh when the warrior and his pony finally left the arena.

"He was showing off," Belle said, "and he should have known better than to try that in this mud." She glanced at Momma. "I don't take stupid chances."

Momma blinked away tears. "I hope not," she said and squeezed Belle's hand. "I sincerely hope not."

"She looks sad. You should be nice." Dora's words sounded in Belle's head and she began to watch her mother's reaction to the performance with new eyes. Dora was right. Momma did look unhappy, but there was more than unhappiness in her expression. She was *afraid*. She flinched at the sound of the guns in the sharpshooting scenes and

started when a pony slipped or a bronc rider got thrown. None of Belle's reassurances seemed to help.

Lightning flashed. The next clap of thunder terrified the horses in the area. One reared up, slipped, and toppled backward. Its rider lay motionless in the mud, his bright blue shirt turning indigo as the heavens opened and sheets of rain poured down.

"Dear God—no." Momma's hand went to her mouth.

"Stay with her," Belle said to Orrin even as she gathered up her skirts and climbed the railing. Lowering herself into the arena, she ran toward Monte.

Oblivious to the rain, the mud, and the crowd, Belle trotted alongside Monte's stretcher. He was still unconscious. Someone had put a folded kerchief over a cut at his hairline. It was already soaked with blood. His left arm curved at an unnatural angle alongside his body. What else might be wrong? She felt sick, almost faint as the stretcher bearers—Ned Bishop, two other wranglers, and one of the cowboy clowns—carried Monte into Dr. Miller's hospital tent and laid him atop one of the tables. No one seemed to know where Dr. Miller was.

"There was a doctor sitting next to me up in the stands," Belle said. "I'll try to get him to c—"

At that very moment David Carter stepped into the tent. Glancing around at the shelves of supplies, he said quietly, "I'll help until someone finds your surgeon," he said. "With your permission?"

He was directing the question to Irma, but Momma spoke up. "Please, doctor," she said.

With a quick nod Carter ordered the lamps be lit. "And I'll need people to hold them up for me so I can see." He felt for a pulse, then lifted the handkerchief and looked beneath it. "I need scissors," he said. Rummaging in Dr. Miller's drawers, Carter found scissors and cut away Monte's bright blue shirt.

"Daddy?"

The doctor glanced over to where George stood, looking frightened.

"It's all right, little man," Carter said. "Daddy has to help this cowboy. You be brave, all right?" He turned back to Monte.

Ned Bishop crouched beside the boy. "We're tough hombres, pardner." He nodded to where Monte lay. "He'll come around. You'll see."

When he looked up at Belle and nodded, she forced a smile. Maybe things would be all right between them again.

After a few more moments the doctor looked up and spoke to Belle and Momma. "He's going to be fine," he said. "He's likely got a concussion, and he needs some stitches and a bone set, but I don't think there's anything seriously wrong. His pulse is regular and strong, and to be quite honest, it's probably better if he doesn't remember what I'm going to have to do in the next few minutes." He looked around him as he said, "I'm going to need to splint this arm. I need boards about like so." He held up his hands to show them. "And bandages."

Momma stepped forward. "You find the doctor's splints," she said to Belle. "And I'll find bandages." She began to look through the supply cabinet. "Are you certain he's going to be all right?" she asked.

Dr. Carter spoke as he worked. "I've got some stitching and some bonesetting to do, but I'm reasonably certain this cowboy will be good as new in a few weeks."

Momma closed her eyes briefly. "Thank God," she said.

"Will these work?" Belle held up the boards she'd selected from a variety of narrow boards leaning in one corner.

Dr. Carter nodded.

Momma set three rolls of bandages out. "Let's see," she said, "you'll want sutures. A needle. Antiseptic." She glanced at the doctor. "A curved needle, I presume?"

He smiled approval. "Indeed. If we can find one." He glanced at Irma. "You didn't tell me your mother had been a nurse."

Before Irma could say anything, Momma forced a laugh. "I'm not, doctor. But we were on the frontier for many years before there was a doctor to call." She shrugged. "We made do."

The rain had let up, and about a dozen wranglers were gathered just outside the tent flap to wait for word of Monte's condition. Ned backed out of the tent and joined them. Momma followed him and addressed the men. "I can't seem to find Dr. Miller's antiseptic," she said. "I've been told Mr. Cody has a rule against alcohol, but I'm guessing someone has some whiskey they've kept about—strictly for medicinal purposes, of course. It would be helpful if we had some to clean the wound before Dr. Carter stitches it up."

"Helpful to my patient when I set his arm, as well," Carter said with a faint smile.

Ned said he'd be back directly.

Belle hadn't realized the performance had ended, but suddenly Shep and Helen and Dora arrived. "He's all right," Belle said. "He needs stitches. And a splint. His arm's broken. But the doctor said he's going to be all right."

Just then Monte groaned. "My *head*. What . . . what happened?"

"You have a headache because you likely have a concussion," Dr. Carter explained.

"Huh?" Monte frowned. He blinked up at Dr. Carter. "Who're you? Where's Doc Miller?"

Someone muttered, "Ain't that the million-dollar question?"

"We don't know where Dr. Miller is," Momma said. "But Dr. Carter was in the audience, and he's taken very good care of you."

"Thank you," Carter smiled, then turned to Monte, explaining, "You've a nasty cut along your hairline, and your arm is broken. A clean break I think—which is better than what we call a compound fracture."

"That's what's *wrong* with me," Monte said. "What *happened?*"

Chuckles rose from the onlookers, and Monte grimaced as he looked around. "Aren't you all supposed to be someplace else?" More chuckles.

Shep drawled, "We're just keeping watch so this sawbones here don't mess up. Nobody knows if he's really a bona fide MD or not." Shep winked at Carter.

He looked down at Monte. "We could haul you onto the ferry and up to the hospital in Manhattan."

"Hospital?" Monte mumbled. "What for? You just said you know how to fix me."

"I do," Carter said.

"Then have at it." Monte paused. "Belle?"

"Right here," Belle said.

He lowered his voice. "Could . . . could you see if Dora might come over?"

The onlookers tittered again and Monte added, in a louder voice, "And would you tell the audience this show is over and they can skedaddle."

"You heard him," Shep said, and began to shoo people away from the tent. Ned returned, slipping Shep a flask. Shep nodded, stuck the flask in his back pocket, and closed the tent flap.

"I could use more light," Dr. Carter said.

"You got it," Shep replied. He handed Momma the flask, then he and Dora and Belle all grabbed lamps and moved in.

"I believe the cowboy asked for you," Momma said to Dora, and got up. "I can hold the lamp."

"Dora?" Monte said.

"I'm h-here," she replied, handing Momma the oil lamp and sitting down in her place.

Monte turned his head so he could see her. He smiled and held up his good hand. "I'd be mighty grateful if you would hold that, ma'am," he said.

Blushing, Dora took his hand and kissed it.

Dr. Carter gave Monte a drink from the flask and began to now. A few minutes later he snipped the thread and stood up. "Fifteen stitches," he said. "That probably equals one pounding headache tomorrow."

When it came time to set the broken bone and the doctor asked Shep to hold Monte down, Dora stood up. "I'll help," she said. "Hold him down, I mean."

"Are you sure?" Dr. Carter seemed doubtful.

Dora nodded. "I d-done it before."

Dr. Carter put a cloth "sausage" in Monte's mouth, directing him to "Bite on that and yell as loud as you want." Before he finished the last word of his instructions, he grabbed Monte's arm and pulled it into place.

Monte yelled, then apologized to Dora. "I guess I'm not as brave as I thought."

Dora kissed his cheek and whispered something in his ear. Whatever it was, it brought the color back to Monte's pale face. When he tried to sit up, Dora put her hand on his chest and ordered him to stay put.

Bill Cody strode into the tent complaining. "People seem to think a cowboy nearly killing himself is just part of the show," he grumbled. "I had to wade through a sea of people before I could get in here. I was almost rude to more than one." His gaze landed on Momma.

"Mrs. Friedrich." He nodded and tipped his hat.

"Bill," Momma said.

Cody looked around after being introduced to Dr. Carter. "It looks as though you all have everything well in hand." He looked down at Monte. "And I'm especially glad to see you're all right, m'boy."

"I'm fine, sir," Monte called, and once again tried to get up.

Dora stood up, put a hand on Monte's shoulder, and pushed him back down. "He h-has a c-conc-cussion," Dora said. She pointed to Monte's scalp. "Fifteen stitches. A b-broken arm." She began to cry softly. "B-but he's going to be all right."

Cody turned to the doctor. "Doc Miller was in the city earlier today. He must have been waylaid by the storm. I imagine he'll be back yet before the night's over, but I'd be grateful if you'd keep an eye on the patient tonight. As a precaution."

Dr. Carter glanced toward his son.

"George," Shep said. "What would you think of bunking with a cowboy tonight?"

George's face lit up. "Y-you mean with *you*?!"

"I'd have to get word to my Aunt Mae," Dr. Carter said, "so she doesn't worry."

"Miss Keen and Irmagard could stay with me at the hotel," Momma said, looking at Bill for approval. "That would free up their quarters for Dr. Carter and his patient."

Cody nodded. "Excellent." He looked to Dr. Carter. "If you can agree to this rather unorthodox arrangement, I'll see that you're well rewarded," he said. "And I'll send you a messenger to take word to your aunt."

CHAPTER 22

--*≈◎ ◎≈*--

THEREFORE DO NOT WORRY ABOUT TOMORROW;
FOR TOMORROW WILL CARE FOR ITSELF.
EACH DAY HAS ENOUGH TROUBLE OF ITS OWN.

Matthew 6:34 NASB

Willa stirred at the sound of laughter in the adjoining room. Fumbling for the locket watch that lay on the bedside table, she opened it and squinted at the dial. *Nearly noon?* It all came back. The rain . . . Monte's accident . . . and the awful next couple of hours. Thank God for Dr. Carter. Thank God Monte was going to be all right. By the time they'd gotten him settled atop Irmagard's cot in the girls' tent, he was complaining about all the fussing and fawning—a sure sign that he would, indeed, be fine. He did not, however, Willa remembered with a smile, complain about Miss Dora Spurgeon's attentions. She was a sweet girl. Charlie and Laura would like her. And they were going to get their son back home. She and Bill had spoken in the tent last night and arranged for Monte to travel with her and Orrin back to Nebraska. *"Until he's recovered,"* Bill had said. They wanted him back with the Wild West for the winter season.

The comings and goings in the tent last night, the laughter, the good-natured ribbing, and above all, the efficiency with which people seemed to shift and adjust to accommodate Monte's needs, had shown Willa a side of the Wild West troupe she'd been told existed but stubbornly refused to believe—until now. Nearly a dozen wranglers had been crowded into that tent before Shep herded them out. It was as if Monte had acquired a set of brothers. The camaraderie among them was evident, and seeing it for herself was beginning to effect a shift in Willa's feelings about the Wild West.

She might never understand Irmagard's determination to turn her back on her home and pursue such an unorthodox life, but perhaps, Willa thought, perhaps she didn't have to *understand* it in order to *accept* it. Could it be that Otto had been right when he extolled the positive aspects of Irmagard's joining the tour? Was part of the attraction the acquiring of a large extended family? Was there more to Irmagard's adventurous spirit than just rebelling against her upbringing?

My plans are not your plans . . . my thoughts are not your thoughts. Maybe Otto had been right when he challenged Willa's certainty over what God wanted for Irmagard. Blast the man, anyway. How could he be right? He had no more interest in spiritual things than . . .

With a sigh, Willa got up, pulled on her dressing gown, and went to the window. The sky was overcast and, while it wasn't raining now, the street below was wet, the park across the street sodden beneath trees dripping moisture. She freshened up, brushing her thick hair until it gleamed and tying it back with a ribbon. Laughter erupted in the adjoining room. Again. She opened the door and immediately saw at least part of the reason for the raucous laughter that had awakened her.

Irmagard gulped down the bite she'd just taken of a pastry. "There was a knock at the door and—" She gestured at the silver coffee service, the pitchers of milk and juice—so much food it barely fit on the table. "They said to call when we were ready for breakfast." She shook her head. "Can you imagine anyone wanting breakfast after this?" She reached for a pastry and held it out. "Try this one, Momma. You'll love it. Apricot filling."

Helen grinned and motioned Willa over. "Set yerself down, ma'am, and dig in—compliments of the management."

Irmagard nodded. "That's what he said when he delivered the cart." She giggled. "And do we ever *like* the management of the Brunswick Hotel!"

Would Bill Cody do this? Willa couldn't imagine why. She cast a glance toward the bouquet on the mantel. *What is going on?*

Someone knocked lightly on the door and slid an envelope into view. Willa retrieved it, read it over, and smiled. "How thoughtful. Bill reports that Dr. Carter checked in with him early this morning. Monte rested well. He's back in the cowboy's domain, and Dr. Carter has rounded up his son and headed back to the city." She glanced up from the note. "Bill is also suggesting that both of you enjoy an extra day of leisure instead of returning to Erastina today. And Dr. Carter hopes we'll be able to join him this evening to make up for missing last night's supper."

"God bless Bill and Dr. David Carter," Helen said, saluting as she reached for another pastry.

Irmagard nodded toward where her muddied dress lay draped across a chair. "Do you suppose they have anyone here who could make that presentable?"

Willa picked it up. "We could probably get it cleaned enough to shop for a new ensemble for this evening." She nodded at Miss Keen. "And I hope you'll join us."

Helen looked doubtful. "I don't know, ma'am. I'm not exactly a Delmonico's kinda gal—if you know what I mean. All those forks and glasses and the like. I wouldn't know what to do with 'em."

"And they wouldn't know what to do with a longhorn." Willa smiled. "May I propose, Miss Keen, that you help me with shopping for whatever Irmagard might need between now and the end of the season, and I'll do my best to cue you when it comes to forks and glasses at the restaurant this evening."

Helen didn't have to think long. She shook Willa's proffered hand. "Agreed."

Willa turned to Irmagard. "Now, before you protest shopping with me, I have something to say. While I may despair of ever *understanding* it, I have determined to do my best to *accept* the reality embraced by Miss Liberty Belle. You have my word that there will be no bustles or corsets urged upon anyone today. And birds on hats are henceforth and forevermore anathema."

———

By that evening one would have thought Helen Keen was Wilhelmina Friedrich's long-lost niece. Or favored daughter. It started with the shopping in the afternoon. The Brunswick concierge directed them to what he called Ladies' Mile, several blocks of department stores and emporiums where the women of New York shopped and dined in opulence.

At Macy's Helen took the lead in appreciating Momma's taste when she suggested Belle try on a Dutch indigo gored walking skirt. And according to Helen, Momma was right again when she matched the skirt with a tucked shirtwaist with bishop sleeves and a banded collar. And then Momma decided to treat Helen to a complete ensemble, from chemise to drawers and petticoat and right on through to a lovely gored walking skirt and waist similar to Belle's. Helen drew the line at the hose suspenders, but when she sashayed out of the dressing room, Momma seemed to consider the shopping trip a complete triumph—in spite of the fact that Belle knew the Macy's prices were horrific. Momma laughed when Helen exaggerated her sashay down Fourteenth Street on their way to the milliner. Both young women emerged with the latest thing in headgear-*sans* fowl-and parasols to boot. Belle couldn't imagine what Helen Keen was going to do with a parasol after today.

Helen's Texas accent had all but disappeared by the time the three of them met Dr. Carter at Delmonico's for a fashionably late supper. And she embarrassed everyone the way she flirted with the doctor. At least Belle felt embarrassed. Momma seemed oblivious to Helen's bad behavior and even joked about not knowing which fork to use for dessert. Momma seemed to have become a different person overnight.

"She's *not* a different person," Helen said when Belle commented on it that night. "You just haven't been able to see her through that haze of whatever old business you're refusing to lay aside. I'm not kidding, Belle, if you don't want her, give her to me, because I wouldn't care if she *was* a little snooty. I'd *love* to have a momma who'd travel halfway across the country just to see if I was all right. Shoot, honey, any of us would. My ma's dead, Mabel's is probably waking up from a two-day hangover in some saloon in Deadwood, and Dora—" Helen bit her lip. "Well, never mind about Dora. You get the point."

Irma did. It was hard to admit it, even to herself, but she realized Helen hadn't been anyone but Helen at dinner, and Momma had always been generous, and the only thing wrong with the way anyone was acting was that she, Irmagard Friedrich, was jealous. Fluffing her pillow, she pretended to be too tired to talk any longer.

On Sunday Belle and Helen moved back to the Wild West grounds. Momma came with them, and together with Shep and Dora and Monte, they attended Sunday Joe's outdoor service, about which Momma had nothing but good to say. By Sunday evening it had been decided that Monte would take Dora with him to Nebraska. It was time she met the family.

"You'll love them," Belle encouraged Dora. "Uncle Charlie and Aunt Laura are wonderful people. And they will love you. It won't be long before the girls will be treating you like a sister."

Dora bit her lower lip and shrugged.

"Dora," Belle said, putting her arm across the girl's shoulders and pulling her aside. "They won't care about a little stutter." When she saw Dora glance toward where Mabel stood talking to a couple of cowboys, she gave her a hug. "My cousins are nothing like Mabel. You'll see."

Dora forced a smile.

And on Monday morning Bill Cody sent word via Shep that, if she wanted it, Liberty Belle would take Dora Spurgeon's place for the remainder of the summer season. Dora would be on hand to watch Monday's shows and review Belle's performance before leaving town with Monte on Tuesday. Belle would ride Rowdy, Dora's spotted horse with the ratty tail.

———

Willa sat looking out on the arena and tried to calm her nerves. Liberty Belle would be in that arena in a few minutes, and then, in less than twenty-four hours, Willa would be headed home. Either event would be reason enough for Willa to feel so distraught. Facing both events within the same twenty-four-hour period was wreaking havoc with her "innards." Willa forced a smile at the word—a Helen Keen expression. What a delightful—if unpolished—young woman. It was comforting to know that Irmagard had Helen in her life. A good friend like that could make such a difference.

Irmagard would have good friends to help her through the next few weeks. There was no doubt in Willa's mind that a relationship was brewing between Shep Sterling and Irmagard. Willa had sensed it back in North Platte when he arrived on the Friedrich doorstep with those roses. How angry she had been. Somehow her feelings about all of that had changed, too. She couldn't quite decide what it was, but she'd become convinced in these few days in New York that there was more to Shep Sterling than met the eye. She wondered what Orrin Knox would have to say about the Wild West after several days of ferreting out new stories. Perhaps he would have insights into Shep Sterling. That would make for interesting conversation on the way home.

Home. How she dreaded going home. What would happen when Irmagard learned of the separation? Whatever Otto might have done to their marriage, he'd been a good father. Willa was determined to never do anything to threaten the father-daughter relationship. She would never expose Otto's philandering. Irmagard must never know about the boy in Denver. Would she blame Willa for everything? The idea made her eyes mist over. *Stop worrying over tomorrow. Today has enough troubles of its own.* Indeed. Today she had to watch her daughter risk life and limb in the Wild West arena. *And of course,* Willa scolded herself, *the dangers of the Wild West are far beyond God's ability to handle.* Willa got a grip on her imagination and forced herself to return to the present.

The band was assembling in its box. She glanced over to see what Orrin Knox was sketching and smiled to recognize Liberty Belle riding proudly, the American flag unfurled above her. "I hope you feel you've had a successful trip, Orrin," Willa said.

"Absolutely," Orrin said. "I . . . ahem . . . with your permission of course, might offer one or two articles to the larger newspapers. I . . . ahem . . . really believe that the Liberty Belle angle will prove quite popular with our Nebraska readers. I'd like to be one of the . . . ahem . . . first to cover it."

She smiled. "As long as you make certain to send copies to Irmagard and Miss Keen for their scrapbooks."

The band began to play. Willa clutched the Wild West program to her bosom and tried to calm her nerves. The sun had been shining all day, and the arena was dry. There was no reason to fear an accident. God could protect Irmagard. She knew that. In her head. But her nerves didn't seem to be listening to logic at the moment.

"Good evening." An elegantly clad woman moved into place on Willa's left. She seemed inclined to chat. Her name was Abigail

Mortimer. She lived in New York City. Was this Mrs. Friedrich's first visit to the Wild West?

When Willa introduced Orrin Knox as a visiting journalist, Mrs. Mortimer asked, "Have you been satisfied with your access to the performers? If not, I might be able to offer some assistance."

"Thank you . . . ahem . . . but I have no complaints. We leave in the morning. I wouldn't . . . ahem . . . have time for further interviews, in any case."

"As it happens," Willa said, "my daughter is one of the performers. She's been very good to see that Orrin met all the right people during out visit."

"Your *daughter*," the woman said, clearly intrigued.

She's probably formulating a mental image of some tobacco-chewing cow.

"I can't imagine the courage it must take for those young women to do the things they do. They are simply stunning, aren't they? You must be very proud."

Proud? "To be quite candid," Willa said, "I'm still in the throes of being terrified my baby will get hurt. I don't know if you heard about the accident on Friday—"

"I did. Thank goodness the young man wasn't seriously hurt."

"Not seriously," Willa agreed, "but he's being sent back to Nebraska to recover."

"Mr. Cody is very good about taking care of his troupe. The injured wrangler will likely recuperate at Scout's Rest. Mr. Cody seems to take a personal interest in things like that."

Willa spoke up. "As it happens, the cowboy, Monte, is my nephew. He's accompanying Mr. Knox and me tomorrow. I promised Bill I'd see to getting him home safely." She shook her head. "But even though Monte is going to be fine, I can't help worrying when I think of my daughter out there." She nodded toward the arena.

"I understand exactly what you're saying," Mrs. Mortimer agreed. "I don't come as often as I might for the same reason. It would be hard enough if my Henry were hurt. But to witness it?" She shuddered. "A mother's worst nightmare. You and I will undoubtedly be scratching our eyebrows at regular intervals this evening." She demonstrated the gesture, which effectively shielded her eyes from the arena. "If Henry ever catches me doing that, I'll never hear the end of it."

"I don't believe I met a Henry Mortimer when Irmagard was introducing me to her new friends," Willa said. "What exactly is your son's role in the production?" She couldn't help the little surge of pleasure at the idea of enlightening this woman as to Irmagard's identity as Liberty Belle. Perhaps she *was* proud after all.

"Oh, Henry doesn't use his given name." Mrs. Mortimer opened the program and showed Willa a photograph. "There he is."

Shep Sterling. King of the Cowboys.

———

All Belle was supposed to do was gallop Dora's horse around the arena and wait in the center, while Helen Keen was introduced. Then the two of them would race. It wasn't much of an act, but Dora's horse was skittish about its new rider. And Momma was up there in the stands recording every second for future retelling at home. Whatever else Momma said about her trip, she simply had to have a good report about Belle's performance. For Daddy.

"Ready, kiddo?" Helen rode up alongside her and winked.

"I didn't think I'd be this nervous." Belle nodded down at the dancing appaloosa. "Is he always like this?"

Helen grinned. "He's about to race and he knows it. You'll do fine. Momma will be impressed."

Finally, the announcer introduced, "Taking the place of Dora Spurgeon this evening . . . from Buffalo Bill's home state of Nebraska, our newest beautiful ranchera—Miss . . . Liberty . . . Belle!"

Her heart pounding, Belle kicked Rowdy and they bolted into the arena. The crowd roared, the band played, and when Rowdy tore around the arena, then stopped abruptly in the center and reared,

Belle nearly lost her balance. She grabbed the saddle horn and hoped no one had noticed.

"And now, the Queen of the Lone Star State, Miss . . . Helen . . . Keen!" Helen's entrance went more smoothly.

"Calm down, kiddo," Helen said as the horses danced about and the announcer explained the rules of the race. "No one noticed."

I bet Momma did.

It was time. The cowboy clowns had set up a series of poles at ten-foot intervals across the length of the arena. First Belle, then Helen, would race in and out of the poles. It was more about skill than speed, and Belle hoped Rowdy would change leads smoothly with a new rider. All she had to do was keep her seat during the weaving in and out—and look competitive.

Helen tore through the course, her pinto's polished black hooves flashing. Willing herself to forget the audience, Belle concentrated on keeping her weight on the balls of her feet, on gripping Rowdy's sides, on having her hands poised so she would jerk on the bit as little as possible. There was hardly time to think. The clown in charge of the race yelled "Go!" and dropped a red flag. Rowdy shot forward, danced in and out of the row of poles and then made a sharp left and tore back to the arena entrance, where he skidded to a stop with all the concentration of a cow pony pulling a rope taut against a struggling calf. The horse knew the routine so well, all Belle ended up having to do was stay on.

Helen took her victory lap. The crowd cheered. Belle took off her hat and bowed as Helen rode by, acknowledging that she'd been beaten. With a wink, Helen reached over and snatched Belle's hat out of her hand, then charged back into the center of the arena and, dropping it in the dust, backed her pony up and motioned for Belle to come and get it. This was not part of the act. Belle didn't move. Helen stood up in the stirrups, stretched out both arms, and taunted her.

Belle patted Rowdy's neck. "Can we do it?" There was only one way to find out.

With a kick and a yelp, Belle and Rowdy headed back into the arena. The crowd cheered. On the first pass, she tried to gauge Rowdy's stride. She didn't even try for the hat. The crowd quieted, thinking Belle had missed.

Helen trotted her horse by. "Go on, hot shot. You can do this. Give 'em something to remember. Your Momma deserves to see more than a pole race and an automatic ride." She leaned over and patted Belle on the head. "Now everybody up there in the stands thinks I'm taunting you some more. It's called milking it for the publicity, hon. We'll plan some other little tricks together as time goes on." She reined her horse away. "Go get 'em."

Belle rode a prancing Rowdy around the perimeter of the arena, aware with every step of exactly when she would ride past Momma. She didn't look. Finally, whirling about, she kicked Rowdy into a gallop and, as they passed her hat, she slipped down and snagged it. The crowd roared. Her heart was pounding, and she was trembling so badly she almost dropped the hat just trying to put it on. She and Helen took a victory lap while the clowns tumbled into view, turning the removal of the poles from the arena into a hilarious act involving dueling poles and racing stick horses.

It was over. After she slid to the ground, Belle had to hold on to a stirrup while she waited to stop shaking.

Helen hopped down. "Good work," she said, and offered a hug.

Belle shook her head. "You made that happen. I was—"

"You were nervous. So what. We make a good team." Helen grinned.

Monte, Dora, and Shep, along with some of the other performers, gathered round, offering congratulations. Shep planted a kiss on her cheek. Ignoring the jeers of some of the cowboys, he whispered, "You were superb." Then he turned toward Helen, shaking a finger at her and scolding, "Bad cowgirl, stealing a girl's hat the first time she's in the arena with a new act."

Helen shrugged and turned to Belle. "Go on now," she said, and motioned toward the stands. "Your momma's gonna be wondering where you are. You tell her I said good-bye and thanks for everything."

"She'll want to see you before she leaves," Belle protested. "You're practically part of the family now. Can't you hornswoggle someone into taking care of the horses again?"

"*Hornswoggle?*" Helen looked horrified as she glanced at Dora. "Did she really just say *hornswoggle?*"

"You g-go," Dora said, and reached for the horses' reins. She stroked Rowdy's neck.

Monte spoke up. "We'll catch up. I think Dora's having second thoughts about leaving."

Dora smiled. "C-come on, cowboy," she said, and together, she and Monte gathered the horses' reins and wove their way through the crowd toward the stables.

———

Momma and Orrin Knox were visiting with a woman who was obviously a high-society New Yorker when Belle and Shep caught up with them. Momma spoke to Shep. "I'm not really certain I'm speaking to you, young man." She eyed him with mock anger. " '*Compliments of the management*' indeed."

Shep ducked his head and mugged guilt. "I deeply regret any appearance of subterfuge, ma'am. I was merely hoping to enhance your opinion of my hometown. And, by association, of myself." He put his hand on his heart and bowed his head.

"You do see what I mean," the elegant stranger said. "Always the actor."

When she extended a hand to Belle and introduced herself as "this ingrate's proud mother," Belle saw where Shep's gorgeous sister had gotten her amazing blue eyes. Mrs. Mortimer looked up at Shep. "You were right, son. She's lovely." She turned back to Belle. "Your mother and I have compared notes and found that we share the same affliction wherein we swing between states of euphoric pride in our children and terrified denial over the danger inherent in what they do for a living. We have also agreed that the only proper treatment for it is for all of us to enjoy a late supper at the Brunswick." She glanced at Shep. "I imagine Edward will be happy to accommodate a request for one of the private dining rooms. He's getting used to giving out favors to family by now."

"I only asked for a nice room," Shep said, somewhat defensively. "And flowers," he added. His mother tilted her head and arched one eyebrow. "Oh, all right. And a breakfast cart. But that was all. And Uncle Edward was happy to do it."

CHAPTER 23

THESE . . . THINGS DOTH THE LORD HATE . . .
A PROUD LOOK, A LYING TONGUE . . .
Proverbs 6:16-17 KJV

It had to be a plot. There was no other explanation for Shep's mother just happening to occupy the seat next to Momma at the Wild West. And if Shep had somehow arranged for his mother to meet her mother, what did that mean? And if it meant what it might mean, how did Belle feel about that? Life was getting confusing. She didn't know how she felt. Or maybe she did, and she just didn't want to think about it. There was so much going on, and now she had more work than ever to do in the arena—which was wonderful. She'd known she would eventually meet Shep's family because he'd talked about it, but here they all were, and Shep was pulling her chair out for her to sit down in this elegant restaurant, and his mother was laughing and chatting with Momma as if they'd known each other for ages. Shep's Uncle Edward had come in and said hello, and as the moments went by, Belle was feeling more and more like she was taking a test for which she hadn't studied.

The entire thing was too ironic for words. Shep's background was more like hers than she'd realized. He, too, had essentially run away from home to join the Wild West. And his father had been a banker—although, as the evening wore on, it became apparent that the Mortimer family's banking concerns were on a much higher rung of the financial world ladder than Otto Friedrich's First Bank of North Platte. It didn't take a genius to figure that out. Everything about Mrs. Mortimer—from the trim on her stylish hat to the tip of her leather-clad boots—said old money and lots of it. Diamond earbobs and jewel-studded bracelets flashed in the restaurant candlelight.

She insisted that Henry must bring Miss Friedrich to the house to meet everyone but said he should wait until Aunt Tillie and Uncle Charlie come back to the city from the summer house. And Aunt Sophie and Uncle Harold would be back from that boat trip down the coast in a few weeks.

"They promised Cook she could go see her family next month, and you know how they are, Henry. They can't get by without Cook." A boat with a cook? And a captain? Mrs. Mortimer might have called their mode of transportation a *boat,* but obviously Aunt Sophie and Uncle Harold had taken a trip on the family *yacht.*

Belle was beginning to have her own *What hath God wrought* thoughts. She could almost envision the hilarity in the upper stratosphere as the angels above got the joke on the girl who ran away from home to find her own way in life, successfully escaping from the world of finishing schools and social graces, only to fall in love with the only man in the Wild West whose family represented everything she had run away from. He even had his own Uncle Charlie. *Whoa. LOVE?*

It hit her just like that. She looked across the table at Shep, who was telling Momma the story about his begging Buffalo Bill for a job, and realized that if she had her way about things, Shep Sterling would have a place at all her tables for the rest of her life. And just at the moment she thought that, Shep glanced her way and winked, and it thrilled her right down to her toes. She winked back. Shep gave a little nod toward Momma, as if he were telling Belle, *I told you I'd win her approval.* And apparently he had, because Momma seemed happier than Belle had seen her in a long, long time.

———

Momma and Orrin came over to the Wild West grounds early Tuesday morning. They would have to leave before noon in order to catch the train home, but Orrin had one last interview to conduct, and so, while he spoke with Ned Bishop, Belle and Momma took a stroll, finally settling on a bench positioned just off the graveled path that circled the Wild West grounds. Once again, Belle asked about Daddy, and once again Momma said that he was in Denver on business. He sent his love. He would be thrilled to learn that the boots he'd had made were working out so well.

"Is there something you're not telling me?" Belle asked abruptly. "Daddy isn't sick, is he? Or is the bank having trouble?"

Momma hesitated. "He's been very busy, Irmagard. To be honest I haven't seen a lot of him in recent weeks. You know how preoccupied he can be when new projects arise." She paused. "I shall tell him he must write more often."

"And you will, too—right?"

"I will," Momma promised. She gestured around them. "I was nervous about coming out here on my own," she said. "I'm so glad I did." She reached for Belle's hand.

"I started a dozen letters to you, Momma. I really did. But somehow, I could never get past *Dear Momma.* I couldn't say I was sorry for being here because I'm not." She paused. "I am sorry, though, for the way it happened. Daddy and I were wrong to go behind your back the way we did."

Momma took a long time to answer. "All any mother wants is for her children to be happy." She squeezed Belle's hand. "I've seen what a life of traveling and performing can do, Irmagard. Based on that, I was completely convinced that this life couldn't possibly make you happy. I was so convinced that I was willing to fight you for as long as it took for your dream to die." She sighed and shook her head. "I was wrong."

"I wish you could feel better about it," Belle said. "Or at least not hate it so much."

Momma let go of her hand. "I don't hate it as much as I worry. About your safety. And other things."

"You do know that a cannon could go off next to Diamond and he'd barely blink."

"I believe you."

"And you know I'm being careful not to take foolish risks in Dora's act."

"Yes."

"Rowdy's a little skittish, but he and I are going to get along fine. You mustn't worry about that."

Momma sighed. "I think I've finally come to realize that you really are quite gifted with horses. I've heard your friends talk about it enough over these past few days. Miss Keen has been especially careful to make certain I realize your talents in that regard. And Mr. Sterling has done his share of praising you, as well."

"Is it Shep who worries you, then?"

"No." She shook her head. "He's from a good family. I believe his intentions are honorable."

"Then why can't you be more like Daddy? Why can't you be happy for me?"

Again, there was a long silence. Finally, Momma took a deep breath. "I haven't ever spoken of this to you, but my mother and my sister were both actresses. They spent their lives traveling from place to place, and . . . I haven't wanted to talk about it because it's just too painful."

Belle shifted on the bench and looked at Momma. But Momma kept looking off into the distance, clearly struggling with her emotions.

"Is that why you always got angry when I'd ask why I didn't have grandparents and aunts and uncles like everyone else?"

Momma nodded. "Perhaps I was wrong not to explain what was behind all my protests. But it's a painful story, and to be quite honest, it makes me ashamed to think about it, much less tell about it. But I know my past is the cause for the fear I feel in here"—she spread her hand across her midsection—"whenever I think of you living this life."

Belle was silent. Waiting.

Taking a deep breath, Momma began. "My earliest memories involve waiting in the corner of a dressing room for my mother to come off stage. Or being jerked awake and dragged aboard a stage coach or a wagon or sometimes a train, en route to the next town. By the time my sister was ten, and I was twelve, our mother was worn-out from drink and . . . things I never want you to know about. As far as I know, neither Olive nor I ever met our fathers. I asked about mine once. My mother slapped me and cursed him. I never asked about him again."

"Oh, Momma—"

"The night my mother died, I took my sister by the hand and walked across town to a little clapboard church. The pastor and his wife took us in. They treated us very well, but neither Olive nor I wanted anything to do with religion. Olive seemed to forget a lot of the terrible things from her childhood, and as she grew older she grew more and more determined to become an actress."

Momma glanced at Belle. "She had red hair and blue-gray eyes. Just like you. She was a stunning beauty and incredibly gifted. Unfortunately, she was also given to 'episodes.' No one knew the answer to her struggles and, it seemed, no one could help her. On stage, she was brilliant. Off it, she would descend into these terrible bouts of depression, and no one could lift her out."

Swiping at the tears on her cheeks, Momma said, "Olive took her own life when you were a baby." She shivered. "And that is why I never wanted you to have anything to do with this life you've run to."

Belle leaned her head on Momma's shoulder. Momma patted her cheek and then said, "I remember reading a Bible verse once that talked about the things in the past happening so that we could learn from them. When you first started talking about the Wild West, I used to quote that verse to myself as justification for why you mustn't be allowed to go through with any such plan. I would tell myself that the past had shown me what happened to women who chose that kind of life, and I believed it was my duty to learn from it and to stop you." She sighed. "But then your father reminded me that it was prideful to presume that I could know positively God's will for another person's life.

"Now don't take this in the wrong way, dear, but you know that your father has never exactly been a religious man. So when he said that, I puffed up and thought what does he know, this man who rarely darkens the door of the church? I didn't think God could possibly be asking me to trust Him that completely. Certainly not with you." She swiped at a tear.

"But He *is* asking me to trust Him completely. I don't like it one bit, but I think I finally realize that's what I'm supposed to do. I'm being asked to trust God with my greatest treasure." She took a deep breath. "So, Miss Irmagard Liberty Belle Friedrich, that's what I'm going to do. With God's help."

They were both teary-eyed. Momma moved first. "My old bones are stiffening up. Let's walk toward the arena and see if we can't find Orrin. It's time we met up with Monte and Dora and headed for the train station."

Soon they were both swept up in the crowd gathered to say good-bye to Monte and Dora. Helen gave Momma an enthusiastic hug, and much to Belle's surprise, Momma put her hands on Shep's shoulders and kissed him on the cheek. When the time came for Momma and Orrin, Monte and Dora to climb aboard the train that would take them first to the ferry landing, and from there on to the train station and home, Belle couldn't keep the tears back.

Momma reached for her and with the last hug whispered, "I am so proud of you. *So proud.*" When Momma stepped back she was crying, too.

Belle watched until the train was out of sight. She and Shep had just turned and started back for the Wild West grounds when Ned Bishop hollered that Bill Cody wanted to see Belle in his tent. Pronto.

———

It was nearly time for the twelve-thirty performance, and the usual crowd of admirers was gathered around Buffalo Bill when Belle walked up. The minute he saw her he said, "Well, folks. If you'll excuse me, I have some business with this lovely young ranchera." He tipped his hat and motioned for Belle to come by him, then offered his arm and led her away. When they were out of earshot, he chuckled. "That wasn't nearly as hard as it usually is. Perhaps I'll have you come rescue me more often."

Belle relaxed a little. He certainly didn't seem upset about anything to do with her.

"Your mother and I had a nice chat early this morning. She had an interesting proposal, and when I agreed to it, she decided I should take care of the details after she left for home." He pulled a note from inside his buckskin coat. "First, I thought you might like to read the note she left me."

July 20, 1886
To the Honorable William F. Cody
Bill: I want to thank you for what you have done to make Irmagard's fondest hopes and childhood dreams come true. Thank you for your assurances and patience with my many questions, doubts, and fears this morning. Having decided on this course of

*action, I find myself, while still easy prey for worry, somewhat hope-
ful for the future. Thank you for being willing to facilitate things.*
   *Sincerely and with my best wishes for a successful winter
season,*

Wilhelmina Friedrich

When Belle glanced up, Cody said, "Your mother wanted to do
something to help you," Cody said. "When I realized she was talking
about some grand gesture, I immediately knew what would qualify as
'grand.' Now, it remains to be seen if this will actually work out, but
if anyone can make it happen, you can." He handed her the piece of
paper he'd been holding back while she read Momma's note. It was
a bank draft payable to William F. Cody. For two *thousand* dollars.
Momma had signed it and written beneath her signature, *payment
in full for one chestnut mare named Blaze. To be given to Irmagard
Manerva Friedrich, also known as Liberty Belle.*

———

Willa's train pulled into the North Platte station on one of those
mid-July days when heat waves rose from the earth and the folks
lucky enough to have an icebox were wont to chip off a piece now
and then just to cool their foreheads. The Mason family was waiting, anxious to see Monte, excited to meet Dora, and eager to haul
everyone home to the ranch. While Orrin Knox chatted with Minnie, and everyone else began to load up, Laura pulled Willa aside.
"We should retrieve your buggy from the livery," she said. "There's
something you need to see."

Willa looked down at her black silk traveling skirt and wondered
at the dictates of fashion. Certainly no one who'd ever lived through
a Nebraska July would ever prescribe black silk as the ideal traveling
suit. "I hope it won't take too long," she said. "I won't last in this
beastly heat."

It didn't take long. Taking the trail to the house, Laura pulled up at the picket fence gate. Looking over the formerly barren yard, Willa managed one word. "Who?"

"I think you know the answer to that," Laura said. "He drove out to the ranch the very day he got back from Denver. Asked me what kind to buy. Said he hadn't listened very well over the years, but he thought I'd know what you'd want."

"What . . . what did you say?"

"You mean after I told him it was going to take more than a dozen trees to make up for his despicable behavior?" Laura paused, then counted on her fingers and recited, "Oak. Maple. Cottonwood. Hackberry. Black walnut. Heavy on the cottonwood, since we know for sure they'll thrive. I told him he'd have to water them every day. He said that wouldn't be a problem."

"But . . . but . . ." Willa kept staring at the trees. "I thought—"

"I know," Laura said. "I thought the same thing when Charlie went looking for him, and Willard told him Otto was in Denver. But we were wrong." Laura reached over and patted Willa on the arm. "He wasn't giving up on this life and going in search of another. He's got everyone in town talking, the way he's tending these trees," Laura said. "And he planted every single one with those soft banker's hands of his." She flicked the reins of the buggy and they headed north to the ranch.

The week after Momma left New York passed in a haze of delightful hard work and unusually long hours. Though she had two horses to manage, Belle was still expected to keep up her commitment to work for Ma Clemmons. As soon as Blaze was transferred to the same stable as Diamond, Belle began to spend as much time as possible simply running her hands over the mare's body and down her legs, over and over again, trying to root out the old expectations and ingrain new trust. "See there?" she'd say. "You can trust me. I'll never hurt you."

While her trust of humans was taking longer than Belle would have liked, Blaze latched on to Diamond like a filly with her dam. Every time Belle took Diamond out to be longed, Blaze carried on to the point that Belle finally took to leading Blaze out first and hitching her to a corral post before going back for Diamond. It worked. Blaze could see Diamond and was content. The wranglers began to tease Belle about the "overgrown weanling with the blaze." Belle wrote Momma about it all, with studied emphasis on how Blaze never kicked or nipped.

If Momma could trust her in spite of her own fears, the least Belle could do was write more often.

On her way to the stables one morning about a week after Momma had left, Belle detoured by the mail office and found two letters. Daddy had finally written, and from the heft of the envelope, it was a long letter. Resisting her first impulse to tear it open on the spot, Belle decided to wait until after supper, when she would have more time to truly savor Daddy's news.

She didn't recognize the handwriting on the other envelope, but it appeared to contain only one sheet of paper, so she opened it and read.

Dear Irma . . . or I suppose I should write "Dear Belle" now. . .

I know we have never been close, but I wanted you to know that you have my profound sympathy. I have always held you and your family in high regard and am grieved every time I drive by the lovely home where my friend Irmagard used to entertain. With its drapes drawn, the dear old place almost seems as if it is mourning its loss. Certainly all of North Platte is deeply saddened by recent events. It is my fondest wish to see restoration accomplished, and I shall pray fervently to that end. I refuse to believe that your parents' separation is permanent, and I shall always be their defender and yours. If I can be of any encouragement to you, do not hesitate to write. In the meantime, please know that you have my best wishes, both for success in the Wild West, and for reunion between your parents. Do not

listen to those who would say otherwise. Your father's recent return
from Denver and new activity at the house in your mother's absence
gives us all hope that healing is at hand and that North Platte will
once again look to Mr. and Mrs. Otto Friedrich as the social leaders
they have always been. Hope on hope ever.

Your friend,
Edna Hertz

P.S. Please thank Mr. Sterling for the autographed photo. I was
so disappointed when my parents were not able to make good on their
promise to see the Wild West in St. Louis. Mr. Sterling's kindness is
greatly appreciated.

Belle ran for her tent. With trembling hands she opened Daddy's letter, but its contents disappointed—or encouraged, depending on how Belle decided to think about it. Daddy said nothing about any difficulties like those Edna Hertz mentioned. Everything in North Platte was just fine according to Daddy. He'd been to Denver on business. The only thing strange about the letter was the absence of any mention of he and Momma having gone to the opera house or visiting the ranch together. Maybe what Edna said was true. Maybe Daddy was trying to spare her feelings.

Daddy's letter lay in her lap and Edna's was atop the table when Shep found her.

———

Shep ducked inside, careful to leave the tent flap up so they were visible to anyone who cared to look. "What's wrong, honey? Helen said she saw you running for the tent. Said something about a letter and tears."

Belle motioned to the table, where she'd thrown Edna's letter.

Shep read the note over twice before setting it back atop the table and, sitting down next to Belle, putting his arm around her. "Do I know Edna Hertz? Name sounds familiar for some reason." When Belle looked up at him he could see disbelief in her eyes.

"Do you *know* her? She practically climbed in your lap the day you brought me those roses."

"Ah." *That one. Ample curves. Nice enough looking. A way of moving that called attention to herself. Trouble just waiting to happen.* He'd been more than a little relieved when she didn't show up in St. Louis. "You know the publicity office sends those autographed photos out when folks request 'em. Right?" He reached for the note and read it a third time. "Anyone who would send a thing like this is no friend of yours. Or mine."

"I never thought of Edna Hertz as a friend," Belle said. "But I didn't realize she *hated* me enough to do something like this." She swiped at more tears and blew her nose. "I *knew* something was wrong when Momma was here. I just had this . . . feeling. All she would say about Daddy was that he was in Denver. 'On business,' she said." Belle shook her head. "And I thought we were finally going to all get along."

"Now, hold on," Shep said and pointed to the note. "You don't know if any of that is true. Other than that your father was in Denver. And your momma told you that."

"It says the house is closed up. Why would she make that up?"

"If your daddy was gone, and your momma was here, why wouldn't they close it up for a few days? There's a reasonable explanation for everything in that letter."

"If she was planning on leaving Daddy, you can be sure I wouldn't know anything about it until the deed was done," Belle said. "That's how she handles things like that." She sniffled again. "In fact, her trip here and buying Blaze and all of that was probably part of her plan to—"

"You're being awful hard on her." Shep frowned and looked down at her. "Especially when you don't know—"

"I know," Belle interrupted him. She told him about being six years old and seeing her mother with another man.

Shep thought for a long while before finally saying, "You never asked her about that?"

"What would have been the point? Daddy came home. Things seemed to be all right."

"Except you've carried the memory, the disappointment, inside you all these years and let it fester without giving your poor mother a chance to defend herself."

"My *poor mother*?!"

Shep could feel her stiffen. She moved away from him on the cot. He gentled his voice. "There's generally two sides to every story, sweetheart. We're all low down at one time or another." He paused. "That's why Sunday Joe has so much to say about forgivin' every time he gets a chance." She let him take her hand but kept her distance. "If there's bad history between your folks, that's a hurtful thing for a child to have to witness. But that was a long time ago, and it seems to me that, if you think it through, you'll realize there's been a lot of goodness piled into both their lives since. If you ask me, it'd be best for you to just let all that stuff about what you saw or didn't see go, so it doesn't taint the present." He put his hand on her shoulder. "Carryin' around something like that doesn't do anybody any good. Like I said before . . . it festers. And that's an ugly thing to have in a life."

Belle sat quietly for a while. Fresh tears began to course down her cheeks. "Even if I think you're right, I don't know *how* to let go of it," she said. "I can't."

"Maybe Sunday Joe could help you figure out how. Want me to see if I can find him?"

Belle reached for the letter. "My father has always been devoted to her. He's given her that house and every other thing she's ever asked for. If this is true—if she's left him—it'll kill him."

"Seems to me there's *two* hearts breaking when a marriage has trouble," Shep said. He offered to go get Sunday Joe again.

"I don't want Sunday Joe," Belle said. "Not right now."

"What then?"

"You," she said. "I want you to hold me."

So he did.

———

"You did great, sweetheart," Shep said as they walked toward the back lot together after the evening performance. "I'm proud of you."

"Can't let a little thing like a life falling apart interfere," Belle said. "The show must go on and all." She sighed. "I just wish I knew what I'm supposed to *do* about it. I mean, do I write Aunt Laura to find out what's going on? Do I telegraph Daddy? Do I get on a train and head home?"

"No," Shep said quickly. "You do *not* get on a train. You stay here and do your job as best you can. Whatever is going on in North Platte, you keep out of it. And when whatever is going on is over, you love them both—warts and all, as they say. If your Momma had wanted to involve you, she had plenty of opportunity to do that when she was here. And besides, for all you know, that letter is pure meanness coming out of what's-her-name." He tied Golden Boy's reins to a hitching post. "And as Sunday Joe would say, this is one of those times when you can do more good prayin' over it than messin' with it anyway."

Belle pulled Rowdy's saddle off and set it atop an empty rack, then grabbed a brush and began to go over the horse's sweat-soaked coat. Maybe Shep was right. Today's performances might not have helped her know what to do, but they'd provided an outlet for her emotions. She was calmer now, and she could see the logic to what Shep was saying. He was right about Sunday Joe's advice, too. She'd talked to the preacher between performances. He'd been short on outrage at Momma over the past and long on Belle's need to forgive. He'd even used the word *fester* and talked about how things kept inside and not given to God ended up hurting people. She needed to forgive the past.

Belle knew he was right. But that didn't mean she could do what he said.

CHAPTER 24

⊷⟴ ⟳⊷

THE WAY OF A FOOL IS RIGHT IN HIS OWN EYES,
BUT A WISE MAN IS HE WHO LISTENS TO COUNSEL.

Proverbs 12:15 NASB

Two weeks after Willa got back from New York, she was helping Laura can garden tomatoes when she heard the clatter of a buggy or wagon come tearing in. Everyone rushed outside just in time to see Orrin Knox jump down and head for the house. He lost his hat in the process, but he let it lay as he charged up and choked out, "Mr. Friedrich—" he gasped—"slumped over his desk. . . . He's . . . at Dr. Sheridan's. . . ."

Willa untied her apron and dropped it on the porch swing. At the bottom of the steps she turned back around. "His horse is worn out," she said. "It'll ruin him to run him back to town in this heat. Can someone hitch up Nellie?"

"Yes," Laura said, "we'll handle it." She and Dora headed for the barn.

Minnie came back outside with a glass of water for Orrin. As she held it out she said, "I'll see to your horse, Mr. Knox, while you

305

help Aunt Willa into town." Orrin gulped down the water, gasped a thanks, and grabbing his hat, went to help hitch up Nellie.

In moments Willa and Orrin were dashing back toward town. The ride seemed to take hours. Orrin said he knew nothing more, and Willa was left to her own thoughts as she hung on, hoping Nellie wouldn't trip, a wheel wouldn't hit a rut and break, and Otto wouldn't die. *Please, God. Not like this. Don't let it end like this.*

The buggy had barely stopped before Willa jumped down and charged through the front doorway of Dr. Sheridan's office, past his desk, and down a narrow hall to the room he called his hospital. It was really only a row of cots separated by folding screens. Otto was the only patient. He lay pale and motionless, and even when Willa spoke his name and grasped his hand, he didn't move.

"I told him he was killing himself," Dr. Sheridan said. "There's not a man on earth who can keep up the hours that man's been working and not suffer for it. He wouldn't listen. Willard found him slumped at his desk when he went in to open the bank this morning."

Willa sat down beside the bed. "Oh, Otto," she whispered, and brushed his forehead with her fingertips. He was breathing evenly. As her fingers traced the line of his jaw, she noticed something different about the left side of his face. She touched the edge of his mouth, where his lips seemed to curve downward. "What is it?"

"A brain hemorrhage, I'm afraid."

"Hemorrhage?" Willa croaked. "Doesn't that mean bleeding?"

"It does," Dr. Sheridan explained, "but in this case, the bleeding is *inside* the brain. Otto has suffered an attack of apoplexy. I won't know the extent of the damage until he regains consciousness."

"When will that be?"

"Only God knows. We must wait. And hope. He's always had the strength of a bull. He doesn't drink to excess. Those are going to be in his favor now, but the entire left side of his body may be affected and there may be some paralysis."

Willa turned in the chair to look at the doctor. "He's *paralyzed?*" She put her hand to her mouth.

"I said there *may* be some paralysis. There may be none at all."

"But it could be serious," Willa said. "And permanent?"

"That's impossible to know right now." The doctor put his hand on her shoulder. "I know you and Otto have had your problems of late, and I am truly sorry. But I also felt certain you'd want to know. And since Mr. Knox knows the family . . . I thought he'd be the one to come for you."

Willa nodded. "Is it all right if I stay with him for a while?"

"As long as you like."

She stroked the back of Otto's hand. "Mr. Knox is probably waiting outside. Would you ask him to come in here?"

"I'll send him right away," the doctor said. "I have to mix up some powders for another patient. I'll be in my office up front. If you notice any change—anything at all—call me right away."

Willa nodded. Orrin came back. "I know it's asking a lot," she said, "but could you possibly take word to Laura and Charlie . . . ? And if I sent a list to Laura, would you bring a few things back into town?"

"Of course," Orrin said. "Whatever you need, Mrs. Friedrich."

She wrote the note. Orrin left. Willa cried.

Willa was in the middle of a nightmarish dream involving all her worst fears about Irmagard and the Wild West when a soft moan brought her fully awake. It was the middle of the night, and at first she didn't know if she should run for the doctor or light the lamp, but as she moved to get up, she realized Otto wasn't having another attack. He was trying to get up.

"Lay back," she said, and grasped his arm. "You've had an attack of apoplexy. Willard found you, and you're at the doctor's clinic. The worst is over. You'll continue to get better now. But it's going to take some time, and—"

He wrested his arm free and grabbed her hand, squeezing it so hard it hurt. She pulled free and lit a lamp, then sat back down and recounted every detail of what Dr. Sheridan had done and said in regards to his care. "Speech is often the last to return," she said. "You must be patient."

He frowned and looked toward the door and then back at her.

"Shall I get Dr. Sheridan?"

With great effort he shook his head. Tears welled up in his eyes.

"There, there," Willa said, and patted his shoulder. She took a deep breath. She'd thought about what she would say when he regained consciousness, but as she stared into his eyes, everything she had practiced seemed irrelevant. One thing seemed certain. She'd been asking God to show her what to do about her marriage, and God had answered in undeniable terms—at least for now. She forced a weak smile. It was the best she could do. "As soon as you're able, I'm going to take you home."

His tears spilled over. She wiped them away. He grabbed her hand again and tried to raise it to his lips. She resisted. "You need me right now, and I will do my duty." Her voice wavered. She looked away. "That will have to be enough." She patted his arm. "Sleep now," she said as gently as she could. As any nurse would.

Feeling stiff from her night propped up in a chair, Willa walked to the front of the clinic while Dr. Sheridan examined Otto. As soon as he joined her, she asked, "Can you keep Otto here for a day or two while I get things ready at the house? As you know I haven't been living there, and—"

"Are you certain you want to do that?" Dr. Sheridan said. "Otto's going to need a great deal of help for the foreseeable future. Maybe even with very basic things for at least a few days. I'm already seeing improvement with his arm and leg this morning, which is a very good sign, but I won't know to what extent he's going to recover for quite some time yet. His speech may be the last thing to return—if it returns at all. It's going to be difficult for him, and Otto's not a man known for his patience. Which means caring for him will likely also be difficult because *he* may decide to be difficult. I don't mean to pry, but if the two of you aren't on the best of terms, perhaps—"

Willa interrupted him. "I hope it isn't common knowledge, doctor, but Otto Friedrich has been *difficult* for much of our married life." She paused. "As to our situation—" She looked away for a moment and then, with a sigh, looked back at the doctor. "I was the one who left. Otto didn't want that. If I decide to return, I have no reason to think he'll be anything but delighted. So if you could bring in a nurse for today and tomorrow, then I'll drive back out to the ranch and pack. It will also give me time to open up the house. There's probably a thick layer of dust over everything, and I'll need to stock the pantry. Otto can stay in Ella Jane's room on the main floor. Stairs won't be an issue."

"You're going to need someone to help you with his daily care," the doctor said.

"I wouldn't know how to go about finding anyone," Willa said. "As you know Ella Jane has married and left town, and I just don't know anyone else to ask."

"One of your nieces, perhaps?"

Willa shook her head. "Otto wouldn't stand for that. His pride wouldn't want them to see him this way." She bit her lip. "Do you think I should wire Irmagard? If there's any danger of—"

"We'll know more in a few days," the doctor said. "I think it's quite all right to wait and see how things go before alarming your daughter. There are no guarantees, of course, but I have a sense that the worst is probably over."

Willa cleared her throat. "Irmagard isn't aware of the situation here, Dr. Sheridan. What I mean is, she doesn't know about me staying out at the ranch and Otto moving into the hotel. To be honest, I wanted some time to think things through before making any kind of pronouncement to the family."

"I understand," Dr. Sheridan said. "Are you sure you don't want me to make other arrangements for Otto's care?"

"Oh, no. No. That wouldn't be right. I couldn't live with myself if I let you do that."

"If you change your mind, you mustn't hesitate to ask for help," the doctor said. "I'll check around to see if anyone might be available for hire. And if two days isn't enough time for you to prepare to take him home, that's all right, too." He patted her arm. "You're a good woman, Willa Friedrich. Otto's blessed to have a woman in his life willing to do this for him—in spite of . . . problems."

Willa nodded, gathered up her things, and headed for the livery. Before leaving town, she swung by the train station and asked Johnny Dolan to ready the barn at the house for Nellie's return. At the last minute she thought to ask if he'd water Otto's trees. And then she headed north to the ranch, wishing with all her heart that she could muster up some semblance of affection for the motionless man in Dr. Sheridan's infirmary.

"I just don't understand why you won't let us send Minnie back with you," Laura said. "We're your family."

Willa laid her everyday apron atop the things in her trunk and closed the lid. With a sigh, she sat down on her cot. "Otto's a proud man, Laura. He'd never forgive me for allowing his own niece to see him like he is. Dr. Sheridan said he might be able to find someone I could hire. I'll hope it pans out. If not, we'll get by."

"Are you going to wire Irma?"

"I don't think so. At least not yet. Dr. Sheridan didn't think it was necessary. He seems to think the worst is over. She'll be coming home in a few weeks for a break after they've finished their fall tour anyway. And I'd much rather he be better before she sees him."

Laura sat down next to her and took her hand. "Are you going to be all right with this?"

"I don't know," Willa replied. "I'm still so angry and hurt I can barely stand to look at him sometimes." She swiped at a tear. "But then he plants *trees*." She began to cry, grateful for the understanding apparent in Laura's quiet presence. Once she'd calmed down, the two of them dragged Willa's trunk through the door. Minnie and Dora came running and helped load it onto Willa's buggy.

Minnie was the first to offer a hug. "I'll pray, Aunt Willa," she murmured. "And you *must* let me come and help if things get too hard."

Dora nodded. "M-me t-t-oo," she said. "I'd be happy to c-clean and wash d-dishes for you. All you need."

Fighting back more tears, Willa hugged them all, climbed into the buggy, grabbed the reins, and headed home. At the top of the rise, she looked behind her at the peaceful ranch. How she would miss the loving family she'd come to know in new ways during the past few weeks.

Father, thank you for the Masons. Thank you for their love. Thank you for the time out here. I don't know if I've learned anything about what I should do. Charlie said you have a plan, I just had to find it. Tell me, Lord God, is Otto's condition part of your plan? I'll try my best to do my duty, if for no other reason than Otto's caring for me for all the years of our marriage. I owe him this. But I need your strength, Father. Maybe even a miracle or three.

Apparently God had spent all His miracles on other supplicants that week. The nurse Dr. Sheridan contacted wasn't available. In fact, the *five* contacts he made about help for Willa weren't available. When, by Saturday, Otto had regained the use of his arm and proven his ability to walk—albeit unsteadily—Willa insisted she take him home. She had cleaned the entire main floor of the house, she'd restocked the pantry, and she told Dr. Sheridan she was tired of sleeping on a cot in the infirmary and tired of having to make a special trip every day to water Otto's trees. "He may not be talking, but he can make his needs known," Willa said. "There's no reason he shouldn't go home."

Otto nodded agreement and motioned for a tablet upon which he wrote, shakily, *Let me go.*

"All right, Otto," the doctor said. "But you see to it you do everything you possibly can for yourself. This is a wonderful woman you have here, and she shouldn't be treated like a servant."

Otto's face turned red at the scolding, whether from embarrassment or anger, Willa couldn't tell. He reached for the cane Dr. Sheridan had provided earlier and, standing erect, wobbled for the door. His left foot dragged.

"See here, Otto," the doctor said. "I'm to go get Mr. Knox when you're ready to go. He's going to help Mrs. Friedrich push you home in this chair." He pointed to the wheelchair he'd rolled out earlier. "It's blistering hot out there. You don't want to walk. Sit down now. It's the best way."

Otto grunted and kept walking. At the front door, he rattled the knob with his nearly useless left hand. When he couldn't work it out, he let go of his cane to use his right hand, lost his balance, and would have fallen if Willa hadn't been there to steady him.

"You don't seem to believe me, Otto," the doctor said. "If you don't sit in this chair and let Mr. Knox wheel you home and help you inside, I won't let you go."

"Please," Willa said. She put her hand on his arm. "It's just this once. Everyone will be delighted to see that you're well enough to leave the infirmary. And the next time they see you, you'll be walking on your own power. And it's much more dignified than having Mr.

Knox and Dr. Sheridan lift you into the buggy. Or into the back of a wagon. Don't you think?"

Otto closed his eyes for a moment. Then, with a grunt and a shrug, he sat down in the wheelchair.

Everything would have been fine, if only Cy Matthews would be reasonable. "He treats me like I'm two years old," Belle said one night when she and Shep took a walk. "At the rate we're going, there's no chance Blaze will even be ready for the parade in October, let alone Madison Square Garden." She gestured as they walked, venting her frustrations. "I think I should talk to Mr. Cody."

"Bill Cody doesn't have time to talk over your disagreement with Cy," Shep said. "He's deep into plans for the Garden performances. Figuring out how to create indoor cyclones and prairie fires is more important right now than whether or not one cowgirl is happy with Cy Matthews."

"So what are you saying I should do?"

"Just settle in and do the job, Belle. Be happy with the way things are for a while. You wanted an audition and you got it. You wanted a job and you got that. You wanted to be a regular part of the performances and you are. You wanted Blaze and you've got her. You're already riding her and she hasn't even tried to buck you off. Not only that, you've got an expert—and I do mean an *expert*—advising you. So train your horse. Do your chores. Perform as expected. Your life is good, Belle. Be thankful."

"I *am* thankful," Belle said. "But I'd be *really* thankful if you'd admit that maybe Cy Matthews is wrong, and I'm right about Blaze."

Shep stopped in midstride. Looking down at her he said, "Honey, I'm going to tell you something now, and it's going to make you mad. But it's for your own good."

"Really?"

"Yes," he nodded. "Really." He put his hand on her shoulder. "You've got more guts than brains if you think you know more than Cy Matthews about training that horse."

Belle glared at him for a moment. When he didn't back down, she turned around and walked off. She didn't know what made her more angry—what Shep had said or the fact that he let her go.

———

"That's good for today," Cy said the following Sunday evening. It had been the shortest session yet.

"Can't I at least take her over to the arena and walk her around in it? There's no one in the stands. She trusts me."

"She trusts you in this corral," Cy said. "We've yet to see what she'll do outside of it. And we're gonna keep it that way until the season closes at the end of the month. Once the company's left on its fall tour and things are quiet around here, I'll start introducing her to new things. And please don't argue with me. I'm gettin' tired of it."

"I'm not arguing," Belle said as she slid out of the saddle and to the ground. "I just don't understand how I'm ever going to have her ready for a parade in October when I haven't so much as ridden her outside this corral yet."

"Been meanin' to talk to you about that," Cy said. "You see to Blaze and then meet me yonder by the arena curtain. I've got to talk to Grady Clemmons about somethin'. I'll be there in a few minutes."

Blaze snuffled Belle's shoulder. She turned around and combed her fingers through the mare's dark mane. "He doesn't know you like I do. Don't let it bother you. We'll figure something out."

A few minutes later Belle had unsaddled Blaze, put her back in the stall next to Diamond, and gone to find Cy.

"I think we both need to face facts, Belle," the older man said. He turned aside and sent a stream of tobacco juice into the dirt. "I'm just as disappointed about it as you are, but that mare just doesn't

314

have the temperament to be a parade horse. Or a trick horse. Now, before you say anything, you let me finish. It ain't your fault. None of it. You were right about her responding to you and you were right about her needing a gentle hand and being a smooth ride. And if she was stabled back in Nebraska there'd be no better saddle horse in the county. But she's got a streak of attitude about her and there's no amount of training in the world that's gonna change that. Blaze was just never meant to *be* what we're asking of her. And it'd be cruel to continue to expect it of her." He spat again.

"But you just said you'd work on gentling her more after we close down."

"Sure I did," Cy said. "She's far from finished, even as a saddle horse. But when she *is* finished, she ought to be shipped home. Your daddy can collect her, and you'll have yourself a nice horse to ride whenever you're back there." His voice gentled. "Now, I know you're disappointed. But trust me. It's best for her and best for you. You can ride Diamond in the parade and I'll talk to Bill and keep my eye out for another arena horse to train for when Diamond needs to retire."

Belle made her way back to Blaze's stall. The mare walked over and nibbled her shirt, looking for sugar. "He's wrong," Belle whispered. "He's wrong about you."

———

It was late that night when Belle slipped out of her tent and made her way back to the stables. All Blaze needed was a chance. They couldn't give up on her. While Belle was willing to concede that a Manhattan parade might be a stretch, she was still convinced that if Blaze were only familiar enough with the arena, if she saw it as little more than a larger corral, where she was secure and where Belle was always in charge, the mare could still prove to be a spectacular trick horse. Enough time had surely passed for her to have forgotten any associations between the arena and bucking. And besides that, Cy hadn't seen Blaze bow. He hadn't seen her raise one hoof to "shake."

Belle was waiting to surprise people with that part of the act. They'd only practiced on nights like this, when everyone else was asleep or disinterested in whatever Liberty Belle was up to over there in the corral with her horse. But if she didn't do something quick, there would never *be* an act for Blaze. As for having a nice saddle mare for when she was at home, Cy had to know what Momma had paid for Blaze. Didn't he realize Belle couldn't just give up like this? Momma would never understand.

At the stables, Belle slid on a hackamore and mounted up bareback. Slowly she walked Blaze across the moonlit grounds, letting the mare take her time. The moonlit tents were the first thing that made her start. Belle patiently urged her forward until Blaze snuffled at a canvas corner, realized it was nothing to fear, and walked on. The fake boulders just inside the arena cast eerie shadows that were a problem for a minute, as well. But again, with Belle's gentle encouragement, Blaze finally walked past them.

"This is it, girl," Belle said. "We're gonna spend a lot of time in here together. And you won't be a bucking bronc ever again. It'll be noisy. But you won't be afraid because I'll be here and I'd never put you in danger. You can trust me. You know that, don't you?" She nudged the mare forward again, and as they walked the perimeter, Belle kept talking. Occasionally the mare would snort and dance sideways, but Belle stayed calm and was always able to settle her. Her heart soared. It was working. Blaze might not be a parade horse, but she would learn to be an arena horse.

And then, as they were leaving the arena, an owl swooped down out of the stands and lighted on one of the false rocks. Blaze snorted, shied, and began to buck. In seconds, Belle was sailing through the air. She landed with a grunt and watched, helpless, as Blaze hurdled over one boulder, stumbled, crashed through the backdrop, and disappeared.

Scrambling to her feet, Belle charged after the horse. Relief flooded through her when she realized the mare had only run back to the corral where they'd been training for weeks. She was waiting at the gate, her sides heaving, her coat flecked with sweat. She seemed to sigh with relief when Belle grasped the hackamore and led her toward the stables. That was when Belle noticed the limp.

CHAPTER 25

·◈─▭ ▭─◈·

BE MERCIFUL, JUST AS YOUR FATHER IS MERCIFUL.

Luke 6:36 NASB

"What in tarnation were you thinking?!" Cy Matthews bent to examine Blaze's leg. "No, don't answer that. I don't want to hear it. In fact," he said, standing upright and putting both hands on his hips, "I don't want to hear anything from you." He grabbed the lead rope. "I need some light to check her over, but if we start hauling lamps out here it'll spook her even more. Let me get her into her spot next to Diamond. He'll calm her down some, and then maybe I can get a better look. I'll come find you when I have something to say."

Belle knew she'd done the right thing to rouse Cy and have him come right away. You didn't just ignore a limp and hope it would get better. But it wasn't easy being the brunt of his temper. Especially when Belle knew that his anger was justified. She could scarcely keep from bursting into tears right there in front of him. As it was, she barely made it halfway to the tent she and Helen shared before she began to blubber. Afraid of waking Helen, she followed the gravel path she and Momma had walked together not three weeks ago, but instead of stopping at the bench they'd shared, Belle headed for the grove of trees where she ended up sitting beneath a towering oak, her knees drawn up, her head down, her mind numb.

Belle woke with a start just as dawn was coloring the eastern sky. For a moment she was disoriented and wondered how it was she'd come to sleep beneath a tree, but then it all came back. As dread clawed at her insides, she made her way to Blaze's stall. The mare seemed all right. Her leg was wrapped, but she didn't seem to be in a lot of pain.

In spite of appearances, Cy's report wasn't good. In fact, it was horrible. Blaze had a bowed tendon. Cy explained that, while she would recover and probably be a great saddle horse, she would never stand up under the demands made of Wild West horses. And as for trick riding?

"Never gonna happen," Cy said. He spit a stream of tobacco juice and swiped his mouth with the back of his hand. "Not that I didn't already tell you that a few hundred times." He stomped off.

By breakfast it seemed that all five hundred people in the Wild West had heard about Liberty Belle ruining a potentially great horse. *You're imagining things,* she told herself, when people seemed to be whispering and looking her way. But she wasn't imagining the fact that Shep didn't have breakfast at all and Helen was unusually quiet. And she wasn't imagining Mabel Douglas's passing up their table to go and sit with Ned Bishop. Not that she missed Mabel Douglas's company. But it was hard to be snubbed by the least-liked person in the troupe.

As the day went on and people continued to give her the cold shoulder, Belle grew increasingly defensive. So much for Sunday Joe's sermons on forgiveness, she thought. Hadn't any of them been listening to him? When she mentioned it to Helen, Helen wasn't sympathetic.

"What you've got to realize, honey, is that the very existence of this Wild West depends on healthy stock. You know how well the animals are treated. And mistreating an animal isn't taken lightly."

"I didn't mistreat Blaze," Belle protested.

"Yes. You did. You asked too much of her too soon. That's mistreating. She trusted you more than anybody, and you let her down."

Belle swallowed hard. "Doesn't everyone know I already feel horrible enough?" She let a tear slide down her cheek.

"Oh, now," Helen said, "it's not the end of the world. Folks'll come around. Just give 'em time."

So Belle gave them time. She kept her head down and worked hard. She begged Cy to show her how to tend Blaze. She was meek and quiet and didn't make any trouble for anyone. And it didn't make a bit of difference. Not even with Shep.

———

Willa's back was so sore that, instead of bending over to pick up the broken pieces, she had to kneel on the kitchen floor. And somewhere between picking up the last bit of broken china and trying to scoop up a lump of oatmeal, she started to cry.

The tears kept flowing as she got up to throw the china into the wastebasket and clean the last bits of oatmeal off the floor. And just when she didn't think she'd ever be able to stop, Otto began to cry, too. Sitting there at the kitchen table with a towel spread across his shirt like a giant bib and bits of oatmeal staining his goatee, Otto wept.

Willa turned her back on him. She gripped the sides of the sink and leaned over and listened to his sobs, but she could not bring herself to move. Finally, the chair he was sitting in scraped across the floor, and she heard him grunt with the effort of standing up. Then she heard his cane fall and hit the floor. She started at the sound and turned around, and there they stood, staring at each other across the kitchen. Finally, she bent and picked up the cane and handed it to him. He took it and just stood there as tears washed down his cheeks and collected in his beard.

She knew she should encourage him not to give up. She should say something about how much better he was doing. And he was. She should tell him she knew he was sick of oatmeal and remind him that it wouldn't be long until he could handle other kinds of food. Dr. Sheridan had told them that only this morning. She should wipe his face and help him to bed. She should do all of those things. But instead, Willa untied her apron and hung it on the hook beside the back door. She opened the door to the porch, stumbled into the nearest chair, and wept. And wept. And wept. And when her sobs had finally been reduced to sniffles, she leaned back and closed her eyes.

And that's where she was when something woke her. She looked toward the front gate, where a woman was lifting the latch and heading up the path to the house. She moved with a stride that spoke of an energy Willa had lost somewhere in the haze of the long hours and endless chores.

The woman strode up onto the porch and held out an envelope. "Vesta McKay," she said. "That there's from Dr. Sheridan himself. I'll wait while you read it." She walked to the edge of the porch and stood, staring toward the horizon.

Willa read Dr. Sheridan's note. Vesta McKay, he said, was the very woman he had had in mind when he suggested Mrs. Friedrich hire help. As it turned out, Mrs. McKay had already been called to attend to the needs of another, a woman experiencing her twelfth confinement. A healthy boy had been delivered and both mother and child were well, so Mrs. McKay had returned to North Platte, and the doctor was taking the liberty to send her over. He hoped Mrs. Friedrich would forgive his doing so without checking with her first, but he was confident she would be pleased if only she would give Mrs. McKay an opportunity to prove her excellent nursing skills.

*You are fast approaching a state of exhaustion that alarms me. As
your physician, I urge you to accept the services of this fine woman.*

When Willa said nothing after reading the note, Mrs. McKay
spoke up. "I've been led to believe that you would benefit from the
services of a nurse. I also do cooking and cleaning for my families. I
pride myself on flexibility, Mrs. Friedrich. And I might also mention
that I'm the soul of discretion."

Willa brushed the hair back out of her face. "I-I'm afraid I don't
know what to say." She looked down at the note. "I was just . . . Earlier
I was thinking that perhaps I should have . . ." She shook her head.
"You'll have to forgive me, Mrs. McKay. I'm not myself." She swallowed and just barely prevented a new onslaught of tears. "I appreciate
that you come very highly recommended, but Mr. Friedrich is a very
private man, and—"

"There are no *buts* in the McKay creed, Mrs. Friedrich. There
is loyalty and friendship. Otto Friedrich helped my dear Ira—may
God rest his soul—when none other in the whole of Lincoln County
would, and it's a joy and a pleasure to be called upon." She smiled,
and for the first time Willa noticed the woman's clear blue eyes. "I'm
thinking what you need is little more than a good night's rest. You
look like you haven't slept in a month of Sundays, dearie." Her chin
trembled with emotion as she said, "Dear Ira McKay was a brawny
man, but when the lockjaw took him down, he was a babe for a while.
I know what you've been dealing with, Mrs. Friedrich. Men like Ira
and your Mr. Friedrich don't make it easy for those who love them
when they're forced to accept help. You've had it hard, I'm thinking.
God bless you for being a faithful wife."

*God bless her? For what? For coming here out of duty? For leav-
ing Otto standing in the kitchen with oatmeal in his beard? For giving
up? For running out on him just now?* With a trembling hand, Willa
handed Dr. Sheridan's note back to Mrs. McKay. "You're hired," she
croaked. "When can you—"

"Why, I've come to stay right now, Mrs. Friedrich." And Mrs. McKay nodded toward the gate. Just the other side of it there was a box, and atop the box, a bag of some kind. Both appeared to have been tied shut with twine.

Willa closed her eyes and took a deep breath. Could it be this easy? Was God finally going to answer some of those prayers she'd uttered? Somehow, Willa thought yes. And with the inner *yes* came a fresh crop of tears.

"Come now, dearie," Mrs. McKay said, and held out her arms. "The Good Lord padded me shoulders for just such times as these. Come have yourself a little cry."

———

Belle felt the first sign of having been forgiven for her selfish behavior on the day Mabel Douglas went back to being herself, taunting and teasing Belle about everything from her propensity for jamming up whatever treadle sewing machine she used to losing every cowgirl race she was in. Belle had developed a thick skin when it came to Mabel's digs, and after the last week of whispered comments and avoidance, it was almost validating to have Mabel be rude again.

One day when Belle was rubbing Blaze down and Ned Bishop walked by, Belle stood up and called him over. "I'm sorry," she blurted out. "For what I did that day. I shouldn't have said that in front of everybody. Even if I was right."

"Which you were," Ned said. "About the mare's needing a light hand."

Belle swallowed. "It doesn't matter now. Not after—" She shrugged. "I just . . . I'm sorry."

Bishop nodded. It was an awkward interchange, but it made things a little better between the two of them, and Belle was grateful.

But even though things were easing up a bit, they still weren't the same. For one thing, Helen didn't trust her anymore. She didn't say

324

it in those words, but it was there in the way she wanted to talk over every move of their act before they rode into the arena together. "Just making sure we're both ready," she would say. When what she was really doing was making sure Belle didn't try anything new and risky. As if Belle would ever do that again. She had learned her lesson.

Not having Helen trust her was hard, but not having Shep around was almost unbearable. He wasn't rude, and he'd stopped avoiding her, but it was as if someone had erected a wall between them. Sometimes when they were in the dining tent or when they were working at the stables at the same time, Belle would look up and see Shep watching her. He'd have this look in his eyes that she didn't know how to interpret. It was terrible to be the fool who'd ruined a good horse, and hard to have lost Helen's trust, but Shep—losing Shep was breaking her heart.

"When are you going to stop punishing that little gal?" Helen sidled up to Shep after an evening performance late in August.

"You think that's what I'm doing?"

"Doesn't matter what I think," Helen said. "It's what *she* thinks. And she's starting to look like a puppy that's displeased its master and doesn't know how to fix it."

"She's the one who stopped talking."

"Yeah, well, that was a couple of weeks ago. And she's started up again. And just about everybody else seems to have decided they've made their point and it's time to do a Sunday Joe and forgive and forget." She pulled him toward where the Wild West train sat on the siding. Grabbing hold of the railing, she climbed onto the platform and motioned for Shep to follow, which he did, sitting down beside her. Dangling one leg off the edge of the platform, he took off his hat and set it on his knee.

"What about you?" Shep said. "All that going over and over

every detail of your act with her every day doesn't exactly look like forgiveness."

"She needed to realize how important it is for us to trust each other. And that I was having trouble trusting her because of her tendency to be reckless. I think she understands that now." She sighed. "She's just a kid, Shep. We had to know she'd have lessons to learn. I didn't think she'd need to learn one quite this big, but I guess I was wrong. Either way, seems to me she's learned it. Shoot, I think *Mabel* even feels a little sorry for Miss Belle."

"What makes you think that?"

"When you were off having dinner with your mother Sunday afternoon, Mabel brought Miss Belle a pastry from that bakery up the road."

"You're kidding," Shep said.

"Not." Helen shook her head. "Even Bishop's being nicer to her. And if Mabel and Ned think its time to be nice, it's time."

"As I just said, *she's* the one who stopped talking to *me*. All I did was tell her the truth."

"What truth was that?"

"That not listening to Cy Matthews proved she had more guts than brains."

Helen raised both eyebrows and stared at him. "You really said that?"

He shrugged. "All right. I probably could have found a better way to put it. I was upset."

"So she isn't the perfect cowgirl. Shoot, I live with the girl. She isn't the perfect *anything*. But I love her anyway, and I'm gonna find her and tell her so. Right now." Helen jumped down and took two steps before turning around and motioning for Shep to follow her. "This is me helping you two kiss and make up, Shepherd. Get your carcass down off that train car and come with me."

———

Helen grabbed a shovel and, coming alongside Belle, began to help her shovel manure into the waiting wagon.

"You don't have to help me," Belle said.

Helen said nothing. Just kept shoveling.

Presently Shep Sterling arrived, shovel in hand.

Belle stood back and looked at them both. They kept shoveling. "Listen," she said. "I know I've messed up just about everything I've tried in one way or another this summer. From bad audition to hackneyed debut in Dora's spot to complete stupidity with Blaze. I've been stubborn, and I wouldn't listen to the people I should have listened to. I've acted like a know-it-all, and I've ignored good advice and—" Clearing her throat, she went back to work. "Shoveling manure is probably the one thing around here I *can* be trusted to do." She tossed a load of manure. And missed the wagon.

Helen and Shep didn't say a word. Belle looked at Helen first. Helen only shrugged. Belle turned toward Shep. "Don't you dare laugh," she said. "Don't you *dare* laugh at me." She went after the errant pile and scooped it up. By the time she got it into the wagon, tears were coursing down her cheeks.

"Now, honey," Helen said, as she gave her a hug, "don't cry over spilled milk. Or manure. I just came over here to tell you I'm sorry I rubbed it in so hard. And I know you're sorry. Let's head back out on the road with a clean slate. What d'ya say?"

Belle swiped at her tears. She nodded. "I say yes. And you can trust me not to pull any stunts in the arena. Ever." She stole a glance at Shep. "And I'm sorry I quit talking to you. What you said was right. Sometimes I *do* have more guts than brains. And I know I messed up, and if you're never going to forgive me, I wish you'd tell me, because if you aren't ever going to talk to me again, I don't know if I can *be* Liberty Belle anymore." She was crying again, and she didn't care because she'd just realized that at some point along the way, being Liberty Belle had stopped being the most important thing in her life.

The most important thing in her life was standing atop this pile of manure with her. Taking her in his arms. Whispering love.

———

"Is something the matter, dearie?"

Vesta came up behind Willa and looked over her shoulder out into the yard.

"He's talking to the trees," Willa said. She nodded at Otto, who was, indeed, standing and looking up at one of the trees he'd planted weeks ago, babbling away. Complete with gestures. "It looks like he's giving a speech."

"And it's worrying you," Vesta said, and returned to her dusting.

Willa turned her back to the window and sat down at the edge of the window seat. "He doesn't talk to *us*."

"Well, of course he does, dear," Vesta said. "A man has a thousand ways of expressing himself. My Ira, may God rest his soul, was never a man of many words, but we never lacked for communication." She finished wiping the top of the dining table and stood, dust rag in hand, smiling down at Willa. "And you can't tell me that after all the years you've been with Mr. Friedrich, you don't know what he's saying most of the time—whether he uses words or not."

Willa sighed. "I used to think I knew. Now I'm not so sure."

Vesta walked around the dining table, pulled out a chair, and sat down opposite Willa. She gestured out the window. "Tell me something you've heard him say in the past few days."

Willa glanced over her shoulder. "He's frustrated."

"And you know that how?"

"By the way he stabs at his food on his plate at dinner. And he won't let me help him down the stairs. He's gentle about it, but if I try he pushes me away."

"Ah, he's *gentle* about it, is he? And what's he saying with that gentle little push?"

Willa looked down at her wedding ring. "He's saying he wants to be left alone."

"No, dear," Vesta said, and put her hand over Willa's. "He's saying, 'I can't stand you seeing me this way. I've always taken care of *you*. This isn't how things are supposed to work and I won't have it.' "

Willa looked into Vesta's blue eyes. "You're reading a great deal into our marriage. And there's a great deal about it you don't know." She looked back outside to where Otto was making the rounds, watering the trees and still pausing every once in a while to jabber away to himself. "Do you think I should talk to Dr. Sheridan about this? There's always the possibility he's had another small stroke. Something none of us noticed. Perhaps he's . . . confused."

"A man who keeps his peace at the table and at every other time except when he's watering trees," Vesta said, "doesn't seem to me to be a man who's confused. If you ask me—" she got up and put the chair back in place before pointing out the window—"that's a man with a plan."

Otto went back to work half days in early September. He devised a system of communicating with abbreviations and hand signals that Willard at the bank learned quickly, and it wasn't long before Willard was no longer a teller at First Bank. He was, instead, the bank president's right-hand man, and, as far as Willa could tell, an excellent one. As Otto's stamina improved, he worked longer hours. His mood improved. He walked. He went to church. He worked in the yard. He kept talking to the trees. He smiled more. Willa suspected he might even be talking to Willard. But he did not talk to her.

"Be patient, dearie," Vesta McKay would say. "When the man has something to say that needs words, he'll use them. Right now he's speaking to you with silence. Working through meals says he needs to get things in order at the bank. Attending church says he

329

wants to get things in order with God. And it's obvious those trees are very important to him. He's been close enough to eternity to look in the door. Give him time to decipher what he wants to do with what he's learned."

Willa tried to be patient, but it was September, and Irmagard would be coming home soon. After a short fall tour, the entire Wild West would disband in St. Louis at the end of the month. And then Irmagard and Helen and Shep would be returning to North Platte for Monte and Dora's wedding. Willa had offered to host the prenuptial dinner. Was she to do all of that with a silent partner? Now that Otto was better, should she write and tell Irmagard about his stroke? And once the wedding was over and Irmagard went back to New York with the Wild West . . . what should she do then?

In the weeks following Otto's stroke, the white heat of her anger against him had burned itself out. Otto Friedrich was not an evil man. He'd provided well for his wife and daughter. As for the boy in Denver, most men would have simply walked away. But not Otto. Otto had felt an obligation and done something about it. Dare she think of it as *honorable*? Perhaps that wasn't the right word, but he'd been right about one thing. The circumstances of his son's birth were not the boy's fault.

There was a great deal of good in Otto Friedrich. He could always be counted on to help those less fortunate. He had never really said an unkind word to Willa. At times over the years, when she'd been near a nervous collapse over this worry or that, it was Otto's mellow voice and strong arms that had always had a steadying influence on her.

As time went on, Willa began to believe that, perhaps—if he ever asked her again—perhaps, she could look past the hurt and find a way to forgive him. *After all, who amongst us is without sin?* Then again, if the man wouldn't talk to her, how could things ever be resolved?

CHAPTER 26

❖⇒◎⇐❖

HOWEVER, THERE IS A GOD IN HEAVEN
WHO REVEALS MYSTERIES.

Daniel 2:28 NASB

"Well, look at you," Helen said and burst out laughing.

Shep feigned indignance as he reached up to straighten his black silk cravat. He touched the brim of his black bowler and inspected Helen. "This is a perfectly normal getup for a New York gentleman headed to Sunday dinner with his family." He fussed with his cuffs and collar. "You don't see *me* laughing at *your* getup," he retorted.

Helen picked up her parasol and feinted a jab in his direction. "That's because I'm armed. You wouldn't dare."

"You feeling all right?" Shep said to Belle. "You look a little pale."

"She's as nervous as a long-tailed cat in a room full of rocking chairs," Helen said.

"I've never *been* to Sunday dinner at a New York brownstone before," Belle said.

Shep smiled at her. "Nothing mysterious about it. We eat. And I've seen proof you know how to do that." He winked. "You look wonderful, by the way." He glanced at Helen. "You both look wonderful."

Helen twirled around. "Thank you, Shepherd. I was telling Belle this mornin' that I could get used to this dressing-up business. Shoot, if a person didn't know better, they might mistake me for a lady."

"If you ask me," Shep said, "you're all the lady anyone in his right mind would ever want."

"That," Helen said, standing on tiptoe and kissing him on the cheek, "was a very nice thing to say." She put her arm through his and brandished the parasol. "So watch out, New York, here we come."

Belle took Shep's free arm and forced a smile. Why *was* she so nervous, anyway? Mrs. Mortimer had seemed nice enough. Belle was glad Helen was coming along, but she had a feeling this invitation to have "Sunday dinner with the family" was probably more about "inspecting the girl from Nebraska to see if she is worthy."

They were on the ferry when Shep took her hand and said, "Relax, honey. It's my *family*. I'm not feeding you to the lions."

———

Even Shep was taken aback when his mother led the three of them into the brownstone's dining room. "Well," he said. "I didn't think we were going to see the *entire* family today."

Belle took in a sharp breath. The dining table had to be twenty feet long, and . . . how many. . . ? Too many Mortimers had gathered.

"This," Mrs. Mortimer said, "is the young woman you've all heard so much about." She indicated Belle. "Miss Irma Friedrich appears with the Wild West as Liberty Belle." She put her hand on Helen's shoulder. "And Shep has also brought his friend Miss Helen Keen." They'd reserved a place for Shep and Belle together. But Helen was all the way down at the opposite end of the very long table, next to a spectacled dark-haired man. As soon as the three Wild Westers had found their places, Mrs. Mortimer began circling the table, introducing people as she went. "Celia and Marie, Shep's sisters. Marie's son, Gabriel. Uncle Charlie and Aunt Tillie. Cousins Helen and Barbara. Shep's Uncle Harold and Aunt Sophie. And this . . ." Mrs. Mortimer put her hand on the shoulder of the squinty-eyed man at the far end of the table. "This is Shep's brother, George."

George stood up and, with the most wooden smile Belle had ever seen, bowed first to her and said, "At last, Miss Friedrich," and then greeted Helen, only he called her "Miss Cream." He cleared his throat. "You must forgive us for overwhelming you today. But one never knows when the entire family can gather. Celia and Marie just got back from the summer house out on Long Island, and Uncle Charlie and Aunt Tillie leave soon for their annual tour in Europe. And then there is Uncle Harold and Aunt Sophie"—when George indicated these two, they nodded—"who have taken to gadding about on that boat of theirs until the rest of us despair of *ever* seeing them."

Feeling her backbone stiffen with what she hoped was a semblance of dignity, Belle said hello. She clasped her hands in her lap, hoping they would stop trembling before she had to actually pick up a fork. Shep reached for her hand beneath the table even as Mrs. Mortimer asked George to say grace.

"We thank thee, divine Providence, for all thy abundant gifts. We thank thee for family bonds that, while often stretched by distance and adventure, are never broken. We ask thy blessing upon this gathering and upon the various endeavors represented around this table. Amen."

As the meal progressed and conversation departed from the initial polite questions directed at Belle and "Miss Cream" to more general discussion, Belle learned that Uncle Charlie was in shipping and apparently owned an entire fleet of oceangoing vessels that imported a vast array of exotic goods into the country. As for Uncle Harold and Aunt Sophie, who liked to gad about in their boat, Belle remembered talk of them from supper at the Brunswick, but it was still impressive to hear them speak of firing the cook or hiring a new captain or of the staff, who were positively unruly at times, in the same tone of voice the Masons spoke of livestock and gardening.

Marie, the gorgeous sister Belle had seen at the Wild West one afternoon, proved to be genuinely friendly. Celia, on the other hand, regarded Belle with a smile that wasn't really a smile. Partway through the meal, Belle began to wish she and Shep had been seated with Helen—not only to get away from Celia's icy stare, but also to have a better view of what was going on down there.

For all his squinting and pompous praying, George Mortimer appeared to be fascinated by Helen. He hardly took his eyes off her through the entire meal, and when dessert was finished, and the men were withdrawing for cigars and the ladies were going for a stroll in the garden, George decided he wasn't ready for a smoke. So he and Shep, Belle and Helen, ended up seated in the gazebo, where George displayed a surprising amount of knowledge of cattle and an equally surprising interest in ranching in the state of Texas. Before the evening was over, George had exacted a promise from Miss Cream to show him the Wild West grounds.

"You haven't been there yet?" Helen said, clearly surprised. "Surely you've seen your brother perform."

"Well . . . yes. Of course I have. But . . . ." George's face reddened as he said, "I anticipate a much more charming companion would make the experience all the more fascinating."

Belle almost laughed aloud at the dandy's obvious flirtation, but then Helen winked at him and said, "Well, how could a girl resist an invitation like that?"

———

Later that night, as she and Helen lay in bed, Belle said something about the dreaded tour with George Mortimer.

"Who's dreading it?" Helen said. "He seems to be a nice enough fella—if a bit of a stuffed shirt." She chuckled. "I bet if a body ever got him out of that starched collar and into a flannel shirt, he'd be almost as nice as his brother. One thing for sure, he knows more about ranching than the average banker."

"A girl could do worse," Belle said.

"Oh, go on," Helen retorted. "George Mortimer isn't interested in me that way." She forced a laugh. "You might find a girl like me polishing the silver in the butler's pantry, but at that table every Sunday?"

Belle didn't argue with her. The Mortimer home was opulent. Elegant. Polished wood and crystal chandeliers, sterling silver and fine china, silk wall coverings and ornately framed oil paintings, inlaid wood and thick carpets, butlers and maids and cooks and— If it weren't for Mrs. Mortimer's kind eyes and welcoming smile, Belle would have been tempted to feign illness just to escape that gargantuan table and the multitude seated around it. But she made it through the night, and as she and Helen and Shep had boarded the ferry to come back to Staten Island a few hours ago, Shep had put his arm around her and said, "And those, sweetheart, are the Mortimers."

"Did I do all right?" Belle asked.

"The more important question would be . . . did *they* do all right?" At her look of confusion, he smiled and winked. "I already approve of you, honey. It don't really matter all that much if they like you. On the other hand, I am hoping you don't want to run screaming out of my life after meeting the entire herd."

Belle looked up at him. She shook her head. "I don't want to run anywhere you aren't."

Shep yelled, "Yee-haw," and sent his bowler hat spinning through the air toward the Statue of Liberty.

———

The Wild West train pulled away from New York in mid-September and wended its way along a short tour route that finally brought them into St. Louis. From St. Louis the troupe disbanded, with the Pawnee, Sioux, and Comanche returning to their various reservations and troupe members scattering to their homes throughout the west.

Belle, Shep, Helen, and Ned Bishop transferred to the Burlington Northern headed for North Platte on Wednesday, September 29. The few weeks before they had to be back in New York to prepare for the Statue of Liberty Parade would go quickly. Monte and Dora's wedding was on Friday, and Helen would leave for Texas the day after. October 6–9 was the Lincoln County Fair, and Bill Cody had asked Shep to participate in a chariot race and help oversee a twenty-five-mile relay race he had planned. Ned Bishop would be riding west to check on some land.

"We're going to feel like we blinked and it was over," Belle said. She opened Minnie's most recent letter and read the clipping Minnie had enclosed. "Listen to this," she said, "It's from the *Register*. 'Let the citizens of Lincoln County give Buffalo Bill the handsomest reception ever known. We have reason to feel proud of the worldwide reputation our honored citizen has received, and it is only right that we show our appreciation.'" Belle scanned the page and then exclaimed, "Oh my goodness . . . Minnie wrote this!" She held the article up. "Look. It says so right there. *Miss Minnie Mason.*"

Belle read on, wondering all the while if Minnie's writing for the newspaper meant that Mr. Orrin Knox had finally opened his eyes. She hoped so. "Minnie says Momma's involved in helping plan the big reception. There's to be a banquet at the Pacific Hotel the night he arrives." She looked up at Shep. "I suppose you'll have to attend?"

"Couldn't say," Shep said. "Bill only mentioned the chariot race. There's plenty of time to find out what he wants me to do after Monte's wedding." He stretched his legs out and, leaning his head back, fell asleep.

———

Everyone in the family met the train. The station was festooned with bunting in preparation for Buffalo Bill's impending arrival, and

Belle noticed that several businesses were flying flags. Uncle Charlie and Aunt Laura were there along with Monte and Dora and the four girls, and in the general pandemonium Belle noticed only one thing. The cane in Daddy's hand.

"Daddy? What happened?"

He hugged her fiercely. But he said nothing. Instead, he looked at Momma.

"Your father had an attack of apoplexy," Momma said, and raised her voice to keep Belle from talking. "He's doing fine. He's back at work, and Dr. Sheridan is very pleased with the way everything has turned out." She hugged Belle and whispered in her ear, "His speech hasn't returned yet, but we remain hopeful. I didn't wire you because there was nothing you could do, and your father didn't want you rushing home to see him that way. Please. Please don't be angry with me."

When Momma released her, she stood back and looked into her eyes with a silent plea, and Belle decided Momma had done what she thought best and there wouldn't be any point to throwing a fit now. When she looked at Daddy, she thought she saw tears in his eyes. She hugged him again and held on to his good arm as together they all walked back to the house. And she saw the trees.

"Your father planted them while I was in New York visiting you," Momma said. "Aren't they wonderful?"

And they were. And so was the knowledge that Shep had been right all along about Edna Hertz's letter being nothing more than a meanspirited attempt to hurt Belle.

The next couple of days were a whirlwind of preparation, and suddenly Monte and Dora were husband and wife driving away in a beribboned buggy toward town and a wedding trip to an undisclosed location. As the buggy disappeared into the distance, a collective sigh went up from the family. It had been a simple wedding performed beneath the overhang of the little log cabin Uncle Charlie and Aunt

Laura had started their married life in. The cabin would be Dora and Monte's new home when they returned from their wedding trip.

For the wedding, the girls had made garlands of fall grasses for the railing and a wreath to hang on the door. There was a wedding supper served outdoors on long planks, and Belle smiled to herself thinking that for one evening the Masons' table rivaled that amazing dining table in Mrs. Mortimer's New York brownstone.

Shep mounted up to ride over to Scout's Rest not long after Monte and Dora drove away. He'd been asked to stay there through the end of the county fair, which meant Buffalo Bill wanted him at his beck and call. Word had it that the new mansion was finished. When Belle wondered aloud if the King of the Cowboys would have a room in the "palace," he laughed and said he hoped not, he'd had trouble enough sleeping in the old house and if he could manage it he was going to bunk with the rest of the hands. If he had to, he said, he'd try out the barn. "I hear it's been known to yield a fair night's sleep for a weary cowboy or cowgirl."

Belle felt lonely the minute he rode away. Lonely and nervous. It was time for her to tell Momma about Blaze.

———

Momma joined Belle on the porch as soon as Daddy had settled in for the night.

"You're right, Irmagard. We need to talk. I've put this off for too long." Momma's voice was shaky, but she seemed determined. "I was only trying to do the right thing. I asked Dr. Sheridan if I should send for you, and he said he didn't think your father was in any further danger. He explained that it would be a matter of time and that Otto would slowly get better. I decided he would much rather you see him in an improved condition. I know you're upset about it, but—"

"No, Momma. I'm not."

Momma turned and looked at her. "You didn't want me out here so you could yell at me about not wiring you about Daddy?"

"No." Belle sighed. "That's not to say I wasn't upset. But after I thought about it, I realized you did what you thought best. And what was I going to do, anyway? Come rushing home and watch? You have the amazing Mrs. McKay, and thank God for her. You did the right thing. But since you brought it up—what does Dr. Sheridan say about his speech? Is he ever going to talk again?"

"Actually," Momma sighed. "I think he *can* talk. He just *won't*." She described seeing Daddy talk while he was watering trees.

"He talks . . . to the *trees?*"

"I know. It sounds crazy. But he's clearly not crazy. I think maybe he's . . . practicing."

"For what?"

Momma shook her head. "I haven't any idea."

"I've ruined Blaze, Momma." There. It was out. "There's no explanation for it other than I was selfish and foolish. I rushed her. Cy Matthews—he's the trainer—told me to wait, but I wouldn't listen. I rushed her. I took her into the arena one night, and she spooked and hurt her leg, and—" Belle broke off. Gulped. "There. That's done. I've been sick with dread over telling you. I know you're angry, and I don't blame you. It's unforgiveable, really. After what you did. All that money, and she'll never be in the Wild West."

"Did they have to . . . destroy her?"

"Oh, no. Nothing like that. But she's done with the Wild West. Cy said she'd be a fine saddle mare, but . . ." Belle sighed. "She'll be the most expensive saddle horse in the country. I'm so sorry, Momma. I know it isn't enough to say that, but I truly am."

"You sound so miserable, Irmagard," Momma said. "It's only a horse."

Belle looked at her, disbelieving. "You can't mean that. You do understand what I just said? Blaze can't perform with me. Ever. Not even in the parade."

"I heard you. I understand. And there's only one thing that concerns me."

339

"Yes?"

"You said it's unforgiveable." Momma reached for her hand. "That's ridiculous. It's a horse, Irmagard. Just a horse."

"But the money—"

"Oh, the money." Momma waved her hand in the air. "There's more money. I can always get more money."

"But Daddy's not well, and—"

"What does Daddy have to do with this?" Momma looked at her. Nodded. "Ah. You think that, while *I* wrote the bank draft, *Daddy* provided the funds. And why wouldn't you think that?" Momma paused, clearly thinking deeply about something. Finally, with a great sigh, she released Belle's hand.

"I told you about my mother and sister when we were together in New York. I didn't tell you about my brother. His name was Philip."

"I have an *uncle*?!"

Momma shook her head. "Let me finish." She thought for a moment before going on. Then taking a deep breath she began. "Philip and I just never found a way to get along. He ran off long before my mother died, and I resented him for that for a very long time. Then, when he *did* try to 'rescue me'—as he put it—I refused." She paused and looked at Belle. "He came here once when your father was away, and you were very young He didn't stay. We had a disagreement—" She broke off. Sighed. "I suppose it would be accurate to say we were 'estranged.' " She moistened her lips. "He was killed in a riding accident not long after we parted, which—" Momma cleared her throat— "will always be one of the great regrets of my life."

Belle reached for Momma's hand.

Momma forced a little smile. "It's all right. He must have believed we'd eventually reconcile, because when he died—" She turned to look at Belle. "Philip was a wealthy man, Irmagard. He left me all of his money. It's a great deal of money, and your father has invested it wisely for me over the years, so really, dear, the money for Blaze was nothing." She smiled. "I can buy you another horse."

CHAPTER 27

My beloved responded and said to me,
Arise, my darling, my beautiful one,
and come along.

Song of Songs 2:10 NASB

Twelve years. For twelve years she had resented, and at times come very close to hating, her own mother over something that had never even happened. What a waste, Belle thought, as she sat in the window seat in her room and watched the moon rise over the prairie. And all the while Momma loved her and tried to do what was best for her. Even when she tried to prevent Belle from living her Wild West dreams, even then Momma did it out of love. What else had she misunderstood about her mother? Who else had she judged wrongly? What a waste of emotion. What a . . . sin.

Dear God. It's Irmagard. And I need help. I need help and forgiveness.

It was a long night, but when the sun rose and the day dawned, Liberty Belle felt brand new inside.

Ten days before she was to leave for New York, Belle awoke and went downstairs to find Shep drinking coffee with her parents in the kitchen.

"Hello, stranger," Belle said. Though she was a new creation, determined to think the best of others until proven wrong, that didn't mean Shep's behavior since Monte and Dora's wedding didn't bother her. He'd hardly been around. Oh, sure, he'd been busy with the fair, and Bill Cody had seemed to pile a lot on him, but still, Belle had expected he would have wanted to have some time together during their break from the Wild West. Finding him in the kitchen on a Sunday morning was a nice enough surprise, but she couldn't resist the "stranger" comment, just to let him know she missed him.

"Hello yourself, stranger," Shep said, and came over and kissed her. On the cheek. Like a sister.

All right, so maybe she shouldn't have expected more than that. Daddy and Momma were, after all, sitting right there smiling at the two of them.

"Mind if I come along with ya to church today?" Shep asked.

"Not a bit," Belle said.

"And maybe we could take a ride after the service?" he said. "It's a nice day. Won't be too many more of those."

"Sure," Belle said. "Except for one thing. Nellie isn't broke to ride."

"I brought a horse for you," Shep said. He grinned. "I was pretty sure you'd say yes."

Who could stay angry with a man whose smile made you feel all . . . whatever it was she felt every time Shep smiled at her. "Well, you were right," Belle said. "I say 'yes'."

————

They crossed the Platte via the town bridge and then headed north up Whitehorse Creek. It wasn't long before it was obvious Shep had more on his mind than a leisurely Sunday afternoon ride. They rode for nearly an hour before coming to a small lake where Shep decided they would have the meal Mrs. McKay had packed. He hobbled the horses while Belle spread out the picnic cloth. They talked of the county fair and laughed anew at the skirmishes between a couple of the men racing for the seventy-five-dollar prize in the long race.

Shep had heard more details about the winter production, which was being called "The Drama of Civilization," and he explained what he knew. "It'll be different from anything we've done before," he said.

"I wish I knew if I was going to be in it," Belle said. "It doesn't make any sense for me to go all the way back to New York just to ride in a parade."

"You'll be in it," Shep said. "I'm sure of it. Helen, too. And Mabel, if she comes back."

Belle frowned. "What do you mean . . . if she comes back?"

"Mabel's unpredictable that way," Shep said.

They ate in silence for a while, and then Belle said, "You were right about Momma," and she told him about her Uncle Philip. "And apparently Momma's rich," she said, then sighed. "But I still hope I can figure a way to pay her back for Blaze someday."

Shep finished his sandwich and lay back, staring at the sky. "It's beautiful here—don't ya think?"

Belle looked around her. "It is. Do you think the lake is spring fed?"

"I know for a fact it is," Shep said. "I've spent a bit of time out here recently." He motioned toward the west. "Good grazing over thataway. Charlie Mason said it'd be a good start for a feller who had a mind to put down roots." He sat up abruptly, looked over to where the horses were grazing. "I better check the hobbles. That paint you're riding tends to be an escape artist. Least that's what Bill said when I picked him out of the corral this mornin'."

As Shep walked toward the horses, Belle looked around her. It really was a beautiful spot. The lake hardly deserved to be called a lake, but the water was clear and cold. Cottonwoods towered overhead. *A place to put down roots.* Shep was right. This would be a good place.

He strolled back slowly, his hands in his pockets, his head down. "Guess we should be headin' back," he said. "Don't want to have to wear out the horses trying to beat sundown."

Belle folded the picnic cloth over her arm, and together they went to fetch the two horses. She stowed the cloth in her saddlebags while Shep removed the hobbles and then she mounted up— There was a ribbon around the saddle horn. And attached to the ribbon was a ring. And there was a very handsome cowboy standing nearby, obviously waiting for a reaction.

"Does it fit?" he finally asked.

Belle slipped it on her finger. She nodded. He walked close. She slid into his arms.

"And the land," he said. "Would that be a good fit, too—for a couple of retired Wild West wranglers? When the time comes."

"Better than good," Belle said. "Perfect."

"Well, I'm glad you think so, 'cause I bought it yesterday." He leaned back and looked into her eyes. "I love you, Liberty Belle. I've loved you since the minute you called me a drugstore cowboy in Bill Cody's barn. I've tried to wait while you chased your dream, but I just couldn't—"

Belle touched his lips. "Stop," she said. Shook her head. "That old dream's gone," she said.

He cocked his head. "Really? You got a new one?"

She nodded.

"You want to tell me what it is?"

"You," she said, and stood on tiptoe to kiss him. "Only you."

CHAPTER 28

✦⟟⟐⟐⟨✦

HUSBANDS, LOVE YOUR WIVES,
JUST AS CHRIST ALSO LOVED THE CHURCH
AND GAVE HIMSELF UP FOR HER.
Ephesians 5:25 NASB

Willa had spent half the morning at a Ladies Aid Society meeting and she was exhausted. She was of a mind to just turn the entire thing over to Carrie Hertz. The woman obviously wanted to run things, and now that Willa thought about it, she didn't really care anymore. It just didn't seem all that important that she be the queen of North Platte society these days.

She and Otto were leaving for New York tomorrow so they could see Liberty Belle ride in the parade. Willa would have thought it too much for Otto, except for the fact that Shep's family owned an office building along the route and they'd be able to watch the entire thing from there without fighting the crowds.

They would meet the entire Mortimer family on this trip, which was somewhat disconcerting. Shep's mother was lovely, but Irmagard had described the brownstone and the family, and Willa couldn't help but feel a bit intimidated. Ah, well. Nothing to be done about that.

She would do the best she could and hope the Mortimers would be understanding of Otto's silence.

Pulling up under the portico, Willa hitched Nellie and went inside, where she was immediately assaulted by the aroma of roses. Whatever Mrs. McKay had done, it had had heavenly results.

"Mrs. McKay? Are you there?" She made her way up the hall, untying her bonnet as she went.

The front hall was filled with bouquets of roses. And in the midst of the roses . . . Otto.

"What on earth?"

"I wanted to give you a garden," Otto said slowly. "I'll dig a real one before winter sets in."

"You . . . you're talking!"

"I am," he said.

"But you . . . you can't talk."

"I can. I was waiting to say this."

"To say what?"

He took a deep breath. "You are the most important thing in my life. I have betrayed you, and I don't deserve your forgiveness. But I humbly beg for it anyway." With painfully slow movements, he got down on his knees. "Please, Willa. Can you please try to—" His voice broke. He took in a ragged breath. "If you will only try, I will spend the rest of my life honoring and cherishing you. I'll never hide anything from you again. I want to start over," he said with a sob. "Please. Will you please forgive me?"

In all her wildest imaginings of Otto apologizing or changing or leaving, Willa had never imagined roses and a man on his knees. She stammered. "I saw you talking. To the trees," she said. "I thought you'd had another stroke."

He was still kneeling.

"For heaven's sake, Otto," she said, and bent down to take his arm. "Get up."

"Forgive me," he said.

She looked at her husband. Her flawed, handsome husband. And she realized something. God had answered her cry for help.

"I already have, you old fool," she said. "I was just waiting for you to ask."

"When did you forgive me?"

She shook her head even as she helped him up. "I think it started with those trees," she said.

And they kissed. And they lived. And they loved.

Now to Him who is able to do exceeding abundantly
beyond all that we ask or think,
according to the power that works within us,
to Him be the glory in the church
and in Christ Jesus
to all generations forever and ever.
Amen.

EPHESIANS 3:20-21 NASB

More From
Stephanie Grace Whitson

Unaware of any family problems, Jacob Nolan creates a list of adventures he wants to experience before college graduation. But his parents receive a wake-up call when tragedy strikes. Jacob's list won't be completed the way he envisioned, but God has His own redemptive plans for the Nolans.

Jacob's List **by Stephanie Grace Whitson**

If You Enjoyed *Unbridled Dreams,* You Might Also Like These

In the late 1860s, three couples carve out a new life in the wild, untamed Colorado Territory. Each person will be called upon to stand on nothing more than faith, risk what is most dear to them, and turn away from the past in order to detect God's plan for the future. By the time Colorado becomes a state, will they be united by love or defeated by adversity?

FOUNTAIN CREEK CHRONICLES **by Tamera Alexander**

Rekindled, Revealed, Remembered

An outspoken Yankee photographer…A former Confederate sharpshooter…A perilous journey to repay a debt… What happens when dreams aren't what you imagined and secrets you've guarded are finally laid bare?

From a Distance **by Tamera Alexander**